"Suspenseful."—*Los Angeles Times*

"Terrific."—*San Francisco Chronicle*

"Irresistible."—*Kirkus Reviews*

"Thrilling."—*The Midwest Book Review*

"Hilariously funny."—*USA Today*

"A blast of fresh air."—*The Washington Post*

"Inventive and fast-paced."—*San Diego Union-Tribune*

"Superb."—*Detroit Free Press*

TEN BIG ONES

&

ELEVEN ON TOP

TWO NOVELS IN ONE

JANET EVANOVICH

St. Martin's Paperbacks

Published in the United States by St. Martin's Paperbacks, an imprint of St. Martin's Publishing Group.

For information, address St. Martin's Publishing Group, 120 Broadway, New York, NY 10271.

www.stmartins.com

ISBN: 978-1-250-62077-4

Our books may be purchased in bulk for promotional, educational, or business use. Please contact your local bookseller or the Macmillan Corporate and Premium Sales Department at 1-800-221-7945, ext. 5442, or by email at MacmillanSpecialMarkets@macmillan.com.

Printed in the United States of America

St. Martin's Paperbacks edition 2020

10 9 8 7 6 5 4 3

TEN
BIG
ONES

This book is an Evanovich/Enderlin
publishing adventure.
Thanks to SuperJen, AKA SuperEditor!

*Thanks to Mitch Adelman
for suggesting the title for this book.*

Chapter
ONE

The way I see it, life is a jelly doughnut. You don't really know what it's about until you bite into it. And then, just when you decide it's good, you drop a big glob of jelly on your best T-shirt.

My name is Stephanie Plum, and I drop a lot of jelly globs, figuratively and literally. Like the time I accidentally burned down a funeral home. That was the mother of all jelly globs. I got my picture in the paper for that one. I'd walk down the street and people would recognize me.

"You're famous now," my mother said when the paper came out. "You have to set an example. You have to exercise, eat good food, and be nice to old people."

Okay, so my mother was probably right, but I'm from Jersey and truth is, I have a hard time getting a grip on the good example thing. A good example in Jersey isn't exactly the national ideal. Not to mention, I inherited a lot of unmanageable brown hair and rude hand gestures from my father's Italian side of the family. What am I supposed to do with that?

My mother's side is Hungarian and from this I get blue eyes and the ability to eat birthday cake and still button the top snap on my jeans. I'm told the good Hungarian metabolism lasts only until I'm forty, so I'm counting down. The Hungarian genes also carry a certain amount of luck and gypsy intuition, both of which I need in my present job. I'm a Bond Enforcement Agent, working for my cousin Vincent Plum, and I run down bad guys. I'm not the best BEA in the world, and I'm not the worst. An incredibly hot guy with the street name Ranger is the best. And my sometimes partner, Lula, is possibly the worst.

Maybe it's not fair to have Lula in the running for worst bounty hunter of all time. To begin with, there are some really bad bounty hunters out there. And more to the point, Lula isn't actually a bounty hunter. Lula is a former hooker who was hired to do the filing for the bail bonds office but spends a lot of her day trailing after me.

At the moment, Lula and I were standing in the parking lot of a deli-mart on Hamilton Avenue. We were about a half mile from the office and we were leaning against my yellow Ford Escape, trying to make a lunch choice. We were debating nachos at the deli-mart against a sub at Giovichinni's.

"Hey," I said to Lula. "What happened to the filing job? Who does the filing now?"

"I do the filing. I file the ass out of that office."

"You're never in the office."

"The hell I am. I was in the office when you showed up this morning."

"Yeah, but you weren't filing. You were doing your nails."

"I was thinking about filing. And if you hadn't needed my help going to look for that loser Roger Banker, I'd still be filing."

Roger was accused of grand theft auto and possession of controlled substances. In layman's terms, Roger got high and went joy riding.

"So you're still officially a file clerk?"

"Heck no," Lula said. "That's so-o-o boring. Do I look like a file clerk to you?"

Actually, Lula still looked like a hooker. Lula's a full-bodied black woman who favors animal print spandex enhanced with sequins. I figured Lula didn't want to hear my fashion opinion, so I didn't say anything. I just raised an eyebrow.

"The job title is tricky since I do a lot of this here bounty hunter stuff but I've never really been given any of my own cases," Lula said. "I suppose I could be your bodyguard."

"Omigod."

Lula narrowed her eyes at me. "You got a problem with that?"

"It seems a little . . . Hollywood."

"Yeah, but sometimes you need some extra firepower, right? And there I am. Hell, you don't even carry a gun half the time. I always got a gun. I got a gun now. Just in case."

And Lula pulled a 40-caliber Glock out of her purse.

"I don't mind using it either. I'm good with a gun. I got an eye for it. Watch me hit that bottle next to the bike."

Someone had leaned a fancy red mountain bike against the big plate glass window in the front of the deli-mart. There was a quart bottle next to the bike. The bottle had a rag stuffed into it.

"No," I said. "No shooting!"

Too late. Lula squeezed off a shot, missed the bottle, and destroyed the bike's rear tire.

"Oops," Lula said, doing a grimace and immediately returning the gun to her purse.

A moment later, a guy ran out of the store. He was wearing a mechanic's jumpsuit and a red devil mask. He had a small backpack slung over one shoulder and he had a gun in his right hand. His skin tone was darker than mine but lighter than Lula's. He grabbed the bottle off the ground, lit the rag with a flick of his Bic, and threw the bottle into the store. He turned to get onto the bike and realized his tire was blown to smithereens.

"Fuck," the guy said. "FUCK!"

"I didn't do it," Lula said. "Wasn't me. Someone came along and shot up your tire. You must not be popular."

There was a lot of shouting inside the store, the guy in the devil mask turned to flee, and Victor, the Pakistani day manager, rushed out the door. "I am done! Do you hear me?" Victor yelled. "This is the fourth robbery this month and I won't stand for any more. You are dog excrement!" he shouted at the guy in the mask. "Dog excrement."

Lula had her hand back in her purse. "Hold on. I got a gun!" she said. "Where the hell is it? Why can't you ever find the damn gun when you need it?"

Victor threw the still lit but clearly unbroken bottle at the guy in the devil mask, hitting him in the back of the head. The bottle bounced off the devil's head and smashed against my driver's side door. The devil staggered, and instinctively pulled the mask off. Maybe he couldn't breathe, or maybe he went to feel for blood, or maybe he just wasn't thinking. Whatever the reason, the mask was only off for a second, before being yanked back over the guy's head. He turned and looked directly at me, and then he ran across the street and disappeared into the alley between two buildings.

The bottle instantly ignited when it hit my car, and flames raced along the side and the undercarriage of the Escape.

"Holy crap," Lula said, looking up from her purse. "Damn."

"Why me?" I shrieked. "Why does this always happen to me? I can't believe this car is on fire. My cars are always getting exploded. How many cars have I lost like this since you've known me?"

"A lot," Lula said.

"It's embarrassing. What am I going to tell my insurance company?"

"It wasn't your fault," Lula said.

"It's never my fault. Do they care? I don't think they care!"

"You got bad car karma," Lula said. "But at least you're lucky at love."

For the last couple months I've been living with Joe Morelli. Morelli's a very sexy, very handsome Trenton cop. Morelli and I have a long history and possibly a long future. Mostly we take it day by day, neither of us feeling the need for documented commitment right now. The good thing about living with a cop is that you never have to call home when disaster strikes. As you might suspect, that's also the bad part. Seconds after the emergency call goes in on the robbery and car fire, describing my yellow Escape, at least forty different cops, EMTs, and fire fighters will track Morelli down and tell him his girlfriend's done it again.

Lula and I moved farther from the fire, knowing from experience that an explosion was a possibility. We stood patiently waiting, listening to the sirens whining in the distance, getting closer by the second. Morelli's unmarked cop car would be minutes behind the sirens. And somewhere in the mix of emergency vehicles my professional mentor and man of mystery, Ranger, would slide in to check things out.

"Maybe I should leave," Lula said. "There's all that filing back at the office. And cops give me the runs."

Not to mention she was illegally carrying a concealed weapon that was instrumental in this whole fiasco.

"Did you see the guy's face when he pulled his mask off?" I asked her.

"No. I was looking for my gun. I missed that."

"Then leaving might be a good idea," I said. "Get me a sub on the way back to the office. I don't think they'll be making nachos here for a while."

"I'd rather have the sub anyways. A car fire always gives me an appetite."

And Lula took off power walking.

Victor was on the other side of the car, stomping around and pulling at his hair. He stopped stomping and fixed his attention on me. "Why didn't you shoot him? I know you. You are a bounty hunter. You should have shot him."

"I'm not carrying a gun," I told Victor.

"Not carrying a gun? What kind of bounty hunter are you? I watch television. I know about these things. Bounty hunters always have many guns."

"Actually, shooting people is a no-no in bond enforcement."

Victor shook his head. "I don't know what this world is coming to when bounty hunters don't shoot people."

A blue-and-white patrol car arrived and two uniforms got out and stood hands on hips, taking it all in. I knew both cops. Andy Zajak and Robin Russell.

Andy Zajak was riding shotgun. Two months ago he'd been plainclothes, but he'd asked a local politician some embarrassing questions during a robbery investigation and had gotten busted back to uniform. It could have been worse. Zajak could have been assigned to a desk in the tower of Irrelevance. Sometimes things could get tricky in the Trenton police department.

Zajak waved when he saw me. He said something to Russell, and they both smiled. No doubt enjoying the continuing calamitous exploits of Stephanie Plum.

I'd gone to school with Robin Russell. She was a year behind me, so we weren't the closest of friends, but I liked her. She wasn't especially athletic when she was in high school. She was one of the quiet brainy kids. And she surprised everyone when she joined Trenton P.D. two years ago.

A fire truck followed Zajak and Russell. Plus two more cop cars and an EMT truck. By the time Morelli arrived, the hoses and chemical extinguishers were already out and in use.

Morelli angled his car behind Robin Russell's and walked across to me. Morelli was lean and hard muscled with wary cop eyes that softened in the bedroom. His hair was almost black, falling in waves over his forehead, brushing his collar. He was wearing a slightly oversize blue shirt with the sleeves rolled, black jeans, and black boots with a Vibram sole. He had his gun on his hip and, with or without the gun, he didn't look like someone you'd want to mess with. There was a tilt to his mouth that could pass for a smile. Then again, it could just as easily be a grimace. "Are you okay?"

"It wasn't my fault," I told him.

This got a genuine smile from him. "Cupcake, it's never your fault." His eyes traveled to the red mountain bike with the destroyed tire. "What's with the bike?"

"Lula accidentally shot the tire. Then a guy wearing a red devil mask ran out of the store, took a look at the bike, tossed a Molotov cocktail into the store, and set off on foot. The bottle didn't break, so Victor pitched it at the devil. The bottle bounced off the devil's head and crashed against my car."

"I didn't hear the part about Lula shooting the tire."

"Yeah, I figured it wasn't necessary to mention that in the official statement."

I looked past Morelli, as a black Porsche 911 Turbo pulled to the curb. There weren't a lot of people in Trenton who could afford the car. Mostly high-level drug dealers . . . and Ranger.

I watched as Ranger angled out from behind the

wheel and ambled over. He was about the same height as
Morelli, but he had more bulk to his muscle. Morelli was
a cat. Ranger was Rambo meets Batman. Ranger was in
SWAT black cargo pants and T-shirt. His hair was dark,
and his eyes were dark, and his skin reflected his Cuban ancestry. No one knew Ranger's age, but I'd guess
it was close to mine. Late twenties to early thirties. No
one knew where Ranger lived or where his cars and
cash originated. Probably it was best not to know.

Ranger nodded to Morelli and locked eyes with me.
Sometimes it felt like Ranger could look you in the eye
and know all the stuff that was inside your head. It was
a little unnerving, but it saved a lot of time since talk
wasn't necessary.

"Babe," Ranger said. And he left.

Morelli watched Ranger get into his Porsche and
take off. "Half the time I'm happy to have him watching over you. And half the time it scares the hell out of
me. He's always in black, the address on his driver's
license is a vacant lot, and he never says anything."

"Maybe he has a dark history . . . like Batman. A
tortured soul."

"Tortured soul? Ranger? Cupcake, the guy's a mercenary." Morelli playfully twirled a strand of my hair
around his finger. "You've been watching Dr. Phil
again, right? Oprah? Geraldo? *Crossing Over* with
John Edward?"

"*Crossing Over* with John Edward. And Ranger's
not a mercenary. At least not officially in Trenton. He's
a bounty hunter . . . like me."

"Yeah, and I really hate that you're a bounty hunter."

Okay. I know I have a crappy job. The money isn't
all that great and sometimes people shoot at me. Still,
someone's got to make sure the accused show up in
court. "I do a service for the community," I told Morelli. "If it wasn't for people like me the police would

have to track these guys. The taxpayer would have to foot the bill for a larger police force."

"I'm not disputing the job. I just don't want *you* doing it."

There was a loud *phooonf* sound from the underside of my car, flames shot out, and a steaming tire popped off and rolled across the lot.

"This is the fourteenth Red Devil robbery," Morelli said. "The routine is always the same. Rob the store at gunpoint. Get away on a bike. Cover your getaway with a bottle bomb. No one's ever seen enough to ID him."

"Until now," I said. "I saw the guy's face. I didn't recognize him, but I think I could pick him out of a lineup."

An hour later, Morelli dropped me off at the bond office. He snagged me by the back of my shirt as I was leaving his unmarked seen-better-days Crown Vic cop car. "You're going to be careful, right?"

"Right."

"And you're not going to let Lula do any more shooting."

I did a mental sigh. He was asking the impossible. "Sometimes it's hard to control Lula."

"Then get a different partner."

"Ranger?"

"Very funny," Morelli said.

He French-kissed me good-bye, and I thought probably I could control Lula. When Morelli kissed me, I thought anything was possible. Morelli was a terrific kisser.

His pager buzzed and he pulled away to check the readout. "I have to go," he said, shoving me out the door.

I leaned in the window at him. "Remember, we promised my mom we'd come for dinner tonight."

"No way. You promised. I didn't promise. I had dinner at your parents' house three days ago and once a

week is my limit. Valerie and the kids will be there,
right? And Kloughn? I'm getting heartburn just thinking about it. Anybody who eats with that crew should
get combat pay."

He was right. I had no comeback. A little over a year
ago my sister's husband took off for parts unknown
with the baby-sitter. Valerie immediately moved back
home with her two kids and took a job with a struggling lawyer, Albert Kloughn. Somehow, Kloughn
managed to get Val pregnant and in nine months' time
my parents' small three-bedroom, one-bathroom house
in the Chambersburg section of Trenton was home to
my mom, my dad, Grandma Mazur, Valerie, Albert
Kloughn, Val's two little girls and newborn baby.

As a short-term fix to my sister's housing dilemma
I volunteered the use of my apartment. I was spending
most of my nights with Morelli anyway, so it wasn't a
total sacrifice on my part. It's now three months down
the road and Valerie is still in my apartment, returning to my parents' house every night for dinner. Once
in a while something fun happens at dinner . . . like
Grandma setting the tablecloth on fire or Kloughn
choking on a chicken bone. But usually it's just flat-out
migraine-inducing bedlam.

"Boy, too bad you'll miss the roast chicken with
gravy and mashed potatoes," I told Morelli in a last-
ditch effort. "Probably pineapple upside-down cake for
dessert."

"Not gonna work. You're going to have to come up
with something better than roast chicken to get me over
to your parents' house tonight."

"What, like wild gorilla sex?"

"Not even wild gorilla sex. It would have to be an
orgy with identical Japanese triplets."

I gave Morelli an eye roll, and I left for the bond
office.

"Your sub's filed under S," Lula said when I swung through the door. "I got you capicolla and provolone and turkey and pepperoni with some hot peppers."

I opened the file and retrieved my sub. "There's only half a sandwich here."

"Well, yeah," Lula said. "Me and Connie decided you wouldn't want to get fat by eating that whole sub all yourself. So we helped you out."

Vincent Plum Bail Bonds is a small storefront office on Hamilton Avenue. Ordinarily a more lucrative location for a bonds office would be across from the courts or the lockup. Vinnie's office is across from the Burg, and a lot of Vinnie's repeat customers are local. Not that the Burg is a bad neighborhood. Truth is, the Burg is possibly the safest place to live if you have to live in Trenton. There's a lot of low-level mob in the Burg and if you misbehave in the Burg you could quietly disappear for a very long time . . . like forever.

It's even possible that some of Connie's relatives might assist in the disappearance. Connie is Vinnie's office manager. She's five foot four and looks like Betty Boop with a mustache. Her desk is positioned in front of Vinnie's small inner office, preventing the unsuspecting from walking in on Vinnie while he's on the phone with his bookie, taking a snooze, or having a private conversation with his johnson. Also behind Connie's desk is a bank of file cabinets. And behind the file cabinets is a small stockroom packed with guns and ammo, office supplies, bathroom supplies, and assorted confiscated booty that mostly runs to computers, fake Rolex watches, and fake Louis Vuitton handbags.

I slouched onto the scarred dung-brown fake leather couch that was positioned against a side wall of the outer office and unwrapped the sub.

"Big day in court yesterday," Connie said, waving a handful of manila folders at me. "We had three guys fail to appear. The bad news is they're all chump change. The good news is none of them have killed or raped in the last two years."

I took the folders from Connie and returned to the couch. "I suppose you want me to find these guys," I said to Connie.

"Yeah," Connie said. "Finding them would be good. Dragging their asses back to jail would be even better."

I flipped through the folders. Harold Pancek. Wanted for indecent exposure and destruction of personal property.

"What's the deal on Harold?" I asked Connie.

"He's local. Moved to the Burg three years ago from Newark. Lives in one of the row houses on Canter Street. Got drunk two weeks ago and tried to take a leak on Mrs. Gooding's cat, Ben. Ben was a moving target and Pancek mostly got the side of Gooding's house and Gooding's favorite rosebush. Killed the rosebush and took the paint off the house. And Gooding says she washed the cat three times and he still smells like asparagus."

Lula and I had our faces frozen in curled-lip grimaces.

"He doesn't sound like much of a threat," Connie said. "Just make sure you stand back if he whips it out to relieve himself."

I took a quick look at the two remaining files. Carol Cantell, wanted for holding up a Frito-Lay truck. This brought an instant smile to my face. Carol Cantell was a woman after my own heart.

The smile turned to raised eyebrows when I saw the name on the last file. Salvatore Sweet, charged with assault. "Omigod," I said to Connie. "It's Sally. I haven't seen him in ages." When I first met Salvatore Sweet he was playing lead guitar for a transvestite rock band. He helped me solve a crime and then disappeared into the night.

"Hey, I remember Sally Sweet," Lula said. "He was the shit. What's he doing now besides beating on people?"

"Driving a school bus," Connie said. "Guess the rock career didn't work out. He's living on Fenton Street, over by the button factory."

Sally Sweet was an MTV car crash. He was a nice guy but he couldn't get through a sentence without using the "f" word fourteen times. The kids on Sally's bus probably had the most inventive vocabularies in the school.

"Have you tried calling him?" I asked Connie.

"Yeah. No answer. And no answering machine."

"How about Cantell?"

"I talked to her earlier. She said she'd kill herself before she'd go to jail. She said you were going to have to come over there and shoot her and then drag her dead body out of the house."

"It says here she held up a Frito-Lay truck?"

"Apparently she was on that no-carbohydrate diet, got her period and snapped when she saw the truck parked in front of a convenience store. Just got whacked out at the thought of all those chips. She threatened the driver with a nail file, filled her car with bags of Fritos, and took off, leaving the driver standing there in front of his empty truck. The police asked him why he didn't stop her, and he said she was a woman on the edge. He said his wife got to looking like that sometimes, and he didn't go near her when she was like that, either."

"I've been on that diet and this crime makes perfect sense to me," Lula said. "Especially if she had her period. You don't want to go through your period without Fritos. Where you gonna get your salt from? And what about cramps? What are you supposed to take for cramps?"

"Midol?" Connie said.

"Well, yeah, but you gotta have some Fritos while you're waiting for the Midol to kick in. Fritos have a calming influence on a woman."

Vinnie stuck his head out the door of his inner office and glared at me. "What are you sitting around for? We got three FTAs in this morning and you already had one in your possession. Four FTAs! Christ, I'm not running a charity here."

Vinnie is my cousin on my father's side of the family and sole owner of Vincent Plum Bail Bonds. He's an oily little guy with slicked-back black hair, pointy-toed shoes, and a bunch of gold chains hanging around his scrawny tanning salon–tanned neck. It's rumored that he once had a romantic relationship with a duck. He drives a Cadillac Seville. And he's married to Harry the Hammer's only daughter. Vinnie's rating as a human being would be in the vicinity of pond slime. His rating as a bonds agent would be considerably higher. Vinnie understood human weakness.

"I haven't got a car," I told Vinnie. "My car got fire-bombed."

"What's your point? Your cars are always getting fire-bombed. Have Lula drive you. She doesn't do anything around here anyway."

"Your ass," Lula said.

Vinnie pulled his head back into his office, and he slammed and locked the door.

Connie rolled her eyes. And Lula flipped Vinnie the finger.

"I saw that," Vinnie yelled from behind his closed door.

"I hate when he's right," Lula said, "but there's no reason we can't use my car. I just don't want to pick up the drunken leaker. If he takes paint off a house, I'm not letting him near my upholstery."

"Try Cantell," Connie said. "She should still be at home."

Fifteen minutes later we were in front of Cantell's house in Hamilton Township. It was a trim little ranch on a small lot, in a neighborhood of similar houses. The grass was neatly cut, but it was patchy with crabgrass and parched from a hot, dry August. Young azaleas bordered the front of the house. A blue Honda Civic was parked in the driveway.

"Don't look like the home of a hijacker," Lula said. "No garage."

"Sounds like this was a once-in-a-lifetime experience."

We approached the front door and knocked. And Cantell answered.

"Oh God," Cantell said. "Don't tell me you're from the bond agency. I told the woman on the phone I didn't want to go to jail."

"This is just a rebooking process," I told her. "We bring you in and then Vinnie bonds you out again."

"No way. I'm not going back to that jail. It's too embarrassing. I'd rather you shoot me and kill me."

"We wouldn't shoot you," Lula said. "Unless, of course, you drew a gun. What we'd do is gas you. We got pepper spray. Or we could zap you with the stun gun. My choice would be the stun gun on account of we're using my car and there's a lot of snot produced if we give you a face full of pepper spray. I just had my car detailed. I don't want the backseat full of snot."

Cantell's mouth dropped open and her eyes glazed over. "I just took a couple bags of chips," she said. "It's not like I'm a criminal."

Lula looked around. "You wouldn't have any of them chips left over, would you?"

"I gave them all back. Except for the ones I ate."

Cantell had short brown hair and a pleasant round face. She was dressed in jeans and an extra-roomy T-shirt. Her age was listed as thirty-two.

"You should have kept your court date," I said to Cantell. "You might have only gotten community service."

"I didn't have anything to wear," she wailed. "Look at me. I'm a house! Nothing fits. I ate a truck full of Fritos!"

"You're not as big as me," Lula said. "And I got a lot of stuff to wear. You just gotta know how to shop. We should go out shopping together some day. My secret is I only buy spandex and I buy it too small. That way it sucks everything in. Not that I'm fat or anything. It's just I got a lot of muscle."

Lula was currently in athletic gear mode, wearing hot pink stretch pants, matching halter top, and serious running shoes. The strain on the spandex was frightening. I was heading for cover at the first sign of a seam unraveling.

"Here's the plan," I said to Cantell. "I'm going to call Vinnie and have him meet us at the courthouse. That way you can get bonded out immediately, and you won't have to sit around in a holding cell."

"I guess that would be okay," Cantell said. "But you have to get me back here before my kids get off the school bus."

"Sure," I said, "but just in case, maybe you want to make alternative arrangements."

"And maybe I can lose some weight before I have to go to court," Cantell said.

"Be a good idea not to hold up any more snack food trucks," Lula said.

"I had my period! I needed those chips."

"Hey, I hear you," Lula said.

After we got Cantell rebooked and rebonded and returned to her house, Lula drove me across town, back to the Burg.

"That wasn't so bad," Lula said. "She seemed like a real nice person. Do you think she's going to show up for court this time?"

"No. We're going to have to go over to her house and drag her to court, kicking and screaming."

"Yeah, that's what I think, too."

Lula pulled to the curb and idled in front of my parents' house. Lula drove a red Firebird that had a sound system capable of broadcasting rap over a five-mile radius. Lula had the sound on low but the bass at capacity, and I could feel my fillings vibrating.

"Thanks for the ride," I told Lula. "See you tomorrow."

"Yo," Lula said. And she took off.

My Grandma Mazur was at the front door, waiting for me. Grandma Mazur rooms with my parents now that Grandpa Mazur is living *la vida loca* everlasting. Grandma Mazur has a body like a soup chicken and a mind that defies description. She keeps her steel gray hair cut short and tightly permed. She prefers pastel polyester pantsuits and white tennis shoes. And she watches wrestling. Grandma doesn't care if wrestling's fake or real. Grandma likes to look at big men in little spandex panties.

"Hurry up," Grandma said. "Your mother won't start serving drinks until you're at the table, and I need one real bad. I had the day from heck. I traipsed all the way over to Stiva's Funeral Parlor for Lorraine Schnagle's viewing, and she turned out to have a closed casket. I heard she looked real bad at the end, but that's still no reason to deprive people from seeing the deceased. People count on getting a look. I made an effort to get there, dressing up and everything. And now I'm not going to have anything to talk about when I get my hair done tomorrow. I was counting on Lorraine Schnagle."

"You didn't try to open the casket, did you?"

"Me? Of course not. I wouldn't do such a thing. And anyway, it was locked up real tight."

"Is Valerie here?"

"Valerie's always here," Grandma said. "That's another reason I'm having the day from heck. I was all tired after the big disappointment at the funeral parlor, and I couldn't take a nap on account of your niece is back to being a horse and won't stop the galloping. And she whinnies all the time. Between the baby crying and the horse thing, I'm pooped. I bet I got bags under my eyes. If this keeps up I'm going to lose my looks." Grandma squinted up and down the street. "Where's your car?"

"It sort of caught fire."

"Did the tires pop off? Was there an explosion?"

"Yep."

"Darn! I wish I'd seen that. I always miss the good stuff. How'd it catch fire this time?"

"It happened at a crime scene."

"I'm telling you this town's going to hell in a handbasket. We never had so much crime. It's getting to where you don't want to go out of the neighborhood."

Grandma was right about the crime. I saw it escalating at the bond office. More robberies. More drugs on the street. More murders. Most of it drug and gang related. And now I had seen the Red Devil's face, so I was sucked into it.

Chapter
TWO

I found my mom at the kitchen sink, peeling potatoes. My sister Valerie was in the kitchen, too. Valerie was seated at the small wood table, and she was nursing the baby. It seemed to me Valerie was always nursing the baby. There were times when I looked at the baby and felt the pull of maternal yearnings, but mostly I was glad I had a hamster.

Grandma followed me into the kitchen, anxious to tell everyone the news. "She blew up her car again," Grandma announced.

My mother stopped peeling. "Was anyone hurt?"

"No," I said. "Just the car. It was totaled."

My mother made the sign of the cross and took a white-knuckled grip on the paring knife. "I hate when you blow up cars!" she said. "How am I supposed to sleep at night knowing I have a daughter who blows up cars?"

"You could try drinking," Grandma said. "That always works for me. Nothing like a good healthy snort before bedtime."

My cell phone chirped, and everyone paused while I answered.

"Are you having fun yet?" Morelli wanted to know.

"Yeah. I just got to my parents' house and it's lots of fun. Too bad you're missing it."

"Bad news. You're going to have to miss it, too. One of the guys just brought in a suspect, and you're going to have to ID him."

"Now?"

"Yeah. Now. Do you need a ride?"

"No. I'll borrow the Buick."

When my Great Uncle Sandor went into the nursing home, he gave his '53 powder blue–and–white Buick Roadmaster to Grandma Mazur. Since Grandma Mazur doesn't drive (at least not legally), the car mostly sits in my father's garage. It gets five miles to a gallon of gas. It drives like a refrigerator on wheels. And it doesn't fit my self-image. I see myself more as a Lexus SC 430. My budget sees me as a secondhand Honda Civic. My bank was willing to stretch to a Ford Escape.

"That was Joe," I told everyone. "I have to meet him at the police station. They think they might have the guy who set fire to my car."

"Will you be back for the chicken?" my mother wanted to know. "And what about dessert?"

"Don't wait dinner. I'll get back if I can, and if not I'll take leftovers." I turned to Grandma. "I'm going to have to commandeer the Buick until I can replace the Escape."

"Help yourself," Grandma said. "And I'll ride with you to the police station. I could use to get out of the house. And on the way home we could stop at Stiva's to see if they got the lid up for the evening viewing. I'd hate to miss out on seeing Lorraine."

Twenty minutes later, Grandma and I cruised into the public parking lot across the street from the cop shop. The Trenton police are housed in a no-nonsense chunk of brick and mortar in a no-nonsense part of town that gives the cops easy access to crime. The building is half cop shop and half courthouse. The courthouse half has a guard and a metal detector. The cop half has an elevator decorated with bullet holes.

I looked at Grandma's big black patent leather purse. Grandma was known to, from time to time, carry a .45 long barrel. "You don't have a gun in there, do you?" I asked.

"Who, me?"

"If they catch you taking a concealed weapon into the building, they'll lock you up and throw the key away."

"How would they know I got a concealed weapon if it's concealed? They better not search me. I'm an old lady. I got certain rights."

"Carrying a concealed weapon isn't one of them."

Grandma pulled the gun out of her purse and shoved it under her seat. "I don't know what this country's coming to when an old lady can't keep a gun in her purse. We got a rule for everything these days. What about the bill of health? It says I can bear arms!"

"That's the Bill of Rights, and I don't think it specifically addresses guns in purses." I locked the Buick and called Joe on my cell. "I'm across the street," I told him. "And I've got Grandma with me."

"She isn't armed, is she?"

"Not anymore."

I could feel Joe smile across the phone line. "I'll meet you downstairs."

Civilian traffic in the building was minimal at this time of day. The courts were closed, and police business was shifting from front door inquiries to back door arrests. A lone cop sat in a bulletproof cage at the end of the hall, struggling to stay awake on his shift.

Morelli stepped out of the elevator just as Grandma and I swung through the front entrance doors.

Grandma looked at Morelli and gave a snort. "He's wearing a gun," she said.

"He's a cop."

"Maybe I should be a cop," Grandma said. "Do you think I'm too short?"

Thirty minutes later, Grandma and I were back in the Buick.

"That didn't take long," Grandma said. "I hardly had a chance to look around."

"I couldn't make an ID. They picked up a guy who was carrying the backpack, but it wasn't the guy who ran out of the store. He said he found the backpack discarded in an alley."

"Bummer. This doesn't mean we're going to have to go back to the house, does it? I can't take any more of the galloping and the baby talk."

"Valerie talks baby talk to the baby?"

"No, she talks it to Kloughn. I don't like to make judgments on people, but after a couple hours of listening to 'honey pie smoochie bear cuddle umpkins' I'm ready to smack someone."

Okay, so I was glad I'd never been there when Valerie called Kloughn cuddle umpkins because I would have wanted to smack someone, too. And my self-restraint isn't as well honed as Grandma's.

"It's too early to go to the viewing," I said to Grandma. "I guess I could stop in on Sally Sweet. He turned up Failure To Appear today on an assault charge."

"No kidding? I remember him. He was a nice young man. Sometimes he was a nice young woman. He had a plaid skirt I always admired."

I pulled out of the lot, right-turned onto North Clinton, and followed the road for almost a quarter mile. At one time in Trenton's history this was a thriving industrial area. The industry had all vacated or drastically downsized and the rotting carcasses of factories and warehouses produced an ambience similar to what you might find in postwar Bosnia.

I left Clinton and wove my way through a neighborhood of small bleak single-story row houses. Originally designed to contain the factory workers, the row houses were now occupied by hardworking people who lived one step above welfare . . . plus there were a few oddballs like Sally Sweet.

I found Fenton and parked in front of Sweet's house. "Wait in the car until I find out what's going on," I said to Grandma.

"Sure," Grandma said, her hands gripping her purse in excited anticipation, her eyes glued to Sweet's front door. The Buick was a car designed for a man, and Grandma seemed swallowed up by the monster. Her feet barely touched the floor, her face was barely visible over the dash. A timid woman might feel overwhelmed by Big Blue. Grandma was a little shrunken, but she wasn't timid, and there wasn't a whole lot that overwhelmed Grandma. Thirty seconds after Grandma agreed to wait in the car, she was on the sidewalk, following me to Sweet's front door.

"I thought you were going to wait in the car?" I said.

"I changed my mind. I thought you might need help."

"Okay, but let me do the talking. I don't want to alarm him."

"Sure," Grandma said.

I knocked on Sweet's front door, and it opened on the third knock. Sally Sweet looked out at me, recognition kicked in, and his face creased into a grin. "Long time no see," he said. "What brings you to my *casa*?"

"We're here to drag your behind back to jail," Grandma said.

"*Fuck*," Sally said. And he slammed the door shut.

"What was that?" I asked Grandma.

"I don't know. It just popped out."

I gave another rap on the door. "Open the door," I said. "I just want to talk to you."

Sally cracked the door and peeked at me. "I can't go to jail. I'll lose my job."

"Maybe I can help."

The door opened wide, Sally stepped to the side to allow us entry, and I gave Grandma a warning glare.

"My mouth is zipped," she said, making a zipping gesture. "And look, I'm locking the zipper and throwing away the key. See me throw away the key?"

Sally and I stared at Grandma.

"Mmmmf, mmmf, mmf," Grandma said.

"So what's new?" I asked Sally.

"I get band gigs on weekends," he said. "Weekdays I drive a school bus. It's not like the glory days when I was with the Lovelies, but it's pretty cool."

"What's with the assault charge?"

"It's bogus, man. I was having a discussion with this dude and all of a sudden he started coming on to me. And I was 'Hey, man, that's not where I live,' you know. I mean, okay, so I was wearing a dress, but that's my professional persona. Wearing a dress is my thing. It's my trademark now. Sure, I was playing support for a rap group, but people still expect me to be in a pretty dress. I'm Sally Sweet, you know? I got a reputation."

"I could see where it might be confusing," Grandma said.

I was trying hard not to look appalled. "So you hit him?"

"Only once . . . with my guitar. Knocked him on his keister."

"Holy cow," I said. "Was he hurt bad?"

"No. But I broke his glasses. The guy was such a

pussy. He started it all, and then he reported it to the police. He said I hit him for no reason. Called me a drugged-out guitar player."

"Were you drugged out?"

"No way. Sure, I smoke weed between sets, but everybody knows weed doesn't count as drugs if you're a guitar player. And I'm real careful. I buy organic. I only do natural drugs, you know. It's okay if they're natural. Natural weed, natural 'shrooms . . ."

"I didn't know that," Grandma said.

"It's a fact," Sally told her. "I think it might even be union rules that guitar players have to do weed between sets."

"That makes sense," Grandma said.

"Yeah," I said. "That would explain a lot."

Sally was out of costume, wearing jeans and ratty sneakers and a faded Black Sabbath T-shirt. He was over six feet tall in flats and close to seven in heels. He had a large hook nose, and he had a lot of black hair . . . everywhere. He was an okay guy, but he was without a shadow of a doubt the ugliest drag queen in the tristate area. I couldn't imagine any man in his right mind coming on to Sally.

"Why didn't you show up for your court date?" I asked Sally.

"I had to drive the little dudes. It was a school day. I take this job very seriously."

"And you forgot?"

"Yeah," he said. "I fucking forgot." He closed his eyes and smacked his head with the heel of his hand. "Darn." He was wearing a thick elastic band around his left wrist. He snapped the elastic against his wrist and yelped. "Ow!"

Grandma and I both did raised eyebrows.

"I'm trying to quit cussing," Sally said. "The little dudes were getting detention for talking trash mouth after getting off my bus. So my boss gave me this elastic band, and I have to snap it every time I cuss."

I looked down at his wrist. It was solid red welts. "Maybe you should think about getting a different job."

"No fucking way. Oh shit! Damn."

Snap, snap, snap.

"That's gotta hurt," Grandma said.

"Yeah, it hurts like a bitch," Sally said.

Snap.

If I brought Sally in now he'd have to overnight and wait for the courts to open before Vinnie could bond him out again. He didn't look like much of a threat to flee, so I decided to give him a break and bring him in during business hours. "I have to get you rebonded," I said to Sally. "We can arrange a time between bus runs."

"Wow, that would be awesome. I always have a couple hours off in the middle of the day."

Grandma looked at her watch. "We better get a move on if we want to get to the funeral home on time."

"Hey, rock on," Sally said. "Who's laid out?"

"Lorraine Schnagle. I went earlier today but they had the lid down on the casket."

Sally made a sympathetic sound. *Tsk.* "Don't you hate that?"

"Drives me nuts," Grandma said. "So I'm going back, hoping the lid will be up for the night viewing."

Sally had his hands in his pockets, and he was nodding his head like a bobble-head doll. "I hear you. Give my best to Lorraine."

Grandma's face lit. "Maybe you want to come with us. Even with the lid down it should be a good viewing. Lorraine was real popular. The place will be packed. And Stiva always puts out cookies."

"I could do that," Sally said, still bobbing. "Just give me a second to get more dressed up."

Sally disappeared into the bedroom, and I made a deal with God that I'd try to be a nicer person if only Sally didn't return in sling-back heels and a gown.

When Sally reappeared he was still wearing the faded T-shirt, jeans, and ratty sneakers but he'd added dangly rhinestone earrings and a vintage tuxedo jacket. I felt like God hadn't totally come through for me, but I was willing to take a shot at honoring the deal anyway.

We all piled into the Buick and headed across town to Stiva's.

"I'm hungry," Grandma said. "I wouldn't mind having a burger. We haven't got a lot of time, though, so maybe we could do a drive-by."

A quarter mile later I swung into the drive-thru lane of a McDonald's and ordered a bag of food. A Big Mac, fries, and a chocolate shake for Grandma. Cheeseburger and Coke for me. A chicken Caesar salad and Diet Coke for Sally.

"I have to watch my weight," Sally said. "I have this to-die-for red gown, and I'd be pissed if I fucking grew out of it." He grimaced. "Oh shit." *Snap, snap, snap.*

"Maybe you should try not to talk," Grandma said. "You're gonna give yourself a blood clot with all that snapping."

I handed the bag of food over to Grandma for distribution and pulled forward. A guy dressed out in a black do-rag, homeboy jeans, new basketball shoes, and a lot of gold jewelry that flashed in the overhead streetlight exited the McDonald's and headed for a car with a high bling rating. It was a brand-new black Lincoln Navigator with gleaming chrome wheel covers and black tinted windows. I rolled closer to get a better look and confirmed my suspicion. It was Red Devil. He was carrying a huge bag of food plus a drink holder with four cups.

Now I know the Red Devil's held up fourteen

deli-marts, and I personally saw him toss a flaming Molotov cocktail into a store. So on the one hand, I had to think that this was a bad guy. Problem was, it was hard to take someone seriously when he was going around doing his robbing wearing a cheap rubber mask, riding on a mountain bike.

"Hey!" I shouted at him. "Wait a minute. I want to talk to you."

When I got close enough to talk, I was going to reach out and choke him until he turned blue. I didn't care all that much about his deli-mart robbing career, but I was really unhappy about my yellow Escape.

He stopped and stared at me and suddenly placed me. "You!" he said. "You're one of the dumb bitches who trashed my bike."

"You're calling *me* dumb?" I yelled back at him. "You're the one going around robbing stores dressed up in a stupid mask, riding a kid's bike. I bet you're too dumb to get a driver's license."

"Dumb bitch," he said again. "Dumb punk-ass bitch."

The passenger side door opened on the Navigator, and I could hear guys laughing inside the car. Red Devil got in, slammed the door shut, and the car came to life.

I was itching to jump out of the Buick, run over to the SUV, wrench the door open, and drag the devil guy out of the car. Since, by my cup tally, there most likely were at least three other people in the Lincoln, and they might all have guns, and they might be cranky about me ruining their dinner, I decided to go with the more conservative plan of getting the license plate number and following at a respectful distance.

"Was that the devil bandit?" Grandma wanted to know.

"Yes."

Grandma sucked in some air. "Let's get him! Ram

him from behind, and then when he stops we'll drag him out of the car."

"I can't do that. I have no authority to capture him."

"Okay, so we don't capture him. How about we just kick him a couple times after we get him out of the car?"

"That would be assault," Sally said. "And it turns out it's illegal."

I hit the speed dial for Morelli's number on my cell phone.

"Is this about the Japanese triplets?" Morelli wanted to know.

"No. It's about Red Devil. I'm in the Buick with Grandma and Sally Sweet, and I'm following the devil guy. We're on State, heading south. I just passed Olden. He's in a new black Lincoln Navigator."

"I'll put it out. Don't approach him."

"No *problemo*." I gave Morelli the license number and put my phone on the seat, next to my leg. I followed the SUV for three blocks and saw a blue-and-white come up behind me. I pulled to the side, the blue-and-white sped past and put his lights on.

Grandma and Sally were mouths open, eyes glued to the cop car in front of me.

"That guy in the SUV isn't stopping," Grandma said.

The SUV ran a light and we all followed. I knew the cop in front of me. It was Eddie Gazarra, riding alone. He was a likeable blond-haired Polish chunk. And he was married to my cousin Shirley-the-Whiner. He was probably looking in his rearview mirror, wishing I'd go away.

The SUV suddenly made a right turn and then a quick left. Eddie stuck to his bumper, and I struggled to stay with Eddie, using my whole body to help muscle the Buick around corners. I was sweating from the exertion. Probably some of the sweat was from fear. I was at the brink of losing control of the car. And I was worried about Gazarra, all by himself, in front of me.

My cell was still on, still connected to Morelli. "We're chasing these guys," I yelled down at the phone, giving Morelli cross streets, telling him Gazarra was in front of me.

"*We?*" Morelli yelled back. "There's no *we*. This is a police chase. Go home."

Sally had himself braced in the backseat, his rhinestone earrings reflecting in my rearview mirror. "He could be right, you know. Maybe we should split."

"Don't listen to him," Grandma said, her blue-veined, bony hands gripping the shoulder strap. "Keep the pedal to the metal! You could be a little careful on the turns, though," she added. "I'm an old lady. My neck could snap like a twig if you whip around a corner too fast."

Not much chance of taking a corner that fast in the Buick. Motoring the Buick around was like steering a cruise ship.

Without warning, the SUV went into a turn in the middle of the road and skidded to a stop. Eddie laid some rubber and pulled up a couple car lengths from the SUV. I two-footed the brake pedal and stopped about a foot from Eddie's back bumper.

The rear side window slid down on the SUV, and there was a flash of rapid gunfire from inside the car. Grandma and Sally hit the floor, but I was too stunned to move. The blue-and-white's windshield crumbled, and I saw Eddie jerk to the side and slump.

"I think Eddie's shot!" I yelled at my phone.

"Fuck," Sally said from the backseat. *Snap.*

The SUV took off, wheels spinning, and was out of sight within seconds. I shoved my door open and ran to check on Gazarra. He was hit twice. A bullet had grazed the side of his head. And he had a shoulder wound.

"Shit," I said to Gazarra. "Don't die."

Gazarra looked at me through narrowed eyes. "Do I look like I'm going to die?"

"No. But I'm not an expert."

"Cripes, what happened? It was like World War III broke out."

"Seemed like the gentlemen in the SUV didn't want to chat with you."

I was being glib, hoping it would keep me from bursting into tears. I'd stripped my T-shirt off and had it pressed to Gazarra's shoulder wound. Thank goodness I was wearing a sports bra, because I'd feel conspicuous if I was wearing my lacy Victoria's Secret Wonderbra when the cops got here. There was undoubtedly a first aid kit in the squad car, but I wasn't thinking that clearly. The T-shirt seemed easier and faster. I was pressing hard enough that my hands weren't visibly shaking, but my heart was racing and my breathing was ragged. Grandma and Sally were standing huddled together in silence by the Buick.

"Is there anything we can do?" Grandma asked.

"Talk to Joe. He's on the cell phone. Tell him Gazarra needs help."

Sirens were screaming in the distance, and I could see the flash of police strobes a block away.

"Shirley's gonna be pissed," Gazarra said. "She hates when I get shot." To my recollection, the only other time Gazarra was shot was when he was playing quick draw in the police station elevator, and his gun accidentally discharged. The bullet ricocheted off the elevator wall and lodged in Gazarra's right buttock.

The first cop car angled in. It was followed by a second blue-and-white and Morelli in his SUV. I took a step back to allow the men access to Eddie.

Morelli looked first to me and then glanced over at Gazarra. "Are you okay?" he asked.

I was covered with blood, but it wasn't mine. "I didn't get hit. Eddie's been shot twice, but I think he's going to be all right."

I guess there are places in this country where cops are always perfectly pressed. Trenton wasn't one of those places. Trenton cops worked hard and worried a lot. Every cop on the scene had a sweat-soaked shirt and grim set to his mouth, including Morelli.

"They opened fire with an automatic weapon from the backseat," I told Morelli. "We were coming out of the McDonald's drive-thru on State, and I saw the devil guy cross the lot and get into the Lincoln. The devil guy got into the front passenger seat, so he wasn't the shooter. He had four drinks with him, so there were probably three other guys in the car. I followed him out of the lot and called you. You know the rest."

Morelli slid an arm around me and pulled me close, resting his cheek on mine. "I don't want to get mushy here in front of the guys, but there was a moment back there when I heard shots fired over the phone . . . and I didn't care a lot about the triplets."

"Nice to know," I said, slumping against him, happy to have someone holding me up. "It happened so fast. No one got out of a car. Eddie was still buckled into his seat belt. They shot him through the windshield."

"The Lincoln was stolen. They probably thought Gazarra was going to bust them."

"No, it was me," I said. "This is all my fault. The Red Devil knew I recognized him."

An EMT truck arrived and parked next to Gazarra. Cops were directing traffic, securing the area, shouting over the static and chatter of the dispatch radio.

"It's uncanny the way you stumble into this stuff," Morelli said. "It's creepy."

Grandma was standing behind us. "Two disasters in one day," she said. "I bet it's a personal record."

"Not even close," Morelli said. His eyes settled on my sports bra. "I like the new look."

"I used my T-shirt as a compress."

Morelli removed his shirt and draped it around my shoulders. "You feel cold."

"That's because my heart stopped pumping blood about ten minutes ago." My skin was pale and clammy, and my forearms were goose-bumpy. "I need to get back to my parents' house and have some dessert."

"I could use some dessert, too," Grandma said. "Probably they don't have the lid up on Lorraine, anyway." She turned to Sally. "I know I promised you a good time at the funeral parlor, but it didn't work out. How about some dessert instead? We got chocolate cake and ice cream. And then we can send you home in a cab. My son-in-law drives a cab sometimes, so we get a break on the rates."

"I guess I could eat some cake," Sally said. "I probably burned off a couple hundred calories just now from fright."

Morelli buttoned me into his shirt. "Are you going to be okay to drive?"

"Yeah. I don't even feel like throwing up anymore."

"I need to check on a few things here, and then I'll follow you over."

My mother was on the front porch when we arrived. She was rigid with her arms crossed over her chest and her lips pressed tight together.

"She knows," Grandma said. "I bet the phone's been ringing off the hook."

"How could she know?" Sally asked. "We were way across town, and it's been less than an hour, start to finish."

"The first call always comes from Traci Wenke and Myron Flatt on account of they listen to the police band on their radios," Grandma said. "And then Elsa Downing probably called. She finds out early because her daughter works as a dispatcher. And I bet Shirley called to see if she could drop the kids off so she could go to the hospital."

I parked the Buick, and by the time I got to my mother her face was white, and I expected steam to begin curling out of her ears at any moment. "Don't start," I said. "I'm not talking about it until I've had some cake."

My mother wheeled around without a word, marched to the kitchen, and sliced me a wedge of cake.

I followed after her. "Ice cream," I said.

She scooped half a tub of ice cream onto my plate. She stepped back and looked at me. "Blood," she said.

"Not mine."

She made the sign of the cross.

"And I'm pretty sure Eddie's going to be okay."

Another cross.

There'd been places left at the table for Grandma and me. I took my place and shoveled in cake. Grandma brought an extra chair from the kitchen for Sally and bustled around filling plates. The rest of the family was silent at the dining room table. Only my father was active, head down, forking up chicken and mashed potatoes. Everyone else was frozen in their seats, mouths open, eyes wide, not sure what to make of me with the blood on my shirt . . . and Sally in his earrings.

"You all remember Sally, don't you?" Grandma asked as introduction. "He's a famous musician, and he's a girl sometimes. He's got a whole bunch of pretty dresses and high heel shoes and makeup. He's even got one of them black leather bustier things with pointy ice cream cone breasts. You don't even hardly notice his chest hair when he's got that bustier thing on."

Chapter THREE

"How can he be a girl sometimes?" Mary Alice wanted to know.

Mary Alice is in third grade and is two years younger than her sister, Angie. Mary Alice can ride a bike, play Monopoly if someone helps her read the Chance cards, and can recite the names of all of Santa's reindeer. She's in the dark on gender crossing.

"I just dress up like a girl," Sally said. "It's part of my on-stage persona."

"I'd want to dress up like a horse," Mary Alice said.

Angie looked at Sally's wrist. "Why are you wearing an elastic band?"

"I'm trying to quit cussing," Sally said. "Every time I cuss I snap the elastic band. It's supposed to make me not want to cuss anymore."

"You should just say a different word than the cuss word," Angie said. "Something that sounds like the cuss word."

"I've got it!" Grandma said. "Fudge. That's what you should say."

"Fudge," Sally repeated. "I don't know . . . I feel silly saying fudge."

"What's the red stuff all over Aunt Stephanie?" Mary Alice wanted to know.

"Blood," Grandma said. "We were in a shoot-out. None of us got hurt, but Stephanie was helping out Eddie Gazarra. He was shot twice, and he had blood spurting all over the place."

"Eeeuw," Angie said.

Valerie's live-in boyfriend, Albert Kloughn, was seated next to me. He looked down at my blood-spattered arm and fainted. *Crash.* Right off his chair.

"He fucking fainted," Sally said. "Oh f-f-fudge." *Snap.*

I was done with my cake, so I went to the kitchen and tried to clean up. Probably I should have cleaned up before coming to the table but I really needed the cake.

When I got back to the table Albert was sitting in his seat. "I'm not squeamish or anything," he said. "I just slipped. It was one of those freak accidents."

Albert Kloughn was about five foot seven, had sandy blond hair showing the beginnings of male pattern baldness, and the chubby face and body of a twelve-year-old. He was a lawyer, of sorts, and he was the father of Valerie's baby. He was a sweet guy, but he felt more like a pet than a future brother-in-law. His office was located next to a Laundromat, and he dispensed more quarters than legal advice.

There was a light rap on the front door, the door opened, and Joe walked in. My mother was immediately running for an extra plate, not sure where she was going to put it. Even with the leaf in, the table could only accommodate eight, and Joe made ten.

"Here," Kloughn said, jumping to his feet, "you can have my place. I'm done eating. I don't mind. Honest."

"Isn't he a cuddle umpkins?" Valerie said.

Grandma hid behind her napkin and made a gagging gesture. Morelli held his response to a benign smile. My father kept eating. And it occurred to me that cuddle umpkins fit Kloughn perfectly. How awful is that?

"Now that everyone's here, I have an announcement to make," Valerie said. "Albert and I have set a date to get married."

This was an important announcement because when Valerie was pregnant she was thinking she might hold out for Ranger or Indiana Jones. This was a worrisome situation since it was unlikely either of those guys would be interested in marrying Valerie. Valerie's opinion of Albert Kloughn improved with the birth of the baby, but until this moment my mother harbored the fear that she'd be saddled with Valerie gossip for the rest of her life. Unwed mothers, horrific painful deaths, and cheating husbands were the favorite topics of the Burg gossip-mongers.

"That's wonderful!" my mother said, clapping a hand to her mouth, her eyes filling with tears. "I'm so happy for you."

"A wedding!" Grandma said. "I'll need a new dress. And we need a hall for the reception." She dabbed at her eyes. "Look at me . . . I'm all teary."

Valerie was crying, too. She was laughing and sniffling back sobs. "I'm going to marry my snuggy wuggums," she said.

Morelli paused, his fork halfway to the roast chicken platter. He slid his eyes to me and leaned close. "If you ever call me snuggy wuggums in public, I'll lock you in the cellar and chain you to the furnace."

Kloughn was standing at the end of the table with a glass of wine in his hand. "I have to make a toast," he said. "To the future Mrs. Kloughn!"

My mother went still as stone. She hadn't totally thought through the consequences of Valerie's marriage to Albert. "Valerie Kloughn," she said, trying not to show her horror.

"Holy crap," my father said.

I leaned close to Morelli. "Now I'm not the only clown in the family," I whispered.

Morelli raised his glass. "To Valerie Kloughn," he said.

Kloughn drained his glass and refilled it. "And to me! Because I'm the luckiest man ever. I found my lovey pumpkin, my one true lovey dovey, my big fat sweetie pie."

"Hey, wait a minute . . ." Valerie said. "Big fat sweetie pie?"

Grandma refilled her wineglass. "Somebody stungun him," she said. "I can't take no more."

Kloughn rushed on. His face was flushed, and he'd started to sweat. "I've even got a baby," he said. "I don't know how that happened. Well, I mean, I guess I know how it happened. I think it happened on the couch in there . . ."

Everyone but Joe sucked in some air. Joe was smiling. "And to think, I almost missed this," he whispered to me.

My mother looked like tomorrow she'd be shopping for a new couch. And my father was studying his butter knife . . . undoubtedly wondering how much damage he could do. Good thing the carving knife was in the kitchen.

"It usually takes Kloughns years to get pregnant," Albert said. "Historically we have a low mobility. Our guys can't swim. That's what my father always said. He said, Albert, don't expect to be a father, because Kloughns can't swim. And look at this. My guys could swim! It's not like I was even trying. I just couldn't figure out how to get the thingy on. And then once I got it on, but I think it had a hole in it, because it seemed like it was leaking. Wouldn't it be something if that was the time? Wouldn't it be something if my guys could swim through the thingy? Like I had Superman guys!"

Poor Snuggy Uggums was motoring down the road to doom, gaining momentum, out of control with no idea how to stop.

"Do something," I said to Joe. "He's dying."

Morelli was still wearing his gun. He took it off his hip and pointed it at Kloughn. "Albert," he said, very calmly. "Shut up."

"Thank you," Kloughn said. And then he wiped the sweat off his forehead with his shirttail.

"What about dessert?" my father wanted to know. "Isn't anyone going to serve dessert?"

It was close to nine when Morelli and I staggered through the front door to his town house. Bob-the-Dog came galloping from the kitchen to greet us, attempted a sliding stop on Morelli's polished wood floor, and slammed into Morelli. This was Bob's usual opening act, and Morelli had been braced for the hit. Bob was a big goofy orange-haired beast who ate everything that wasn't nailed down and had more enthusiasm than brains. He shoved past us and bounced out the door, in a rush to tinkle on Morelli's minuscule front yard. This was always Bob's first choice of bathroom, and as a result the grass was scorched brown. Bob returned to the house, Morelli closed and locked the front door, and we stood there for a moment sucking in the silence.

"This wasn't one of my better days," I said to Morelli. "My car was destroyed, I was involved in a shooting, and I just sat through the dinner from hell."

Morelli slung an arm around me. "Dinner wasn't that bad."

"My sister talked cuddle umpkins to Kloughn for two hours, my mother and grandmother cried every time someone mentioned the wedding, Mary Alice whinnied nonstop, and the baby threw up on you."

"Yeah, but aside from that . . ."

"Not to mention, Grandma got completely snookered and passed out at the table."

"She was the smart one," Morelli said.

"You were the hero."

"I wouldn't actually have shot him," Morelli said. "Not to kill, anyway."

"My family is a disaster!"

Morelli grinned. "I've called you Cupcake for as long as I can remember, but I'm rethinking it after listening to the two hours of cuddle umpkins."

"Just exactly what is a human-type cupcake?"

"It's like a cream puff but not as squishy. It's dessert. It's soft and sweet . . . and it's good to eat."

The eating part gave me a rush that went straight to my doodah.

Morelli kissed me just below my earlobe and told me a few things about the right way to eat a cupcake. When he got to the part about licking the icing off the top, my nipples shrunk to the size and hardness of steel ball bearings.

"Boy, I'm really tired," I said. "Maybe we should be thinking about going to bed."

"Good idea, Cupcake."

I've been living with Morelli for several months now, and it's been surprisingly easy. We still like each other, and the magic hasn't gone out of the sex. Hard to imagine it ever would with Morelli. He's nice to my hamster, Rex. He doesn't expect me to make him breakfast. He's neat without being freaky about it. And he remembers to close the lid on the toilet . . . most of the time. What more can you ask from a man?

Morelli lives on a quiet street in a small, pleasant

house he inherited from his Aunt Rose. The house mirrors my parents' house and every other house on Morelli's street. When I look out his bedroom window I see neatly parked cars and two-story red-brick attached town houses with clean windows. There are small trees and small shrubs in small yards. And behind the front doors are frequently large people. Food is good in Trenton.

The bedroom window in my apartment looks out at a blacktop parking lot. The apartment building was constructed in the seventies and is totally lacking in charm and amenities. My interior decorating style is one step away from college dorm. Decorating takes time and money. And I have neither.

So it's a mystery why I would miss my apartment, but the truth is, sometimes I felt homesick for the depressing mustard and olive green bathroom, the hook in the entrance area where I hang my jacket, the cooking smells and television noise from the neighboring apartments.

It was nine in the morning and Morelli was off, ridding the city of bad guys, protecting the populace. I rinsed my coffee cup and set it in the dish drain. I tapped on Rex's cage and told him I'd be back. I hugged Bob and told him to be good and not eat any chairs. After I hugged Bob I had to use the lint roller on my jeans. I was rollering my jeans when the doorbell bonged.

"Howdy," Grandma Mazur said when I answered the door. "I was out for a walk, and I was in the neighborhood, so I thought I'd stop by for a cup of coffee."

"That's a long walk."

"Your sister came over first thing with her laundry, and the house got real crowded."

"I was just going out," I told Grandma. "I have some people to pick up this morning."

"I could help! I could be your assistant. I'd be good at it. I can be real scary when I try."

I grabbed my shoulder bag and denim jacket. "I don't actually need anybody scary, but you can ride along if you want. My plan is to stop at the office to say hello. And then I'm going to get Sally so he can reschedule."

Grandma followed me out the front door, to the curb. "This sure is a pip of a car," Grandma said, taking the Buick in. "I feel like one of them old-time gangsters when I ride in this car."

I feel poor when I ride in the car, since I'm the one buying the gas. No car in the history of the world guzzled gas better than the Buick.

Lula was at the door when I parked in front of the bonds office. "Don't bother trying to get that boat docked just right," she said. "We got an emergency call. Remember the chip lady? Well, she's having some kind of a breakdown. Connie just got off the phone with the chip lady's sister, and Connie said we should go over there and see what's happening."

Sometimes part of my job falls under the category of preventive care. If you know something's going wrong in a bondee's life, it's best to check in with him from time to time rather than wait for him to flee.

"Hell-*o*," Lula said, peeking in the car window. "We got Grandma on board."

"I'm helping Stephanie this morning," Grandma said. "What's a chip lady?"

"It's some woman held up a Frito-Lay truck," Lula said. "And then she ate the chips."

"Good for her," Grandma said. "I've always wanted to do that."

Lula climbed into the backseat. "Me, too. You read those adult magazines and they're always talking about sex fantasies, but I say chip fantasies are where it's at."

"I wouldn't mind combining them," Grandma said. "Suppose you had some good-looking naked man feeding you the chips."

"No way," Lula said. "I don't want to be distracted by no man when I'm eating chips. I'd rather have dip. Just get out of my way when I see the chips and dip."

"It's good you have priorities," Grandma said.

"Know thyself," Lula replied. "Someone famous said that. I don't remember who."

I took Hamilton to Klockner, passed the high school in Hamilton Township, and turned into Cantell's neighborhood. A woman was standing on Cantell's front porch. She took a startled step back when she saw the three of us emerge from Big Blue.

"Guess she's never seen a '53 Buick before," Grandma said.

"Yeah," Lula said, hitching up her fuchsia and black animal print spandex pants. "I'm sure that's it."

I approached the porch and handed the woman my business card. "Stephanie Plum."

"I remember you," the woman said. "You had your picture in the paper when you burned the funeral home down."

"It wasn't my fault."

"It wasn't my fault either," Grandma said.

"I'm Cindy, Carol's sister. I know she's been having a hard time so I called her this morning. Just checking in, you know? And as soon as I heard her I knew something was wrong. She didn't want to talk on the phone, and she was real secretive. So I came over here. I only live two blocks away. She wouldn't answer her door when I knocked, so I went around back and that door was locked, too. And the shades are all drawn. You can't see into the house at all."

"Maybe she just wants to be alone," Lula said. "Maybe she thinks you're nosey."

"Put your ear to the window," Cindy said.

Lula put her ear to the front window.

"Listen real close. What do you hear?"

"Uh oh," Lula said. "I hear the crinkle of a chip bag. I hear crunching."

"I'm afraid she's held up another truck!" Cindy said. "I didn't want to call the police. And I didn't want to call her ex-husband. He's a real jerk. If I'd been married to him, I'd be a little nutty, too. Anyway, I remembered Carol saying how nice you all were, so I thought maybe you could help."

I rapped on the front door. "Carol. It's Stephanie Plum. Open the door."

"Go away."

"I need to talk to you."

"I'm busy."

"She's going to jail," Cindy wailed. "She's a habitual offender. They're going to lock her up and throw away the key. She's a chip junkie. My sister's an addict!"

"We don't want to get carried away with this," Lula said. "Last I looked, Fritos weren't on the list of controlled substances."

"Maybe we should shoot the lock off the door," Grandma said.

"Hey, Carol," I yelled through the door. "Did you rob another Frito-Lay truck?"

"Don't worry," Cindy called out. "We'll get you a good lawyer. Maybe you can plead insanity."

The door flew open and Carol stood in the doorway, holding a bag of Cheez Doodles. Her hair was smudged with orange doodle dust and stood out from her scalp like an explosion had gone off inside her head. Her mascara was smudged, her lipstick eaten off, replaced with orange doodle stain. She was dressed in a nightgown, sneakers, and a warm-up jacket. Doodle crumbs stuck to the jacket and sparkled in the morning sunlight.

"Whoa," Lula said. "It's fright night."

"What is it with you people?" Carol screeched. "Don't you have lives? Go away. Can't you see I'm having breakfast?"

"What should we do?" Cindy asked. "Should we call 911?"

"Forget 911," Lula said. "Call an exorcist."

"What's the deal with the Cheez Doodles?" I asked Carol.

"I slipped. I fell off the wagon."

"You didn't rob another truck, did you?"

"No."

"A store?"

"Absolutely not. I paid for these. Okay, maybe a couple bags got stuck in my jacket, but I don't know how that happened. I don't have any memory of it, I swear."

"You're a nut," Lula said, prowling through the house, gathering up stashed bags of chips. "You got no self-control. You need Chips Anonymous." Lula opened a bag of Doritos and scarfed a few.

Grandma held out a grocery bag. "I found this in the kitchen. We can put the chips in it and take them with us so she isn't tempted to eat any more."

"Put the chips in the bag and give them to Cindy," I told Grandma.

"I thought it might be a good idea if *we* took them," Grandma said.

"Yeah," Lula said. "That's a much better idea than making poor Cindy cart them off."

I wasn't great in the willpower department. Even as I was standing there, I could feel the Cheez Doodles calling my name. I didn't want a whole grocery bag of doodles and chips in the car with me. I didn't want to end up looking like Carol.

"Give all the chips to Cindy," I said. "The chips should stay in the family."

Grandma looked over at Carol. "Are you gonna be okay if we give her *all* the chips? You aren't gonna flip out, are you?"

"I'm okay now," Carol said. "Actually, I feel kind of sick. I think I'm going to lie down for a while."

We filled the grocery bag with the remaining chips and left Carol standing at the door, the pallor of her skin looking slightly green under the orange doodle dust. Cindy drove off with the chips. And Grandma and Lula and I stuffed ourselves into the Buick.

"Hunh," Lula said, settling in. "We could have taken a few bags with us."

"I had my eye on that bag of barbecue chips," Grandma said. "It's gonna be hard for me to keep up my strength without some chips."

"Uh oh," Lula said. "Look at this, a couple of bags of chips somehow got in my big ol' purse . . . just like what happened to Carol."

"Chips are devilish like that," Grandma said.

"Yeah," Lula said. "Guess we should eat them so they don't go to waste."

"How many bags do you have?" I asked her.

"Three. You want one?"

I blew out a sigh, and Lula handed me a bag of Fritos. Not only was I going to eat them . . . I was secretly glad she snitched them.

"Now what?" Lula wanted to know. "I'm not going to have to go back to the filing, am I?"

"Sally Sweet's next up," I said.

"I'm in," Lula said.

Sally lived on the opposite side of town. By the time we got there, he'd be done with his morning bus run, and it'd be a good time to bring him in and get him rebonded.

I called Morelli on the way over to get a report on Eddie Gazarra.

"He's going to be okay," Morelli said. "He'll probably get released from the hospital tomorrow."

"Anything new going on?"

"There was another devil holdup last night. This time the firebomb worked and the store burned down."

"Anyone hurt?"

"No. It was late at night, and the store was empty. The night manager got out the back door. The word on the street is that the Comstock Street Slayers are bragging about the cop shooting."

"I didn't realize we had Slayers in Trenton."

"We've got everything in Trenton."

"If you rounded up all the Slayers, I might be able to identify the Red Devil," I said to Morelli.

"To the best of our knowledge there are twenty-eight active Slayers, and they're about as easy to round up as smoke. And probably the twenty-eight figure is low."

"Okay, suppose I rode around in their neighborhood, looking for the guy?"

"Honey, even *I* don't ride around in that neighborhood."

I disconnected and turned onto Fenton Street. It was easy to find Sally's house. A big yellow school bus was parked at the curb. I pulled up behind the bus, and we all trooped out.

Sally opened the door with the security chain still in place. "I've changed my mind," he said. "I don't want to go."

"You have to go," I told him. "It's the law."

"The law's bogus. I didn't do anything wrong. And now if I go with you I'm going to have to pay more money, right? Vinnie's gonna have to write another bond, right?"

"Uh . . . yeah."

"I haven't got more money. And anyway, I'm not even the one who should have been arrested. They should have arrested that jerk Marty Sklar. He's the one who started all this."

I felt my eyebrows shoot halfway up my forehead. "Marty Sklar is the guy who made a pass at you?"

"Do you know him?" Sally asked.

"I went to school with him. He was a big macho football player. And he married Barbara Jean Biabloki, the pom-pom queen." It was a perfect match. They deserved each other. Sklar was a bully, and Barbara Jean thought she could walk on water because she grew perfect breasts. Last I heard, Sklar was working in his father-in-law's Toyota dealership, and Barbara Jean had porked up to biblical proportions. "Was Sklar drunk?"

"Fuckin' A. Oh crap!" *Snap, snap.*

"You gotta remember about fudge," Grandma said.

Sally nodded. "Fudgin' A."

We all did a mental *eeyeuuw.* Fudgin' A didn't sound tasty coming out of Sally's mouth.

"Maybe fudge don't work for that one time," Grandma said.

If I could get Sklar to drop the charges against Sally, and we had a sympathetic judge, I could save Sally the expense of a second bond. "You're not going anywhere," I said to Sally. "I don't need to bring you in today. I'll talk to Sklar and see what I can do about getting the charges dropped."

"No shit!" *Snap.*

"You better clean up your mouth, or you're gonna lose that hand," Lula said to Sally. "You're gonna amputate yourself."

"F-f-fudge," Sally said.

Grandma looked down at her watch. "You're going to have to take me home now. I have a beauty parlor appointment this afternoon, and I don't want to be late. I got a lot of ground to cover today what with the shooting and all."

This was a good deal for me because the negotiation with Marty Sklar would go better without Grandma present. In fact, I'd prefer to do it without Lula but I didn't think that was going to happen. I pointed the Buick toward the Burg and motored across town. I dropped Grandma off in front of my parents' house. My sister's car was still in the driveway.

"They're planning the wedding," Grandma said. "Ordinarily I'd be right there, but it looks to me like this is going on for days. They spent two hours this morning talking about what kind of suit Mr. Cutie Uggums was going to wear. I don't know how your mother does it. That woman has the patience of a saint."

"Who's Mr. Cutie Uggums?" Lula wanted to know.

"Albert Kloughn. He and Valerie are getting married."

"That's scary," Lula said.

Melvin Biabloki's Toyota dealership took up half a block on South Broad Street. It wasn't the biggest or the best dealership in the state, but according to Burg gossip it made enough money to send Melvin and his wife on a cruise every February and to give a job to his son-in-law.

I parked in the area reserved for customers, and Lula and I went searching for Sklar.

"This here's a butt-ugly showroom," Lula said. "They should buy some new carpet. And what's with the nasty plastic chairs? For a minute there I thought I was back at the office."

A guy in a sports coat ambled over, and it took me a moment to realize it was Marty Sklar. He was shorter than I remembered. His head was balding. He was wearing glasses. And his six-pack stomach had turned to a keg. Marty wasn't aging well.

"Stephanie Plum," Marty said. "I remember you.

Joe Morelli used to write poems on bathroom walls about you."

"Yeah. I'm living with him now."

Sklar touched his index finger to my lip. "Then all those things he said must be true."

He'd caught me flat-footed. I wasn't expecting the touch. I slapped his hand away, but it was too late. I had Marty Sklar cooties on my lip. Yuk. I needed mouthwash. Disinfectant. I was going to rush home and take a shower. Maybe two showers.

"Hey," Lula said. "Don't you touch her. Did she say you could touch her? I don't think so. I didn't hear her give you permission. You keep your nasty-ass hands to yourself."

Sklar cut his eyes to Lula. "Who the hell are you?"

"I'm Lula. Who the hell are you?"

"I'm Marty Sklar."

"Hunh," Lula said.

I tried not to think about the lip cooties and pushed forward. "Here's the thing, Marty. I want to talk to you about Sally Sweet."

"What about him?"

"I thought you might want to drop the charges. It turns out he's hired a really good lawyer. And the lawyer's found a bunch of witnesses who've officially stated you came on to Sweet."

"He hit me with his guitar."

"That's true, but I thought you might not want it to go public about the sex thing."

"What sex thing?"

"The witnesses said you wanted to have sex with Sally."

"That's a lie. I was just busting his balls."

"It's not going to sound like that at the trial."

"Trial?"

"Well, he's got this lawyer now. And all the witnesses . . ."

"Shit."

I looked at my watch. "If you move fast and make a phone call, you can stop the process before it gets out of control. Probably your father-in-law would be upset to learn that you propositioned a transvestite."

"Yeah," Lula said. "That's like a double cheat. You were gonna cheat with a guy in a dress. Father-in-laws hate that."

"What's the name of this hotshot lawyer?" Sklar asked.

"Albert Kloughn."

"And he's supposed to be good? I never heard of him."

"He's a shark," I said. "He's new to the area."

"So what's your interest in this?" Sklar asked me.

"Just being a friend, Marty. Since we went to school together and all."

And I left the showroom.

Lula and I didn't say anything until we were out of the lot.

"Girl, you can lie!" Lula yelled when I turned the Buick onto Broad. "You are the shit. I almost gave myself a hemorrhoid trying not to laugh back there. I can't believe how good you can lie. I mean, I've seen you lie before, but this was like Satan lying. It was inspired lying."

Chapter
FOUR

I drove two blocks up Broad and pulled into a Subway shop.

"This is a good place to eat lunch," Lula said. "They got them low-carb sandwiches. And they got them low-fat sandwiches. You could lose a lot of weight eating here. The more you eat, the more you lose."

"Actually, I chose Subway because it was next to Dunkin' Donuts."

"Friggin' A," Lula said.

We each got a sub. And then we each got six doughnuts. We sat in the car and ate the sub and the doughnuts in silence.

I crumpled my wrappers and shoved them into the doughnut bag.

"Do you know anything about the Slayers?" I asked Lula.

"I know they're bad news. There's a whole bunch of gangs in Trenton. The Comstock Street Slayers and the Bad Killer Cuts are the two big ones. Used to be you only heard about Slayers on the West Coast, but they're everywhere now. Kids join up in prison, and then they bring it back to the street. Comstock Street is gangland these days."

"I talked to Morelli a while ago. He said the Slayers are bragging about shooting Eddie Gazarra."

"Bummer. You better watch out on account of you disrespected Red Devil, and he was hanging with those guys. You don't want to get on the bad side of a Slayer. I'd be real careful of that if I was you."

"You're the one who shot up the devil guy's tire!"

"Yeah, but he didn't know it was me. He probably thought it was you. You're the big-deal bounty hunter. I'm just a file clerk."

"Speaking of file clerk, I should get you back to the office so you can do some filing."

"Yeah, but who's gonna watch out for your ass then? Who's gonna help catch the bad guys? You know what we should do? We should go take a look around Comstock Street. Maybe we could get the Red Devil."

"I don't want to get the Red Devil. He shoots at people. He's a police problem."

"Boy, what's with you? Everything's a police problem these days."

"I enforce bail bond requirements. That's the extent of my authority."

"Well, we don't have to actually get him. We could just do some investigating. You know, like we could ride around in the neighborhood. Maybe talk to a couple people. I bet we could find out who the devil guy is. You're the only one who knows what he looks like."

Lucky me. "To begin with, I don't know where the devil guy lives, so it would be hard to ride around in his neighborhood. And if that isn't enough, even if we found his neighborhood and went asking questions, no one would talk to me."

"Yeah, but they'd talk to me. Everyone talks to me. I got a winning personality. And I look like I belong in a gang-infested neighborhood." Lula scrounged in her big black leather purse, found her cell phone, and punched in a number.

"Hey," she said when the connection was made. "It's Lula, and I need some information." Pause. "Your ass," she said. "I'm not doing that no more." Another pause. "I'm not doing that either. And I'm especially not doing that last thing. That's disgusting. Are you gonna listen to me, or what?"

There were about three more minutes of conversation, and Lula dropped her phone back into her bag.

"Okay, I got some gang boundaries now. The Slayers are between Third and Eighth Streets on Comstock. And Comstock's one block over from Stark," Lula said. "I used to work part of that area. My corner was on Stark, but I got a lot of customers from the south side. It wasn't so bad back then. That was before the gangs moved in. I figure we just mosey on over there and take a look around."

"I don't think that's a good idea."

"How bad could it be? We're in a car. We're just driving through. It's not like we're in Baghdad, or something. And anyway, the gangs aren't out during the day. They're like vampires. They only come out at night. So during the day the streets are real safe."

"That's not true."

"Are you calling me a fibber?"

"Yeah."

"Well, okay, maybe they aren't *real* safe. But they're safe enough in a car. What could happen to you in a car?"

Problem was, Lula and I were sort of the Abbott and Costello of law enforcement. Things happened to us all the time. Things that weren't normal.

"Give me a break," Lula said. "I don't want to go back and file. I'd rather ride through hell than file."

"Okay," I said on a sigh. "We'll do a drive-through."

Abbott and Costello weren't all that bright. They were always doing stupid things like this. And more to the point, I felt guilty about Eddie Gazarra. I felt like he got shot because I'd acted impulsively. I felt like I owed him. Anyway, Lula was probably right. It was daytime. It was probably reasonably safe. I could do a simple ride through the Slayer's neighborhood and maybe I'd get lucky. If I could find the Red Devil, the police might have a chance at getting the guy who shot Eddie.

I cut through the center of the city and turned up Stark Street. Stark Street started out bad and got worse. The gang graffiti increased with each block. By the time we were at Third the buildings were solid slogans and signs. The sidewalks were spray-painted. The street signs were spray-painted. First-floor windows were laced with iron security bars, and the bars and pawn shops were behind partially closed security gates.

I turned right at Third and drove one block to Comstock. Once off Stark there were fewer businesses and the streets narrowed. Cars were parked on both sides of Comstock, reducing the road to barely two lanes. We passed a couple guys on a corner. They were young, dressed in baggy jeans and white T-shirts. Their arms and hands were tattooed. Their expressions were sullen and watchful.

"Not a lot of people out," Lula said. "Except for the two sentries we just passed."

"It's the middle of the day. People are working."

"Not in this neighborhood," Lula said. "Most of these people don't got jobs unless you count holding up liquor stores as a profession."

I checked my rearview mirror and saw one of the corner watchers put a cell phone to his ear.

"I'm getting a bad feeling," I said.

"That's because you're a minority here."

"You mean being white?"

"No. I mean you're the only one for blocks not packin' a gun."

I cruised past Fifth and started looking for a way out. I didn't want to go deeper into the 'hood. I wanted to get back to Stark and head for city center. I turned left onto Sixth and realized the truck in front of me wasn't moving. It was double-parked. No one at the wheel. I put the Buick into reverse and inched back. I was about to pull onto Comstock when a kid appeared from out of nowhere. He was in his late teens, and he looked like a clone of the guys on the corner.

He approached the car and rapped on the driver-side window. "Hey," he said.

"You might want to ignore him," Lula said. "And it might not be a bad idea to back up a little faster."

"I'd like to back up faster, but there are a couple really nasty-looking guys at my bumper. If I back up I'll run over them."

"So what's your point?"

"I know you," the kid at my window said, his face inches from the glass. "You're a fucking bounty hunter. You busted my uncle. You were with some Rambo guy. And you're the one fingered Red Devil."

The car started to rock, and I realized the guys in the back were on the bumper. More faces pressed against the side windows.

"Step on the freaking gas," Lula said. "It don't matter if you run these clowns over. They've been run over lots of times. Look at them. Don't they look like they've been run over?"

"The guy at your window is saying something. What's he saying?"

"How would I know?" Lula said. "It's gangsta talk shit. Something about kill the bitches. And now he's licking the glass. You're gonna have to Clorox this car if we ever get outta here."

All right, I have three options. I can call Joe and have him send the police. That would be really embarrassing, and they might not get here in time to stop the bitch killing. The second choice is that I call Ranger. Equally embarrassing. And there might be bloodshed. Not mine, probably. Or I could run over a couple of these fine, upstanding young men.

"I'm getting real nervous about this," Lula said. "I think you might have made a bad decision to come into this neighborhood."

I felt my blood pressure edge up a notch. "This was your idea."

"Well, it was a bad idea. I'm willing to admit that now."

The Buick bounced around a little, and I could hear scraping, thumping sounds overhead. The idiots were jumping up and down on the roof.

"Your grandma's not gonna like it one bit if they scratch her car," Lula said. "This here's a classic."

"Hey," I yelled to the guy with his face pressed against my window. "Back off from the car. It's a classic."

"Classic this, bitch," he said. And he pulled a gun out of his baggy pants and aimed it at me, the barrel about an inch from the window glass.

"Holy shit," Lula said, eyes the size of duck eggs. "Get me the fudge out of here."

Option number three, I thought. And I mashed the accelerator down to the floorboard. The car sucked gas and roared back like a freight train. I didn't feel any bumps under the tires indicating that I'd run over a body. I took that as a good sign. I wheeled backward onto Comstock and screeched to a stop to change gears. Three guys flew off my roof. Two bounced off the right front fender onto the road. And one smacked onto the hood and grabbed hold of a windshield wiper.

"Don't stop now," Lula yelled. "And don't worry about the hood ornament. You'll lose him on the next turn."

I rammed the car into drive and took off. I could hear a lot of noise behind me. A lunatic mix of yelling and gunfire and laughter. The guy on the hood stared in at me, the pupils of his eyes dilated to the size of nickels.

"Think he got a pharmaceutical problem going," Lula said.

I leaned on the horn, but the hood rider didn't blink.

"This here's like having an insect stuck on your windshield," Lula said. "A big ugly drugged-out praying mantis."

I hauled the Buick around into a looping left turn onto Seventh, and the insect silently sailed off into space and crashed into a rusted-out van that was parked at the curb. I resumed breathing when I got to Stark.

"See, that worked out okay," Lula said. "Too bad we didn't find the devil guy, though."

I gave her a sideways glance. "Maybe you want to go back tomorrow and try again?"

"Maybe not tomorrow."

I called Connie and told her we were on our way back to the office and asked her to run a search for me.

"If I give you some street boundaries, can you check our files for guys in that neighborhood?" I asked her.

"I can search by zip code, and I can search by street. As long as the area isn't too big, I can do the *by street* search."

I felt a responsibility to Eddie, and I thought chances were decent that the devil guy had a record. I'd declined to go through mug shots at police headquarters. I'd done that drill for other crimes and found it to be spectacularly unhelpful. After looking at a hundred head shots, I tended to forget the face of the perp. A search by neighborhood would produce a much smaller pool of potentials.

Connie was pulling files when Lula and I swung through the front door. "I got seventeen hits for the boundaries you gave me," she said. "None are outstanding. It's not really our neighborhood."

Lula looked through the pile of files on Connie's desk. "Hey, this is the guy who was stuck to the hood of your car," Lula said, holding a photo for me to see.

Connie grabbed a file and closed the drawer with her foot. "That's Eugene Brown. He's been arrested so many times we have a personal relationship. Never been convicted of anything but possession."

"Looks like we bonded him out for armed robbery and vehicular manslaughter," Lula said.

"Eyewitnesses have a way of disappearing when Eugene's involved," Connie said. "And there's a lot of sworn testimony recanting. What was he doing on the hood of your car?"

"We were sort of cruising up Comstock Street . . ." Lula said.

Connie's eyes got wide. "Where on Comstock?"

"Third."

"Do you have a death wish? That's Slayerland."

"We were just riding through," Lula said.

"The two of you? In what car? The Buick? The powder blue–and–white Buick? You can't go past Third on Comstock in a powder blue car! That's Cut's colors. You don't go into gang territory with another gang color."

"Well, yeah, but I didn't think it counted for cars. I just thought it counted for clothes. For, like, do-rags and shirts and shit," Lula said. "And it's hard to believe anybody'd take Cut serious with a color like powder blue. Powder blue is a sissy color."

I took the files from Lula and shuffled through them. No devil guy. Connie handed me the remaining four files. No devil guy there either. This left me with three possibilities. The devil guy didn't have a record. Or the devil guy used a different bond agent. Les Sebring, maybe. Or the devil guy gave an address outside of Slayerland.

I saw Connie and Lula go still and fix their eyes on the door behind me. Either someone walked in with a gun in his hand or else Ranger was here. Since no one ducked for cover, I was betting it was Ranger.

A warm hand settled at the base of my neck, and I felt Ranger lean into me. "Babe," he said, softly, his right arm snaking around me to take the file from my hand. "Eugene Brown," he read. "You might not want to spend a lot of time with Eugene. He's not a fun guy."

"I sort of bounced him off the hood of the Buick today," I told Ranger. "But it wasn't my fault."

Ranger tightened his hold on my neck. "You want to be careful with Eugene. He hasn't got much of a sense of humor, Babe."

"I don't suppose you know the identity of the devil guy who's robbing all the deli-marts?"

"Don't suppose I do," Ranger said. "But it's not Eugene. There'd be more bodies on the floor if it was Eugene."

Vinnie's inner office door opened, and Vinnie stuck his head out. "What's up?"

"I'm going out of town for a couple weeks," Ranger said. "Tank will be on the job, if you need him." Ranger dropped the Brown file on Connie's desk and turned to me. "I want to talk to you . . . outside."

It was late afternoon and the sky was overcast, but the autumn air was still warm in spite of the gloom. Ranger's customized black Ford F-150 FX4 was parked curbside. A black SUV with tinted windows was parked behind the truck. The SUV had its motor running.

I followed Ranger out of the office, glancing first at the SUV and then at the heavy traffic on Hamilton. Rush hour in Trenton.

"What if *I* need something?" I asked Ranger, doing a little flirting, feeling brave because I was on a public street. "Should I call Tank?"

He ran a fingertip along my hairline and tucked a stray curl behind my ear. "It depends what you need. Did you have anything special in mind?"

Our eyes held, and I felt the first licks of panic. I should know better than to play with Ranger. He never got rattled, and he never backed down. I, on the other hand, frequently got rattled with Ranger and almost always backed down.

"How about if I need a car?" I asked, searching for something legitimate to change the tone. There'd been times past when I'd needed a car, and Ranger had provided one.

Ranger pulled a set of keys from his pocket and dropped them into my hand. "You can take my truck. I can get a ride back with Tank."

A narrow alley separated Vinnie's office from the neighboring business. Ranger nudged me into the shadow of the alley, pressed me against the brick wall, and kissed me. When his tongue touched mine my fingers curled into his shirt, and I think I might have momentarily lost consciousness.

"Hey," I said, when consciousness returned. "You're poaching."

"And?"

"Stop it."

"You don't mean that," Ranger said, smiling.

He was right. A woman would have to be dead not to want to kiss Ranger. And I wasn't even close to dead.

I gave the keys back to him. "Nice gesture but I can't take the truck."

"Call Tank if you change your mind. And be careful. Don't try to play with Eugene."

And he was gone.

Lula and Connie were shuffling papers, trying to look busy, when I returned to the office.

"Is he gone?" Lula wanted to know.

"Yeah."

"Lord, he makes me nervous. He is so hot. I got flashes. Look at me. I'm having a flash. I'm not even in menopause, and I'm hot flashing."

Connie rolled back in her chair. "Did he tell you where he was going? How long he'd be away?"

"No."

Connie had a problem. When Ranger was gone she was left with me and a couple part-time BEAs. If a high-stakes bond went south, she'd be in a bind. The case would have to go to me. At least temporarily. I was okay at my job, but I wasn't Ranger. Ranger had skills that went way beyond the normal parameters of human ability.

"I hate when he does this," Connie said.

"I been noticing the last two times he took off there was a coup in Central America," Lula said. "I'm going home, and I'm watching CNN."

I left the office and headed home to Joe's house. Somehow I'd managed to keep busy all day, but it didn't feel like I'd accomplished much. I stopped at Giovichinni's deli on Hamilton and picked up some lunch meat, sliced provolone, a medium container of potato salad, and a loaf of bread. I added a couple tomatoes and a small tub of chocolate ice cream.

It was a bad time to stop at Giovichinni's, but it was my only option if I wanted to eat. St. Francis Hospital was a block away, and half the hospital emptied out into Giovichinni's at this hour.

Mrs. Wexler came up to me while I was standing in line. "My goodness," she said, "I haven't seen you in an age. I understand your sister is getting married. Isn't that nice for her, but it must be a very stressful time for you. Is that a cold sore on your lip, dear?"

My hand immediately flew to my lip. I didn't have anything on my lip when I left the house this morning, but yes, there was definitely something erupting on my mouth. I dug in my purse for a mirror. "I've never had a cold sore," I told Mrs. Wexler. "I swear to God."

"Well, it does look like a cold sore," Mrs. Wexler said.

I squinted into my mirror. Yikes! There it was . . . big and red and angry looking. How did this happen? And then it hit me. Marty Sklar and his cooties! I studied my lip. No. Wait a minute, it wasn't a cold sore. It was a boo-boo.

I'd gnawed a hole into my lip on the way across town, worrying about Eugene Brown and God knows what else. Okay, and the fact that I was attracted to two men didn't help. Probably I loved both of them. How sick is that?

"It's a cut," I said to Mrs. Wexler. "I got it this afternoon."

"Of course," Mrs. Wexler said. "I can see that now."

My mother called on my cell phone. "Mrs. Rogers just called," my mother said. "She said you're in Giovichinni's, and you have a cold sore."

"It's not a cold sore. It's a cut."

"Well, that's a relief. Could you pick up a couple things for me while you're there at Giovichinni's? I need a pound of olive loaf, an Entenmann's raspberry swirl coffee cake, and a quarter pound of Swiss. Make

sure they don't slice the Swiss too thin. It all sticks together if it's too thin."

I scurried off to the deli counter, got my mother's
stuff, and got back into line.

Leslie Giovichinni was working the register.
"Gosh," she said, when I stepped in front of her. "You
poor thing. You've got a big herpes!"

"It's not a herpes," I said. "It's a *cut*. I got it this
afternoon."

"You should put ice on it," she said. "It looks real
painful."

I paid Leslie and slunk out of the store. I hunched
behind the wheel of the Buick and turned into the
Burg. I had to park in the driveway when I got to my
parents' house because there was a big yellow school
bus at the curb.

Grandma was at the door, waiting for me. "Guess
who's here?" she said.

"Sally?"

"He came over because he was so excited that the
charges were dropped. And he's been real helpful on
account of Valerie's still here, and we've been dis-
cussing the bridesmaids' dresses. Valerie wants pink,
but Sally thinks they should be a fall color since it's
fall."

Valerie was in the kitchen, sitting at the table with
the baby hanging from her neck in a kind of sling ap-
paratus. My mother was at the stove, stirring a pot of
marinara.

Sally was sitting across from Valerie. His long black
curly hair was Medusa meets Howard Stern. He was
wearing a Mötley Crüe T-shirt, jeans with the knees
torn out, and red lizard cowboy boots.

"Hey, man, thanks for getting the charges dropped,"
Sally said. "I got a call from the court. And then Sklar
called me just to make sure I wasn't gonna go ahead

with the lawyer. I didn't know what to say at first, but I just went with it. It was real good."

I put the cheese and lunch meat in the fridge, and I set the coffee cake on the table. "Glad it worked out."

"So what do you think of the dresses?" Valerie wanted to know.

"Are you sure you want to have a big wedding?" I asked Valerie. "It seems like a lot of work and expense. And who will you have for bridesmaids?"

"You'll be my maid of honor. And then there's Loretta Stonehouser. And Rita Metzger. And Margaret Durski as bridesmaids. And the girls can be junior bridesmaids."

"I'm thinking pumpkin would be a good color for the bridesmaids' gowns," Sally said.

I cut myself a large wedge of coffee cake. It was going to take a lot of cake to improve my mood on the pumpkin gown.

"You know what we need?" Grandma said. "We need a wedding planner. Like that movie. Remember where Jennifer Lopez is the wedding planner?"

"I could use help," Valerie said. "It's hard to find the time for everything, but I don't think I can afford a wedding planner."

"Maybe I could help plan the wedding," Sally said. "I have extra time between my bus runs."

"You'd be a perfect wedding planner," Grandma said. "You have a real eye for color, and you got ideas about all that seasonal stuff. I would never have thought to have pumpkin gowns."

"It's settled then. You're the wedding planner," Valerie said.

My mother's attention wandered to the pantry. She might have been taking a mental inventory, but more likely, she was contemplating the whiskey bottle hidden behind the olive oil.

"How's the house search going?" I asked Valerie. "Any luck?"

"I haven't had a lot of time to put to it," she said. "But I promise to start looking."

"I sort of miss my apartment."

"I know," Val said. "I'm really sorry this is taking so long. Maybe we should move back here with Mom and Dad."

My mother's back went rigid at the stove. First the wedding planner and now this.

I cut another piece of cake and headed out. "I have to go. Joe's waiting."

Joe and Bob were on the couch, watching television. I dropped my purse on the small hall table and took the grocery bag into the kitchen. I made sandwiches and spooned out the potato salad.

"I'm thinking about getting a cookbook," I told Morelli when I handed him his plate.

"Wow," he said. "What's that all about?"

"I'm getting tired of sandwiches and pizza."

"A cookbook sounds like a big commitment."

"It's not a commitment," I said. "It's a stupid cookbook. I could learn how to cook a chicken or a cow, or something."

"Would we have to get married?"

"No." Jeez.

Bob finished his sandwich and looked first to me and then to Morelli. He knew from past experience that it wasn't likely we'd share, so he put his head down on his paw and went back to watching *Seinfeld*.

"So-o-o," I said. "Did you hear about Eugene Brown?"

"What about him?"

"I bounced him off my car today."

Morelli took a forkful of potato salad. "Am I going to hate the rest of this story?"

"It's possible. It was sort of a hit-and-run."

"So this falls under the category of making an official police report?"

"Unofficial police report."

"Did you kill him?"

"I don't think so. He was latched on to the hood of the Buick, hanging on to the windshield wiper, and he got pitched off when I turned the corner. I was at Seventh and Comstock, and I didn't think it was a good idea to get out of the car to check his vital signs."

Morelli collected the three plates and stood to take them to the kitchen. "Dessert?"

"Chocolate ice cream." I followed after him and watched while he scooped. "That was too easy," I said. "You didn't yell or tell me I was stupid, or anything."

"I'm pacing myself."

I rolled out of bed with Morelli at the crack of dawn.

"This is getting scary," Morelli said. "First you're thinking about buying a cookbook. And now you're getting up with me. Next thing you'll be inviting my grandmother over for dinner."

Not likely. His Grandma Bella was nuts. She had this Italian voodoo thing going that she called the eye. I'm not saying the eye worked, but I've known people who got the eye to coincidentally lose their hair, or skip their period, or break out in an unexplained rash. I was half Italian, but none of my relatives could give the eye. Mostly, my relatives gave the finger.

We showered together. And that involved some fooling around. So before Morelli even had breakfast he was already a half hour late.

I had coffee going by the time he came downstairs. He chugged a cup while he did the gun and badge routine. He dropped a blueberry into Rex's cage. And he dumped two cups of dog crunchies into Bob's bowl.

"What's the reason for the early start?" he asked. "You aren't going back to Comstock Street, are you?"

"I'm checking out real estate. Valerie isn't doing anything about finding her own place, so I thought I'd do some searching for her."

Morelli looked over his cup at me. "I thought you were all settled in here. What about the cookbook?"

"I like living with you, but sometimes I miss my independence."

"Like when?"

"Okay, maybe independence is the wrong word. Maybe I just miss my own bathroom."

Morelli grabbed me and kissed me. "I love you, but not enough to add a second bathroom. I'm not budgeted for any more renovations." He set his cup on the counter and headed for the front of the house. Bob ran with him, woofing, jumping around like a rabbit.

"Bob needs to go out," I said.

"Your turn," Morelli said. "I'm late, and besides, you owe me for the shower."

"What? What do you mean I owe you for the shower?"

He shrugged into a jacket. "I did your favorite thing today. Almost drowned doing it, too. And I think I got a bruise on my knee."

"Excuse me? What about that thing I did for you last night? I was just getting payback this morning."

Morelli was grinning. "They're not nearly equal, Cupcake. Especially since I did it in the shower." He took his keys off the hall table. "Come on. Be a sport. I'm really late."

"Fine! Go. I'll walk the dog. Yeesh."

Morelli opened the front door and stopped. "Shit."

"What?"

"We had visitors last night."

Chapter
FIVE

I tightened my robe and peeked around Morelli. There was graffiti on the sidewalk and graffiti on the Buick. We both stepped out onto the small porch. The graffiti was on the front door.

"What are these marks?" I asked. "They look like little kitty paws."

"These are gang symbols. The Comstock Street Slayers are affiliated with Crud and Guts. Sometimes Crud and Guts is known as Cat Guts. So you have CSS with a paw print." Morelli was pointing as he was talking. "The GKC on the door would stand for Gangsta Killer Cruds."

I moved off the porch, over to the Buick. Every square inch of the car was spray-painted. "Slay the bitch" and "Crud Money" were prevalent themes. Morelli's SUV had been left untouched.

"Seems like there's a message here," I said to Morelli. I wasn't all that fond of the Buick but I hated seeing it defaced. The Buick had from time to time saved my butt. And probably this is a weird thing to say, but sometimes I had the feeling there was more there than just a car. Not to mention, the slogans seemed directed at me. And I suspected they weren't indicators of affection.

"'Slay the bitch' is self-explanatory," Morelli said. His no-expression cop face was in place with only the tight corners of his mouth giving him away. Morelli wasn't happy. "'Crud Money' describes the gangster lifestyle of extortion and drug sales. In this case, it could be putting you on notice that you're marked for retribution."

"What does that mean? Retribution?"

Morelli turned to me and our eyes held. "Could be anything," he said. "Could be death."

A greasy wave of undefined emotion slid through me. I suspected fear was heavy in the mix. I didn't know a lot about gangs, but I was coming up to speed fast. I hadn't felt especially threatened by gang-related crime three days ago. Now it was sitting at my curb, and it didn't feel good.

"You're exaggerating, right?" I asked.

"Executions are a part of gang culture. Gangs have been steadily on the rise in Trenton, and the murder rate has been rising with them. It used to be that the gangs were small and composed of kids looking to have a local identity. Now the gangs have their roots in the prison system and have national affiliations. They control the drug sales and territories. They're violent. They're unpredictable. They're feared in their communities."

"I knew there was a problem. I didn't know it was that bad."

"It's not something we like to talk about since we're at a loss how to fix it." Morelli pushed me into the house and closed the door. "I want you to stay here today until I get some intel on this. I'm going to have the Buick picked up and impounded in the police garage, so someone from the street gangs task force can take a look at it."

"You can't take the Buick. How will I get to work?"

Morelli tapped me gently on the forehead with his index finger. "Anybody home in there? Look at that car. Do you want to drive that car around?"

"I've driven around in worse." And that was the honest-to-God sad truth. How pathetic is that?

"Humor me, okay? Stay in the house. You should be safe here. To my knowledge, the Slayers have never burned down a house."

"Just a deli," I said.

"Yeah. A deli."

We both thought about that for a moment.

Morelli took my car keys from my purse and left. I locked the front door and went to the living room window to watch Morelli pull away in his SUV.

"How are we going to go for a walk?" I asked Bob. "How am I going to do my job? What will I do all day?"

Bob was pacing in front of the door, looking desperate.

"You're going to have to do it in the backyard today," I said, not all that unhappy about missing the walk. Bob pooped *everywhere* in the morning, and I got the privilege of carting it home. It's hard to enjoy a walk when you've got a big bag of poop in your hand.

I hooked Bob up to his backyard leash and tidied the kitchen. By one o'clock the bed was made, the floors were clean, the toaster was polished, the laundry was washed, dried, and folded, and I was cleaning out the fridge. At some point when my back was turned, the Buick disappeared from the curb.

"Now what?" I said to Bob.

Bob looked thoughtful, but he didn't come up with anything, so I called Morelli. "Now what?" I said to Morelli.

"It's only one o'clock," he said. "Give me a break. We're working on it."

"I polished the toaster."

"Un hunh. Listen, I have to go now."

"I'm going nuts here!"

There was a disconnect and then a dial tone.

I still had the phone in my hand when it rang.

"What's going on?" Connie wanted to know. "Are you sick? You always check in at the office by now."

"I have a car problem."

"And? You want me to send Lula?"

"Sure. Send Lula."

Ten minutes later, Lula's red Firebird was idling in front of Morelli's house.

"Looks like Morelli got his house decorated," Lula said.

"It appears Eugene Brown didn't enjoy getting flipped off my hood."

"I didn't get none of this gang crap on my house, so it looks like you're the only one he's holding a grudge against. I guess that's on account of I was just an innocent passenger."

I gave Lula the squinty-eyed death glare.

"Don't you look at me like that," Lula said. "You should be happy for me that I'm not involved in this. Anyways, Vinnie's not happy either. He said there's just five days left to get Roger Banker's ass hauled into court, or he's gonna be out the bond."

If I had a quarter for every time I tried to snag Roger Banker, I could go to Bermuda for a week. Banker was as slippery as they come. He was a repeat offender, so he knew the drill. I couldn't feed him a load of baloney about just going down to the court to reschedule. He knew once the cuffs were on him, he was going to jail. He was unemployed, living off an indeterminate number of loser girlfriends and loser relatives. And he was hard to spot. Banker had no memorable features. Banker was like the invisible man. I once stood next to him at a bar and didn't recognize him. Lula and I had been collecting photographs of him and committing the photographs to memory with hopes that would help.

"Okay," I said, "let's make the rounds. Maybe we'll get lucky."

The rounds consisted of Lowanda Jones, Beverly Barber, Chermaine Williamson, and Marjorie Best. There were other people and places to include in the Banker hunt, but Lowanda, Beverly, Chermaine, and Marjorie were my top picks. They all lived in the projects just north of the police station. Lowanda and Beverly were sisters. They lived four blocks apart, and they were a car crash.

Lula cruised into the projects. "Who's first up?" Lula asked.

"Lowanda."

The projects covered a large chunk of Trenton real estate that was less than prime. *A lot* less than prime. The buildings were red-brick, government-issue low rise. The fencing was industrial chain-link. The cars at the curb were junkers.

"Good thing for the gang graffiti or this would be real drab," Lula said. "Wouldn't you think they could grow grass? Hell, plant a bush."

I suspected even God would have a hard time landscaping the projects. The ground was as hard and as blighted as the lives of the people who lived here.

Lula turned onto Kendall Street and parked two doors down from Lowanda's garden apartment. The term *garden* being used loosely. We'd been here before so we knew the layout. It was a ground-floor unit with one bedroom and seven dogs. The dogs were of varying sizes and ages. All of indeterminate breed. All of them horny buggers willing to hump anything that moved.

We got out of the car cautiously, on the lookout for the pack of beasts.

"I don't see any of Lowanda's dogs," Lula said.

"Maybe they're locked up in the house."

"Well, I'm not going in if they're in the house. I hate those dogs. Nasty-assed humpers. What's she thinking, anyway, to keep a pack of pervert dogs like that?"

We knocked once. No answer.

"I know she's in there," Lula said. "I can hear her talking, doing business."

Lowanda did phone sex. She didn't look like she was rolling in money, so I was guessing she wasn't all that good at the job. Or maybe she just spent her money on beer, cigarettes, and chicken nuggets. Lowanda ate a lot of chicken nuggets. Lowanda ate chicken nuggets like Carol Cantell ate Cheez Doodles.

I knocked again and tried the doorknob. The door wasn't locked. I held the door open a crack, and Lula and I peeked in. No dogs in sight.

"Not likely Banker's in here," Lula said, following me through the front door. "The door would be locked up. And anyway, jail would look good compared to this pigpen."

We stepped over a suspicious stain on the rug and stared into the jumbled mess that passed for Lowanda's home. There was a mattress on the floor in the far corner of the living room. The mattress was covered with a tattered yellow chenille spread. An open, empty pizza delivery box was on the floor by the mattress. Clothes and shoes were scattered everywhere. A couple rickety folding chairs had been set up in the living room. The backs of the chairs said "Morten's Funeral Parlor." A big brown leather recliner had been placed in front of the television. The recliner had a gash in one arm and in the seat, and some of the stuffing was spilling out.

Lowanda was in the recliner with her back to us, a phone to her ear and a bucket of chicken nuggets balanced on the roll of fat that circled her waist. She was wearing gray sweats decorated with ketchup stains.

"Yeah, honey," she said into the phone. "That's good, baby. Oh yeah. Oh-h-h-h yeah. I just got myself all naked for you. An' I got love oil on myself 'cause I'm gonna get hot."

"Hey!" Lula said. "Lowanda, you paying attention here?"

Lowanda jumped in her seat and whipped around to look at us. "What the hell?" she said. "What are you doing scaring me like that when I'm trying to earn a honest living?" She returned to the phone. "Excuse me, sugar. Lowanda's got a small problem. Could you just work on yourself some? I be right back." She covered the phone with her hand and got up, some of the chair stuffing sticking to her double-wide ass. "What?"

"We're looking for Roger Banker," Lula said.

"Well, he isn't here. Does it look like he's here?"

"Maybe he's hiding in the other room," Lula said.

"You got a search warrant?"

"We don't need a search warrant," Lula said. "We're bounty hunters."

"Whatever," Lowanda said. "Just do your search and get out. I gotta get back to my caller. Soon as you stop talking to Mr. Stiffy he turns into Mr. Softy. And I get paid by the job. I do a volume business here."

Lula moved through the house while I stayed with Lowanda.

"I'm willing to pay for information," I told Lowanda. "Do you have any information?"

"How much you paying?"

"Depends on the information," I said.

"I got an address. I know where he's at if you hurry over there." She handed the phone over to me. "You talk to this guy, and I'll write down the address."

"Wait a minute . . ."

"Hello?" Mr. Stiffy said. "Who's this?"

"None of your business."

"I like that," he said. "Spunky. I bet you'd like to spank me."

"Wait a minute. I know your voice. Vinnie?"

"Stephanie? Christ." Disconnect.

Lowanda came back with the paper. "Here it is," she said. "This is where he's staying."

I looked at the paper. "This is your sister's address."

"And? What happened to my caller?"

"He hung up. He was done."

Lula returned to the living room. "Lowanda," she said, "you better do something about your kitchen. You got a cockroach as big as a cow in there."

I gave Lowanda a twenty.

"This is it? This is all I get?" Lowanda said.

"If Banker's at Beverly's house, I'll be back with the rest of the money."

"Where's the dogs?" Lula wanted to know.

"Out," Lowanda said. "They like to go out when the weather's nice."

Lula opened Lowanda's door and looked around. "How far out do they go?"

"How the hell do I know? They go *out*. And they stay out all day. *Out* is *out*."

"Just asking," Lula said. "No need to get touchy. You don't exactly have the best-mannered dogs, Lowanda."

Lowanda had her hands on her hips, lower lip stuck out, eyes narrowed. "You dissin' on my dogs?"

"Yeah," Lula said. "I *hate* your dogs. Your dogs are rude. Those dogs hump everything."

"Wasn't so long ago people was saying that about *you*," Lowanda said. "You got some nerve coming around here asking for information and then dissin' my dogs. I got a mind to never give you no more information."

I grabbed Lula before she removed Lowanda's eyes from her eye sockets, and I shoved Lula out the door.

"Don't provoke her," I said to Lula. "She's probably got guns."

"I got a gun," Lula said. "And I got a mind to use it."

"No guns! And get moving. I don't like standing out here in the open where the dogs can find us."

"I think she insulted me," Lula said. "I'm not ashamed of my past. I was a damn good ho. But I didn't like the tone of her voice just now. It was an insulting tone."

"I don't care what tone she had . . . move your butt to the car before the dogs get us."

"What's with you and the dogs? Here I just been insulted, and all you can think about is the dogs."

"Do you want to be standing here when those dogs come running around the corner of the building?"

"Hunh. I could take care of those dogs if I had to. It's not like I'm *afraid* of those dogs."

"Well, *I'm* afraid of those dogs, so haul ass."

And that was when we heard them. Yipping, yipping, yipping in the distance. On the move. Getting closer. Somewhere out of sight, to the side of the building.

"Oh shit," Lula said. And Lula started running for the car, knees up, arms pumping.

I was two steps in front of her, running for all I was worth. I could hear the dogs round the corner. I turned to look, and I saw them galloping after us, eyes wild, mouths open, tongues and ears catching wind. They were closing ground fast, the biggest of them in the lead.

Lula let out a shriek. "Lord help me!"

I guess the Lord was listening because they ran past Lula and took me down. The first dog hit me square in the back, sending me to my knees. Not a good position to be in when you're attacked by a pack of humpers. I tried to regain my footing, but the dogs were on me, and I couldn't get up. I had humpers on both legs, and a bulldog that looked like Winston Churchill humping my head. There was a humper on a humper.

"Keep going. Save yourself!" I yelled to Lula. "Tell my mother I love her."

"Get up!" Lula yelled at me. "You gotta get up! Those dogs'll hump you to death."

She was right. The pack was vicious. It was in a humping frenzy. Dogs in inferior humping positions were snarling and nipping, jockeying for better locations. The leg humpers held tight, grimly determined to finish the job, but the head humper kept losing his grip. The head humper was drooling and panting hot dog breath in my face. He'd hump some and slide off, and then he'd come scrambling back, trying to hump again.

"I can't get up!" I said. "I've got seven humping dogs on me. *Seven*. Do something!"

Lula was running around, hands in the air. "I don't know what to do. I don't know what to do."

"Get the dog off my head," I yelled. "I don't care about the leg humpers. *Just get the dog off my head!*"

"Maybe you should let them have their way with you," Lula said. "They'll go away as soon as they're done. That's the way it is with male humping."

"Maybe you should goddamn grab this horny humping bulldog and get him the hell off my freaking head!"

The door to Lowanda's apartment crashed open, and Lowanda yelled out to us. "Hey!" she said. "What are you doing to my dogs?"

"We aren't doing nothing," Lula said. "They're humping Stephanie."

Lowanda had a bag of dog kibble in her hand. She shook the bag and the dogs stopped humping and looked around. Lowanda shook the bag some more and the dogs gave a couple last halfhearted humps and took off for the kibble.

"Dumb-ass bounty hunters," Lowanda said, disappearing into the house with the dogs, slamming and locking the door behind her.

"I thought you were a goner," Lula said to me.

I was on my back, breathing heavy, eyes closed. "Give me a minute."

"You're a mess," Lula said. "Those dogs humped all over you. And you got something in your hair from that bulldog."

I got to my feet. "I'm going with drool. It looks like drool, right?"

"If you say so."

Lula and I moved to the safety of the car, and Lula drove the distance to Beverly's apartment. Beverly's apartment looked a lot like Lowanda's, except Beverly didn't have a recliner. Beverly had a couch hauled up to her television. The couch was partially covered with a blue sheet, and I feared there was a gross stain under the sheet, too terrible for even Beverly to overlook.

"You can't come in here now," Beverly said, when she opened the door. "I'm busy. I got my honey here, and we were just getting it on."

"More information than I need," Lula said. "I just watched a pack of dogs hump Stephanie. I about reached my humping limit for the day."

"Those must be Lowanda's dogs," Beverly said. "I don't know what the deal is with those dogs. I never seen anything like it. And three of them is female."

"We're looking for an FTA," I said to Beverly.

"Yeah, that's what you're always doing here," Beverly said. "But I'm not FTA. I didn't do nothing wrong. Swear to God."

"It's not you," I said. "I'm looking for Roger Banker."

"Hunh," Beverley said. "That's inconvenient. You gonna arrest him?"

"We're going to take him to the station to get re-bonded."

"Then what? Then you gonna let him go?"

"Do you want us to let him go?" Lula asked.

"Well, yeah."

"Then that's what we'll do," Lula told her. "He'll be in and out. And on top of that, we'll give you a twenty if we get to take him in."

Lowanda and Beverly would give their mother up for spare change.

"Okay, I guess I could tell you then," Beverly said. "He's the honey in the back room. And he might be a little indisposed."

"Roger," Beverly called out. "I got a couple ladies out here want to see you."

"Bring them back," Roger said. "I can handle them. More is better when it comes to ladies."

Lula and I looked at each other and did some eye rolling.

"Tell him to get dressed and come out here to meet us," I said to Beverly.

"You should put some pants on and come out here," Beverly said. "They don't want to meet up with you in the back room."

We could hear some rustling and fumbling, and Banker strolled out. He was wearing khaki pants and sneakers. No socks, no shirt. I was betting on no underwear.

"Roger Banker," Lula said. "This here's your lucky day, on account of we come to give you a free ride to the clink."

Banker blinked once at Lula and once at me. And then he whirled around and ran for the kitchen door.

"Cover the crappy car in the front," I yelled to Lula.

"It's probably Banker's." And I took off after Banker, pushing around Beverly, following Banker out the back door. Banker was running fast, long legs gobbling up ground. He jumped a section of chain-link and disappeared around the end of the building. I scrambled to follow and got snagged on a piece of wire as I cleared the top of the fence. I ripped myself free and kept going. Banker was maybe half a block ahead of me, but I had him in view. He was on the street, doubling back, running toward his car. And he was slowing down. Good thing, too, because I was dying. I really needed to do more aerobics. The only time I actually worked out was when I was in bed with Morelli. And even then I spent a lot of time on my back.

Lula was between Banker and the car. She was in the road, looking like a big pissed-off bull about to charge. If I was Banker I would have thought long and hard about getting around Lula, but I guess Banker didn't feel like he had a lot of options, because he never broke stride. Banker ran straight on, into Lula. There was a sound like a basketball hitting against a brick wall. Lula went on her ass, and Banker bounced back about five feet.

I tackled him from behind, and we both went down. I had cuffs in my hand, and I was trying to grab a wrist, but Banker was flailing around.

"Help me!" I yelled to Lula. "Do something."

"Out of my way," Lula said.

I rolled free of Banker, and Lula sat down hard on him, simultaneously expelling every molecule of air out of both ends of Banker's body.

"Ooooff," Banker said. And then he went dead still, spread-eagled on his back, looking like roadkill.

I cuffed him, and stood free. His eyes were open but glazed, and he was breathing shallow.

"Blink if you're okay," I said.

"Fuck," Banker whispered.

"Well, what were you thinking?" Lula asked down at him, hands on hips. "You don't just run into a woman like that. Didn't you see me standing there? I got a mind to sit on you again. I could squash you like a bug if I wanted."

"I think I messed myself," Banker said.

"Then you aren't riding in my car," Lula told him. "You can walk your sorry behind all the way to the police station."

I hauled Banker up onto his feet and searched his pockets for his car keys. I found the keys plus twenty dollars. "Give the money to Beverly," I told Lula. "I'll drive him to the station in his car, and you can follow."

"Sure," Lula said.

I dragged Banker to the crappy car parked curbside and turned to Lula. "You're going to wait for me at the police station, right?"

"Are you implying I don't always wait?"

"You never wait."

"I can't help it. I got a thing about police stations. It's from my troubled past."

An hour later I had Banker securely behind bars, and I had the body receipt in my hand, guaranteeing that Vinnie wouldn't be out his bond money. I searched the parking lot, but I couldn't find Lula. Big surprise. I called her cell phone. No answer. I tried the office.

"Sorry," Connie said. "She's not here. She stopped in to say that you had Banker, but then she took off again."

Great. I had half the ass ripped out of my jeans, my shirt was covered with grass stains, and I didn't even want to think about the state of my hair. I was standing in the middle of the public parking lot across from the police station, and I had no car. I could call my father. I could call Morelli. I could call a cab. Problem was, they were all a temporary fix. When I woke up tomorrow I would be back to square one with no car.

Of course there was still one more choice available to me. Ranger's truck. It was big and black and brand new. It came fully loaded with all sorts of toys and customized options. And it smelled like expensive new leather and Ranger . . . an aroma second only to chocolate chip cookies baking in the oven. Too bad there were a lot of really good reasons not to use the truck. At the top of the list was the fact that Joe would be nuts.

My cell phone chirped in my bag. "It's me," Connie said. "Vinnie just left for the day, and his last directive was that you're responsible for Carol Cantell. He doesn't want any screw-ups."

"Sure," I said. "You can count on me." I disconnected, blew out a sigh, and dialed Ranger's man, Tank. The conversation with Tank was short. Yes, Ranger had given him instructions to turn the truck over to me. Delivery would take about twenty minutes.

I put the time to good use by rationalizing my actions. I had no choice. I had to take the truck, right? How else would I do my job? And if I didn't do my job I wouldn't get paid. And then I wouldn't be able to make my rent payment. True, my sister was paying the rent these days on my apartment, and I was living rent-free with Morelli. But that could change at any moment. Suppose Valerie suddenly moved out?

What then? And it wasn't as if I was married to Morelli. We could have a big fight, and I could be on my own again. In fact, now that I was getting the truck a big fight was almost a certainty. This was an exhausting thought. Life was fudging complicated.

The truck arrived exactly on time, followed by the black SUV. Tank got out of the truck and handed me the keys.

To say that Tank is a big guy is oversimplification.
Tank is a tank. His freshly shaved head looks buffed up
with Pledge. His body is perfectly toned and fat free.
His ass is tight. It's rumored that his morals are loose.
And his black T-shirt looks painted onto him. Hard to
tell what Tank thinks of me. Or, for that matter, if Tank
thinks at all.

"Call me if there's a problem," Tank said. Then he
got into the SUV and took off.

Just like that . . . I had a truck. Not just any old
truck, either. This was a wicked, bad-ass, four-door supercrew with oversized cast aluminum wheels, a whole
herd of horses under the hood, tinted windows, and
GPS. Not to mention a slew of gadgets about which I
was clueless.

I'd ridden with Ranger, and I knew he always had a
gun tucked away, hidden from view. I climbed behind
the wheel, felt under the seat, and found the gun. If it
had been my truck and my gun, I'd have removed the
gun. Ranger left it in place. Trusting.

I cautiously turned the key in the ignition and eased
the truck into the flow of traffic. The Buick drove like
a refrigerator with wheels. The truck drove like a monster Porsche. I decided if I was going to drive the truck
I was going to need a whole new wardrobe. My clothes
weren't cool enough. And I needed more basic black.
And I should trade in my sneakers for boots. And probably I needed sexier underwear . . . a thong, maybe.

I crossed town, drove a couple blocks on Hamilton,
and slipped into the Burg. I was taking the long way
home to Joe's house. Always procrastinate the unpleasant. Morelli wouldn't be happy about me going off with
Lula, but he'd understand. Going off with Lula when
he'd asked me to stay in the house would generate the
sort of anger that could be worked off with a half hour

of vicious channel surfing. The truck was going to provoke a full-blown contest of wills.

I turned the corner onto Slater and felt my heart roll over in my chest. Morelli was home. His SUV was parked in front of the house. I lined up behind the SUV and told myself it might not be so bad. Morelli was a reasonable guy, right? He'd see that I had no choice. I had to take Ranger's truck. It was the sensible thing to do. And besides, it was my business. Just because you lived with someone didn't mean they ran your life. I didn't tell Morelli how to conduct his business, did I? Well, okay, maybe once in a while I stuck my nose in there. But he never listened to me! That's the important point here.

Problem was, it wasn't actually about the truck. It was about Ranger. Morelli knew he might not be able to help me if I was standing next to Ranger when Ranger was operating outside the law. And Morelli had enough of his own wild years to understand the feral side of Ranger's sexuality. Another good reason not to have me standing too close to Ranger.

I swung out of the truck, beeped it locked, and marched up to the house. I opened the door, and Bob rushed up to me and bounced around. I gave him some hugs and got some Bob slobber on my jeans. I didn't mind about the slobber. It seemed like a small price to pay for unconditional love. And besides, you could hardly notice the slobber mixed in with the grass and dirt stains and God knew what else. Bob sniffed at the God knew what else and backed off. Bob had standards.

Morelli didn't rush to greet me. He didn't bounce around or slobber or exude unconditional love. Morelli was slouched on the couch, watching the Three Stooges on television. "So," he said when I came into the room.

"So," I answered.

"What's with the truck?"

"What truck?"

He cut his eyes to me.

"Oh," I said. "That truck. That's Ranger's truck. He's letting me borrow it until I get the Buick back."

"Has the truck got a VIN?"

"Of course it has a VIN."

Is the VIN legitimate? would have been a better question. Ranger has a seemingly inexhaustible supply of new black cars and trucks. The origin of these vehicles is unknown. The vehicle identification tag is almost always in place, but it seems possible the Bat Cave might contain a metal shop. Not that Ranger or any of his men would actually steal a car, but maybe they wouldn't ask too many questions upon delivery.

"You could have borrowed my SUV," Morelli said.

"You didn't offer it to me."

"Because I wanted you to stay in the house today. One day," Morelli said. "Was that too much to ask?"

"I stayed in the house for most of the day."

"Most of the day isn't all of the day."

"What about tomorrow?"

"It's going to be ugly," Morelli said. "You're going to be on a rant about women's equality and personal freedom. And I'm going to be waving my arms and yelling, because I'm an Italian cop, and that's what we do when women are irrational."

"It's not about women's equality and personal freedom. This isn't political. It's personal. I want you to support my career choice."

"You don't have a career," Morelli said. "You have a suicide mission. Most women try to avoid murderers and rapists. I have a girlfriend who goes out trying to find them. And if murderers and rapists weren't bad enough, now you've pissed off a gang."

"These gang people should get a grip. The least little thing and they're all bent out of shape. What's the deal with them?"

"That's how they have fun," Morelli said.

"Maybe the police should try to get them involved in a hobby, like woodworking, or something."

"Yeah, maybe we could get it to replace all the drug dealing and killings they're doing now."

"Are they really that bad?"

"Yes. They're really that bad."

Morelli shut the television off and came over to me. "What the hell happened to you?" he said, looking more closely at my jeans.

"I had to run Roger Banker down."

"What's this in your hair?"

"I'm hoping it's dog drool."

"I don't get it," Morelli said. "Other women are happy to stay home. My sister stays home. My brothers' wives stay home. My mother stays home. My grandmother stays home."

"Your grandmother is insane."

"You're right. My grandmother doesn't count."

"I'm sure there'll be a time in my life when I want to stay home. This isn't it," I said.

"So I'm ahead of my time?"

I smiled at him and kissed him lightly on the lips. "Yeah."

He pulled me close to him. "You don't expect me to wait, do you?"

"Yep."

"I'm not good at waiting."

"Deal with it," I said, pushing away.

Morelli narrowed his eyes. "Deal with it? Excuse me?"

Okay, maybe I said it a little more authoritatively than I'd intended. But my day hadn't been all that great, plus I was feeling just a tad defensive over the foreign substance in my hair that might have been drool, but then, maybe not. I could have ended the conversation there, but I didn't think it was smart to back down on the issue. And truth is, I was working my way out of Morelli's house.

"I'm not staying home. End of discussion."

"The hell this is the end," Morelli said.

"Oh yeah? Well end *this*." And I gave him the finger and headed for the stairs.

"Very adult," Morelli said. "Nice to know you've thought this through and have it reduced to a hand gesture."

"I've thought it through, and I have a plan. I'm leaving."

Morelli followed me upstairs. "Leaving? That's a plan?"

"It's a temporary plan." I took the laundry basket from the closet and started putting clothes in it.

"I have a plan, too," Morelli said. "It's called you're staying."

"We'll do your plan next time." I emptied my lingerie drawer into the basket.

"What's this?" Morelli said, picking out lavender string bikini underpants. "I like these. You want to fool around?"

"No!" Actually, I sort of did, but it didn't seem in keeping with the current plan.

I gathered up some things from the bathroom, added them to the basket, and carted the basket downstairs. Then I lugged the hamster cage from the kitchen and put it on top of the clothes in the basket.

"You're serious about this," Morelli said.

"I'm not going to start every day off with an argument about hiding in the house."

"You don't have to hide in the house forever. Just

lower your visibility for a few days. And it would be nice if you'd stop looking for trouble."

I hefted the laundry basket and pushed past him to the door. "On the surface that sounds reasonable, but the reality of it is that I give up my job and hide."

I was telling the truth. I didn't want to start every day off with an argument. But, I also didn't want to wake up to more graffiti on Joe's house. I didn't want a firebomb thrown through his front window. I didn't want a Slayer breaking in when I was alone and in the shower. I needed a place to stay that was unknown to the Slayers. Not Morelli's house. Not my parents' house. Not my apartment. I wouldn't feel completely safe in any of those places. And I didn't want to put anyone in danger. Maybe I was making a big thing out of nothing . . . but then, maybe not.

So, here I was idling at the corner of Slater and Chambers with a pleasant, perfectly designed, color-coordinated Martha Stewart laundry basket on the seat beside me, filled with all the clean clothes I could find, a hamster cage wedged into the seat behind me . . . and no place to go.

I'd told Morelli I was going home to my parents' house, but it had been a fib. The truth was, I walked out without totally thinking the whole thing through.

My best friend Mary Lou was married and had a pack of kids. No room there. Lula lived in a closet. No room there either.

The sun was setting, and I was feeling panicky. I could sleep in Ranger's truck, but it didn't have a bathroom. I'd have to go to the Mobil station on the corner to use the toilet. And what about a shower? The Mobil station didn't have a shower. How was I going to get the drool out of my hair? And Rex? This was so pathetic, I thought. My hamster was homeless.

A flashy black Lexus SUV made its way up Slater. I slid low in the seat and held my breath as the Lexus rolled forward. Hard to see through the SUV's tinted windows. Could be anyone driving, I told myself. Could be a perfectly nice family in the Lexus. But in my gut I worried that they were Slayers.

The Lexus stopped in front of Morelli's house. The bass from the SUV stereo thumped down the street and beat against my windshield. After a long moment the SUV moved off.

Looking for me, I thought. And then I burst into tears. I was in emotion overload, feeling sorry for myself. A bunch of gang guys were out to get me. The police had Big Blue. And I'd moved out on Morelli . . . for the umpteenth time.

Rex had come out of his soup can and was hunkered down on his wheel, myopically surveying his new surroundings.

"Look at me," I said to Rex. "I'm a mess. I'm hysterical. I need a doughnut."

Rex got all perky at that. Rex was always up for a doughnut.

I called Morelli on my cell and told him about the Lexus. "Just thought you should know," I said. "Be careful when you go out of the house. And maybe you shouldn't stand in front of any windows."

"They're not out for me," Morelli said.

I nodded agreement in the dark truck and disconnected. I drove a half mile down Hamilton and pulled into the drive-thru lane at Dunkin' Donuts. Is this a great country, or what? You don't even have to get out of your car to get a doughnut. Good thing, too, because I looked a wreck. Besides the grass-stained, ripped-up clothes, my eyes were all red and splotchy from crying. I got a dozen doughnuts, parked in the back of the lot, and dug in. I gave Rex part of a jelly doughnut and a piece from a pumpkin spice doughnut. I figured pumpkin was good for him.

After eating half the bag I was sick enough not to care about Morelli or the gang guys. "I ate too many doughnuts," I said to Rex. "I need to lie down or burp or something." I checked out my shirt. Big glob of jelly on my boob. Perfect.

The engine was off and the only diode blinking was for the antitheft system. I turned the key and the dash lit up like Christmas. I touched one of the buttons and the GPS screen slid into place. After a few seconds a map appeared, pinpointing my location. Very slick. I touched the screen and a series of commands appeared. One of the commands was return route. I touched the screen and a yellow line took me from Dunkin' Donuts back to Morelli's house.

Just for the hell of it I pulled out of the lot and followed the line. Minutes later, I was at Morelli's house. Interesting thing is, the line didn't stop there. I continued to follow the line and after a couple blocks I got really excited because I knew where I was going. The line was taking me to the police station. And if the line led me to the police station, maybe it would also retrace the route Tank took when he brought the truck to me. If the computer stored enough information, there was the possibility that it might take me to the Bat Cave.

Chapter
SIX

I reached the police station and sure enough the yellow line kept going. I was moving back toward the river, into an area of renovated office buildings and street-level businesses. Now I had a new problem. The yellow line could go on forever. It could go right past the Bat Cave, and I'd never know. And just as I was thinking this, the yellow line stopped.

I was on Haywood Street. It was a side street with minimal traffic, two blocks away from the noise and frustration of city center rush-hour gridlock. A series of four-story town houses ran along the north side of the street. A couple office buildings occupied the south side. I had no idea where to go from here. None of the town houses had an attached garage and there was no on-street parking. I circled the block, looking for an alley with rear-access parking. None. This was a good central location, and one of the town houses would make a good Bat Cave, but I couldn't see Ranger parking his truck any distance from his house. I was idling in front of an office building with underground parking. Ranger could park in the underground garage, but even then he'd have to cross the street to get to the town house. Not a big deal for an ordinary person. Seemed out of character for Ranger. Ranger sat with his back to the wall. Ranger never left himself exposed.

The other possibilities weren't as much fun. The computer could simply have run out of allotted space, and Haywood Street meant nothing. Or Tank could have taken Ranger's truck and parked it convenient to the Tank Cave.

Lights were on in most of the town houses. The office buildings were mostly dark. The building with parking was a relatively small seven-story structure. The foyer plus floors six and five were lit. I rolled back a couple feet, so I could see through the large glass double door. The foyer looked newly renovated. Elevators to the rear. Reception desk to one side. There was a uniformed guy behind the reception desk.

A two-lane entrance to the underground parking garage sat like a black gap in the building façade. I pulled into the parking garage entrance, but I was stopped by a machine that demanded a passkey. A heavy iron gate barred my way. I squinted into the dark interior and got a rush. I was pretty sure I was looking at a black Porsche parked nose-in to the back wall.

I hit my high beams, but the angle of the truck didn't splash a lot of light around the garage. Fortunately, Ranger carried a full array of bounty hunter toys. I retrieved a three-pound Maglite from the backseat, swung out of the truck and played the light across the expanse of the garage. The back wall held a stairwell and elevator. There were four parking spaces in front of the elevator. The first two were empty. Ranger's Porsche Turbo filled the third. A Porsche Cayenne filled the fourth. His Mercedes was missing. And I had the truck. Two black SUVs were parked on the side wall.

"It's the Bat Cave," I said to Rex when I got back behind the wheel.

Kind of fun to finally have found it ... but now what? Ranger was off somewhere, and I still didn't have a place to spend the night. I stared into the dark garage. I had no place to stay, and dollars to doughnuts, sitting in front of me was a building with a vacant apartment. Don't even think about it, I said to myself. That's like a death wish. This man is fanatical about protecting his privacy. He won't be happy to find you've broken into his apartment and done the Goldilocks thing.

There was a part of my brain that was in charge of stupid ideas. When I was seven it told me to jump off my parents' garage roof to see if I could fly. It also encouraged me to play Choo Choo with Joe Morelli when I was a kid. Morelli was the originator of Choo Choo. Morelli was the choo choo train, and I was the tunnel. And as it turned out it was necessary for the train to spend a lot of time under my skirt. Later in life the stupid idea part of my brain encouraged me to marry Dicky Orr. Orr was a slick talker who had a roving eye. Less than a year after the wedding, other body parts that belonged to Orr started roving as well. And that was the end of that marriage.

The stupid idea part of my brain was now telling me I might be able to break in and go undetected. Just for one night, it said. Do it for Rex's sake. Poor Rex needs a place to spend the night.

I backed out of the garage entrance and drove around the block, hoping the stupid idea department would shut down. Unfortunately, it was still up and running when I returned to Ranger's building. I had his truck. He hadn't bothered to remove his gun. Maybe he hadn't bothered to remove his passkey. I checked the visor and the console. I checked the side-door pockets and the glove box. I was looking for a plastic credit card–type key that would slide into the machine. I backed out a second time, drove to the corner, and parked under a streetlight so I could better see the interior of the truck. Still couldn't find the passkey.

I looked down at the key in the ignition. There was an extra key and two small black plastic devices attached to the key ring. One was a remote to unlock the truck. The second was also a remote of some sort. I circled the block, pulled into the garage entrance, pushed a button on the second remote, and the gate slid open.

Stephanie, I said to myself, if you have any sense at all, you'll turn tail and get out of here as fast as possible. Yeah, right. I'd gotten this far—how could I not want to explore further? I mean this was the Bat Cave, for crying out loud.

There were two SUVs parked to the side. That meant Ranger wasn't the only person to use this garage. It would be awkward for Tank or one of Ranger's other men to discover Ranger's truck had wandered home, so I retreated from the driveway and parked on the next block. Then I walked back to the garage, let myself in, and remoted the iron gate closed. I stepped into the elevator and looked at the panel. Seven buttons plus garage. I bypassed the security guard at the desk on the first floor and pressed number two. The elevator rose two floors and the doors opened to a large darkened reception area that I assumed led to offices. Floors three and four were similar. I skipped five and six since these were the lighted and presumably occupied floors. And the seven button wouldn't work. The elevator would go down, but it wouldn't go all the way up to seven.

The penthouse, I thought. The dragon's lair. It needed a passkey. Just for the hell of it, I aimed the garage remote at the panel and hit the remote button. The elevator silently rose to floor seven and opened. I stepped out to a small reception area with a patterned white-and-black marble floor and off-white walls. No windows, a breakfront on one of the walls, one door in front of me.

I'd like to say that I was very cool about all this, but the truth is, my heart was pounding so hard it was blurring my vision. If the door opened and Ranger looked out at me, I'd fall over dead on the spot. And what if he had a woman with him? What would I do? I wouldn't do anything, I reasoned, because I'd be dead, remember?

I held my breath and remoted the door. I turned the knob. Couldn't get in. I looked more closely at the door. It had a deadbolt. I inserted the extra key and the door opened. Now I had a real dilemma. Up to this point I wasn't feeling especially invasive. I'd discovered the location of Ranger's base of operations. In truth, not such a big deal. However, once I crossed the threshold in front of me, I was in Ranger's private space, and I was uninvited. This was officially breaking and entering. Not only was it illegal . . . . it was rude.

The stupid part of my brain kicked in again. Yes, it said, but how about all those times Ranger let himself into *your* apartment? Half the time you were asleep, and he scared the bejeebers out of you. Can you ever remember one time that he knocked first?

Maybe one time, I answered. It stood to reason that he'd knocked at least once. But hard as I tried I couldn't recall him ever knocking. Ranger slipped in like smoke under the door.

I took a deep breath and stepped over the threshold. "Hello," I called softly. "Anybody home? Yoohoooo?"

Nothing. Not a sound. The reception area had been lit, but the apartment was dark. I was standing in a small hallway foyer. An antique wood sideboard was against the wall to my right. There was a tray on the sideboard that looked like it was supposed to hold keys, so I dropped Ranger's keys in the tray. I flipped the switch by the door and two side-by-side candlestick lamps, also on the sideboard, blinked on.

The foyer area was defined by an arch and beyond the arch the living room opened directly in front of me. Kitchen and dining area to the right of the living room. Bedroom suite to the left. The apartment was larger than mine and miles more opulent. Ranger had furniture. Expensive furniture. It was an eclectic mix of antique and modern. Lots of wood and black leather. Marble in the small powder room off the foyer.

Hard to imagine Ranger moving through these rooms dressed in SWAT black. The apartment felt masculine, but more like cashmere sweater and Italian loafers than bounty hunter fatigues. Okay, maybe jeans and boots and cashmere sweater but that was a stretch. The jeans would have to be excellent.

The kitchen was gourmet and stainless steel. I peeked in the refrigerator. Eggs, fat-free milk, four bottles of Corona, a plastic container of rustic olives, and the usual condiments. Apples, limes, and eating oranges in the crisper. Brie and cheddar in the dairy drawer. All jars and shelves were immaculate. Nothing but ice cubes in the freezer. Spartan, I thought. I looked through the cupboards. Organic unsweetened granola, a jar of honey, an unopened box of crackers, green tea, a foil bag of Kona coffee beans, a foil pack of smoked salmon, and a foil pack of tuna. Yeesh. No Cap'n Crunch, no peanut butter, no Entenmann's coffee cake. How could anyone live like this?

I prowled through the living room into the bedroom area.

There was a small sitting room with a comfy, clubby couch and large-screen plasma TV. The bedroom opened off the sitting room. King-size bed, perfectly made. Four king pillows in shams, matching the ivory sheets trimmed with three narrow ribbons of dark brown piping. All looked like they'd been ironed. A lightweight down comforter encased in a matching dark brown duvet covered the bed. No spread. Blanket chest at the foot of the bed. Brass lamps with black shades on tables. Fabrics on chairs and curtains were earth tones. Very subdued and classy. I'm not sure what I expected from Ranger, but it wasn't this.

In fact, I was having some doubts that he lived here. It was a great apartment, but there were no personal touches. No photographs in the living room. No book on the nightstand next to the bed.

The master bath and dressing room attached to the bedroom. I stepped into the bath and went momentarily breathless. The room very faintly smelled like Ranger. I prowled around and discovered the scent was from the soap. Again, as in the rest of the house, nothing was out of place. Towels were neatly stacked. Ivory and dark brown, matching the sheets. Very plush. The thought of them next to a naked Ranger gave me a rush that buckled my knees.

The double sink was soap scum–free and set into a marble countertop. Toiletries were displayed to the left. Straight edge and electric razor to the right. No tub, but there was a large marble-and-glass walk-in shower. White terry robe on a hook by the shower.

The dressing room was filled with clothes. A mix of work and casual. I recognized the work clothes. The Ranger who wore the casual hadn't been a part of my life. Everything was neatly hung or folded. No dirty socks on the floor. Everything perfectly pressed. Thank God, no ladies' lingerie. No birth control pills or box of tampons.

I decided there were two possibilities. Either Ranger lived with his mother, or else he had a housekeeper. I didn't see any evidence of a little Cuban lady in residence, so I was going with the housekeeper theory.

"So," I said to the empty apartment, "nobody'd mind if I stayed here tonight, right?"

Since no one objected, I took it as a positive sign. Ten minutes later, I was back in the apartment with Rex and a change of clothes. I set Rex's cage on a kitchen counter and gave him a chunk of apple. I ate the rest of the apple and wandered into the sitting room. I sunk into the comfy couch and picked up the remote for the television. Total space age. I hadn't a clue what to do with all the buttons. No wonder Ranger said he never watched television.

I gave up on the television and migrated into the bedroom. I was tired and the bed looked inviting, but the thought of sliding between Ranger's sheets had me in a cold sweat.

Get over it, I told myself. It's not like he's here.

Yes, I answered, but these are his sheets, for cripes' sake. His personal sheets. I did some chewing on my lower lip. On the other hand, they'd obviously been laundered since he'd slept in them. So it wasn't all that personal, right?

Problem number two: I didn't want to contaminate the sheets with the gunk in my hair. This meant I'd have to shower in Ranger's bathroom. A shower meant I'd have to get naked. And the thought of being naked in Ranger's bathroom brought back the cold sweat.

Just do it, I told myself. Be an adult. Unfortunately, being an adult was part of the dilemma. I was having a *very adult* reaction to getting naked in the shower. An uncomfortable mix of desire and acute embarrassment. I ordered myself to ignore it all. I squinched my eyes closed and took my clothes off. I opened my eyes, adjusted the water, and stepped under the spray. Serious. Down to business. Get the gunk out of my hair. Get out of the shower.

Halfway through lathering with Ranger's shower gel

I was barely able to focus. The scent seemed to swell around me. I was hot and slippery with shower gel, and I was surrounded by Essence of Ranger. Agony. Ecstasy. I was living a wet dream. *Yikes.* Next time I broke into Ranger's apartment I would bring my own soap.

I scrubbed my hair with a vengeance, rushed out of the shower, and toweled off. Yes, these were Ranger's towels and God only knows what they've touched, *so don't go there!* This was not exactly a silent thought. This was more of a mental shriek.

I got dressed in undies and T-shirt and marched off to bed. I slipped under the covers. I closed my eyes and groaned. It was heaven. Like floating on a seven-hundred-thread-count cloud. Total comfort, except for the uneasy feeling of impending doom.

The room was still dark when I awoke the next morning. Curtains were drawn throughout the apartment, and I wasn't about to open them. Didn't want to broadcast my presence. I rolled out of bed and went straight to the shower. It was daytime. I was feeling much more brave. And God help me, I was looking forward to Ranger's shower. I was a shower gel slut!

After the shower, I had an orange and some granola for breakfast. "I got through the night, and I survived the shower," I said to Rex, sharing a slice of orange with him, dropping some granola in his food dish. "I don't know why I was so worried. Probably Ranger wouldn't even mind that I was here. After all, he's slept in my bed and used my shower. Of course, I was in them at the time. Still, what's good for the gander is good for the goose, don't you think?" The apartment was quiet and comfortable, and I was feeling less like an intruder. "This isn't too different from living with Morelli," I told Rex. "I was a guest there. And I'm a guest here." The fact that Ranger didn't know I was a guest was starting to seem like a technicality. "Don't worry," I said. "I'm going to get our apartment back. All I have to do is find a place for Valerie. And hopefully the Slayer problem will go away."

I didn't expect Ranger would be home anytime soon, but I wrote a note of explanation, just in case, and propped it on Rex's cage. I closed Ranger's front door behind me and remoted it locked. Then I took the stairs, stopping periodically to listen for footfalls, keeping alert for the sound of a fire door opening above or below me.

I cracked the door to the garage and peeked out. Ranger's two cars were still in place. The SUVs had multiplied overnight. There were now four of them parked side by side. No humans walking around, so I scuttled across the garage, opened the gate, and hurried up the street to the truck.

I hauled myself up behind the wheel, locked the doors around me, and sat for a moment in the silence, inhaling the delicious aroma of leather seats and Ranger.

I sniffed my arm and groaned. The Ranger smell was coming from me. He'd given me his truck, and I'd moved into his home. I'd slept in his bed, and I'd showered with his shower gel. I couldn't imagine what would follow if he found out.

Ranger rarely showed emotion. He was more a man of action . . . throwing people against walls and out windows, never breaking a sweat, his face perfectly composed. Now you've made me mad, he'd calmly say. And then bodies would fly through the air. The bodies always belonged to scumbags who'd done really bad things, so the carnage wasn't totally unjustified. Still, it was a scary and awesome spectacle to watch.

I didn't think Ranger would throw me against a wall or out a window. My fear was more that we'd stop being friends. And there was also a small fear that retribution would be sexual. Ranger would never do anything that wasn't consensual. Problem was, once Ranger truly invaded my space there wasn't a lot I didn't eventually consent to. Ranger was very good in close.

Okay, so what's up for the day? Harold Pancek was my only outstanding case. I needed to work at finding Pancek. Probably I should check up on Carol Cantell. I should stay out of Slayerland. And I needed to find an apartment for Valerie.

A call to Morelli was in the number one slot.

"Hey," I said when he answered. "Just wanted to make sure you're okay."

"Where are you?"

"I'm in the truck on the way to work. Any new damage from the Slayers?"

"No. It was a quiet night . . . after you left. So what's the deal, are you coming back?"

"No. Never."

We both knew that was a big fib. I always came back.

"One of these days we should probably grow up," Morelli said.

"Yeah," I said, "but I don't think we should feel rushed into it."

"I'm thinking I might ask Joyce Barnhardt out on a date."

Joyce Barnhardt was a total skank and my archenemy. "That would be a definite detour off the road to maturity," I told him.

Morelli gave a snort of laughter and hung up.

Half an hour later, I was in the office, and Connie and Lula were standing noses pressed to the front window.

"That vehicle sitting at the curb looks like Ranger's personal truck," Lula said.

"It's a loaner," I told her.

"Yeah, but it's Ranger's, right?"

"Yep. It's Ranger's."

"Oh boy," Connie said.

"No strings attached," I told them.

Lula and Connie smiled. There were always strings attached.

They'd plotz if they knew about the Bat Cave. For that matter, I was having a hard time not plotzing when I thought about the Bat Cave.

"Today is Harold Pancek Day," I said.

"He's a no-brainer," Connie said. "I've been checking on him. He works at the multiplex. Shows up every day at two and works until ten. If you can't get him at home, you can get him at work."

"Have you tried calling him?"

"I reached him once, and he told me he'd come in for rescheduling. He was a no-show on that. And now I get a machine when I call."

"I vote we get him tonight at the multiplex," Lula said. "There's a movie I want to see. It's that one where the world gets blown up and there's only mutants left. I saw the ad on television, and one of those mutants is really fine. We could go to the movie and then snag ol' Harold on the way out." She was thumbing through the paper on Connie's desk, searching for the entertainment page. "Here it is. That movie starts at seven thirty."

The plan had a lot going for it. It would give me the entire day to try to find a place for Valerie. And it would take up some of my night. I didn't want to go back to Ranger's apartment until the building was in low- to no-traffic mode. Plus I'd seen those ads Lula was talking about and the mutant was extremely fine.

"Okey dokey," I said. "We'll go tonight. I'll pick you up at six thirty."

"You're gonna be in the Bat Truck, right?"

"It's all I've got."

"I bet you get a tingle when you sit in it," Lula said. "I can't wait. I want to try behind the wheel. I bet you feel like a real badass behind the wheel."

Mostly I felt like I was wearing someone else's underpants. Considering it was Ranger's underpants (figuratively speaking), the feeling wasn't entirely unpleasant.

"What are you doing for the rest of the day?" Lula wanted to know.

I took Connie's paper and turned to real estate. "I'm looking for an apartment for Valerie. She's not showing a lot of motivation to vacate mine, so I thought I'd help her out."

"I thought you were all settled in with Morelli," Lula said. "Uh oh, is there trouble in paradise?"

I started circling rentals. "No trouble. I just want my own space back."

I was concentrating on the paper, not looking up, not wanting to see Lula's and Connie's reactions.

I finished circling, folded the paper, and put it in my shoulder bag. "I'm taking the back end of your paper," I said to Connie. "And there's no trouble."

"Hunh," Lula said. She leaned forward and sniffed. "Damned if you don't smell good. You smell just like Ranger."

"Must be the truck," I said.

I'd barely gotten out the door when my cell phone rang.

"It's your mother," my mother said. As if I wouldn't know her voice. "Everybody's here, and we were wondering if you could stop by for just a second to take a look at some dress colors. We picked out a gown, but we need to make sure it's okay with you."

"Everybody?"

"Valerie and the wedding planner."

"The wedding planner? You mean Sally?"

"I never realized he knew so much about fabric and accessorizing," my mother said.

Grandma Mazur was at the door, waiting for me, when I parked behind the big yellow school bus, in front of my parents' house.

"Now that's a truck," she said, eyeballing Ranger's Ford. "I wouldn't mind having a truck like that. I bet it's got leather seats and everything." She leaned forward and sniffed. "And don't you smell good. What is that, a new perfume?"

"It's soap. And it won't go away."

"It smells sort of . . . sexy."

Tell me about it. I was in love with myself.

"They're all in the kitchen," Grandma said. "If you want to sit you have to bring a chair from the dining room."

"Not necessary," I told her. "I can't stay long."

My mother, Valerie, and Sally were having coffee at the kitchen table. There were some fabric samples, next to the coffee cake, and Valerie had a couple pages torn from a magazine in front of her.

"Sit," my mother said. "Bring a chair."

"Can't. Got things to do."

Sally handed one of the pages to me. "This is a picture of the bridesmaids' dresses. Your dress will be the same, but a different color. I'm still thinking pumpkin."

"Sure," I said. "Pumpkin would be terrific." Anything would be okay at this point. I didn't want to be a party pooper, but I had other things on my mind.

"What things do you have to do?" Grandma wanted to know.

"Bounty hunter things."

My mother made the sign of the cross.

"You should see Stephanie's new truck," Grandma

Mazur said. "It looks like a truck the devil himself would drive."

This got everyone's attention.

"It's a loaner from Ranger," I said. "I had some problems with the Buick, and I haven't got the insurance money from the Escape yet."

Another sign of the cross from my mother.

"What's sticking out of your bag?" Grandma asked me. "Looks like the want ads in the paper. Are you looking for a car? I could go with if you're looking for a car. I like cars."

"I'm not looking for a car today. Val's been too busy with the new baby to look for an apartment, so I thought I'd help her out. I saw a couple places in the paper that looked interesting."

Valerie reached out and took the paper from my bag. "No kidding? Wow, that's really nice of you. Is there anything good in here?"

My mother scooted around so she could look at the paper with Valerie.

"Here's one that's a house for rent. And it says it has a Burg location. That would be perfect," my mother said. "The girls could stay in the same school." She looked over at me. "Did you call the number? Do you know where this is?"

"I called on the way here. It's a duplex on Moffit Street. The house next to Gino's Tomato Pie. The owner lives in the other half. I told her I'd stop around this morning."

"I know that house," Grandma said. "It's pretty nice. Lois Krishewitz used to own that house. She sold it two years ago when she broke her hip and had to move into assisted living."

Valerie was on her feet. "Just give me a minute to get a few things together for the baby, and then we can go look at it. We wanted to buy, but we can't seem to scrape together a down payment. This would give us more space in the meantime."

"I'll get my purse," my mother said.

"I'll come, too," Sally said.

"Me, too," Grandma said.

"We can take my bus," Sally said. "We'll have more room."

"This is gonna be cool," Grandma said, starting for the door. "We're gonna be just like the Partridge Family. Remember when they all traveled around in that bus?"

Don't panic, I told myself. We're just going a short distance. If you sit low in your seat no one will see you.

Valerie had the baby in a carrier on her back and the big patchwork quilt diaper bag over her shoulder. "Where's my purse?" she asked. "I need my purse."

Grandma handed Val her purse. And Val draped her big shoulder bag over her free shoulder.

"Jeez, Val," I said, "let me give you a hand with some of that."

"Thanks," she said, "but I'm balanced this way. I do this all the time."

I don't mean to sound cynical, but if Val ever needed fast cash we could probably get her a job as a pack animal. She could work alongside the mules that take people into the Grand Canyon.

"I've got my checkbook," my mother said, closing the door behind us. "Just in case we like the house."

Valerie lumbered down the porch steps, followed by Grandma.

"I want the front seat," Grandma said, hurrying along. "I don't want to miss anything."

It was a crisp blue-sky morning, and Sally's big hoop earring gleamed gold in the sunlight as he took the wheel. He was wearing a Buzz Lightyear T-shirt, his usual ratty sneakers, and ripped jeans. He had a shark tooth necklace around his neck, and the volume of his hair seemed to have increased since I saw him last. He settled little heart-shaped Lolita-type sunglasses on his big hook nose, and he started the bus.

"You gotta turn at the corner," Grandma told him. "Then you go two blocks and make a right."

Sally took the first corner wide, and Grandma slid off her seat, onto the floor.

"Fuck," Sally said, looking down at Grandma. *Snap*.

"Don't worry about me," Grandma said, righting herself. "I just didn't remember to hold on. I don't know how all those little kids do it. These seats are slippery."

"The kids are all over the fucking bus all the time," Sally said. "Oh shit." *Snap, snap*.

"Sounds like you're having a relapse," Grandma said to Sally. "You were doing real good for a while there."

"I have to concentrate," Sally told her. "It's hard to stop doing something that took me years to perfect."

"I can see that," Grandma said. "And it's a shame you have to give up something you're so good at."

"Yeah, but it's for a good cause," Sally said. "It's for the little dudes."

Sally eased the bus up to the curb in front of the rental house and opened the door with a *whoosh* of the hydraulic. "Here we are," he said. "Everybody out."

I tagged along after my mother, Grandma Mazur, Valerie and the baby, and Sally as they all hustled up to the front porch.

My mother knocked on the landlord's door, and everyone quieted down for a moment. My mother knocked a second time. Still, no one opened the door.

"That's odd," Grandma said. "I thought she was supposed to be home."

Sally put his ear to the door. "I think I hear someone breathing in there."

Probably she was on the floor, having a coronary. A

herd of lunatics just got out of a big yellow school bus and descended on her porch.

"You better open up if you're in there," Grandma yelled. "We got a bounty hunter out here."

The door cracked open, the security chain in place. "Edna? Is that you?" the woman asked.

Grandma Mazur squinted at the eyes behind the door. "Yep, it's me," she said. "Who are you?"

"Esther Hamish. I always sit by you at bingo."

"Esther Hamish!" Grandma said. "I didn't know you were the one who bought this house."

"Yep," Esther said. "I had some money socked away from Harry's insurance policy, God bless him, may he rest in peace."

Everyone made the sign of the cross. Rest in peace, we all said.

"Well, we come to see about the rental," Grandma told Esther. "This here's my granddaughter. She's looking for a place."

"How nice," Esther said. "Let me get the key. You had me going for a minute there. I've never had a school bus park in front of my house before."

"Yeah," Grandma said. "It's new to us, too, but we're getting used to it. I like that it's a nice cheery yellow. It's a real happy color. Problem is, it blocks the view of the street. Of course I guess it could be worse. We could have our view blocked by one of those vans that carries aliens around. I was listening to news on the radio, and they said a bunch of aliens were found dead from heatstroke in one of them vans yesterday. Imagine that. Here these poor creatures travel through space to get to us, all those light years and galaxies away, and then they die from heat stroke in a van."

"What a shame," Esther said.

"I'm just glad it wasn't in front of my house," Grandma said. "I'd feel terrible if I had to find E.T. dead in a van."

Chapter
SEVEN

Esther Hamish's rental was a lot like my parents' house. Living room, dining room, kitchen on the ground floor. Three small bedrooms and bath on the second floor. Narrow backyard. Minuscule front yard. A stand-alone, two-car garage to the rear of the property.

The interior was clean but tired. The bathroom and kitchen were serviceable but dated. Again, a lot like my parents' house. And clearly the house was occupied.

"When will it be available?" Valerie asked.

"Two weeks," Esther said. "I have a young family in here now, and they just bought a house. They'll be moving in two weeks."

"Wait a minute," I said. "The paper said immediate occupancy."

"Well, two weeks is almost immediate," Esther said. "When you get to be my age, two weeks is nothing."

Two weeks. I'll be dead in two weeks! Valerie needs to move out of my apartment now.

Valerie turned to my mother. "What do you think?"

"It's perfect," my mother said.

Esther looked at Sally. "Are you the son-in-law?"

"Nope," Sally said. "I'm the bus driver and the wedding planner."

"The son-in-law is a lawyer," my mother said proudly.

Esther perked up when she heard that.

"You should take it," Grandma said to Valerie.

"Yeah," Sally said. "You should take it."

"Okay," Valerie said. "It's a deal."

So here we go again, there's good news, and there's bad news. The good news is I'm getting my apartment back. The bad news is I'm not getting it back soon enough.

"I need a doughnut," I said, more to myself than anyone else.

"That's a good idea," Grandma said. "I could go for a doughnut."

"Back to the bus," Sally said. "We're all going for doughnuts."

Five minutes later, Sally was parked in front of Tasty Pastry. The doors *whoosh*ed open and everyone tramped out for celebratory doughnuts. Grandma picked out two, my mother picked out two, Valerie got two, and Sally got two. And I got a dozen. I said they were for the office, but if my day didn't improve there was a good chance I'd eat every last one of them.

Renee Platt was behind the counter. "Wow, it's really brave of you to take on the Slayers," she said to me. "I sure wouldn't want to mess with any of those guys."

"Who are the Slayers?" my mother wanted to know.

"Nobody special," I told my mother. "And I didn't take them on."

"I heard you went into their territory with a tank and ran over a bunch of them," Renee said. "Including the head guy. And I heard you're the only one who can identify the Red Devil. And that you've sworn a blood oath to get him."

"Omigod," I said. "Who did you hear that from?"

"Everybody knows," Renee said. "It's all over town."

My mother crossed herself and ate her two doughnuts on the spot.

"It's the Hungarian side of the family," Grandma
said. "We're tough. We come from a long line of army
deserters and nasty alcoholics."

"Probably we should be going home now," I said.
My mother looked like the two doughnuts didn't do
it. My mother had her lips pressed so tight together her
face was turning blue. I was a trial to my mother.

We all trooped out to the bus and took our seats.
"Let me know if you need help rounding up those
Slayers," Grandma said to me. "I don't know what
they are, but I bet I could kick some Slayer butt."

"They're a gang," Sally said. "A really bad gang. I
have to go through their territory to pick up a couple
kids on my bus route, and it's like going through a war
zone. They have sentries on the corners and soldiers
patrolling the streets. And I don't know what it is, but
these guys never smile. They just stand there, staring,
like the living dead."

"What do gangs do?" Grandma wanted to know.

"They act tough," Sally said. "And these days they
control a lot of the drug traffic. And they kill each
other."

"I don't know what this world's coming to," Grandma
said. "Used to be the mob did that. What's left for the
mob to do? No wonder Lou Raguzzi looks so bad. I
saw him the other day at Stiva's and his shoes were all
run down at the heel. He probably can't afford to buy
shoes."

"Lou's doing fine," my mother said. "He's being
audited by the IRS. He got those shoes special so he
wouldn't look too successful."

Everyone crossed themselves at the mention of the
IRS. Street gangs and the mob paled in comparison to
fear of the tax code.

"I'm going to have to take off," Sally said, stopping in front of my parents' house. "I have to get across town to start picking the little dudes up."

"Thanks for the ride," Grandma said, making her way down the bus steps. "Maybe I'll see you tonight. There's a good viewing at Stiva's. Charley Whitehead's laid out, and the Knights of Columbus should be there tonight. They always put on a good show. They're the best of the lodges."

I took Valerie's diaper bag, and my mother took Valerie's purse, and we all followed Grandma off the bus and up to the house.

"I have to go, too," I said, depositing the diaper bag in the hallway.

"It was nice of you to help your sister find a place," my mother said to me.

I hiked my own bag onto my shoulder. "Thanks, but it was self-serving."

"It would have been self-serving to order her out of your apartment. Finding her a house was a nice thing to do."

I took my bag of doughnuts, called good-bye to everyone, and let myself out. I climbed into Ranger's truck, and I sat there for a moment, trying to calm myself. I was going to be in big trouble if the rumors got back to the Slayers. The Slayers wouldn't like being run over and hunted down by a pasty-faced white woman. It wasn't the sort of thing that earned gangland prestige points. Not much I can do about it now, I thought. The best I could do was to stay away from them and try to keep a low profile. With any luck, the Slayers would be busy selling drugs and shooting each other and not have time for me.

I rolled the engine over, drove the length of the block, turned at the corner, and headed for Joe's house. Security check. I wanted to see for myself that the house was still standing, that no further damage had been done. I'd moved out of the house, but there were still ties. Just as there were still ties to Morelli. Truth was, I'd broken up with him so many times it was beginning to feel like the normal thing to do. For that matter, I wasn't sure if we'd actually broken up. It felt more like a reorganization.

Morelli's street was pretty much deserted, except for a van in front of Morelli's house. The van belonged to Joe's cousin, Mooch. Mooch was covering the graffiti, painting Joe's front door a bright red. The graffiti was still on the sidewalk, but it didn't look as if anything new had been added. I slowed but I didn't stop. Mooch didn't look around from his work, and I didn't call out.

Next stop was Carol Cantell. I wasn't obligated to check on her *every* day, but I'd become attached to Carol. How could you not like someone who held up a Frito-Lay truck and then ate the evidence?

I parked in front of the Cantell house and walked to the porch. Carol's sister, Cindy, opened the door before I rang the bell.

"We were in the front room, and we saw you pull up in the truck," Cindy said. "Is something wrong?"

I looked around Cindy to Carol. "Social visit. I wanted to make sure everything was okay."

"I'm feeling a lot better," Carol said. "I think I got the chips out of my system."

Cindy leaned closer. "Boy, you smell great," she said to me. "You smell like . . . I don't know. Not exactly perfume."

"It's shower gel," I said. "I borrowed it from a guy I know."

Carol came over and sniffed at me. "Is he married?"

"No."

"Would he like to be?"

The question stuck with me until I was well out of

Cantell's neighborhood. I hadn't a clue to the answer.
I worked with Ranger, I drove his truck and I was living in his apartment, and yet I knew almost nothing
about him. A few facts. He'd been married when he
was very young, and he had a daughter in Florida. He'd
dropped out of college to join the army. While in the
army, he'd been Special Forces. That was about it. He
never shared his thoughts. He rarely showed emotion.
A smile once in a while. His apartment yielded little.
He had good taste in furniture, leaning toward earth
tones, and he had great taste in soap.

It was lunchtime, and I hadn't any idea what to do
next, so I parked in the Shop n Bag lot and ate two of
the doughnuts. I was scraping a blob of custard off my
shirt when my phone rang.

"Where are you?" Morelli wanted to know.

"I'm in the Shop n Bag lot, and I'm eating lunch."

"Have you heard the rumors?"

"There are so many. Which ones are you talking
about?"

Morelli gave an exasperated sigh.

"Oh," I said. "Those rumors. Yeah, I heard those rumors."

"What are you going to do about them?"

"I'm sort of hiding."

"You'd better hide really well, because I'll put you
under house arrest if I find you."

"On what charges?"

"Reckless endangerment of self and driving me
nuts. Where are you hiding? You're not staying with
your parents. I checked."

"I'm staying at a friend's place."

"Is it safe?"

"Yep." Except from the friend.

"I'd feel better if you sounded more scared," Morelli
said. "These guys are crazy. They're unpredictable and

irrational. They operate under a whole different set of rules."

Morelli disconnected and it was my turn to give an exasperated sigh. I was trying hard *not* to be scared.

I decided as long as I was in the lot I might as well do some food shopping, so I locked the truck and ambled into the store. I got a box of Frosted Flakes, a loaf of nice mushy white bread, a jar of peanut butter (the good kind that's been hydrogenated and is full of trans fats and sugar), and a jar of nongourmet olives.

I was pushing my cart down the sanitary products aisle when Mrs. Zuch spotted me.

"Stephanie Plum!" she said. "I can't remember when I last saw you. I see your grandmother all the time, and I hear all about your exploits."

"Whatever Grandma said, it's not true."

"And this business about the Slayers . . ."

"That's especially not true."

"Everyone's talking about it. How you single-handed put them out of business. It's a shame about the killer."

"Killer?"

"You know, the contract that's out on you. I hear they brought someone in from California. I'm surprised you're out and about like this. You don't even look like you're wearing a bulletproof vest, or anything."

Was she serious? "It's all rumor," I said. "None of it's true."

"I understand," Mrs. Zuch said. "And I think it's admirable that you're being so brave and so modest. But if it was me, I'd be wearing the vest."

"I don't think the Slayers spend a lot of time in Shop n Bag."

"You could be right," Mrs. Zuch said. "But just in case, I think I'll move on now."

And Mrs. Zuch put distance between us.

I made an effort not to furtively look over my shoulder while I wheeled my shopping cart to check out.

My phone rang when I got to the truck.

"What's all this noise about a contract killer?" Connie wanted to know. "Have you talked to Joe?"

"I talked to Joe, but he didn't say anything about a killer."

"Vinnie just wrote a bond on a kid from Slayerland, and all the kid could talk about was how you're going down."

I rested my forehead on the steering wheel. This was out of control. "I can't talk now," I told Connie. "I'll call you back."

I dialed Morelli, and I did some deep breathing while I waited.

"Yeah?" Morelli said.

"It's me. You know when you asked me if I heard the rumors? Just exactly what rumors were you referring to?"

"Your vow to rid the world of Slayers rumor. Your vow to identify the Red Devil rumor. Oh yeah, and the contract killer rumor. That's my personal favorite."

"I just heard about the contract killer. Is it true?"

"Don't know. We're checking. Are you still in the Shop n Bag lot?"

A little alarm went off in my brain. He wouldn't actually try to catch me and lock me up in his house, would he?

"I did some grocery shopping, and I'm on my way back to the office," I told him. "Let me know if you hear anything."

I disconnected, plunged the key into the ignition, and took off, driving in the opposite direction of the office. This was dandy. Now I had to hide out from the Slayers *and* from Morelli.

I had time to kill before I met Lula for our movie
date and capture, so I headed for the mall. When in
doubt . . . shop. I parked at the Macy's entrance and me-
andered through the shoe department. My credit card
was pretty much maxed out, and I didn't see anything
worth going to debtors' prison over, so I wandered out
of Macy's and hit the Godiva store. I collected all the
loose change in the bottom of my bag, and I got two
pieces of chocolate. If you buy chocolate with loose
change the calories don't count. And anyway, one of
the pieces was a raspberry truffle, so it was fruit. And
fruit is healthy, right?

My cell phone rang while I was eating the second
truffle.

"I thought you were going back to the office," Morelli said.

"Changed my mind at the last minute."

"Where are you?"

"Point Pleasant. I had some time, so I thought I'd
take a walk on the boardwalk. It's such a nice day. A
little windy here, though."

"Sounds like there are a lot of people there."

"I'm in a pavilion."

"Sounds more like a shopping center."

"And you called, why?" I asked.

"They've released your car. I had it detailed and all
the graffiti came off. You can pick it up anytime."

"Thanks. That's great. I'll send my dad over for it."

"You can run, but you can't hide, Cupcake," Morelli
said. "I'll find you."

"You are such a cop."

"Tell me about it."

I disconnected and left the mall. It was almost six,
so I headed for Lula's house. I ate the rest of the doughnuts while I sat in traffic on Route 1.

Lula was outside, sitting on her stoop, waiting for

me. "You're late," she said. "We're gonna miss the beginning of the movie. I hate that."

"Traffic," I told her. "And anyway, I'm only five minutes late. We have lots of time."

"Yeah, but I gotta get popcorn. You can't watch no mutant movie without popcorn. And probably I need soda and some candy to balance out all that salt and grease on the popcorn."

I parked in the multiplex lot and took a last look at the Pancek file. "Harold Pancek," I read to Lula. "Twenty-two years old. Blond hair, blue eyes, Caucasian. Chunky build. Five feet ten inches tall. No identifying characteristics. This is the guy who took a leak on the rosebush. He's got a low ticket bond. We're not going to make a lot of money on him, but we need to bring him in anyway."

"On account of we're professionals," Lula said.

"Yeah. And if we want to keep the job, we haven't got a choice."

I pulled the file photo, and Lula and I studied it.

"He reminds me of someone," Lula said. "I can't put my finger on it."

"SpongeBob SquarePants. Yellow hair. No neck. Body by Lego."

"That's it. Skin like a sponge."

I slipped the photo and the authorization to capture into my shoulder bag. I also had cuffs, a stun gun, and defense spray in the bag. My gun was in Morelli's cookie jar. Ranger's gun was in the truck. God knows what Lula had in her bag. Could be a loaded rocket launcher.

We crossed the lot and entered the theater. We got our tickets, our popcorn, our soda, our M&Ms, Jujubes, Twizzlers, and Junior Mints.

"Look there," Lula said. "SpongeHead is collecting tickets."

The smart thing would be to cuff him now. Any number of things could go wrong if I waited. He could go home sick. He could recognize me and leave. He could decide he hated his job and quit, never to be seen again.

"I've been dying to see this movie," Lula said, her arm wrapped around a tub of popcorn that was big enough to feed a family of eight.

"We really should cuff him now. If we wait he could get away."

"Are you kidding me? I got my popcorn. I got my soda. I got my Twizzlers. And on top of that, we've never been to a movie together. We never do anything together except work. I think this here's quality bonding time. And what about that hot mutant? Don't you want to see the mutant?"

She had me there. I wanted to see the mutant. I approached Pancek and handed him my ticket. I looked him in the eye and smiled. He smiled back, blank-faced, and tore my ticket in half. He did the same to Lula. No glimmer of recognition for either of us.

"This is gonna be a snap," Lula said, taking a seat. "On our way out we'll clap the cuffs on ol' Harold and trot him off to jail."

After ninety minutes of mutant action, Lula was ready to bag Pancek.

"We could be as good as those mutants," Lula said to me. "You know the only difference between us and those mutants? Costumes. They had cool costumes. I'm telling you, you can't go wrong with capes and boots. And you need an insignia. Maybe we should get an insignia. Something with a lightning bolt."

Pancek was in the aisle directing people to the exit. Lula walked past Pancek, turned, and stood at his back. I was a few steps behind Lula.

I smiled at Pancek. "Harold Pancek?" I asked. Like I was some long-lost friend.

"Yeah," he said. "Do I know you?"

"Stephanie Plum," I said. "I'm a recovery agent for Vincent Plum Bail Bonds." And *click*, the cuff was on his wrist.

"Hey," he said. "What the hell do you think you're doing?"

"You failed to show for a court hearing. I'm afraid I'm going to have to take you in to get rescheduled."

"I'm working."

"You're leaving an hour early today," I told him.

"I gotta tell my boss."

I snapped the second bracelet on him and gave him a nudge toward the door. "We'll make sure your boss knows."

"No, wait a minute. On second thought, I don't want anyone to know. This is embarrassing. Jeez, is everyone looking?"

"Not everyone," Lula said. "I think there's a guy over by the popcorn counter who's not looking."

"It's all a big mistake, anyway. I'm not the one who killed her rosebush."

"I suppose it was the phantom leaker," Lula said.

"It was Grizwaldi's dog. He lifts his leg on that bush every day. This is discrimination. I don't see Grizwaldi's dog getting hauled into court. Everybody knows he pisses on everything, but it's okay because he's a dog. It's not fair."

"I see your point," Lula said. "Not that it makes any difference. We're still gonna cart your chunky ass off to jail."

Pancek dug his heels in. "No way. I'm not going to jail."

"You're making a scene," I told him.

"Fine. I'll make a scene. I have a cause."

"The mutants would never have stood for this," Lula said. "Those mutants didn't put up with anything."

I gave Pancek a yank forward and maneuvered him through the lobby, up to the exit door. I was talking to him all the way, trying to get him to cooperate. "It's not like you're going to get locked away," I said. "We have to bring you to the station to reschedule. That's just the way it's done. We'll get you bonded out again as soon as possible."

I held the door open and nudged Pancek out the door, into the lot. Cars were at least ten rows deep, parked under the glare of the overhead security lights. I was parked five rows back.

Lula and I led Pancek through three rows of cars and stopped. An SUV was idling in the aisle between parked cars. A silver compact was nose-to-nose with the SUV. A black guy in a silky white oversized warm-up suit was standing beside the SUV, talking to a white male dressed head to toe in Abercrombie & Fitch. Both men were late teens. From what I could see of the silver car, there was a couple in the backseat and a girl in the passenger-side front seat.

"We don't want to be seeing this," Lula said. "Used to be you had to go looking for the dope, and now the dope comes to you."

I called the Hamilton Police and told them they had a problem in the multiplex lot. Then I called the theater and told them to send security into the lot.

The guy in the silky suit and the kid kept talking. The silky suit was stoic and the white kid was agitated. The girl in the front passenger seat got out of the car. Impatient.

"This isn't good," Lula said. "She should never have got out of the car. These are gang guys. They got a philosophy about women makes Eminem sound like he's writing nursery rhymes."

Three big guys in homey clothes, all wearing red scarves flying from pants pockets, got out of the SUV and did their *I'm a big bad gang member* shuffle over to the negotiation. One of the big guys jabbed a finger into the Abercrombie & Fitch kid's chest and got into his face. The kid pushed back. The gang guy took out a gun and held it to the kid's head.

"Crap," Lula said on a sigh.

I looked over my shoulder, wondering what was taking security so long. Probably this happened all the time and no one wanted to come into the lot until the police arrived.

The girl's eyes were wide. Deer caught in the headlights. The remaining gang members turned on her, walking her backward, trapping her against Ranger's truck. Another gun was drawn. A knife appeared.

I pressed the panic button on the truck's remote and the truck alarm went off.

Everyone jumped.

The SUV guys piled into their car, backed up, and left the lot, burning rubber.

I did a double hit on the panic button, and the alarm went silent. I turned to Lula and realized Pancek was missing. We'd forgotten to keep watch over Pancek. Worse than losing Pancek, he'd taken off wearing a sixty-dollar pair of cuffs.

Lula was looking around, too. "Don't you hate when they take off like that?" she said. "If there's one thing I can't stand it's a sneaky felon."

"He can't have gone far. You take one side of the lot and I'll take the other, and we'll meet in the theater."

There was the sound of a car engine coming to life in the second row. A car was gunned out of its parking space, and the car roared off toward the exit. I caught a glimpse of yellow hair on the guy behind the wheel.

"Guess we don't have to search the lot no more,"

Lula said. "Bet it's hard to drive with those cuffs on.
Think you should have cuffed him behind his back like
the book says."

"He didn't seem dangerous. I was trying to be nice
to him."

"See where that gets you. Never be nice to people."

I unlocked the truck and climbed in. "Maybe he's
dumb enough to go home," I said to Lula. "We'll check
out his house."

We pulled out of the lot, and I saw two Hamilton
Township PD cars angled into the curb, lights flashing,
half a block down. One was a squad car and the other
was unmarked. The SUV was in front of the squad car.
The occupants of the SUV were palms down on the
SUV hood, getting searched.

I eased past the police cars and recognized Gus Chianni. He was standing back, letting the uniforms do
their job. Most of the Hamilton cops were strangers to
me. I knew Chianni because he was one of Morelli's
longtime drinking buddies.

I stopped and powered my window down. "What's
going on?" I asked Chianni.

"Speeding," he said, smiling. "We were answering
your call and ran across this SUV doing eighty in a
twenty."

"It's the car I called in."

His smile widened. "I figured." He took a step back
and looked at Ranger's truck. "You steal this?"

"Borrowed."

"Bet Joe's happy about that."

All the cops knew Ranger's truck.

"Gotta go," I said. If Chianni was here, Morelli
wasn't far behind.

The guy in the white silk warm-up suit turned his
head sideways and stared at me. His face held no expression, but his eyes were like still pools in the river

Styx. Black and bottomless and terrifying. He gave a slight nod, as if to say he knew who I was. His right hand lifted off the SUV hood and he made the sign of a gun, thumb up, index finger extended. He mouthed the word *bang* at me.

Chianni saw it, too. "Be careful," he said to me.

I went out to the highway and drove in the opposite direction to what I would ordinarily take to get to the Burg.

"This is bad," Lula said when we were on the highway. "That guy recognized you. He knew who you were. And it wasn't because he saw you in the lot just now, either. None of them saw us in the lot. That guy was no-shit evil, and he knew who you were."

I pushed it aside and concentrated on driving. I didn't want the fear to grab hold of me. Careful was good. Scared was counterproductive. I went a couple miles out of my way, but I was able to reach Pancek's house without running into Morelli.

Pancek's house was dark, and his car wasn't in sight. I slowly drove around several blocks looking for the car. Big zero. He could have stashed the car in a friend's garage, and he could be hiding in his dark house, but I didn't think that was the case. I suspected he'd gone to someone he trusted and was trying to get out of the cuffs.

I took Lula home, and then I went back to Ranger's apartment on Haywood Street. I parked the truck on a side street and walked the distance to the underground garage. I looked up at the building. Again, floors five and six were lit. I remoted myself through the security gate and scurried across the garage to the elevator. Ranger's Turbo and the Porsche Cayenne were still in place. A black Ford Explorer was parked on the side wall, plus a black GMC Sonoma was parked next to the SUV.

I stepped into the elevator, remoted myself up to the seventh floor, and held my breath. The elevator doors opened to the austere foyer, and I jumped out.

I listened at the door to Ranger's apartment, didn't hear anything, held my breath, and let myself in. Everything seemed just as I'd left it. Very calm. Temperature a little on the cool side. Dark—like Ranger. I flipped the lights on as I walked through the apartment. I said hello to Rex in the kitchen and set the grocery bags on the counter. I plugged my cell phone in to recharge, and I put the food away.

I wondered about floors five and six. For two nights now, they'd been lit. A variety of black cars were coming and going in the garage. So I was guessing floors five and six were offices. Although I suppose they could also be apartments. Either way I needed to be careful where I parked the truck and careful when I moved about the building.

I made a peanut and olive sandwich and washed it down with one of Ranger's Coronas. I shuffled off to the bedroom, dropped most of my clothes on the floor, went into the bathroom to brush my teeth and smell Ranger's soap, and then I crawled into bed.

It had been a really weird day. Not that I haven't had weird days before. Weird days were getting to feel normal. The disturbing part about *this* weird day was that there'd been steadily escalating indicators of personal danger. I'd done my best to stay sane, to keep my fear in check, but the fear was actually riding very close to the surface. I'd been involved in some scary situations in the past. This was the first time a contract to kill me had been put into motion.

Chapter
EIGHT

I opened my eyes and had a moment of panicky confusion. The room was dark and felt unfamiliar. The sheets were smooth and smelled like Ranger. And then it all clicked into focus. Again, I was the one who smelled like Ranger. I'd washed my hands and face before bed and the scent had lingered.

I switched the bedside light on and checked the time. It was almost eight A.M. My day hadn't even started, and already I was late. It was the bed, I decided. It was the best bed I'd ever slept in. And, while I worried about Ranger returning, when I was in the apartment I felt safe from everything else. Ranger's apartment felt serene and secure.

I rolled out of bed and padded into the bathroom. It was Friday. Most people are happy on Friday because their workweek ends. I had the sort of job that never ended. Connie worked a half day on Saturday. Vinnie worked when he didn't have anything better to do. We weren't sure when Lula worked. And I worked all the time. Okay, so it wasn't always nine-to-five working. But it was always looking. Opportunities for capture popped up where you least expected—at supermarkets, airports, shopping malls, and movie theaters.

And while on the subject of movie theaters, if I was

a better bounty hunter I could probably take weekends off. When you botch a capture, like I did last night, you have to work twice as hard to make repairs. Pancek knew what I looked like now. And he knew I was after him.

I'd had plenty of opportunity to buy shower gel yesterday, but I'd conveniently forgotten. So now I had to once again use Ranger's shower gel. What a hardship, eh? And then I had to dry off with one of his thick, superabsorbent towels. Another hardship I forced myself to endure. All right, I admit it, I was liking Ranger's lifestyle. And even more difficult to admit, I was liking the stolen intimacy. I was going to have to say a lot of Hail Marys for that one.

And I was going to pay a price when Ranger returned. Even if I was long gone by the time he walked through his front door, even if I washed and ironed his sheets and replaced his shower gel, Ranger would know his home had been violated. The guy was a security expert. Probably there were cameras everywhere. Not in his apartment, I was guessing. But chances were good that there were cameras in the garage, the elevator, and his outer foyer. No one had come up to bust me, so I had to assume that either the cameras weren't monitored or else Ranger had been contacted and was allowing me to stay.

I got dressed in sneakers and jeans and a stretchy white scoop-neck T-shirt. I swiped some mascara on my lashes, and I headed for the kitchen. I dropped a handful of Frosted Flakes into Rex's food dish, and I poured out a bowl for myself. I was late so I didn't take time to make coffee. I needed to stop at the office first thing. I'd get coffee there.

I unplugged my phone, grabbed my short denim jacket and shoulder bag, and locked up behind myself. I took the elevator to the garage, suffering through the moment of fear when the elevator doors parted and I was exposed. Even if I'd been discovered on camera, I wanted to delay confrontation as long as possible. No sense pushing the issue and jeopardizing my tenancy. I needed a place to stay, and I was already in trouble with Ranger. Might as well get the most out of it, right?

I looked out and saw no one. I stepped out, the doors closed behind me, and I heard voices in the stairwell.

Ranger's two cars were directly in front of me. There were three black SUVs to my right. And there was a blue Subaru SUV and a silver Audi sedan to my left. I made an instinctive choice and jumped behind the Subaru, crouching low, hoping I was out of sight. I didn't know who had access to the garage, but I figured Ranger's men would belong to the black SUVs.

The door to the stairwell opened, and Tank and two other men came out. All three got into one of the black SUVs and left the garage. I waited a couple beats before I scuttled across the floor, remoted the gate open, and made my escape.

The bonds office was on Hamilton, in the middle of the block. A one-lane alley ran behind the office, servicing a rear entrance and parking for two cars. I parked Ranger's truck on a side street, and I entered the office through the back door . . . just in case Morelli was on the prowl. I was in a mood to avoid the unpleasant.

"Uh oh," Lula said when she saw me. "It's never good when you gotta sneak in through the back."

I went straight for the coffeepot. "I'm being careful."

"I can appreciate that," Lula said. "What's the plan for the day?"

"I need a different car. I can't blend in when I drive Ranger's truck." To be more specific, I can't blend in when I park the truck for the night. Ranger's men were constantly traveling the streets around the Bat Garage.

I didn't want to take a chance on one of them spotting the truck. "I was hoping you could follow me to my parents' house. I'm going to leave the truck in their garage. And then we can go car shopping."

"Car shopping! I love car shopping."

I added creamer and sipped some coffee. "You're not going to love this kind of car shopping. I have no money. I'm looking for a wreck." I turned to Connie. "And while we're on the subject of no money, as I'm sure you already know . . . Pancek ran off with my only cuffs."

"Lula told me. Take a pair from the S and M box in the back when you leave."

There used to be a thriving sex shop on Carmen Street. Rumor had it they were the biggest supplier of dildos, whips, and body chains for the tristate area. Nine months ago, the owner decided he was tired of paying his insurance premium to the mob and told his collection agent to take a hike. Shortly after that, the store mysteriously burned to the ground. An entire crate of cuffs came out of the fire almost completely unscathed, and Vinnie bought the crate on the cheap.

"How come you're going to leave the truck at your parents' house?" Lula wanted to know. "Why don't you just give it back?"

"I thought I'd keep it a while longer, just in case. You never know when you might need a truck." And I can't get into Ranger's apartment if I hand the keys back to Tank.

"A couple new skips came in this morning," Connie said. "I'll get the paperwork together later today, and you can pick the files up tomorrow."

"I suppose after you get your new car you're going to want to go looking for Harold Pancek," Lula said.

"I suppose I am."

"And I suppose I should go with you since he's so slippery."

I looked at the stack of files on the filing cabinet. At least a month's worth. "What about the filing?"

"I can do the filing any old time. It's not like filing's a matter of life or death. I got good priorities. I take our friendship seriously. When you're going out on these dangerous manhunts, I feel an obligation to ride along and protect your skinny ass. Just 'cause a man looks like SpongeBob doesn't mean he can't turn violent."

"You're pathetic," Connie said to Lula. "You'll do anything to get out of filing."

"Not anything," Lula said.

Ten minutes later, I had Ranger's truck safely tucked away in my parents' garage.

My dad had retrieved Uncle Sandor's Buick from the police and the Buick and Ranger's truck were now locked up together.

"What a nice surprise," Grandma said when she saw me at the kitchen door.

"I can't stay," I told Grandma and my mother. "I just wanted to tell you I'm leaving Ranger's truck in the garage."

"What about *our* car?" my mother wanted to know. "Where's your father going to park the LeSabre?"

"You never use the garage. The LeSabre is always parked in the driveway. Look outside. Where is the LeSabre? *In the driveway.* I had to drive around it to get to the garage."

My mother was cutting vegetables for soup. She stopped cutting and looked over at me, wide-eyed. "Holy mother. There's something wrong, isn't there? You're in trouble again."

"Did you steal the truck?" Grandma asked hopefully.

"I'm not in trouble, and there's nothing wrong. I told Ranger I'd take care of his truck while he's out of town. I was going to use it, but I've changed my mind. It's too big."

My mother didn't really want to know the truth, I told myself. The truth wasn't good.

"It is big," Grandma said. "And you know what they say about the size of a man's truck."

"I'm off," I said. "Lula's waiting for me."

Grandma trotted after me. She stopped at the front door and waved at Lula. "What are you girls doing?" Grandma asked. "Are you chasing down a killer?"

"Sorry," I said. "No killers today. I'm going car shopping. I need something to tide me over until I get the insurance check from the Escape."

"I'd love to go car shopping," Grandma said. "Wait a minute while I tell your mother and get my purse."

"No," I said. But she was already running around the house, gathering her things.

"Hey," Lula yelled from the curb. "What's the holdup?"

"Grandma's coming with us."

"The Three Musketeers ride again," Lula said.

Grandma bustled out of the house and climbed into the Firebird's backseat. "What have you got?" Grandma asked Lula. "You got 50 Cent? You got Eminem?"

Lula slid Eminem into the slot, punched up the sound system, and we motored off like distant thunder.

"I've been thinking about your car problem," Lula said, "and I know a guy who's got cars to sell. He don't ask a whole lot either."

"I don't know," I said. "If you buy a used car at a lot you usually get a guarantee."

"How much do you want to spend?" Lula asked.

"A couple hundred."

Lula slanted a look at me. "And you want a guarantee for that kind of money?"

She was right. A guarantee was unrealistic. In fact, it was unrealistic to think I could find a car that actually ran for that kind of money.

Lula hauled out her cell phone, scrolled through the phone book, and dialed a number. "I have a friend who needs a car," she said when the phone connected. "Un hunh," she said. "Un hunh, un hunh, un hunh." She turned to me. "Do you need a registration?"

"Yes!"

"Yeah," Lula said into the phone. "She'd like one of those."

"Isn't this fun?" Grandma Mazur said from the backseat. "I can't wait to see your new car."

Lula disconnected, turned out of the Burg, and headed across town. When we got to Stark Street Lula hit the automatic door locks.

"Don't worry," Lula said. "I'm just locking the doors for good measure. We aren't going into the bad part of town. Well, okay, maybe it's a *bad* part of town, but it's not the *worst* part of town. We're not going into gangland. This here is the part of town where the unorganized criminals live."

Grandma had her nose pressed to the glass. "I've never seen anything like this," she said. "Everything's got writing on it. And there's a building that's been all burned out and now it's boarded up. Are we still in Trenton? Does the mayor know about this? How about Joe Juniak? Now that he's a congressman he should be looking into these things."

"I used to work on this street when I was a ho," Lula said.

"No kidding?" Grandma said. "Isn't that something. Are there any working ladies out now? I sure would like to see one."

We kept a lookout for working ladies but none turned up.

"Slow time of the day," Lula said.

Lula made a right onto Fisher, went one block, and parked in front of a narrow two-story house that looked like it was decaying from the bottom up. Clearly it had once been part of a row of attached houses, but the houses on either side had disappeared and only their connecting walls remained. The lots had been mostly cleared of debris, but the landscaping was war zone. An occasional piece of pipe remained, mixed into smatterings of crushed rubble that hadn't made the last truck out. A nine-foot-high razor wire fence had been erected around each of the lots. Refrigerators, washing machines, gas grills, lawn furniture, and a couple ATVs, all with varying degrees of rust, were displayed in the one lot. The second lot was filled with cars.

"These lots are owned by a guy named Hog," Lula said. "Besides the lots he's got a garage on the next block. He buys junker cars at auction, fixes them up enough to get them running, and then sells them to dummies like us. Sometimes he gets cars from other sources, but we don't want to talk about that."

"Those would be the cars without registration?" I asked.

"Hog can get a registration for any car you want," Lula said. "It's just you gotta pay extra for it."

Grandma was out of the Firebird. "Those lawn chairs with the yellow cushions look pretty nice," she said. "I might have to take a look at them."

I jumped out after her and grabbed her by the purse strap. "Don't leave my side. Don't wander off. Don't talk to anyone."

A large guy with skin the color of hot chocolate and a body like a cement truck strolled over to us. "Lula tells me somebody wants to buy a car," he said. "You be happy to know you came to the right place because we got some fine cars here."

"We don't want too fine a car," Lula said. "We're sort of shopping for a bargain."

"How much of a bargain?"

"Two hundred dollars and that includes plates and registration."

"That don't even cover my overhead. I got expenses. I got middlemen."

"Your middlemen are all in jail," Lula said. "The only expenses you got is filling your car with gas so you can drive over to the workhouse to pick up your sorry-ass relatives."

"Ouch," Hog said. "That's nasty. You're getting me all excited."

Lula gave him a smack on the side of the head.

"I love when you do that," Hog said.

"Do you have a car, or what?" Lula said. "Because we can go down the street to Greasy Louey."

"'Course I got a car," Hog said. "Don't I always have a car? Have I ever failed you?" He looked at Grandma and me. "Which of you lovely ladies is buying this car?"

"Me," I said.

"What color you want?"

"A two-hundred-dollar color."

He turned and considered the motley collection of cars huddled together behind the razor wire. "Two hundred dollars don't get you much of a car. Maybe you be better to rent a car from Hog." He walked over to a silver Sentra. "I just got this car. It needs some body work, but it's structurally sound."

Needs some body work was a gross understatement. The hood was crumpled and attached to the car with duct tape. And the left rear quarter panel was missing.

"The thing is," I said to Hog, "I need a car that blends in. People would notice this car. They'd remember that they saw a car with only three fenders."

"Not in this neighborhood," Hog said. "We got lots of cars look like this."

"Look at her," Lula said. "She look like she gonna spend a lot of time in this neighborhood?"

"How about this car?" Grandma called out from across the lot. "I like this car."

She was standing in front of a purple Lincoln Town Car that was about a block long. It had terminal rust creeping up from the undercarriage, but the hood was attached in the normal fashion, and it had all its fenders.

"You could put a whole pack of killers in this car," Grandma said.

"I didn't hear that," Hog said. "Don't matter to me who you hang with."

"We don't hang with them. We arrest them," Grandma said. "My granddaughter's a bounty hunter. This here's Stephanie Plum," she said proudly. "She's famous."

"Oh crap," Hog said, eyes bugged out. "Are you shitting me? Get out of here. You think I want to die?" He craned his neck, looking beyond us, up and down the street. "Not only would the brothers like to get hold of her, I hear they brought someone special in from the coast." He scrambled behind a car, putting some distance between the two of us. "Go away. Shoo."

"Shoo?" Lula said. "Did I hear you say *shoo*?"

"Some Slayer ride by here, I be a dead man," Hog said. "Get her off my lot."

"We came here to buy a car, and that's what we're gonna do," Lula said.

"Fine. Take a car," Hog said. "Take anything. Just go away."

"We want this pretty purple car," Grandma said.

Hog gave Grandma another of the bug-eyed looks. "Lady, that's an expensive car. That's a Lincoln Town Car. That's no two-hundred-dollar car!"

"We wouldn't want to cheat you," Lula said. "So we'll just wander around awhile and see if we like something less expensive."

"No. Don't do that," Hog said. "Take the friggin' Lincoln. I got the keys in the house. I'll just be a minute."

"Don't forget the plates and the registration," Lula said.

Five minutes later, I had a temporary plate taped to my rear window, Grandma was strapped into the passenger seat, and Lula was a car length ahead of us, en route back to the office.

"I feel like a movie star in this car," Grandma said. "It's like a big limousine. Not everybody can afford a car like this, you know. It must have belonged to somebody special."

A gangster or a pimp, I thought.

"And it rides real smooth," Grandma said.

I had to admit the ride was smooth. The car was about the same size as Sally's bus and took two lanes to make a corner, but the ride was smooth.

Lula and I parked in front of the bonds office, and we all got out to reorganize.

"Now what?" Lula said. "Are we going after Harold Pancek?"

"Yeah," Grandma said. "Are we going after Harold Pancek?"

"Lula and I are going after Harold Pancek," I said. "I should take you home first."

"No way! What if you need an old lady to quiet him down?"

My mother would cut me off from pineapple upside-down cake for the rest of my life if she knew I took

Grandma on a bust. Then again, I'd just driven Grandma down Stark Street, so I was most likely screwed already.

"Okay," I said. "You can go with us, but you have to stay in the car."

I felt obligated to say this but it was an empty demand because Grandma never stayed in the car. Grandma was always the first out of the car. I was taking her along because I really didn't think we were going to find Pancek at home. Pancek had been here for a couple years but hadn't seemed to put down roots. According to Connie's background search, Pancek's relatives and long-time friends were in Newark. I was guessing that after last night Pancek skipped back to Newark.

A gray late-model sedan drove by, hooked a U-turn in the middle of traffic, and parked behind the purple Lincoln. Morelli.

"Uh oh," Lula said to me. "You got that look."

"What look is that?"

"That *oh shit* look. That's not a look from a woman who got some last night."

"It's complicated."

"I've been hearing that a lot lately," Lula said.

Morelli got out of the car and walked over, looking like a cop who'd just gotten rear-ended. The anger was tightly controlled, and the gait was deceptively relaxed.

"Isn't this a nice coincidence," Grandma said to Morelli. "I didn't expect to see you until tomorrow night."

Neither rain, nor sleet, nor snow, nor shoe sale at Macy's could get me out of Saturday dinner with my parents. Like a spawning salmon, I was expected to return to my birthplace. Unlike a salmon, I didn't die, although sometimes I wished I could, and the migration took place weekly.

"I need to talk to Stephanie," Morelli said with his best effort at a pleasant smile, his hand at my neck, his fingers curled into the back of my shirt to discourage escape.

"Gee, we were right in the middle of something," I said. "Can it wait?"

"Afraid not," Morelli said. "We need to talk *now*."

I followed him to his car, and we stood with our backs to Lula and Grandma to keep them from eavesdropping.

"Gotcha," Morelli said.

"Now what?"

"Now I take you back to my house and lock you in the bathroom. If you're real nice to me, I'll bring the television in for you."

"You're not serious."

"About the television? Afraid not, I've only got one, and I'm not lugging it up the stairs."

I gave him one of those looks that said *Get real*.

"There's a contract on you," Morelli said, "and I ride by and see you standing here like a duck in a shooting gallery. A dead girlfriend doesn't do me much good."

Well, at least he thought I was still his girlfriend. "I was hoping the contract was just rumor."

"My sources tell me there's a guy in town from L.A. He goes by the street name Junkman, and it's widely believed he was brought in by the Slayers to take you out. From all reports, this is a very bad guy. Lots of talk about him. Virtually no useable information. At this point, we don't even have a description."

"How do you know he's real?"

"The sources are good. And the brothers on the street are scared. Just so you don't feel too special, it appears you aren't the only one on his list. It's said to include a cop and two rival gang members."

"Who's the cop?"

"Someone in gang intelligence. We don't have a name."

"I think it's sweet of you to want to lock me in your bathroom, but it doesn't fit into my plans. And last time I was in your house we had a major disagreement over all this."

Morelli ran a fingertip around the scoop neckline of my T-shirt. "First of all, it wasn't much of a dis-agreement. A disagreement in my family involves restraining orders and bloodshed. Second, I like this little white T-shirt." He hooked a finger into the neck-line and looked inside.

"Excuse me?" I said.

"Just checking." More of the smile.

"You wouldn't really lock me in your bathroom, would you?"

"Yep."

"That might be considered kidnapping."

"Your word against mine."

"And it's disgustingly arrogant and macho."

"Yeah," Morelli said. "That's the best part."

I looked back at Grandma and Lula. "How do you expect to accomplish this?"

"I thought I'd drag you into my car and carry you kicking and screaming into my house."

"In front of Grandma and Lula?"

"No," Morelli said. "I can't do it in front of your grandmother." The smile faded. "Can we get serious? This isn't just rumor. These guys are out to get you."

"What am I supposed to do? I live here. I can't go into hiding for the rest of my life."

Morelli's pager buzzed, and he looked at the read-out. "I hate this thing," he said. "You're going to be careful?"

"Yes."

"You're going to get off the street?"

"Yes."

He gave me a fast kiss on the forehead and took off.

Grandma and Lula watched Morelli drive away.

"I don't usually like cops," Lula said, "but he's hot."

"He's a looker all right," Grandma said. "And he's got a way about him. There's nothing like a man with a gun."

"He don't get his way from a gun," Lula said. "His way is natural born."

I did some mental knuckle cracking and sidled up to the big purple Lincoln, hoping it would shield me from potential sniper fire. Morelli had done a good job of rattling my nerves. Stating the obvious to Morelli, that I lived in Trenton and couldn't hide for the rest of my life, wasn't a declaration made from bravery. It was a declaration tinged with desperation and maybe even a little hysteria. I was backed into a corner, the victim of circumstances. And I was at a loss how to fix it.

The best I could come up with on short notice was a temporary survival plan. Hide out in Ranger's apartment at night. Search for Pancek by day. The Pancek search was a good thing because I suspected after our initial trip to Canter Street, the search would shift to Newark, far away from the Slayers.

"Everybody in the car," I said. "We're going on a Harold hunt."

I docked the Lincoln in front of Pancek's row house, and we all got out and stood on the stoop while I rang the bell. There was no answer, of course. I rang again. I dialed his number on my cell phone. We could hear the phone ring on the other side of the door. The machine picked up. I left a message.

"Hi, this is Stephanie Plum," I said. "I need to talk to you." I left my cell number and disconnected.

I tried Pancek's next-door neighbor.

"He left early this morning," she said. "Must have been around seven. I went out to get the paper, and he was loading up his car. Usually you take grocery bags into the house, but he was taking them out."

"Did he say anything?"

"No. But that wasn't unusual. He's sort of an odd guy. Not real friendly. Lived in there all alone. I never saw anyone else go in. Guess he didn't have a lot of friends."

I left my card with her, and I asked her to call if Pancek returned.

"Now what?" Grandma wanted to know. "I'm ready to catch this guy. Where do we go next?"

"Newark. His family is in Newark."

"I don't know if I can go with you," Grandma said. "I'm supposed to go to the mall with Midgie Herrel at one o'clock."

I took Route 1 to Route 18 and got on the Jersey Turnpike. Grandma was home, waiting for Midgie. Sally, Valerie, and my mom were busy planning the wedding. Lula was sailing along with me in the purple Lincoln, riding shotgun, nosing through a big bag of food we bought before leaving Trenton.

"What do you want first?" she asked. "You want a sandwich or a Tastykake?"

"The sandwich." We had about forty Tastykakes. We couldn't choose which kind we wanted, so we got a bunch of everything. I have a cousin who works at the Tastykake factory in Philadelphia, and she said they make 439,000 Butterscotch Krimpets a day. I intended to eat three of them when I was done with the sub. And maybe I'd follow them up with a coconut layer cake. It's important to keep your strength up on a manhunt.

By the time we got to Newark, Lula and I had almost emptied the food bag. My jeans were feeling unusually tight and my stomach felt seasick. I suspected the queasy stomach was more fear of death than overeating. Still, it would have been good if I'd stopped after the third Tastykake.

Pancek's mother had posted the bond. I had her address plus the address of Pancek's former apartment. I knew Pancek drove a dark blue Honda Civic, and I had his plate number. It would be nice to find the Civic parked in front of one of the addresses.

Lula was reading a map, directing me through Newark. "Turn left at the next corner," she said. "His momma's house is on the first block, two houses in on the right side."

Lula and I were in a neighborhood that looked a lot like parts of the Burg. The homes were modest red-brick row houses, their front stoops set into sidewalk. Cars were parked on both sides, narrowing the street to barely two lanes. It was early afternoon and not much was happening. We drove past Pancek's mother's house, looking for the Civic. We did a four-block grid but came up empty.

By late afternoon we'd talked to Pancek's mother, two former neighbors, his former girlfriend, and his best buddy from high school. No one was giving Pancek up, and we hadn't run across his car.

"We're all out of Tastykakes," Lula said. "It's either time to go home or time to go shopping."

"Time to go home," I said.

Pancek's best buddy was married, and I couldn't see the wife putting up with Pancek. The girlfriend thought Pancek should rot in hell. That was a direct quote. His neighbors barely knew him. That left his mother. I had a feeling Mrs. Pancek knew more than she was telling us, but from today's performance it was obvious she wasn't ready to rat on her son.

We'd run down all our leads, and there wasn't anything left to do short of staking out the mother's house.

I was all in favor of a job well done, but Pancek wasn't worth a stakeout. A stakeout was a major bummer.

Morelli called on my cell phone. He didn't waste time with hello or how are you. Morelli got right to the heart of it. "Where are you?"

"I'm in Newark, looking for a skip."

"I don't suppose you'd consider staying there. Maybe getting a room."

"What's up?"

"We have a dead guy here. Gunned down on the street, and then had his nuts surgically removed."

"Gang member?"

"Big time. Cut. Had a J freshly carved into his forehead."

"Would that be J for Junkman?"

"That would be my guess," Morelli said. "Are you scared yet?"

"I'm always scared."

"Good. I'm drinking Pepto-Bismol by the case. I hate this. Every time my pager goes off I get an eye twitch, terrified that someone found your body."

"At least we don't have to worry about me getting my nuts surgically removed."

There was a moment of silence. "That's sick," Morelli finally said.

"I was shooting for levity."

"You failed." And he disconnected.

I told Lula about the killing, and we went in search of the turnpike.

"These gang guys are crazy," Lula said. "It's like they're alien invaders, or something. Like they don't know how to live on planet Earth. Hell, they're not even hot aliens. Not that it would matter, but if they were hot looking they'd at least be interesting, you see what I'm saying?"

I wasn't seeing what she was saying. I was taking

slow, even breaths, and I was working at controlling my heart rate.

I dropped Lula off at the office, and I drove to Ranger's building. I could see someone in the lobby, talking to the guard at the desk. A car pulled out of the garage, and the gate slid back into place. Too much activity, I thought. Too early for me to sneak inside.

I parked halfway down the block, and I watched the people coming and going. I called Connie, gave her the Haywood Street address, and asked her to check on the building.

"That's Ranger's building," Connie said.

"You know about it?"

"The RangeMan offices are there. Ranger moved his business into that building about a year ago."

"I didn't know."

"Well, it's not like it's the Bat Cave," Connie said. "It's an office building."

So what was with the top-floor apartment? It was filled with Ranger's clothes. Clearly he lived there at least part-time. I was disappointed, and I was relieved. I was disappointed because I hadn't discovered some big secret place. And I was relieved because maybe I hadn't invaded Ranger's private space. The relief was unwarranted, of course. His clothes were there. His shower gel, his deodorant, his razor was there. It might not be the Bat Cave, but it was Ranger's private space.

"Anything else?" Connie wanted to know.

"Nope," I said. "That was it. See you tomorrow."

By seven o'clock the building looked just about empty. The fifth and sixth floors were lit, but the lobby door appeared locked, and garage traffic seemed to have stopped. I locked the Lincoln, walked the short distance to the garage, and let myself into Ranger's apartment.

I dropped my keys into the dish on the sideboard

and went to the kitchen to say hello to Rex. I had a beer and a peanut butter sandwich, and I moved to the den to take another crack at the television. After ten minutes of pushing buttons on the remote I had the picture up but no sound. I went to school with a guy who owned an appliance store. I called him at the store, and he gave me a remote lesson. Hooray, now I could watch and *hear* television. Home sweet home.

I'd set the alarm on the bedside clock, so I could get out earlier in the morning. It was Saturday, but I suspected the security industry didn't slow for weekends, and I didn't want to take a chance on getting kicked out of the one place I felt safe.

I borrowed a black hooded sweatshirt from Ranger's closet. The sweatshirt was miles big, but it was the best I could do by way of disguise. I pulled the hood up, rode the elevator down, and I reached the Lincoln without a problem. Connie wouldn't be in the office for a couple hours, so I crossed the river into Pennsylvania and headed for Yardley. Yardley was just a short distance from Trenton, but it was light years from Slayerland. Junkman would not be patrolling Yardley looking for Stephanie Plum.

I parked in a public lot, locked my doors, and powered my seat back. It was 7:30 A.M., and Yardley was sleeping in.

I called Morelli at nine o'clock. "What are you doing?" I asked.

"Bob and I are at the car wash. Then we're going to Petco to get some dog food. It's a pretty exciting morning."

"I can hear that. Anything new going on?"

"Nothing you want to know about. I hope you're some place far away."

"Far enough. I'll be on my cell phone if you have

breaking news. And don't forget, my mother's expecting us to show up for dinner tonight."

"You're going to have to pay up, Cupcake. I don't do dinner without reimbursement."

"I'll run a tab for you." And I disconnected.

Truth is, I missed Morelli. He was sexy and smart and his house felt homey. His house didn't have the aphrodisiac shower gel, but it had Bob. I really missed Bob. Go figure that one. Okay, so I had to carry his poop in a plastic bag back to the house. It didn't seem like such a big deal anymore.

I left the lot and cruised through town. I turned onto Hamilton, drove past the office, and parked on a side street. Then I entered the office through the back door.

Connie looked up from her computer when I walked in. "Using the back door again?"

"I'm trying to decrease my visibility."

"Good call."

Vinnie rarely came in on a Saturday, and Lula was always late. I poured myself a cup of coffee, and took a seat across from Connie. "Any new shootings, firebombings, rumors of my imminent death?"

"Nothing new." Connie slid the mouse across the mouse pad and clicked. "I've got three new skips. I'm printing out the search results for you now. The original paperwork is somewhere in the mess of unfiled documents stacked on the cabinets."

Oh boy. Lula hadn't filed anything in so long there were more files on top of the cabinets than there were in the drawers.

"We have to go through those stacks," Connie said, coming out of her chair. "And we might as well file them while we search. We're looking for Anton Ward, Shoshanna Brown, and Jamil Rodriguez."

An hour later, we had the documentation for all

three skips, and we'd filed more than half of the outstanding cases.

The front door crashed open, and Lula marched in. "What's going on here?" she asked. "I miss anything?"

Connie and I gave Lula a cold ten-second stare.

"Yeah?" Lula asked.

"We just spent an hour doing your filing so we could find the paperwork on three new skips," Connie said.

"You didn't have to do that," Lula said. "I got a system."

"You weren't here," Connie said. "Where the hell were you? You were supposed to be here at nine."

"I'm never here at nine on Saturdays. I'm always late on Saturdays. Everybody knows that." Lula poured herself a cup of coffee. "Did you hear the news? I was listening to the radio on the way in and they said the Red Devil robbed the deli-mart on Commerce Street this morning. And he shot the clerk ten times in the head. That's a lot of times to get shot in the head."

The Red Devil again. Getting more bold. More ruthless. It seemed like years had passed since my Escape got fried and Eddie got shot. I dropped into my seat at the desk and added Connie's search information to the three files.

Shoshanna Brown was wanted for possession. She was a repeater. I'd picked Shoshanna up for priors, and I knew she wouldn't be hard to find. Probably she didn't have a ride to court.

Jamil Rodriguez was caught shoplifting a variety of electronics from Circuit City. When they searched him they found a loaded Glock, a box cutter, a sandwich bag filled with Ecstasy, and a human thumb in a sealed vial of formaldehyde. He claimed to have no knowledge of the thumb.

Anton Ward had a high bond. He'd gotten into a

fight with his girlfriend and had stabbed her repeatedly with a steak knife. The girlfriend had lived, but she wasn't happy with Anton. Anton had made bail but had failed to show for court. He was nineteen with no priors. Or at least no priors as an adult. Vinnie had a notation on Ward's bond document that there were gang tattoos on Ward's arm. One of the tattoos was a paw print accompanied by the letters CSS. Ward was a Comstock Street Slayer.

I paged through the file, looking for the photo. The first photo was a profile. The second was full on. I saw the second photo and froze. Anton Ward was the Red Devil.

"You don't look too good," Lula said. "Are you okay? You look whiter than usual."

"This is the devil guy."

Connie grabbed the file. "Are you sure?"

"It's been five days, but I'm pretty sure that's him."

"I didn't give him to you when I ran the neighborhood check because I couldn't find him," Connie said. "I didn't have time to go through the stacks of unfiled folders."

"Oops," Lula said.

Connie looked through the folder and read from the computer search. "Anton Ward. Dropped out of high school when he was sixteen. No work history. Lives with his brother." She flipped to the bond document. "His bond was secured by someone named Francine Taylor. She put her house up as collateral. Vinnie has a note that the daughter, Lauralene, is very pregnant, very young, and expecting to marry Anton Ward." Connie handed the file back to me. "I hate to give this to you. Ordinarily this would go to Ranger."

"No problem," I said. "I'm turning it over to the police." Trenton PD didn't have the manpower to pursue every skip. This was fine by me because it meant my job was secure. Anton Ward would be different. He was involved in a cop shooting and a possible murder. Trenton PD would find the manpower to go after Anton Ward.

I called Morelli and told him about Ward.

"I don't want you anywhere near this guy," Morelli said.

I felt the muscles knot around my spine. Morelli's a cop. He's Italian, I told myself. He can't help himself. Cut him some slack.

"Could you rephrase that?" I asked Morelli. "I think what you meant was *Be careful*."

"I said exactly what I meant. I don't want you anywhere near Anton Ward."

So here's the unfortunate truth. I called Morelli because I didn't want to go anywhere near Anton Ward. Problem is, when Morelli issues it as a demand my ears go flat against my head, my eyes narrow, and I take a stance with my head down, ready to lock horns. I don't know why I do this. I think it might have something to do with curly hair and being born in Jersey. And needless to say, this isn't the first time it's happened.

"And I suppose it's okay for you to go after him?" I said to Morelli.

"I'm a cop. We go after criminals. That's why you called me, right?"

"And I'm a fugitive apprehension agent."

"Don't take this the wrong way," Morelli said, "but you're not a great apprehension agent."

"I get the job done."

"You're a magnet for disaster."

"Okay, hotshot," I said. "I'll give you twenty-four hours to get him . . . and then he's mine."

I put my phone back into my bag and looked over at Lula.

"Guess you told him," Lula said. "If it was me I

would have given him forever. To begin with, those
people all live over in Slayerland. And if you want to
think about something else, Anton hasn't got a lot to lose
being that he just made Swiss cheese outta someone's
head."

"I got carried away."

"No shit. And how are you expecting to find someone Morelli can't find? Morelli's good."

Morelli'd issued his ultimatum before I'd finished
giving him all the information. "Morelli doesn't know
about Lauralene Taylor. And, as we all know, the girlfriend is always the ticket to the skip."

"I'm hoping he don't need Lauralene on account of I
don't want to have to follow your ass into Slayerland,"
Lula said.

I tucked the three new files into my bag. "Lauralene doesn't live in Slayerland. She lives on Hancock
Street."

"Hey, that's my neighborhood," Lula said.

Lula leaned over me and sniffed. "Boy, that Ranger
truck smell stays with you. You've been outta that truck
for a whole day, and you still smell like Ranger." She
took a step back. "There's something different about
you. I can't put my finger on it."

"She's fat," Connie said.

Lula's face creased into a broad smile. "That's it.
Look at those chubby cheeks and that bootie. And you
got love handles that go all the way around. You go,
girl, you're on your way to being a big woman like
Lula."

I looked down at myself. They were right! I had
a roll of fat hanging over the waistband of my jeans.
Where'd that come from? I was almost certain it wasn't
there last night.

I ran into the bathroom and examined my face in
the mirror. Definite chubbiness. Apple cheeks. Two

chins. Shit. It was the stress. Stress released a hormone that made you fat, right? I was pretty sure I read that somewhere. I checked out my jeans again. I'd had a stomachache all morning. Now I knew why. I popped the top snap and felt some relief as more fat oozed out.

I went back to Lula and Connie. "It's the stress," I said. "It's releasing hormones that are making me fat."

"Good thing I brought doughnuts with me," Lula said. "Have one of the chocolate-covered cream-filled and you'll feel better. Don't want to let that stress grab hold of you."

Connie let me out the back door and locked up after me. We'd filed the remaining folders and eaten all the doughnuts. Connie was going to a baby shower at the firehouse this afternoon. Lula had a hair appointment. I was going to spend the day being careful.

I slipped out of the alley, wearing the hooded sweatshirt with the hood up, and I did a fast scan of the side street. No gang guys in baggy pants and do-rags waiting to gun me down. Good deal.

I cruised into the Burg, and I parked one street over from my parents' house. I walked head down around the block, cut through the Krezwickis' yard, and hopped the fence into my parents' backyard.

My mother shrieked when she saw me at the back door. "Holy mother," she said, hand over her heart. "I didn't recognize you at first. What are you doing with the hood up on that sweatshirt? You look like a maniac."

"I was chilly."

She put her hand to my forehead. "Are you coming down with something? There's a lot of flu going around."

"I'm fine." I removed the sweatshirt and hung it over the back of a kitchen chair. "Where is everybody?"

"Your father's running errands. And Valerie took the girls shopping. Why?"

"Just making conversation."

"I thought maybe you were going to make a big announcement."

"What would I announce?"

"It's getting obvious," my mother said.

"Okay, so I've moved out of Morelli's house. It's not like it's the end of the world. We haven't even totally broken up this time. We're still talking to each other."

"You moved out? But aren't you pregnant?"

I was stunned. Pregnant? Me? I looked down at my belly. Yikes. I *did* look pregnant. I was on the pill, but I guess there could have been a slip-up. I did a fast calculation and stifled a sigh of relief. I wasn't pregnant.

"I'm *not* pregnant," I said.

"It's the doughnuts," Grandma said. "I know a doughnut butt when I see one."

I looked around for a knife. I was going to kill myself. "I've been under a lot of stress," I said.

"You could get that fat sucked out," Grandma said. "I saw a show on it last night. They showed a doctor sucking a whole load of fat out of some woman right on television. I almost threw up watching it."

The front door crashed open, and Mary Alice galloped in. Valerie followed with the baby. Angie followed Valerie.

Angie and Mary Alice immediately went to the television. Valerie brought the baby into the kitchen with her.

"Look who's here," Grandma said to Valerie. "Stephanie came early, and she's not even going to leave right away."

Valerie set the diaper bag on the floor and looked at me wide-eyed. "Oh my gosh," she said. "You're pregnant!"

"That's what we thought, too," Grandma said. "Turns out she's just fat."

"It's stress," I said. "I need to relax. Maybe I'm drinking too much coffee."

"I'm telling you, it's the doughnuts," Grandma said. "The Plum side of the family finally caught up with you. You don't watch out you're going to look like your Aunt Stella."

Stella had to have someone else tie her shoes.

"Your pants aren't buttoned," Mary Alice said to me as she galloped through. "Did you know that?"

Okay. Fine. I'll never eat again. Not ever. I'll drink water. But wait a minute, suppose the Junkman finds me and I get shot. I could end up on life support, and I could need the extra fat. Maybe the extra fat is a good thing. An act of God!

"What have we got for dessert?" I asked my mother.

"Chocolate cake and vanilla ice cream."

If God had wanted me to lose weight, he would have made sure there was creamed spinach for dessert.

Albert Kloughn arrived at six o'clock sharp.

"I'm not late, am I?" he asked. "I was working, and I lost track of time. I'm sorry if I'm late."

"You're not late," my mother said. "You're just in time."

We all knew who was late. Joe. The pot roast and green beans and mashed potatoes were set on the table, and Joe's chair was empty. My father sliced up the roast and took the first piece. Grandma plopped a glob of potatoes onto her plate and passed right. My mother looked at her watch. No Morelli. Mary Alice made horse sounds with her tongue and galloped her fingers around her water glass.

"Gravy," my father said.

Everyone jumped to attention and passed him the gravy.

I had a plate heaped with meat and potatoes smothered in gravy. I had a buttered roll, four green beans, and a beer. I'd taken the food, but I hadn't yet dug in. I was having an inner dialogue with my stupid self. Eat it, the stupid self was saying. You need it to keep up your strength. And suppose you get run over by a truck tomorrow and die? What then? You'll have dieted for nothing. Eat and enjoy!

My mother was watching. "You're not that fat," she said. "I always thought you were too thin."

Kloughn picked his head up and looked around. "Who's fat? Am I fat? I know I'm a little roly-poly. I've always been like that."

"You're perfect, Snuggy Uggums," Valerie said.

Grandma knocked back her glass of wine and poured another.

A car door slammed shut at the curb, and everyone sat straight and still in their seat. A moment later, the front door opened, and Morelli walked in.

"Sorry I'm late," he said to my mother. "I was stuck at work." He moved next to me, dropped a friendly kiss on the top of my head, and took his seat.

There was a collective sigh of relief. My family feared Morelli was my last shot at marriage. Especially now that I was fat.

"What's new?" I asked Morelli.

"Nothing's new."

I made a show of looking at my watch.

"Don't push it," Morelli said softly, smiling for the family. "Are you still driving the truck? I didn't see it out front."

"It's in the garage."

"Are you really going after Ward?"

"It's my job."

Our eyes locked for a moment, and I felt the handcuff clamp around my left wrist.

"You've got to be kidding," I said, holding my wrist up for inspection, the remaining bracelet dangling loose.

"Private joke," Morelli said to the rest of the table. Then he clicked the other half of the cuffs onto his right wrist.

"Kinky," Grandma said.

"I can't eat like this," I told Morelli.

"You eat with your right hand, and I cuffed the left."

"I can't cut my meat. And besides, I have to go to the bathroom."

Morelli gave his head a single shake. "That is so lame," he said.

"I do," I said. "It's the beer."

"Okay," Morelli said. "I'll go with you."

Everyone sucked in some air. A piece of pot roast fell out of my father's mouth, and my mother's fork slipped from her fingers and clattered onto her plate. We weren't the sort of family who went to the bathroom together. We barely admitted to *using* the bathroom.

Morelli looked around the table and gave a small defeated sigh. He reached into his shirt pocket, extracted the key to the cuffs, and released me.

I popped out of my seat and ran upstairs to the bathroom. I locked the door, opened the window, and climbed out onto the roof over the back stoop. I'd used this escape route since junior high. I was good at it. I dangled myself off the roof, and I dropped to the ground.

Morelli grabbed me, spun me around, and trapped me against the back of the house. He leaned into me and grinned. "I knew you'd go out the window."

In a perverse way, I liked that Morelli had me figured out. It was reassuring to know he paid attention. "Very clever of you."

"Yep."

"Now what?"

"We go back to the table. And when dinner is over, we go home . . . together."

"And what happens in the morning?"

"We sleep late, read the Sunday paper, and take Bob for a walk in the park."

"And Monday?"

"I go to work, and you stay home and hide."

I did a major head slap. "Unh," I said.

His eyes narrowed. "What?"

"To begin with, I'm afraid to hide in your house. I'm afraid to hide in my apartment or in my parents' house. I don't want to endanger anyone, and I don't want to make it easy for the bad guys to find me. And if that isn't enough, I *hate* when you order me around. I'm in law enforcement, too. I'm key to this mess. We should be working together."

"Are you crazy? What did you have in mind? I should use you for bait?"

"Maybe not bait."

Morelli grabbed the front of my shirt, pulled me to him, and kissed me.

It was a great kiss, but I didn't know what the heck it meant. It seemed to me a breaking-up kiss would have had less tongue.

"So," I said, "do you want to explain that?"

"There's no possible explanation. I am so messed up. You frustrate the shit out of me."

I knew the feeling. I was the mess-up queen. There was a contract on my head, and I was weirdly involved with two men. I didn't know which was more frightening.

"I'm going to take the coward's way out and leave," Morelli said. "That whole thing with the handcuffs got a little freaky. I should go back to work anyway.

We have a twenty-four-hour watch on Ward's brother's house, so stay far away. I swear if I see you anywhere near there I'm going to have you arrested."

I did another eye roll and returned to the house. I was doing so many eye rolls these days I was getting head pains.

Sunday morning I took a good look at myself in the mirror in Ranger's bathroom. Not a pretty sight, I decided. The fat had to go. I showered and got dressed, borrowing a black T-shirt from Ranger. The T-shirt was nice and roomy and hid the fat roll.

It had been easy to find the T-shirt. It was perfectly folded and stacked on a shelf, along with twenty other perfectly folded black T-shirts. It had been easy to find the hooded sweatshirt I'd previously borrowed. The hooded sweatshirt had been perfectly folded and stacked on a shelf, along with six other perfectly folded black hooded sweatshirts. Doubly impressive because it's damn hard to perfectly fold a hooded sweatshirt. I counted thirteen black cargo pants, thirteen black jeans, thirteen perfectly ironed long-sleeved black shirts that matched the cargo pants. Black cashmere blazer, black leather jacket, black jeans jacket, three black suits, six black silk shirts, three lightweight black cashmere sweaters.

I started opening drawers. Black dress socks, black and dark gray sweat socks. Assorted black athletic clothes. There was a small safe and a locked drawer. I was guessing the locked drawer held guns.

None of this especially interested me. The ugly truth is, I'd finally lost the fight for dignity, and I was searching for Ranger's underwear. Not that I was going to do anything kinky with it. I just wanted to see what he wore. Hell, I thought I'd shown a lot of restraint to have gone this long without snooping.

I'd now searched the entire dressing room, and unless Ranger kept his underwear in his safe, it appeared to me that he went commando.

I did one of those stupid fanning motions with my hands that women used to do in movies back in the forties to signify heat. I had no idea why I did it. It did nothing to cool me off. I was thinking about Ranger in his black cargo pants, and my face felt sunburned. I had other body parts that were pretty warm, too.

I had one drawer left. I slowly opened the drawer and peeked inside. A single pair of black silk boxers. Just one pair. What the heck did that mean?

I was feeling a little perverted, so I carefully closed the drawer, went into the kitchen, opened the refrigerator door, and let the cold air wash over me.

I looked down and couldn't see my toes past my belly. Mental groan. "No more junky breakfast cereal," I told Rex. "No more doughnuts, chips, pizza, ice cream, or beer."

Rex was in his soup can so it was hard to tell what he thought of the plan.

I got the coffee going, fixed myself a small bowl of Ranger's cereal, and added skim milk. I like this cereal, I told myself. This is delicious. And it would be even more delicious with some sugar and chocolate. I finished the cereal and poured out a mug of coffee. I took the coffee into the den, and I turned the television on.

By noon I was bored with television, and the apartment was starting to feel claustrophobic. I hadn't heard a word from Morelli, and I took that as a bad sign both romantically and professionally. I dialed his cell and held my breath while it rang.

"What?" Morelli said.

"It's Stephanie. I'm just checking in."

Silence.

"Since I haven't heard from you I'm assuming you don't have Ward."

"We've been watching the brother's house, but so far Anton's a no-show."

"You're watching the wrong house. You need to get to him through the girlfriend."

"I don't have any leverage with the girlfriend."

"I do. The girlfriend's mother used her house as collateral on the bond. I can threaten the mother with foreclosure."

More silence. "You could have told me this yesterday," he finally said.

"I was sulking."

"Good thing you're cute when you sulk. What's the plan?"

"I'll visit the mother and apply some pressure. I'll pass whatever information I get on to you, and you can do the takedown."

Chapter
TEN

Anton Ward's girlfriend, Lauralene Taylor, lived at home with her mother on Hancock Street. I wanted to question the Taylors, and I thought it was best to do it alone. Less threatening that way, and I didn't think I'd need help. This was basically a fishing trip in a neighborhood that was hard times but not in the red zone on the danger meter.

Houses were small, in varying degrees of disrepair, and largely multiple family. The population was ethnically mixed. The economy was a hair above desperate. Mostly the inhabitants were working poor.

I drove past Francine Taylor's house, didn't see any activity, and decided it was safe to approach. I parked the Lincoln a couple houses away, locked up, and walked back.

The Taylor house was better than most in the neighborhood. The exterior was a faded lime green, halfway between bare wood and fresh paint. Shades looked inexpensive, but had been neatly raised to the same level on all windows. The small porch was covered with green indoor-outdoor carpet. Porch furnishings consisted of a rusted metal folding chair and a large glass ashtray filled with butts.

I hesitated a moment, listening before knocking. I didn't hear any yelling behind the closed door, no gunshots, no big dog snarling. Just the muffled hum of a television. So far, so good. I rapped once and waited. I rapped a second time.

A very pregnant kid opened the door. She was a couple inches shorter than me, dressed in pink sweats not designed for maternity. Her face was round and smooth with baby fat. Her hair had been straightened and bleached honey blond. Her skin was dark, but her eyes had an Asian tilt. Much too pretty for Anton Ward, and much too young to be pregnant.

"Yeah?" she said.

"Lauralene Taylor?"

"You're either a cop or social services," she said. "And we don't want none."

She tried to close the door, but my foot was in the way.

"I represent Anton's bond agent. Is Anton here?"

"If Anton was here, you'd be dead."

Lauralene sounded like she thought that would be a good thing, giving me pause to rethink my opinion of her. "Anton needs to reschedule his court date," I said.

"Yeah, like that's gonna happen."

"Your mother used this house as collateral. If Anton doesn't show up for court, your mother will lose her house."

"Anton will take care of us."

Mrs. Taylor came to the door, and I introduced myself.

"I have nothing to say to you," Francine Taylor said. "You're talking about the father of my unborn grandchild. You need to take this up with him."

"You signed the bond document," I said. "You used your house as collateral. If Anton doesn't show up for court, you'll lose this house."

"He won't let that happen," Francine said. "He has connections."

"He has no connections," I said. "If he stays in the area we'll catch him, and he'll go to jail. His only other option is to run. And if he runs, he's not going to take a pregnant woman with him. And he's not going to care if you keep this house. You'll be on the street with nothing."

It was the truth. And I could see that Francine knew it. She wasn't as dumb as her kid.

"I knew I shouldn't have put the house up for him," Francine said. "It was just I wanted him to turn out good for Lauralene."

"This dump isn't worth nothing anyway," Lauralene said.

"I work hard to make my payments on this house," Francine said. "It's a roof over your head. And it's gonna be the only roof over your baby's head. And I'm not losing it for no worthless Anton Ward."

"It don't matter what anyone thinks," Lauralene said. "I'm not giving up Anton, and there's nothing you can do about it. He's gonna marry me. And he's gonna take me out of this hole. We got plans."

I gave Francine my card and asked her to call if she had information on Ward. I wished Lauralene luck with the baby, and she told me to kiss her ass. I try not to be judgmental, but it was a little frightening that Lauralene Taylor and Anton Ward were reproducing.

I returned to the Lincoln and sat there awhile, watching the Taylor house. I'd had a bowl of rabbit food for breakfast and nothing for lunch. I was starving and there was no food in the Lincoln. No Krispy Kremes, no Big Mac, no supersize fries.

I had two new skips, but I wasn't motivated to find them. And Harold Pancek was out there, but truth is, I didn't care much about him either. I cared about Anton Ward. I wanted to see Ward locked up. I would have preferred not to be the one doing the capture, but at the moment I felt relatively safe. So I decided to sit tight.

I was still watching the Taylor house at four o'clock. I was bored out of my mind and hungry enough to eat the upholstery. I called Lula, told her I was on Hancock, and asked her to bring me something nonfattening to eat.

Five minutes later, the Firebird pulled to the curb behind me, and Lula got out. "What's happening?" she asked, handing over a brown paper lunch bag. "Did I miss anything?"

"I'm hanging out to see if Lauralene has a date tonight."

I looked in the bag. It contained a bottle of water and a hard-boiled egg.

"You gotta stay away from the carbs," Lula said. "That's how I lost all my weight. I went on that protein diet. Then I sort of fell off the wagon and gained all the weight back, but it was still my favorite diet, except for the time I ate two pounds of bacon and threw up."

I ate the egg and drank the water. I thought about eating the bag, but I was worried it was carbohydrate.

"I guess I should stay with you in case something dangerous happens, and you need someone to squish somebody," Lula said.

I looked over at her. "Nothing better to do?"

"Not a damn thing. I'm between men right now. And there's nothing on television worth watching." She pulled a deck of cards out of her purse. "I figured we could play rummy."

At six o'clock Lula said she had to have a bathroom break. She took off in the Firebird, and she returned a half hour later with powdered sugar on her shirt.

"That's really rotten," I said. "You've got a lot of

nerve sneaking out to get food and not bringing any
back for me."

"You're on a diet."

"It's not the starvation diet!"

"Well, I was going to stop home to use the bathroom, and then I thought why not use the bathroom
at Dunkin' Donuts? And then I couldn't very well use
their bathroom without buying some doughnuts. That'd
be rude, right?"

I gave her an Italian hand signal that didn't mean
left turn.

"Boy, you get cranky when you don't get a doughnut," Lula said.

A little over an hour later, streetlights were on, and
Hancock Street was settled in for the night. Lula and I
couldn't play cards in the dark, so we were passing the
time with twenty questions.

"I'm thinking of something that's animal," Lula
said. "And my ass is asleep. What makes you so sure
Lauralene's gonna have a date tonight?"

"She's got news for Anton, and I'm betting she's
going to use it to make him come see her."

Just then, the Taylors' front door opened and Lauralene stepped out.

"You're pretty smart," Lula said. "You're always
thinking. You know all about manipulative female
shit."

Lauralene looked right and left, and Lula and I froze.
We were just a couple houses down. Easily in sight. Fortunately, we weren't under a streetlight, and Lauralene
didn't appear to have picked us out. She was wearing
the same pink sweat suit. She wasn't carrying a purse.
She set off down the street, walking away from us.

"She's going to meet him," Lula said. "And she don't
want her mama to know."

Lauralene turned the corner, and I started the car

engine. I left my headlights off, and I carefully followed after Lauralene. She walked two blocks and got into the backseat of a parked car. The car was in shadow, hard to tell the make, impossible to see the occupants at this distance. It looked to be a compact, possibly dark green.

I stopped several houses back and idled at the curb. There were no cars parked between Lauralene and me.

"We're sort of exposed, sitting here like this," Lula said. "She could turn around and see us."

I agreed, but I didn't want to drive past Lauralene and risk having her recognize me. Better to take our chances being parked in the dark.

After a short time, the car in front of us started to rock.

"Look at this," Lula said. "She's seven months pregnant, and they're doing the nasty in the backseat of a friggin' compact. They didn't even bother to go out of the neighborhood."

"They must have been in a hurry," I said.

"Well, excuse me, but I think that's tacky. He could at least of had the courtesy to steal something with a bigger backseat. This here's a pregnant woman he's slippin' it to. I mean, how much effort does it take to find a Cadillac? All those old people over in Hamilton Township got Caddies. Those cars are just sitting around waiting to get stolen."

"He's doing more than slippin'," I said. "I've never seen a car rock like that."

"He's gonna ruin the shocks if he keeps this up."

Some loud groaning sounds carried back to us, and Lula and I rolled our windows down so we could hear better.

"Either he's real good or else she's going into labor," Lula said. She leaned forward and squinted. "Am I looking at a moon? What the hell is he doing? How'd he get his ass plastered against the rear window like that?"

The sight was both horrifying and mesmerizing.

"Maybe we should go get him before he finishes up," Lula said. "It'll be easier to get the cuffs on him when he's got a boner and can't move real fast."

Lula was probably right, but I couldn't see myself slapping cuffs on Anton Ward while his flag was flying. Last month Morelli and I rented a porno flick, and there was some boinking in it. And okay, so it was fun in a car crash kind of way. But that was film, and this is Anton Ward in the flesh, rocking the car with pregnant Lauralene Taylor. Yikes. I was as close as I wanted to get.

"Uh oh," Lula said. "The car's stopped rocking."

We stuck our heads out and listened. Quiet.

"He don't impress me as being the type to stick around," Lula said.

We jumped out of the Lincoln and scurried up to Ward's car. I had cuffs shoved into the waistband of my jeans, and I was holding Ranger's Maglite in one hand and pepper spray in the other. Lula was fumbling in her purse, looking for her gun as she ran.

I took a deep breath, prayed to God that Anton and Lauralene had their clothes on, and flashed the Maglite into the car interior.

"What the fuck?" Anton Ward said, bare ass gleaming under the Maglite.

"Oops," I said. "Sorry, I thought you were done."

"Guess they must have been changing positions," Lula said, looking into the car.

"You fat cow," Ward yelled at Lauralene. "You set me up." And he punched her in the face.

I dropped the Maglite and the spray, and reached into the car to secure Ward, but he was a man in motion, and I only succeeded in grabbing his pants. He wriggled out of the pants, hurled himself out of the opposite side of the car, and took off running.

I ran after him, down the street to the corner. He turned the corner and kept going. He was younger and probably in better shape than me, but he was running buck naked with the exception of socks. I figured eventually the socks were going to slow him down, not to mention the outdoor plumbing swinging in the breeze.

I could hear Lula pounding the pavement half a block back. Nice to know someone was slower than me.

Ward cut through a narrow alley between houses, jumped a fence, and fell when he caught his foot on the top of the fence. He scrambled to his feet, but he'd lost ground to me. I went over the fence and tackled him.

He wasn't a real big guy, but he was a nasty fighter. We rolled around on the ground, swearing and clawing. Turns out it's not that easy to grab hold of a naked guy. Not that I was feeling fussy about where to grab, mostly I just couldn't get a grip on anything. He caught me with a knee to the stomach, and I rolled off him in a rush of pain.

"Stand clear," Lula yelled. "I've got him!" And Lula fell on top of Anton Ward, doing a perfect repeat of Roger Banker.

There was a woof of air that got squished out of Anton Ward's body when Lula made contact, and then Ward didn't move. He was on his back, spread-eagled, eyes open and fixed.

Lula toed him. "You aren't dead, are you?"

Ward blinked.

"He isn't dead," Lula said. "Too bad, hunh?"

I cuffed him, and Lula and I hauled him to his feet.

"Guess we don't have to search him for weapons," Lula said. "That's a big advantage to chasing down a naked guy."

"Come on," I said to Ward. "We're going back to the car."

"I'm not going nowhere," he said.

"Don't mess with me," I told him. "I've only had an egg to eat today, and I'm feeling really vicious."

"Not only that, but I wouldn't mind having a reason to sit on you again," Lula said. "I'm working at perfecting my technique. That was my new special move. I'm even going to give it a name. You know how the Rock has all them wrestling moves like the *People's Elbow* and the *Rock Bottom*? I'm gonna call mine the *Lula Bootie Bomb*."

Ward did some mumbling and started walking. "You're as good as dead," he said to me.

"We're so scared, we're shaking," Lula said. "Look at me. I'm shaking. We're getting threatened by some ugly-ass naked guy. You think we're scared of you? You can't even keep your baggy-ass clothes on."

"You mess with me, and you mess with the Nation," Ward said. "Only reason bounty hunter bitch hasn't tasted the brothers so far is she's being saved for Junkman." Ward smiled at me. "You're gonna like Junkman. They tell me he's got a way with bitches."

We turned the corner, and I could see the Lincoln at the curb, but no Ward car.

"Fuck," Ward said. "That cow took off with my car."

No big disaster, except his clothes were in the car. Lula and I both looked at Ward.

"He isn't going in my Firebird like this," Lula said. "I'm not sitting his nasty bare ass on my Firebird seat."

I didn't want his bare ass on my upholstery, either. I wasn't in love with the Lincoln, but it was all I had right now.

"I'll call Morelli," I said. "They can come pick him up."

"You have Ward in cuffs?" Morelli said, after a deadly pause.

"Yeah, and I thought you could come get him."

"You were supposed to call me for the takedown."

"I forgot. It happened kind of fast. You know, took me by surprise."

Ten minutes later, two squad cars pulled up. Robin Russell got out of the first car and walked over to me.

"Oh man," she said, "he's naked. I'm not getting paid enough for this job."

"Wasn't our fault he's naked," Lula said. "We caught him in the act. He was in the backseat of a Hyundai, humping like a big dog."

Carl Costanza followed Russell. He checked Ward out and grinned at me. "You want to tell me the details?"

"No," I said. "You're going to have to make them up as you go."

"Joe's gonna love this," Costanza said.

"Where is he?"

"He's waiting at the station. He was afraid he'd be up for homicide if he didn't calm down before he saw you."

Robin slung a friendly arm around Costanza's shoulders. "I have a real big favor to ask . . ."

"No way."

Robin Russell narrowed her eyes. "You don't even know what I was going to say."

"You were going to try to sweet-talk me into putting this guy's bare ass in my squad car."

"I was not," Russell said. "Well, all right, I was." She locked eyes with Costanza. "What would it take?"

Costanza smiled at her.

"You're a disgrace to the uniform," Russell said to Costanza.

"I try."

Russell wrapped her hand around Ward's arm and tugged him forward. "I'm going to sit you on my Trenton *Times*," she said to Ward. "And I don't want to see your butt move off that newspaper."

"That was fun," Lula said. "That was worth waiting for."

It was satisfying to have captured Ward, but I don't know if I'd classify the experience as fun. I dropped Lula at her Firebird, thanked her for her help, and then I went on to the police station. I would have preferred to crawl back to Ranger's apartment and let my mind go numb in front of his big-screen TV, but I had to make sure I was credited for the capture. And I had to pick up my body receipt.

The police station isn't in the high-rent part of town, and the public lot is across the street and unguarded. It was too late, too dark, and I was too worried to take a chance on the public lot, so I parked illegally in the lot reserved for cop cars. I had myself buzzed in through the back door, and I went directly to the desk. Ward was there, chained to a wooden bench, still naked. Someone had draped a towel over his lap.

"Hey, bitch," Ward said to me. "Want to take a peek under the towel? Take one last look at the big boy?"

Then he made slurpy kissy sounds at me.

I'd already seen more of the "big boy" than I wanted, and it wasn't that big or that fascinating. And the kissy sounds were really getting on my nerves. I kept my head down at the desk, waiting for my paperwork. I didn't want to see Morelli. I didn't know if he was in the building. If I got out before he found me, that would be cool. I figured time and space were my friends at this point.

There was a new cop behind the desk, going slow, making sure he was getting it right. I had a hard time not ripping the body receipt out of his hands.

"In a hurry?" he asked.

"Things to do."

I took the receipt from him, turned on my heel, and marched out of the building. I avoided eye contact with Ward, just in case the towel had slipped or, even worse, was moving. The back door closed behind me, and I shrieked when Morelli grabbed me and pulled me to one side.

"Jeez," I said, hand over my heart. "You scared the crap out of me. Don't sneak up on me like that." Although, truth is, I'm not sure I shrieked because I *didn't* know who it was or because I *did* know who it was.

"Are you okay?"

"Yeah, I think I'm okay. I'm just having some heart palpitations. I have them a lot these days."

"Now that you've had a chance to see Ward up close, are you sure he's the Red Devil?"

"Yes."

"And he was in the car when Gazarra got shot?"

"Yes."

A patrol car pulled up to the back door for delivery. Morelli and I stood aside while two cops hauled Lauralene out of the backseat.

"What did she do?" I asked.

"Ran a red light in a stolen car, driving without a license."

Lauralene's eyes were red from crying.

"She's had a bad night," I said to Morelli. "And she's pregnant. Maybe you can talk to her. She looks like she could use a friend."

I called Francine and told her Ward had been captured. Then I told her Lauralene was at the cop shop.

"Now what?" Morelli said.

"I'm going home. Stick a fork in me, I'm done."

"And home is where?"

"It's a secret."

"I could find you if I put some energy to it," he said.

"I'd tell you if I thought I could trust you."

Morelli sent me a tight smile. He couldn't be trusted. We both knew it. He'd drag me out of my hiding place against my wishes if he thought it was the right thing to do.

"Do you need an escort out of here? Are you in public parking?"

"No, I'm illegally parked in the chief's spot."

Morelli looked over at the reserved space. "The Lincoln? What happened to the truck?"

"Too high profile."

My cell phone rang at six forty-five Monday morning.

"Junkman tagged the second gang member on his list," Morelli said. "You don't want to know the details, but it took us less time to locate all the body parts this time since we knew where to look."

Not good information on an empty stomach.

I rolled out of bed and went to the kitchen to say good morning to Rex. I made coffee and drank it with my meager bowl of healthy, tasteless cereal. After two cups of coffee I still wasn't motivated to start my day, so I went back to bed.

The phone rang again at eight o'clock. It was Connie.

"You remembered about Carol Cantell, right?"

"Sure. What was I supposed to remember?"

"She's got court today."

Shit. I'd completely forgotten. "What's her court time?"

"She's supposed to be there at nine, but her case probably won't be heard until after lunch."

"Call her sister and have her go over to Carol's house. I'll pick Lula up at the office in a half hour."

No time for a shower. I borrowed a hat and another shirt from Ranger and pulled on my one remaining pair of clean jeans. I was in the elevator when I realized I'd buttoned the top snap on the jeans. Hooray. The diet was working. Good thing, too, because I was hating every minute of it and would love an excuse to quit.

I remoted the gate open and ran to the car. I was parking closer now that I was driving the Lincoln. Not as afraid of discovery by Ranger's men. I was on the cell phone at the first red light, calling Cantell.

"What?" she yelled into the phone. "What?"

"It's Stephanie Plum," I said, in my most reassuring, soothing voice. "How are things going?"

"I'm fat . . . that's how it's frigging going. I have nothing to wear. I look like a blimp."

"You remembered your court date?"

"I'm not going. I can't get into any of my clothes, and everyone's going to laugh at me. I ate a truckful of chips, for crying out loud."

"Lula and I are coming over to help. Just hang in there."

"Hurry up. I'm losing it. I need salt. I need grease. I need something crunchy in my mouth. I'm running a fever here."

Cindy was sitting on Carol's front porch when we drove up.

"She won't let me in," Cindy said. "I know she's in there. I can hear her pacing."

I rapped on the front door. "Carol, open the door. It's Stephanie."

"Have you got food?"

I crinkled a bag of Cheez Doodles so she could hear it through the door. "Lula and I stopped on the way over and bought Doodles to get you through the court session."

Carol cracked the door. "Let me see."

I shoved the Cheez Doodles at her. She grabbed the

bag from me, ripped it open, and shoved a handful of doodles into her mouth.

"Oh yeah," she said, sounding a lot like Lowanda doing phone sex. "I feel better already."

"I thought you were over the doodle craving," Lula said.

"I'm not good with stress," Carol said. "It's a glandular thing."

"It's a mental thing," Lula said. "You're a nut."

We all followed Carol upstairs to her bedroom.

"I did my hair, and I put on my makeup, and then I went to get dressed, and I just sort of had a brain fart," Carol said.

We stood at the doorway and surveyed the disaster area. It looked like her closet exploded, and then her room was ransacked by monkeys.

"Guess you couldn't decide what to wear," Lula said, stepping over the clothes carnage that littered the floor.

"Nothing fits!" Carol wailed.

"Would have been good if you'd discovered that yesterday," Lula said. "You ever think of preparing ahead?"

I was picking through the crumpled piles of clothes on the floor, looking for slacks with elastic waistbands, bulky tops, scarves that matched. "Help me out here," I said. "Let's start with the slacks. Black would be good. Everything goes with black."

"Yeah, and it don't show the cellulite lumps," Lula said. "Black is real slimming."

Ten minutes later we had Carol squashed into black slacks. The button was open at the waist but you couldn't see it under the hip-length dark blue cotton shirt.

"Good thing you got this nice big roomy shirt," Lula said to Carol.

Carol looked down at it. "It's a nightgown."

"Do you have any roomy shirts that aren't night-gowns?" I asked her.

"They all have doodle stains on them," she said. "It's hard to get those orange smudges out of stuff."

"You know what I think?" I said. "I think this outfit looks good. No one will know you're wearing a night-gown. It looks just like a shirt. And the color is good for you."

"Yeah," Lula and Cindy said. "The color is good."

"Okay," I said, "we're ready to go."

"I've got her purse and jacket," Cindy said.

"I've got a towel so she don't get doodle crumbs on herself on the way to the courthouse," Lula said.

"I can't do it!" Carol sobbed.

"Yes, you can," we all said. "You can do it."

"Hit me," Carol said. "I need a hit."

I gave her a new bag of Cheez Doodles. She tore the bag open and scarfed a handful of doodles.

"You gotta pace yourself," Lula said to Carol. "You got a long day ahead of you, and you don't want to run out of doodles."

Carol clutched the bag to her chest and we nudged her forward, down the stairs, out to the car.

I got Carol Cantell settled in at the courthouse and then I left. Lula and Cindy were with Cantell. Cindy had four unopened bags of doodles. Lula had cuffs and a stun gun. They promised to call me if a problem developed.

I would have stayed with Cantell to see how things turned out but I was feeling grungy. I needed a shower. And I needed to put distance between me and the Cheez Doodles. Ten more minutes with Cantell and I would have wrestled her for the remaining bags.

I drove past Ranger's building, but there was too much activity to chance a run for the elevator. So, what are the alternative shower and lunch possibilities?

Morelli's house was one alternative. I had a key to the house, and I still had some clothes there. Convenient but not smart, I thought. Not a good time to return. Too many unresolved issues. And Junkman could be watching the house.

Better to go to my parents' house. It was easier to sneak in through the back, and I could feel relatively confident that I wasn't seen.

Chapter

ＥＬＥＶＥＮ

It was close to noon when I cruised into the Burg. Sally's bus was parked in front of my parents' house, and my father's car was missing from the driveway. Probably there was a big wedding discussion going on, and my father was hiding out at the Elks Lodge.

On first pass I didn't see any Slayers with boom boxes or automatic weapons. Of course, if someone was skinny enough he could be crouched behind Mrs. Ciak's hydrangea bush. I thought better safe than sorry, and I did my Saturday night routine, driving halfway around the block to park. I had the sweatshirt on again with the hood up. I locked the Lincoln, and once again, I cut through the Krezwickis' yard.

I didn't want my mother to do another freak-out, so I took the sweatshirt off before I opened the back door.

Sally, Valerie with the baby, my mother, and Grandma Mazur were at the kitchen table.

"You're hiding from someone, aren't you?" my mother said to me. "That's why you keep sneaking in the back."

"She's hiding from them gang members who want to kill her," Grandma said. "Does anyone want that last piece of cake?"

"That's ridiculous," my mother said. "We don't have gangs in Trenton."

"Wake up and smell the coffee," Grandma said. "We got Bloods and Craps and Latin Queens. And that's just to name a few."

"I was in a rush this morning, and I didn't have time to take a shower," I said to my mother. "Is it okay if I shower here?"

"Of course it's okay," my mother said. "Did you really break up with Joseph again?"

"I moved out of his house. I'm not sure how broken up we are."

My mother went still, radar humming. "If you're not living with Joseph, where are you living?"

This got everyone's attention.

"I'm staying in a friend's apartment," I said.

"What friend?"

"I can't say. It's . . . a secret."

"Omigod," my mother said. "You're having an affair with a married man."

"I'm not!"

"Isn't that something," Grandma said.

Sally snapped the band on his wrist.

"What was that for?" Grandma asked.

"I thought a really bad word," Sally said.

Yeesh. "I'm not going to discuss this," I told everyone. "This is stupid." And I flounced off to take a shower.

An hour later, I was showered and shampooed, and I was peering into my mother's refrigerator. I didn't have nearly so much blubber hanging over the waistband of my jeans today. Amazing how the fat disappears when you stop eating. The downside was that I felt mean as a snake.

"What are you looking for?" my mother wanted to know. "You've been standing there with the door open for ten minutes."

"I'm looking for something that won't make me fat."

"You're not fat," my mother said. "You shouldn't worry."

"She's got to be careful of the Plum side of the family," Grandma said. "This is when it starts. Remember how Violet was always so thin? Then she hit her thirties and ballooned up. Now she has to buy two seats when she gets on an airplane."

"I don't know what to eat!" I said, arms flapping. "I've never had to worry about weight before. What the hell am I supposed to friggin' eat?"

"Depends what kind of diet you're doing," Grandma said. "Are you doing Weight Watchers, Atkins, South Beach, The Zone, The Slime Diet, The Sex Diet? I like the Slime Diet, myself. That's where you're only allowed to eat things that got slime . . . like oysters and slugs and raw bull's balls. I was going to try the Sex Diet, but I couldn't figure out some of the rules. Every time you get hungry you're supposed to have sex. Only thing is, they didn't say what kind of sex you're supposed to have. Like, whether you should have it alone or with someone else. And what about that oral sex stuff? I never did a lot of that personally. Your grandfather wasn't much for experimenting," Grandma said to me.

My mother went to the cupboard, poured herself a tumbler of whiskey, and chugged it.

"So what kind of diet are you on?" Grandma asked me.

"I'm on the Tastykake diet," I said, helping myself to a Butterscotch Krimpet.

"Good for you," Grandma said. "That's a good choice."

"I'm going back to work," I told everyone, putting my hood up, ducking out the back door.

Mrs. Krezwicki was at her kitchen window when I scuttled through her yard. She leveled a gun at me, sighting with one eye. I pushed the hood back and waved, and she lowered the gun and reached for the wall phone. Calling my mother, no doubt.

I got into the Lincoln and drove to the office.

"I heard from Lula at the courthouse," Connie said. "Cantell's doing okay."

"How about Ranger? Have you heard from Ranger?"

"Not a word."

Rats. He wasn't supposed to be back for at least another week, but I didn't want to take any chances on being caught in his bed. Or even worse, in his shower!

Connie's eyes fixed on my hat. "That looks like Ranger's hat."

"He gave it to me." It was a perfectly good fib. If he gave me his truck, why not his hat?

Connie looked like she bought it.

"I wish Ranger would get his butt back here," Connie said. "I'm not happy about you going after Rodriguez. What kind of a person would carry a thumb around with him?"

"A crazy person?"

"It's creepy. If you want, I can call Tank to go with you."

"No!" Last time I went out with Tank he broke his leg. Then his substitute got a concussion. I was hell on Ranger's Merry Men. Bad enough I was squatting in his apartment, I didn't want to compound the damage by wiping out his workforce. And if I was being totally honest, I'd have to admit that time spent with Tank was uncomfortable. Tank was Ranger's right-hand man. He was the guy who watched Ranger's back. He was entirely trustworthy, but he rarely spoke, and he never shared his thoughts. I'd reached a sort of telepathic state with Ranger. I hadn't a clue what was in Tank's mind. Maybe nothing at all.

"I'm a lot more worried about Junkman than I am about Rodriguez," I said to Connie.

"Have you seen Junkman?"

"No."

"Do you know what he looks like?"

TEN BIG ONES   183

"No."

"Do you know why you're on his list?"

"Does there have to be a reason?"

"There's usually a reason," Connie said.

"I can identify Ward as the Red Devil, and I bounced Eugene Brown off my Buick."

"That could be it," Connie said. "Or it could be something else."

"Like what?"

Connie shrugged. "I don't know gangs, but I know something about the mob. Usually when someone's targeted for takeout, it's about power . . . keeping it or getting it."

"How does that relate to me?"

"If it's an entire gang that's out to get you, you move far away. If it's only one member, you can eliminate the problem by eliminating the member."

"Are you suggesting I kill Junkman?"

"I'm suggesting you try to find out why Junkman has you on his list."

"I'd have to penetrate the Slayers."

"You'd have to catch one and make him talk to you," Connie said.

Catch a Slayer. It sounded like a kid's game.

"You could hide out until Ranger gets back," Connie said.

What she meant was, I could hide out until Ranger gets back and eliminates Junkman for me. Ranger was good at solving problems like that. And it was tempting to let him solve mine, but that's not the sort of thing you do to someone you like. That's not even the sort of thing you do to someone you hate. Not when the problem is solved by murder.

I'd already been there, and it didn't feel great. I was pretty sure Ranger had once killed a man to protect me. The man had been insane and determined to end my life. His death had been ruled a suicide, but in my heart, I knew Ranger had stepped in and done the job. And I knew there'd been an unspoken agreement between Ranger and Morelli. Don't ask, don't tell.

Morelli was a cop, sworn to uphold the law. Ranger had his own set of laws. There were things that fell in the gray zone between Morelli and Ranger. Things Ranger was willing to do if he felt it necessary. Things Morelli could never justify.

"I'll think about it," I told Connie. "Let me know if you hear from Ranger."

I'd parked in the small lot behind the bonds office. I left through the back door, got into the Lincoln, and I called Morelli.

"What's happening with Anton?" I asked. "Did he make bail?"

"It's set high. I don't think anybody's going to step forward for him."

"Have you talked to him? Did he tell you anything interesting? Like about Junkman?"

"He's not talking," Morelli said.

"Can't you make him?"

"I could, but I misplaced my rubber hose."

"You said Junkman was a hired gun, right? That he was from L.A."

"We're not sure if that information is right anymore. The source hasn't turned out as reliable as we'd hoped. We know there's a guy out there who uses the tag Junkman. And we know he's working his way through a list. That's really all we're sure of."

"And I'm on the list."

"That's what we were told."

And that's what Anton confirmed. "It would be helpful to know why I'm on the list."

"Whatever the reason, it would help your cause if you'd quit your job and look like a nonthreatening housewife. Or maybe go away for a couple months. These guys have a short attention span."

"Would you miss me if I went away?"

There was a long silence.

"Well?" I asked.

"I'm thinking."

I called Lula next.

"Carol's up in about ten minutes," Lula said. "How are we supposed to get home?"

"I'm on my way. Parking's a pain. Call me when you're on the sidewalk in front of the building, and I'll swing by and pick you up."

I reached the courthouse and drove around the block. My phone rang on the second pass.

"We're out," Lula yelled. "We got Carol with us, too. And we all need a bar!"

"How did she do?"

"Probation and counseling. It was her first offense, and she'd already paid for all the Fritos she ate. We had a lady judge who weighed about two hundred pounds and was real sympathetic."

I turned the corner and saw them at the curb. Lula and Cindy were smiling. Carol looked shell-shocked. She was ghostly white, clutching a bag of Cheez Doodles to her chest, and she was visibly shaking.

They all piled into the backseat, with Carol sitting between Cindy and Lula.

"Carol doesn't know the court session is over," Lula said, grinning. "Carol's in a state. We gotta get Carol a big-ass margarita."

I drove over to the Burg, and I parked in front of Marsilio's. It was a nice safe place to get a drink. If anybody messed with you at Marsilio's, Bobby V. would kick their butt. Or even worse, he'd make sure they didn't get a table.

We guided Carol into Marsilio's, sat her at a table, and used the napkin to brush some of the doodle dust off her.

"Am I going to jail?" Carol asked.

"No," Cindy said. "You're not going to jail."

"I was afraid I was going to jail. Who would take care of my kids?"

"I'd take care of your kids," Cindy said. "But you don't have to worry about it, because you're not going to jail."

Alan, the owner, rushed over with a margarita for Carol.

"Am I going to jail?" she asked.

Three margaritas later, we poured Carol into the Lincoln, and I dumped her at Cindy's house.

"Boy," Lula said. "She was really hammered."

With any luck she'd throw up a bag or two of doodles. Don't get me wrong, I love doodles, but they aren't exactly diet food when you snarf them by the truckload.

It was late afternoon, so I took Lula to the office. I parked in the rear lot, and we went in through the back door.

Connie was on her feet when she saw us. "I've got a bunch of files," she said. "Everyone take a couple and put them away. I don't want another file mess."

I took my stack of files and arranged them alphabetically. "Joe tells me no one bonded out Anton Ward this time."

"He's being held on a big bucks bond, and no one has the collateral to cover it. His brother called, but Vinnie wouldn't take the bond. The only way Ward's going to get out is with a signature bond, and no one's going to write a signature on Anton Ward."

"What's the charge?"

"Armed robbery and accessory."

"Ain't no justice in this world," Lula said. "That

scrawny piece of garbage will plea-bargain and get off with a couple years."

Connie filed the last of her folders. "I don't think he'll plea-bargain. I don't think he'll talk at all. If he gives up any Slayers, he's as good as dead."

There was a burst of rapid-fire gunshots from the back of the building, and we all instinctively went to the floor. The shooting stopped, but we stayed down.

"Tell me I'm hallucinating," Lula said. "I don't want to believe this."

After a couple minutes we got to our feet and tiptoed to the back door. We put our ears to the door and listened.

Perfectly quiet.

Connie cracked the door and peeked out. "Okay," she said. "It makes sense now."

Lula and I peeked out, too.

The Lincoln was totally spray painted with gang graffiti and riddled with bullet holes. The tires were shot out, and the windows were shattered.

"Hunh," Lula said. "Guess you're going to need alternative transportation."

What I needed was a new life. I felt myself gnawing on my lip again and immediately forced myself to stop.

"You're kind of white," Connie said to me. "Are you okay?"

"They found me. I was driving a new car, and I parked in the back, and they figured it out."

"Probably watching the office," Lula said.

"I'm trying real hard not to freak," I told them.

"Play the role," Lula said. "That's what we do. We pick a role and we play it. What role you want to play?"

"I want to be smart, and I want to be brave."

"Go for it," Lula said.

Connie closed and locked the door. She went to the

ammo storage area, rummaged through boxes, and came up with a Kevlar vest.

"Try this on for size," she said to me.

I slipped it on, flattened the Velcro closures, and covered the vest with the hooded sweatshirt.

Lula and Connie stood back and looked at me. I was wearing Ranger's black hat, black T-shirt, black sweatshirt.

"It's the damnedest thing," Lula said. "Now you don't just smell like Ranger, you're even starting to look like him."

"Yeah," Connie said. "How come you still smell like Ranger?"

"It's this new shower gel I bought. It smells like Ranger." Can I fib, or what?

"I'm gonna go buy a gallon," Lula said. "What's it called?"

"Bulgari."

I was back to using Ranger's truck. I was parked two blocks from his building, waiting for the sun to set and the building to clear out. Another couple minutes and I thought it would be safe for me to make a move. I'd been waiting for over two hours. That was okay. It had given me time to think.

Connie was right. I needed to find out why I was on the list. Eventually, Street Crimes or the Criminal Intelligence unit would get the information, but I was having a hard time finding the patience for "eventually."

I'd had a stupid, crazy idea while I was at the bonds office. It was so stupid and crazy I couldn't bring myself to say it out loud. Trouble was, the idea wouldn't go away. And I was beginning to think it wasn't so stupid and crazy.

What I needed was a snitch. I needed to find a Slayer who could be bribed into talking. I didn't have a lot of money to use as a bribe, so I figured I'd have to resort to violence. And then I needed to find this Slayer outside of Slayerland. No way was I getting caught within Slayer boundaries.

So how am I going to catch a lone Slayer out of his 'hood? Turns out there's one sitting in jail. Anton Ward. All I have to do is bond him out, and he's mine. Okay, so I don't have all the details worked out, but it has potential, right?

The sun was down, and the streets were empty. Time to take a look at the building, I decided. I locked the truck, I pulled the hood over Ranger's ball cap, and I walked the two blocks to the gate. Floors five and six were lit. And there was a single window showing light on the fourth floor. Only the night guard was left in the lobby. Now or never, I thought. I remoted myself through the gate, crossed the garage, and took the elevator without a hitch. I let myself into the apartment and relaxed.

The apartment was nice and empty. Just as I'd left it. I dropped the keys to the truck in the dish on the sideboard. I shrugged out of the sweatshirt and vest and went to the kitchen.

Rex was running on his wheel. I tapped on the side of the cage and said hello. Rex paused for a moment, whiskers twitching. He blinked once and went back to running.

I opened the refrigerator and looked inside. Then I looked down at my waistline. Still some fat oozing over the top of my jeans, but there was less fat than yesterday. I was moving in the right direction. I closed the refrigerator door and hustled out of the kitchen before the beer got to me.

I watched television for a while, and then I took a shower. I told myself I was taking a shower to relax, but the truth was, I wanted to smell the soap. Sometimes I was able to forget I was living in Ranger's

space. Tonight wasn't one of those times. Tonight I was
very aware that I was using his towels and sleeping in
his bed. It was a kind of Russian roulette, I thought.
Each night I walked into the apartment and spun the
barrel. One of these nights Ranger would be here waiting for me, and I was going to take it between the eyes.

I toweled off and went to bed in panties and T-shirt.
The sheets were cool and the room was dark. The panties and T-shirt felt skimpy in Ranger's bed. I would be
much more comfortable if I was fully dressed. Socks,
jeans, two or three shirts buttoned to the neck, tucked
into the jeans. Maybe a jacket and hat.

It was the shower, I decided. The hot water and the
delicious soap. And the towel. It had me all overheated.
I could fix that . . . but I'd go blind. At least that was the
threat when I was growing up in the Burg—you abuse
yourself and you'll go blind. It hadn't totally stopped
me—but it had me worried. I really didn't want to go
blind. Besides, what if I was in the middle of something and Ranger walked in? Actually, that sounded
pretty good.

No! It didn't sound good. What was I thinking? I
was sort of attached to Joe. Maybe. So where the heck
was he when I needed him? He was at home. Probably.
I could go over there, I thought. I could walk in and tell
him I'd just taken a shower with this great soap that always makes me feel sexy. And then I'd explain to him
how I got carried away with the towel . . .

Good grief. I switched the light on. I needed something to read, but there were no books, no magazines,
no catalogues. I wrapped myself in Ranger's robe,
curled up on the couch, and turned the television on.

I woke up to the *Today* show. I was still in Ranger's
robe. I was on the couch. And I was feeling cranky. It
didn't help that Al Roker was on the television screen,

talking to some woman from Iowa, and Al was looking happy as could be. Al always looked happy. What's
with that?

I said good-bye to Al and beamed the television
off. I dragged myself into the bathroom but decided to
forgo the shower. I brushed my teeth and got dressed in
the clothes on the floor.

I was desperate for coffee, but it was almost eight
o'clock, and I needed to get out of the building. I clapped
Ranger's hat on my head, stuffed myself into the vest and
sweatshirt, and took the elevator to the garage. The elevator doors opened just as a car approached the gate. I flattened myself against the side and returned to the seventh
floor. I waited in the seventh-floor foyer for ten minutes,
and I tried it again. This time the garage was empty.

I left the garage, and I walked to the truck. The sky
was overcast and a misting rain had started to fall. The
buildings on either side of Comstock were red brick
and cement. No trees, no shrubs, no lawns to soften the
landscape. It felt nicely urban when the sun was shining. Today it felt grim.

I drove to the office and parked the truck in full
view on the street. Connie was already at work. Lula
hadn't yet arrived. I saw no sign of Vinnie.

I went straight to the coffeepot and poured out a cup
for myself. "I haven't seen a lot of Vinnie lately," I said
to Connie. "What's the deal?"

"He's got hemorrhoids. He comes in for an hour to
bitch and complain, and then he goes home to sit on his
rubber doughnut."

Connie and I both smiled at this. Vinnie deserved
hemorrhoids. Vinnie *was* a hemorrhoid.

I sipped my coffee. "So you're the one writing bonds
now?"

"I'm doing the low money bonds. Vinnie gets off his
doughnut to do guys like Anton Ward."

"I need a favor."

"Uh oh," Connie said. "I got a bad feeling about this."

"I want you to help me bond out Anton Ward. I need to talk to him."

"No way. Un uh. Nope. No can do. Forget it."

"This was your idea! You were the one who said I had to find out why I was on Junkman's list."

"And you think Ward is going to tell you out of gratitude?"

"No. I was planning on beating it out of him."

Connie considered that. "Beating might work," she said. "Who's going to slap him around?"

"Me and Lula. You could do it, too, if you want."

"So let me get this straight," Connie said. "We bond him out. Then we escort him from the jail to the trunk of Lula's Firebird and take him somewhere for further discussion."

"Yeah. And then when we're done we can revoke his bond."

"I like it," Connie said. "Did you think of this all by yourself?"

"Yep."

"Think of what all by herself?" Lula said, swinging through the front door. "Man, it's crappy out there. It's gonna rain cats and dogs all day."

"Stephanie's got a plan to bond out Anton Ward and beat some information out of him," Connie said.

Lula's mood changed to smiley face. "No shit? Are you messin' with me? That's inspired. You aren't gonna leave me out, are you? I'm good at smackin' people around. And I'd just love to smack Anton Ward around."

"You're in," I said to Lula. "We just have to figure some things out first. Like, where are we going to take him for his beating?"

"It has to be someplace isolated, so no one hears him screaming," Lula said.

"And it has to be cheap," I said. "I haven't got any money."

"I have just the place," Connie said. "Vinnie has a house in Point Pleasant. It's right on the beach, and no one's going to be around now. The season's over."

"That's a great plan," Lula said. "The arcade will still be open, and in between beatin' on Anton Ward I can play the claw machine."

"Do you think we'll have to beat him a lot?" I asked Connie. A bunch of her relatives were mob, and I figured she knew about these things.

"I hope so," Lula said. "I hope he don't talk for days. I love Point Pleasant. And I haven't beat on anyone in a while. I'm looking forward to this beating."

"I've never actually beat anyone," I said.

"Don't you worry about it," Lula said. "You just stand back and leave it to me."

"We have to do this right," Connie said. "We don't want anyone to know we have Ward. We're going to have to make it look like he just disappeared."

"I've already thought it through," I said. "You can call Ward's brother back and tell him we'll bond Ward out if he agrees to wear a personal tracking unit. We just got one in from iSECUREtrac, right?"

"We haven't used it yet," Connie said. "Haven't even taken it out of the box."

"If Ward agrees to the PTU we say we have to have him released into our custody so we can install the unit. Then we tell everybody we have to install the transmitter here, at the office. We tell them after the unit is in place Anton is free to go.

"We cuff Anton on his release and bring him back to the office, but instead of strapping the transmitter on him, we dump him in Lula's trunk. All she has to do is back up to the rear door, and Anton's off to Point Pleasant. Then we pretend Anton escaped. We can say he used the lavatory at the office, and he went out through the window."

"Brilliant," Lula said. "You're a criminal genius."

"I like it," Connie said. "Let's do it."

We all did a high five.

"It'll take me some time to set this up," Connie said. "I'll arrange it for the end of the business day. Then it won't be suspicious if we close the office down and disappear. In the meantime, you two should take a drive to Point Pleasant and make sure it's okay to use the house." She took a key from a mess of keys she kept in her top drawer. "This is the key to the house. He doesn't have a security system. It's just a little bungalow on the beach." She wrote the address on a sticky note and gave it to me.

Lula and I didn't do a lot of talking on the way to Point Pleasant. Hard to say why Lula fell into silence. Mine was brought on by a mixture of disbelief and terror. I couldn't believe we were going to do this. It was insane. And it was all my idea.

I was driving Ranger's truck, and Lula was reading the map. We'd reached the ocean, and we were looking for Vinnie's street. The rain was steady and the little shore houses that seemed cute and colorful in July sunshine looked sad in the dismal gray gloom.

"You turn left onto the next street," Lula said. "And you go all the way to the end. It's the last house on the right. Connie says it's painted salmon and turquoise. I'm hoping she's wrong about the paint."

"This is like a ghost town," I said. "Not a single house has a light on."

"Better for us," Lula said. "But it feels spooky, don't

it? It's like we're in some horror movie. *Nightmare in Point Pleasant.*"

I got to the last house on the right and darned if it wasn't painted salmon with turquoise trim. It was a small two-story bungalow that faced the ocean. No garage, but there was a driveway separating Vinnie's house and an almost identical bungalow next to him. At this time of year a car parked in the driveway would be reasonably well hidden.

I pulled the truck into the driveway, and I cut the lights. Lula and I squinted through the rain to the bungalow's back door. Above the door was a hand-painted sign that said SEA BREEZE.

"Bet Vinnie had to think a long time to come up with that name," Lula said.

I put my hood up, and Lula and I sprinted through the rain and huddled together on the small back stoop while I fumbled with the key. I finally got the door open, we both jumped inside, and I slammed the door shut behind us.

Lula shook her corn-rowed head, sending water flying. "Could we possibly have picked a crappier day to do this?"

"Maybe we should wait a couple days until the weather is better." The heartfelt, cold-feet statement of the year.

"I don't want to be no alarmist or nothing, but you wait a couple days and you might not be around to beat on this guy."

Chapter
TWELVE

The back door to Vinnie's beach bungalow opened
to the kitchen. The floor was yellow-and-white linoleum that looked relatively new. The counters were red
Formica. The cabinets were painted white. The appliances were also white. GE. Mid-grade. A small white
wood table, covered with a blue-and-white checked
plastic tablecloth, sat to one side. There were four chairs
at the table.

Beyond the kitchen was a combination living room
and dining room. The carpet was gold and showing wear. The dining room table was white and gold,
French provincial. Probably confiscated from a bad
bond. The living room furniture was overstuffed brown
velour. Tasteful in an upper-end whorehouse sort of
way. End tables were dark fruitwood, Mediterranean
style. Hand-stitched pillows with messages were everywhere. KISS ME I'M ITALIAN. HOME IS WHERE THE
HEART IS. SUMMER STARTS HERE.

There was a downstairs bathroom and a small downstairs bedroom. Both rooms looked out at the driveway.

"Here's where we'll beat Anton," Lula said, standing in the bathroom. "Just in case there's blood, it'll be
easy to clean up with all this tile."

Blood? My stomach went sick and little black dots floated in front of my eyes.

Lula kept going. "And there's only that one little frosted window over the tub. So nobody can see us. Yep, this is gonna be good. Nice and private. No neighbors around. That's important on account of he's probably gonna be screaming in pain, and we don't want no one to hear."

I sat down on the toilet and put my head between my legs.

"You okay?" Lula asked.

"I've been dieting. I think I must be weak from hunger."

"I remember when I was dieting, and I felt like that," Lula said. "And then I discovered that protein diet, and I was eating all those pork roasts. I felt real good on the protein diet. Except sometimes I'd overdo it. Like when I found that sale on boiled lobsters. And I was eating all those lobsters and melted butter. I'm telling you that butter went through me like goose grease."

I didn't want to hear about goose grease right now. I stayed on the toilet, taking deep breaths, and Lula went exploring upstairs.

"There's two bedrooms and a bathroom up there. Nothing special. Looks like it's for kids and guests," Lula said, returning to the bathroom. "Maybe we should get you food."

I didn't need food. I needed someone to intervene and stop me from kidnapping a guy and beating him bloody. I left the bathroom and walked through the living room to the front door. I opened the door and stepped out onto the covered front porch. There was a minuscule front yard, just big enough for an aluminum and nylon webbed chaise and a small table.

A boardwalk ran the length of the beach for as far as

the eye could see. Beyond the boardwalk, the wet sand was the color and texture of fresh concrete. The ocean was loud and scary. Big gray rollers crashed onto the beach, conjuring visions of tsunamis barreling in, gobbling up Point Pleasant.

The wind had picked up, driving the rain across the porch in sheets. I retreated back into the house and locked the door. We pulled every shade and closed every curtain and then we left.

I called Connie when we hit White Horse. "What's up?" I asked.

"It's all set," Connie said. "Ward and his brother bought the whole enchilada. Ward's being held at the prison on Cass Street. I have to get there before four o'clock to bond him out."

I picked Connie up at three thirty and dropped her at the prison. We decided Ward might not be happy to see Lula and me, so we waited in the truck. In a half hour, Connie emerged with Ward, his hands cuffed behind his back. Ranger's truck was a four-door supercrew cab with a full backseat and steel rings conveniently bolted into the floor, just right for securing leg shackles. Connie got in back with Ward, and I swung the truck out into traffic.

Ward didn't say anything. And I didn't say anything. And Lula didn't say anything. All of us being careful not to rock the boat. Ward thinking he was going home. And Lula and Connie and me thinking we were going to beat the crap out of him.

I parked curbside when I reached the office. We took our time off-loading Ward, making a show of it as best we could in the rain. We wanted people to witness the fact that we'd brought him this far. The whole time I was having heart palpitations, and I couldn't get the phrase "harebrained scheme" out of my head.

We finally brought him inside and sat him in the

chair in front of Connie's desk. The plan was to give him a shot at talking to us. If he refused to cooperate we'd hit him with the stun gun, blindfold him, and trundle him out to the Firebird.

"I want to know about Junkman," I said.

He was slouched in the chair. Hard to do when your hands are cuffed behind your back, but he managed. He cut his eyes to me under half-lowered lids. Sullen. Insolent. He didn't say anything.

"Do you know Junkman?" I asked.

Nothing.

"You better answer her," Lula said. "Otherwise we might get upset, and then I'd have to sit on you again."

Ward spat on the floor.

"That's disgusting," Lula said. "We don't put up with that. You don't watch your step, I'll give you enough volts to make you pee your pants." And she showed him her stun gun.

"What the hell is this?" Ward said, sitting up straighter. "I thought I was supposed to get hooked up to a monitor. What's with this stun gun bullshit?"

"We thought you might want to talk to us first," Lula said.

"I got rights, and I'm being violated," Ward said. "You got no business keeping me cuffed. Either put the fucking monitor on me or turn me loose."

Lula got into his face and wagged her finger at him. "Don't you use that language in front of ladies. We don't tolerate that."

"I don't see no ladies," Ward said. "I see a big fat black . . ." And he used the *c* word. The mother of all swear words. Even better than the *f* word.

Lula lunged at him with the stun gun, and Ward jumped out of his chair.

Connie was on her feet, too, trying to contain the disaster. "Don't let him get to the door!" she yelled.

I sprang into action, blocking his way. He turned and ran for the back door. Connie and Lula both had stun guns in hand.

"I got him. I got him," Lula shouted.

Ward lowered his head, and gave Lula a head butt to the stomach that knocked her on her ass. Connie rounded on him in a crouch, and they sized each other up. Ward sidestepped and bolted around her. He wasn't smart, but he was nimble.

I took a flying leap and tackled him from behind. We both went down, I rolled off, and Connie swooped in and tagged him with the stun gun.

"Unh," Ward said. And he went inert.

We all popped our heads up to see if anyone was looking in the front window.

"We're in the clear," Connie said. "Quick, help me drag him behind the file cabinets before someone sees him."

Ten minutes later we were set to go. Ward was cuffed and shackled. We wrapped him in a blanket and carted him out the back door to Lula's car. We dumped him in the trunk, and we all made the sign of the cross. Then Connie slammed the trunk lid shut.

"Holy Mary Mother of God," Connie said. She was breathing heavy, and her forehead was beaded with perspiration.

"He isn't going to die in there, is he?" I asked Connie. "He can breathe, right?"

"He'll be fine. I asked my cousin Anthony. Anthony knows these things."

Lula and I didn't doubt for a moment that Anthony knew all about stuffing bodies in trunks. Anthony was an expediter for a construction company. If you treated Anthony right, your construction project moved along without a hitch. If you decided you didn't need Anthony's services, you were likely to have a fire.

Connie locked the office, and we all piled into the Firebird. Twenty minutes into the trip Anton Ward came to life and started yelling and kicking inside the trunk.

It wasn't that loud from where I was sitting, but it was unnerving. What must he be feeling? Anger, panic, fear. What was I feeling? Compassion? No. In spite of Connie's expert assurances, I was worried Ward would die, and we'd have to bury him in the dark of night in the Pine Barrens. I was going straight to hell for this, I thought. It was all adding up. I was for sure beyond Hail Marys.

"This guy's creeping me out," Lula said. She punched a number on her CD player and drowned Ward out with rap.

Ten minutes later I could feel my cell phone vibrating. It was hooked to my Kevlar vest, and I couldn't hear the ring over the rap, but I could feel the vibration.

I flipped the phone open and yelled, "What?"

It was Morelli. "Tell me you didn't bond out Ward."

"There's a lot of static here," I said. "I can't hardly hear you."

"Maybe it would help if you turned the radio down. Where the hell are you, anyway?"

I made crackling, static sounds, disconnected, and shut my phone off.

Hard to tell when the yelling and kicking stopped, but there were no sounds coming from the trunk when Lula parked in Vinnie's driveway and cut the engine.

It was still raining, and the street was dark. No lights shining from any of the houses. The ocean roiled in the distance, the waves thundering down onto the sand and then swooshing up the beach.

It was pitch black when we huddled around the rear

end of the Firebird. I had a flashlight. Connie had the stun gun. Lula was hands free to open the trunk.

"Here goes," Lula said. "Here's the plan. Soon as I get the lid up we want Stephanie to shine the light in his eyes in case the blanket's come undone, and then Connie can zap him."

Lula opened the trunk. I switched the light on and aimed it at Ward. Connie leaned forward to zap Ward, and he kicked out at Connie. He caught Connie square in the chest and knocked her back four feet onto her keister. The stun gun flew out of Connie's hand and disappeared into the darkness.

"Shit," Connie said, scrambling to get to her feet.

I ditched the flashlight, and Lula and I wrestled Ward out of the trunk. He was bucking and swearing, still wrapped in the blanket. We lost our grip and dropped him twice before we got him into the house.

As soon as we were in the kitchen, we dropped him again. Connie closed and locked the kitchen door, and we stood there breathing hard, dripping wet, gaping at the pissed-off guy writhing around on the linoleum. He stopped wriggling when the blanket fell away.

He had big baggy homey pants that had slipped off his boney ass and were around his knees. He was wearing cotton boxers with red and white stripes. His oversize four-hundred-dollar basketball shoes were unlaced in hood fashion. He looked pretty bad, but it was an improvement over the last time I saw him.

"This is kidnapping," he said. "You can't do this, bitch."

"Of course we can," Lula told him. "We're bounty hunters. We kidnap people all the time."

"Well, maybe not *all* the time," I said.

Connie looked pained. Kidnapping wasn't actually allowed. We could detain and transport people if we had the right documentation.

"If you stop flopping around we'll stand you up and sit you on a chair," I told him.

"We'll even pull your pants up, so we don't have to look at Mr. Droopy hanging out," Lula said. "I've seen enough of Mr. Droopy to last a long time. It's not that great."

We dragged him to his feet, pulled his pants up, and plopped him onto one of the wooden kitchen chairs, securing him with a length of rope that we wrapped and knotted around his chest and the chair back.

"You're at our mercy now," Lula said. "You're going to tell us what we want to know."

"Yeah, right. I'm real scared."

"You should be scared. If you don't start talking about Junkman, I'm gonna hit you one."

Ward gave a bark of laughter.

"Okay, that's it. I guess we have to persuade you," Lula said. "Go ahead, Stephanie, make him talk."

"What?"

"Go ahead and hurt him. Slap him around."

"You're going to have to excuse us for a moment," I said to Ward. "I need to talk to my associates in private."

I pulled Lula and Connie into the living room. "I can't slap him around," I said.

"Why not?" Lula wanted to know.

"I've never slapped anyone around before."

"So?"

"So, I can't just walk up to him and hit him. It's different when someone attacks you, and you get lost in the heat of the moment."

"No, it's not," Lula said. "You just be thinking he hit you first. You just walk up to him, and you imagine him punching you in the face. And then you punch him back. Once you get started, I bet you'll like it."

"Why don't you hit him?"

"I could if I wanted," Lula said.

"Well, then?"

"I just don't think it's my place. I mean, you're the one needs to know about Junkman. And you're the bounty hunter. I'm just a bounty hunter assistant. I figured you'd want to do it."

"You figured wrong."

"Boy, I never had you figured for chicken," Lula said.

Unh. I walked back to Ward and stood in front of him. "Last chance," I said.

He waggled his tongue at me and spat on my shoe.

I made a fist, and I told myself I was going to hit him. But I didn't hit him. My fist stopped just short of his face, and my knuckles sort of bumped against his forehead.

"That's pathetic," Lula said.

I dragged Lula and Connie back into the living room.

"I can't hit him," I said. "Someone else is going to have to hit him."

Lula and I looked at Connie.

"Fine," she said. "Get out of my way."

Connie marched up to Ward, squared her shoulders, and gave him a light slap.

"Jeez," Lula said. "Is that bitch slap the best you can do?"

"I'm an office manager," Connie said. "What do you want from me?"

"Well, I guess it's up to me," Lula said. "But I'm pretty rough when I get going. He'll be all bruised and bloody and cut up and stuff. We might get into trouble for that."

"She has a point," I said to Connie. "It'd be best if he didn't look too beat up."

"How about if we all kick him in the nuts?" Lula said.

We repaired to the living room.

"I can't kick him in the nuts," Connie said.

"Me either," I said. "He's just sitting there. I can't kick a guy in the nuts when he's just sitting there. Maybe we should turn him loose. Then we could chase him around the house and get into the moment."

"No way," Connie said. "He already knocked me on my ass once tonight. I'm not giving him another shot at it."

"We could burn him with lighted cigarettes," Lula said.

We looked at each other. None of us smoked. We didn't have any cigarettes.

"How about if I get a stick," Lula said. "Like a broomstick. And then we could hit him like he was a piñata."

Connie and I did a grimace.

"You could really hurt someone like that," Connie said.

"So what we want to do is inflict maximum pain without hurting him?" Lula asked. "Hey, how about sticking him with a needle? I hate when I get stuck with a needle. And it only makes a tiny hole in you."

"That has potential," Connie said. "And we can stick him in places that won't show."

"Like his dick," Lula said. "We could use his dick for a pincushion."

"I'm not touching his dick," I said.

"Me either," Connie said. "Not even with rubber gloves. How about his feet? You could stick the needle between his toes and then nobody would see it."

"I bet you got that idea from Anthony," Lula said.

"Dinner table conversation," Connie said.

We fanned out and looked for a needle. I took the

downstairs bedroom and found a sewing kit in the closet. I selected the biggest needle in the kit, and I brought it into the kitchen.

"Who's going to do this?" I asked.

"I'll take his shoe off," Connie said.

"And I'll take his sock off," I said.

That left Lula with the sticking.

"I bet you think I can't do it," Lula said.

Connie and I made some encouraging sounds.

"Hunh," Lula said. And she took the needle.

Connie took Ward's shoe off. I removed his sock. Then Connie and I stepped back to give Lula room to operate.

Ward was looking nervous, and he was shuffling his shackled feet around.

"This here's a moving target," Lula said. "I can't do my best work like this."

Connie got another length of rope and tied Ward's ankles to the chair legs.

"This little piggy went to market," Lula said, touching the little toe with the tip of the needle. "And this little piggy stayed home . . ."

"Just stick him," Connie said.

Lula grabbed Ward's big toe, closed her eyes, and rammed the needle into Ward dead center between two toes. Ward let out an unearthly scream that raised every hair on my body.

Lula's eyes flew open. Her eyes rolled back into her head, and she crashed over in a dead faint. Connie ran into the bathroom and threw up. And I staggered outside and stood in the rain, on the front porch, until the clanging stopped in my head.

By the time I got back to the kitchen, Lula was sitting up. The back of her shirt was soaked in sweat and sweat beaded on her upper lip.

"Must have been something I ate," she said.

The toilet flushed and Connie joined us. Her hair was a wreck, and she'd washed off most of her makeup. It was a sight that was more frightening than Lula with the needle.

Ward's eyes were dilated black. If looks could kill, we'd all be dead.

"So, are you ready to talk?" Lula asked Ward.

Ward shifted the death look to Lula.

"Hunh," Lula said.

We all went into the living room.

"Now what?" I asked Connie and Lula.

"He's pretty tough," Lula said.

"He's not tough at all," I said. "He's a jerk. We're a bunch of wimps."

"How about if we lock him up here and don't give him any food," Lula said. "I bet he'll talk when he gets hungry."

"That could take days."

Connie looked at her watch. "It's getting late. I should be heading for home."

"Me, too," Lula said. "I gotta get home to feed the cat."

I looked over at Lula. "I didn't know you adopted a cat."

"It's more like I'm thinking about it," Lula said. "I'm thinking of stopping at the pet store on the way home and getting a cat, and then I'm going to have to feed him."

"So what are we going to do with this idiot?" Connie asked.

We swung our attention back to Ward.

"I guess we leave him here for now," I said. "Maybe we can think of something overnight."

We cut the ropes away, stood Ward up, shoved him into the bathroom, and cuffed him to the main pipe of the pedestal sink. He had one hand free, and he was

within reach of the toilet. We removed everything from
the medicine chest. We left the ankle bracelets in place
and attached an extra length of chain to the shackle and
wrapped the extra chain around the base of the toilet.
Then we closed the door on him.

"This feels a little like kidnapping," I said.

"No way," Lula said. "We're just detaining him.
We're allowed to do that."

"I'm thinking about changing careers," Connie said.
"Something more sane . . . like being the detonator on
the bomb squad."

We turned the lights out and locked up. We piled
into Lula's car and left Point Pleasant.

"I never even got to play the claw machine," Lula
said.

Ranger's truck was still parked in front of the bond office. It wasn't covered with graffiti or riddled with bullet holes. I thought that was a good sign. I got out of the
Firebird and unlocked the truck with the remote. Then
I stood back, held my breath, and started the truck with
the remote. I blew out a sigh of relief when the truck
didn't explode.

"You're in business," Lula said. "See you tomorrow.
Be careful."

I got into the truck and locked the doors. I sat there
for a moment in the dark, enjoying the silence, not sure
what to think of the day. I was tired. I was depressed. I
was appalled.

I jumped when someone rapped on the driver-side
window. I sucked in some air when I saw the guy. He
was big. Over six feet. Hard to tell his build in the dark.
But I was guessing he was heavily muscled. He was
wearing an oversize black hooded sweatshirt, and his
face was lost in shadow inside the hood. His skin in
the dark looked as black as the sweatshirt. His eyes

were hidden behind dark glasses. He could be one of Ranger's men. Or he could be a messenger from the dead. Either way, he was freaking scary. I released the emergency brake and put the truck in gear in case I needed to lay rubber.

I cracked the window an inch. "What?" I asked.

"Nice truck."

"Un hunh."

"Yours?"

"For now."

"You know who I am?"

"No."

"You wanna know?"

"No."

Pretty amazing that my voice was staying steady, because my heart was racing, and I had a cramp in my large intestine.

"I'll tell you anyway," he said. "I'm your worst nightmare. I'm Junkman. And I'm not just gonna kill you . . . I'm gonna eat you alive. You can take that as a literal promise."

His voice was deep, the inflection serious. No smile in his voice, but I knew he was getting off on the moment. I'd run into his type before. He fed off fear, and he was hoping to see fear in my face. I was looking into his mirrored lenses, my face reflecting back at me. I decided my face wasn't showing much. That was good. I was learning from the men in my life.

"Why do you want to kill me?" I asked.

"For fun. And you can think about it for a while because I gotta cut the balls off a cop before I let myself enjoy *you*."

There was more to it than fun, I thought. He wasn't a kid. He probably got the muscle and the attitude in prison. He was brought in by the Slayers, and I thought Connie was right, Junkman wanted something from these killings besides satisfying his blood lust. Not to trivialize the blood lust. I was guessing Junkman liked to kill. Probably emasculated his victims for a show of power over the enemy, and I was betting he also liked the blood on his hands.

He gave me some kind of gang sign language and stepped back from the truck. "Make the most of your last hours on earth, bitch," he said.

A black Hummer came out of nowhere and pulled up beside me. Junkman got in, and the Hummer disappeared down the street. No chance to get the plate.

I sat perfectly still and rigid until I could no longer see the Hummer taillights. The instant the lights vanished from my field of vision, all my bravado vanished as well. Tears poured out of my eyes, and it was painful to swallow. I didn't want to die. I had more doughnuts to eat. I had nieces to spoil. If I died, poor Rex would be orphaned. And Morelli. Don't even go there, I thought. I didn't know what to think about Morelli, but I wished I'd told him I loved him. I'd never said it out loud. I'm not sure why not. Just never felt right, I guess. And I always thought I'd have lots of time. Morelli had been a part of my life since I was a kid. It was hard to imagine a life without him, but sometimes it was equally hard to imagine his role in my future. I couldn't get past two months of cohabitation with him without going nutty. Probably not a good sign.

I had a dilemma now. My eyes were leaking, and my nose was running. I was trying real hard not to progress to openmouthed sobbing. *Stop it!* I told myself. Get a grip. Easier said than done. I was feeling vulnerable and incompetent. The vulnerable and incompetent Stephanie wanted to run to Morelli. The stubborn Stephanie hated to give in. And the halfway intelligent Stephanie knew it would be a bad thing to leave Ranger's truck sitting in front of Morelli's house. Junkman would recognize it if he rode by, and Morelli's house would be a target for God knows what.

I took the path of mindless action. I stepped on the gas, and I let the truck take me someplace. Of course, it took me to Ranger's building. I parked in my usual spot, two blocks from the garage entrance. I reached under the seat and helped myself to Ranger's gun. It was a semiautomatic. I was pretty sure it was loaded. To say I wasn't a gun person was a gross understatement. I wasn't sure I knew how to fire the gun, but I figured I might be able to scare someone with it.

I retreated into my hooded sweatshirt, locked the truck, and walked head down in the rain to the garage. Minutes later I was in Ranger's apartment with the door bolted behind me. I left the gun and the truck keys on the sideboard. I ditched the sweatshirt, hat, and Kevlar vest. I removed my wet shoes and socks. My jeans were soaked from the knee down, but I'd lived with them like that for the entire day, and I could endure a few minutes more. I'd stopped whimpering, and I was starving.

I stuck my head into Ranger's refrigerator and pulled out one of his low-fat plain yogurts. No way was I going to die with a roll of fat hanging over my waistband.

I scraped the last smidgen of yogurt from the cup and looked at Rex. "Yum," I said. "I'm stuffed."

Rex was running on his wheel and didn't bother to respond. Rex was a little slow. He didn't always see the humor in sarcasm.

"Probably I should call Morelli," I said to Rex. "What do you think?"

Rex was noncommittal on the subject, so I dialed Morelli.

"Hey," Morelli said.

I gave him my smiley voice. "It's me. Sorry we had a bad connection this afternoon."

"You've got to practice your crackle. You've got too much phlegm in it."

"I thought it was pretty good."

"Second rate," Morelli said. "What's up? Are you going to tell me about Ward? It seems he's disappeared."

"He escaped from us."

"Apparently he escaped from everybody. His brother hasn't seen him either."

"Hmmm. That's interesting."

"You didn't kidnap him, did you?"

"Kidnap is an ugly word."

"You didn't answer my question," Morelli said.

"You don't really want me to, do you?"

"Jesus."

"I have something else to tell you before this conversation goes down the drain. I met Junkman today. About an hour ago. I was in Ranger's truck, parked in front of the office, and Junkman rapped on my window and introduced himself."

There was a long empty space where nothing was said, and I could feel the electric mix of emotion traveling the phone line. Astonishment that this had happened. Fear for my safety. Anger that I'd allowed contact. Frustration that he couldn't fix the problem. When he finally spoke it was in his flat cop voice.

"Tell me about it," Morelli said.

"He was big. Around six foot two. And he was chunky. It looked like muscle, but it was hard to tell for sure. I didn't get to see his face. He was wearing dark glasses. And he had a big oversize sweatshirt hood over his head."

"Caucasian, Hispanic, African-American?"

"African-American. Maybe some Hispanic. He had a slight accent. He said he was going to kill me, but he had to kill a cop first. He said he was doing it for fun, but I think that's just part of it. When he left he gave me a hand signal. Probably some gang thing. Definitely not Italian."

"It's almost ten o'clock. What were you doing in front of the bonds office at nine o'clock?"

"Lula and Connie and I were out looking for Ward."

"Where were you looking?"

"Around."

There was another big silence and I sensed things were going to deteriorate now, so I moved to wrap it up. "Gotta go," I said to him. "Turning in early tonight. I just wanted to check with you. And I wanted to tell you I . . . uh, like you." *Shit.* I chickened out! What was it with me that I couldn't say the big *L* word? I am such a dope.

Morelli sighed into the phone. "You are such a dope."

I returned the sigh and disconnected.

"That went well," I said to Rex. *Yeesh.*

Chapter THIRTEEN

It was ten o'clock at night, and I was bone tired. I'd been cold and wet all day. I had just had an embarrassing phone conversation with Morelli. And one cup of nonfat, unfruited, unsweetened, unchocolated yogurt wasn't doing it for me.

"Sometimes sacrifices need to be made," I told Rex. "Sometimes you have to sacrifice weight loss for the pleasure of eating a peanut butter sandwich on worthless white bread."

I felt a lot better after I ate the peanut butter sandwich on the worthless white bread, so I passed on the milk with the 2 percent butterfat and drank a glass of Ranger's watery, tasteless skim. Am I righteous, or what?

I said good night to Rex, and I switched the light off in the kitchen. I was too tired and cold for television. And I was too grungy just to crawl under the covers. So I dragged myself to the shower.

I stood in the shower until I was pruney and toasty warm. I pulled on red bikini undies and dropped one of Ranger's black T-shirts over my head. I dried my hair, and I climbed into bed.

Heaven. Too bad the bed, the shirt, the whole comfy apartment wasn't actually mine. Too bad it belonged to a guy who could be a little scary. This brought me around to thinking about the lock on the front door. Did I throw the bolt when I came in?

I got out of bed, padded to the front door, and checked the locks. All locked. Not that it mattered with Ranger. He had a way with locks. Didn't matter if it was a deadbolt, a slide bolt, a chain. Nothing stopped Ranger. Fortunately, Ranger wasn't due home. And the average garden-variety thief, rapist, murderer, gang guy didn't have Ranger skills.

I slumped back to bed and closed my eyes. I was safe for at least a couple more days.

I struggled out of sleep thinking something was wrong. I was caught at the edge of a dream, and something was pulling me awake. It was the light, I thought. Dim but annoying. I'd fallen asleep and left a light burning somewhere in the apartment. Probably did it when I checked the locks. Probably I should get up and turn the light off.

I was on my stomach with my face smushed into the pillow. I squinted at the bedside clock. Two o'clock. I didn't want to get out of bed. To quote Grandma Mazur, I was snug as a bug in a rug. I closed my eyes. The hell with the light.

I was trying hard to ignore the light when I heard the faint rustle of clothing from the far side of the room. If I was a man this would have been the point where my gonads ran for cover and hid inside my body. Since I didn't have any gonads, I kept my eyes closed and hoped death came quickly.

After about twenty seconds of this I got impatient with waiting for death. I opened my eyes and rolled onto my back.

Ranger was leaning one shoulder against the doorjamb, his arms loosely crossed over his chest. He was dressed in his usual working outfit of black T-shirt and black cargo pants.

"I'm trying to decide if I should throw you out the window, or if I should get in next to you," Ranger said, not looking especially surprised or angry.

"Are there any other options?" I asked him.

"What are you doing here?"

"I needed a safe place to stay."

His mouth curved at the corners. Not quite a smile but definite amusement. "And you think this is safe?"

"It was until you came home."

The brown eyes were unwavering, fixed on me. "What scares you more . . . getting thrown out the window or sleeping with me?"

I sat up in bed, pulling the covers up with me. "Don't flatter yourself. You're not that scary." *Liar, liar, pants on fire!*

The almost smile stayed in place. "I saw the gun and the flak vest when I came in."

I told him about the death threat from Junkman.

"You should have asked Tank for help," Ranger said.

"I don't always feel comfortable with Tank."

"And you feel comfortable with me?"

I hesitated with my answer.

"Babe," Ranger said. "You're in my bed."

"Yes. Well, I guess that would indicate a certain comfort level."

His attention dropped to my chest. "Are you wearing my shirt?"

"I have to do laundry."

Ranger unlaced his boots.

"What are you doing?"

He looked over at me. "I'm going to bed. I've been up since four this morning, and I just drove nine hours to get home. Half of it in pouring rain. I'm beat. I'm going to take a shower. And I'm going to bed."

"Um . . ."

"Don't look so panicked. You can sleep on the couch, or you can leave, or you can stay in the bed. I'm not going to attack you in your sleep. At least it's not my plan right now. We can figure this out in the morning."

And he disappeared into the bathroom.

Heaven help me, I didn't want to give up the bed. It was warm and comfy. The sheets were silky smooth. The pillows were soft. And the bed was big. I could stay on my side, and he could stay on his side, and we'd be fine, right? Clearly, he didn't think my staying was a sexual invitation. We were adults. We could do this.

I turned on my side, face to the wall, back to the bathroom, lulled into sleep by the distant sound of the shower and the rain on the window.

I came awake slowly, thinking I was back at Morelli's house. I could feel the warmth from the man next to me, and I edged closer. I reached out, and the instant my fingertip touched skin I realized my mistake.

"Oops," I said.

"Babe," Ranger said, wrapping his arms around me, gathering me close to him.

I meant to push away, but I was distracted by the scent of the sexy shower gel mingled with warm Ranger. "You smell great," I told him, my lips brushing against his neck as I spoke, my mind suddenly not totally connected to my mouth. "I thought of you every time I took a shower. I *love* this stuff you use."

"My housekeeper buys it for me," Ranger said. "Maybe I should give her a raise."

And he kissed me.

"Oh *shit*," I said.

"Now what?"

"I'm sorry. I'm having a major guilt attack over Morelli."

"While we're on the subject, why aren't you in *his* bed?"

"Same old, same old."

"You had a fight, and you moved out."

"More like a disagreement."

"I'm seeing an unhealthy pattern of behavior here, Babe."

Tell me about it. "I didn't want to move back home because Junkman was looking for me, and I didn't want to endanger my family." Plus they'd drive me crazy. "I was going to sleep in the truck, but it led me here. The GPS was on. I just followed it backwards."

"And broke into my apartment?"

"I had a key. You don't seem especially upset or surprised that I borrowed your apartment."

"With the exception of the seventh floor, the entire building inside and out is monitored. Tank called me when you pulled up to the gate. I assumed you had a good reason for needing the apartment, so I told him to let you stay."

"That was nice of you."

"Yeah, I'm a nice guy. And I'm late for work." He rolled out of bed, stood at bedside, pressed speaker phone, and hit a button.

A woman's voice came on. "Good morning," she said. "Welcome home."

"Breakfast for two this morning," Ranger said. And he disconnected.

I looked over at him. He was wearing the black silk boxers. They sat disturbingly low on his hip, and his hair was mussed from sleep. How I'd managed to stop kissing him and give in to the guilt was a mystery. Even now, I was having a hard time not jumping across the bed and grabbing him.

"What was that?" I asked, thankful my voice didn't sound as breathless as I felt.

"Ella and Louis Guzman manage this building for

me. I work here, and sometimes I sleep here. That's about it. Ella makes it easy for me. She does the cooking, the cleaning, the laundry, the shopping."

"And she brings you breakfast?"

"She'll be at the door in ten minutes. I've never had a woman here before, so she's going to be curious. Just smile and endure it. She's a very nice lady."

I was dressed and had my teeth brushed when Ella rang the bell. I opened the door to her, and she bustled in carrying a large silver tray.

"Hello. Good morning!" she said, all smiles as she swept past me.

She was small and robust with short black hair and bright bird eyes. Early fifties, I thought. She was wearing bright red lipstick. No other makeup. She was dressed in black jeans and a black V-neck knit shirt. She set the tray on the dining room table and laid out two place settings.

"This is Ranger's usual breakfast," Ella said to me. "If you would like something different, I'd be happy to make it for you. Maybe some eggs?"

"Thank you. This will be fine. It looks lovely."

Ella excused herself and retreated, closing the door behind herself. She'd brought hot coffee in a silver pot with matching cream and sugar, a platter of sliced fruit and berries, a small silver dish of lox, and two small pots of cream cheese. A white linen napkin covered a basket of sliced, toasted bagels.

Ranger was in the bedroom, lacing his boots. He was dressed in his usual uniform, hair still damp from the shower.

"What is *that*?" I said, arm straight, finger pointing to the dining room.

He rose out of the chair and walked to the doorway. "Breakfast?"

"You eat like this every day?"

"Every day that I'm here."

"What about the tree bark and wild roots?"

He poured the coffee and took some fruit. "Only when I'm in a third world jungle. And I'm almost never in one of those."

"I've been eating that cardboard cereal in your cupboard."

Ranger cut his eyes to me. "Babe, I looked in my cupboard. You've got Frosted Flakes in there."

"So," I said, "is this the Bat Cave?"

"This is an apartment I keep in my office building. I have similar buildings and apartments in Boston, Atlanta, and Miami. It turns out security is big business these days. I supply a variety of services to a wide range of clients. Trenton was my first base of operation, and it's the place I spend most of my time. My family is still in Jersey."

"Why all the secrecy?"

"We're not secretive about the office buildings, but we try to keep a low profile."

"We?"

"I have partners."

"Let me guess—the Justice League. The Flash, Wonder Woman, and Superman."

Ranger looked like he was thinking about smiling.

"Okay, forget the partners," I said. "I want to get back to the Bat Cave. Is there a Bat Cave?"

Ranger took a bagel and speared some lox onto it. "You're going to have to work harder for that one. It's not in the phone book, and GPS isn't going to take you there."

A challenge.

Ranger glanced at his watch. "I have five minutes. Tell me about Junkman."

"Not much to tell. He wants to kill me. I told you everything I know last night."

"What are you doing about it?"

"Connie and Lula and I kidnapped a Slayer. The plan was to get him to talk to us about Junkman, but we haven't had any luck."

Ranger finished his bagel and pushed back from the table to finish his coffee. "Kidnapping a Slayer is good. Why wouldn't he talk?"

"He didn't want to."

Ranger paused with the coffee cup halfway to his mouth. "You're supposed to persuade him."

"We were going to slap him around, but when we got him tied to the chair it turned out none of us could hit him."

Ranger burst out laughing and coffee sloshed out of his cup onto the table. He put the coffee down and reached for his napkin, trying not to laugh, not having a lot of luck at it.

"Jeez," I said. "I think that's the first time I've ever seen you laugh like that."

"There's not a lot to laugh about when you're knee deep in garbage. And that's where we usually operate." He swiped his napkin across the table, blotting up the coffee spill.

"If you have all this, why do you still do fugitive apprehension?"

"I'm good at it. And someone has to do the job."

I followed him into his dressing room and watched him open the locked drawer and remove a gun. I was working hard at keeping my eyes focused above his waist, but I was thinking *No underwear!*

"Do you still have your Slayer hidden away?" he asked.

"Yes."

"Is he secure?"

"Yes," I said.

"My day is filled, but we can talk to him tonight.

In the meantime, don't have any contact with this guy. Don't feed him. Let him worry." He clipped the gun to his belt. "I need the truck. Use one of the Porsches. The keys are in the plate on the sideboard. The communication room and gym are on the fifth floor. Feel free to use the gym. Ella and Louis live on the sixth floor. You can intercom number six if you need anything. She'll be in today to make the bed and clean and pick up laundry. She'll do your laundry if you leave it out for her." He glanced at his watch again. "I have a meeting scheduled. I'm assuming you want to live here a while longer?"

"Yes." I didn't have a lot of good choices.

His mouth curved into the almost smile. "You're going to be indebted to me, Babe. You want to start working on that guilt problem."

Oh boy.

He grabbed me and kissed me, and I felt my toes curl. And I wondered how long it would take me to get him undressed. And just exactly how many minutes did he have before the meeting? I didn't think I needed a lot of time. After all, he wasn't wearing any undies. That would help, right?

"I have to go," he said. "I'm late."

Thank God, he was late. There were no minutes. No time to cheat on Joe. No time to send myself straight to hell. I smoothed the wrinkles from his shirt where my fingers had gripped the material. "Do you know where the truck is?"

"It's in the garage. I had Tank bring it in last night. All the cars and trucks are equipped with GPS tracking. We always know where they are."

Great. Really glad I went to the trouble to park two blocks away.

I showered and dressed and left the apartment, being careful not to run into any of the men. I suspected they were also careful not to run into me. The arrangement felt awkward.

I chose the Turbo, parking at the curb when I got to the office, so I could keep an eye on the car. It was one thing to lose a bargain-basement Lincoln; I didn't want to get a bunch of unnecessary holes in Ranger's megabucks Porsche.

"Holy crap," Lula said, staring out the window at the Porsche. "Is that Ranger's Turbo?"

"Yes. He's back, and he needed the truck, so he gave me the 911. He's going to talk to our friend tonight. He said we shouldn't have any contact with him. And he didn't want us to feed him."

"Fine by me," Connie said. "I'm not anxious to repeat yesterday's performance."

"Yeah," Lula said. "That was embarrassing."

"Anything new on the books?" I asked.

"No, but you have three outstandings," Connie said. "Shoshanna Brown, Harold Pancek, and the thumb guy, Jamil Rodriguez. Maybe you want to leave Rodriguez for Ranger."

"We'll see how it goes," I said. "I'm going to pick up Shoshanna Brown this morning."

Lula looked at me hopefully. "Need any help?"

"Not with Brown. I've picked her up before. She's usually cooperative." And to make things even easier, I'd chosen the flashy Turbo. Shoshanna would be at home smoking weed in her rat-trap apartment, watching the Travel Channel on her stolen television, and she'd happily trade her freedom for a ride in the Porsche.

Shoshanna lived in the projects on the other side of town. I took Hamilton to Olden and wound my way around, avoiding known Slayer territory. I parked in front of Shoshanna's building and called her. Ordinarily, I'd march up to Shoshanna's front door and encourage her to come with me in person. If I did that today, alone and in the Porsche, the car would be gone the instant I turned my back.

"Yeah, what?" Shoshanna said, answering the phone.

"It's Stephanie Plum. I want you to look out your front window."

"This better be good. I'm watching a show on the best bathrooms in Vegas."

"I came to take you for a ride in Ranger's Turbo."

"Are you shitting me? The Porsche? You came to pick me up in the Porsche? Hold on. I'll be right out. I just gotta put on some lipstick for my new photo. I've been waiting for you anyway. I'm hoping I get sent to the workhouse on account of I got a tooth that's killing me, and they got a good dentist there. I won't have to pay for it or nothing."

Two minutes later, Shoshanna burst out of her apartment and angled herself into the Porsche. "Now this is class," she said. "I hope some of my neighbors are watching. I don't suppose you could drive me past my friend Latisha Anne's apartment so she could see?"

I drove Shoshanna past Latisha Anne's apartment, Shirelle Marie's apartment, and Lucy Sue's apartment. And then I drove her to jail.

Shoshanna was cuffed to the bench when I left with my paperwork. "Thanks," she said. "See you next time."

"You might want to think about staying out of trouble."

"It's no *problemo*," she said. "I only get caught when I need dental."

Morelli was waiting for me outside. "Nice car," he said.

"I borrowed it from Ranger to get Shoshanna. She jumped right in."

"Clever."

I was choking on guilt. My throat was dry and my

chest was hot. I could feel sweat beginning to prickle at the roots of my hair. I happen to be excellent at rationalizing away acts of dumbness, but this one had me for a loss. I'd slept with Ranger! Not sexually, of course. But I'd been in his bed. And then there was the evil shower gel. And the kisses. And heaven help me, there'd been desire. A lot of desire.

"It was all because of the shower gel," I said.

Morelli's eyes narrowed. "Shower gel?"

I made a major effort not to sigh. "Long story. You probably don't want to hear it. Out of morbid curiosity, what sort of a relationship do we have?"

"It looks to me like we're in the *off* stage of *on again, off again*. Or maybe we're still *on again* . . . but in a remote sort of way."

"Suppose I wanted to change it to full-time *on again*?"

"For starters, you'd have to get a new job. Or even better, no job at all."

"No job?"

"You could be a housewife," Morelli said.

Our eyes locked in stunned disbelief that he'd suggested such a thing.

"Okay, maybe not a housewife," Morelli said.

I sensed a slur on my ability to housewife. "I could be a housewife if I wanted. I'd be a good one, too."

"Sure you would," Morelli said. "Eventually. Maybe."

"It's just that I was surprised because marriage is usually a prerequisite to being a housewife."

"Yeah," Morelli said. "Isn't that a frightening thought?"

Lula and Connie had their noses pressed against the front window when I got out of Ranger's Cayenne.

"Where's the Turbo? What happened to the Turbo?" Lula wanted to know. "You didn't destroy the Turbo, did you?"

I gave Connie the body receipt. "The Turbo is fine. I swapped it out after I dropped Shoshanna at the police station. It was good for luring Shoshanna out of her house, but it didn't suit my purposes for this afternoon. I thought we'd go looking for Pancek again, and we need a backseat in case we get lucky."

I was standing with my back to the door, and I saw Connie's eyes go wide.

"Be still my heart," Lula said, looking past me, through the window to the sidewalk.

I figured they were looking at either Johnny Depp or Ranger. My money was on Ranger.

The door opened, and I glanced over my shoulder, just in case, not wanting to miss Johnny Depp. But then not entirely disappointed when it turned out to be Ranger.

He crossed the room and stood close behind me, his hand at my back, heating the skin beneath his touch.

"Tank said you wanted me to stop by," he said to Connie.

Connie took the Jamil Rodriguez file from her desktop. "I originally gave this to Stephanie, but she's got a lot on her plate right now."

Ranger took the file and flipped through it. "I know this guy. The thumb belongs to Hector Santinni. Santinni stiffed Rodriguez on a drug sale, so Rodriguez chopped Santanni's thumb off and put it in a jar of formaldehyde. Rodriguez carries the thumb everywhere. Thinks the thumb gives him an edge."

"So much for the edge," Connie said. "The police have the thumb."

"A lot more where that came from," Ranger said. His hand moved to the base of my neck. "Your call, Babe," he said to me. "Do you want him?"

"Is he a gang guy?"

"No. He's an independent nut case."

"I'll keep him."

"He's probably looking for a new thumb," Ranger said. "So be careful. Most afternoons you can find him at the bar on the corner of Third and Laramie."

His fingertips trailed the length of my spine, triggering feelings I was determined to ignore. And he was gone.

"Damn," Lula said, doing thumbs up, eyes fixed on the thumbs. "I don't know if I want to go after a guy who's going big game hunting for a thumb. I'm real attached to mine."

I made chicken sounds and did wing flaps.

"Hunh," Lula said. "Smart-ass. What makes you so brave all of a sudden?"

For starters, every move I made in the Cayenne was tracked at RangeMan Central. And if that wasn't enough, I suspected I was being followed. Ranger and Morelli always ran neck and neck in the *vote of no confidence* race. The only difference being in the level of sneakiness. Ranger always won out on sneaky. When there's a code-red danger alert, Morelli rants and raves and tries to lock me away. Ranger just assigns a goon to watch over me. Sometimes the goons are visible. Sometimes the goons are invisible. Whatever the state of visibility, they stick to me like glue, preferring death to the hideous task of informing Ranger they've lost me.

I turned and looked out the window in time to see Ranger pull away in the big bad truck. A shiny black SUV with tinted windows was left idling at curbside behind the Cayenne. "That's what makes me so brave," I said.

"Hunh," Lula said, following my eyes to the SUV. "I knew that."

Lula and I left the bonds office and climbed into the Cayenne. "I thought we'd drive past Pancek's house first," I said. "See if he's returned."

"Are you gonna try to lose the SUV?"

"I can't lose the SUV as long as I'm in this car. It's hooked into a GPS tracking system."

"I bet there's a way to disable it," Lula said. "This is one of Ranger's personal cars, and I bet there's times Ranger doesn't want anyone to know where he's going."

I'd had the same thought, but for now I didn't want to disable the system. And I didn't want to lose my bodyguard. I had the flak vest and sweatshirt in the backseat and Ranger's loaded gun in my purse. I thought I was relatively safe until Junkman made his third hit, but I wasn't taking unnecessary chances.

I glanced back at the SUV. "To tell you the truth, I'm happy to have the added protection."

"I hear you," Lula said.

I drove a block down Hamilton, left-turned into the Burg, and followed the maze of streets that led to Canter. I didn't see the blue Honda Civic parked anywhere near Pancek's apartment. I parked two houses down, put my Kevlar vest on under the sweatshirt, got out of the car, and walked to Pancek's door. I rang the bell. No answer. I rang two more times and returned to the car.

"No luck," I told Lula.

"Are we going back to Newark?"

"Not today. Ranger told me where I can find Rodriguez. I thought I'd go after him while I have an escort."

"On the one hand, that sounds good," Lula said. "Like, we got some help if we need it. On the other hand, if we screw up we got a witness laughing his ass off."

Lula had a point. "Maybe we won't screw up."

"I just hope it's not Tank back there. I wouldn't mind taking Tank home with me someday, and it would put a crimp in my plans to embarrass myself with a lame bust."

The SUV was half a block back. Too far for us to see its occupants. We were debating the embarrassment potential when my phone rang.

"Where are you?" Sally wanted to know. "We've been waiting for twenty minutes."

"Waiting?"

"You were supposed to meet us to get your dress fitted for the wedding."

Crap. "I forgot."

"How could you forget? Your sister's getting married. It's not like this happens every day. How do you expect me to plan this wedding if you forget things?"

"I'll be right there."

"We're at the Bride Shoppe next to Tasty Pastry."

"What'd you forget?" Lula wanted to know.

"I was supposed to go for a fitting for my bridesmaid dress. They're all waiting for me. This will only take a minute. I'll run in and run out, and we can go look for Rodriguez."

"I love wedding dresses," Lula said. "I might buy one even if I never get married. I like the bridesmaid dresses, too. And you know what else I like? Wedding cake."

Chapter

FOURTEEN

I put the Cayenne in gear and raced off, doubling back to Hamilton. I took the turn to the parking lot on two wheels and diagonal-parked the SUV next to my mother's Buick LeSabre.

Lula and I jumped out of the car and sprinted for the Bride Shoppe. Ranger's men in the SUV barreled in after us. The guy in the passenger seat had one foot on the ground when I turned and pointed at him.

"Stay!" I said. And then Lula and I hustled through the front door.

The Bride Shoppe is run and owned by Maria Raguzzi, a dumpling of a woman in her late fifties. Maria's got short black hair and long black sideburns and fine black hair on her knuckles. She always wears a fat round pincushion on a Velcro wrist bracelet, and for as long as I've known her, she's had a yellow tape measure draped around her neck. She's been married and divorced three times, so she knows a lot about weddings.

Loretta Stonehouser, Rita Metzger, Margaret Durski, Valerie, Grandma Mazur, my mother, and the "wedding planner" were all crammed into the little showroom. Maria Raguzzi and Sally were bustling around, distributing dresses.

Margaret Durski was the first to see me. "Stephanie!" she shrieked. "Omigod, it's been so long. I haven't seen you since Valerie's first wedding. Omigod, I see you in the paper all the time. You're always burning something down to the ground."

Rita Metzger was right behind her. "Stephane*eeee*!" she said. "Is this so awesome? Here we are all together. Is this cool, or what? And have you seen the dresses? The dresses are to die for. Pumpkin. I love pumpkin."

My mother stared at me. "Are you still gaining weight? You look so big."

I unzipped the sweatshirt. "It's the vest. It's bulky. I was in a hurry and forgot to take it off."

Everyone gaped.

"What is that thing you're wearing?" Rita wanted to know. "It like squashes your boobs. It's very unflattering."

"It's a bulletproof vest," Grandma said. "She's gotta wear one of them on account of she's an important bounty hunter, and there's always people trying to kill her."

"There's not always people trying to kill her," Lula said. "Just sometimes . . . and this is one of them times," she added.

"Omigod!" Margaret said.

My mother squelched a groan and made the sign of the cross.

"The fudging vest wasn't in the fudging plan," Sally said. "What the fudge am I supposed to do with this? It's gonna fudging ruin the fudging line of the fudging gown."

"It's a flak vest, not a chastity belt," I told him. "It comes off."

"Cool," he said.

"You should chill," Lula told him. "You're gonna get a embolism you keep that up."

"This is a fudging responsibility," Sally said. "I take my wedding planning seriously." He took a gown off the rack and handed it over to me. "This is yours," he said.

Now it was my turn to gape. "What happened to pumpkin?"

"The other girls are wearing pumpkin. The maid of honor has to have a different color. This is eggplant."

Lula gave a burst of laughter and clapped her hand over her mouth.

Eggplant. Great. As if pumpkin wasn't bad enough. I ripped my vest off and unlaced my shoes. "Where do I go to try this on?"

"There's a dressing room through the pink doorway," Sally said, leading the way, carrying Valerie's gown, staggering under the weight of it.

Five minutes later we were all zipped up. Three pumpkins and an eggplant. And Valerie, who was wearing enough glaring white to make everyone snow-blind. Her breasts bulged out of the bodice neckline, and the back zipper valiantly struggled to hold the dress together. The skirt was bell shaped, meant to disguise leftover baby fat. In actuality, the skirt emphasized her hips and ass.

Valerie tottered over to the three-way mirror, took a look at herself, and shrieked. "I'm fat!" she yelled. "My God, look at me. I'm a whale. A big white whale. Why didn't someone tell me? I can't go down the aisle like this. The aisle isn't even *wide* enough."

"It's not so bad," my mother said, trying to smooth away the fat bulge at the waistline. "All brides are beautiful. You just need to see yourself with the veil."

Maria came running with the veil, draping the gauze fabric over Val's eyes. "See how much better it looks through the veil?" Maria said.

"Yeah, and if you want to really feel better, you

should get a load of Stephanie in the eggplant," Lula said.

"It didn't seem that vegetable when we were looking at swatches," Sally said, eyeing my gown.

"She needs a different makeup palette," Loretta said. "Some eggplant on her eyes to balance the dress. And then some glitter under the brow to open the eye. And more blush."

"A *lot* more blush," Lula said.

"What am I doing getting married anyway?" Valerie said. "Do I really want to get married?"

"Of course you want to get married," my mother said, the panic clear in her voice, her life flashing in front of her eyes.

"Yes," Valerie said. "But do I want to get married to Albert?"

"He's the father of your child. He's a lawyer, sort of. He's almost as tall as you." My mother drew a blank after that and looked to Grandma for help.

"He's cuddle umpkins," Grandma said. "And oogie-boogie bear and all them things. What about that?"

"I love this," Lula said, big grin on her face. "I thought I was gonna lose a thumb this afternoon, but here I am in the middle of cuddle umpkins' pumpkin patch." Lula turned to Sally. "What are you going to do? Does the wedding planner get to be an attendant, or something? Or do you just gotta be the wedding planner?"

"I'm singing," Sally said. "I have a lovely russet satin gown. I thought it would continue the fall theme."

"Maybe we should get the Trenton *Times* to cover this," Lula said to me. "Or MTV."

Maria had been jumping from one gown to the next, pinning and tucking. "All done," she said.

Sally took me aside. "You remember about the wedding shower, right? Friday night at the VFW hall."

"Sure. What time?"

"Seven. And it's a surprise, so be careful what you say to Valerie."

"My lips are sealed."

"Let me see you make the zipper," Grandma said. "I always like when a person makes the zipper and throws the key away."

I zipped my lips, and I threw the key away.

Lula swiveled in her seat. "Ranger's guys are still back there."

It was the second time I drove past the bar at the corner of Third and Laramie. Most of the street was residential, if you can call warehousing human misery in squalid brick cubes residential. There were no public parking lots, and curbside parking was nonexistent. Half the cars parked at the curb looked like they hadn't been moved in years.

I double-parked directly in front of the bar, and Lula and I got out. I didn't bother to lock the Cayenne. Ranger's men weren't going to let anything happen to his car. I had cuffs tucked into the back of my jeans. I was wearing the Kevlar vest under the sweatshirt. I had pepper spray in my pocket. Lula was half a step behind me, and I didn't ask what she was carrying. Best not to know.

Heads turned when we entered the bar. This wasn't a place where women went voluntarily. We took a moment to allow our eyes to adjust to the dark interior. Four men at the bar, one bartender, a lone man sitting at a scarred round wood table. Jamil Rodriguez. He was easy to recognize from his photo. A medium-sized black man in a rhinestone do-rag. Cheesy mustache and goatee. A nasty scar etched into his cheek, looking like an acid burn.

He slouched back in his chair. "Ladies?"

"You Jamil?" Lula asked.

He nodded his head yes. "You got business with me?"

Lula looked at me and smiled. "This fool thinks we're gonna buy some."

I pulled a chair up next to Rodriguez. "Here's the thing, Jamil," I said. "You forgot to show up for court." And I slapped a cuff on him.

"You sit around and wait and good things come to you," Rodriguez said. "I been looking for a new thumb." And he pulled a big Buck knife out of his pocket.

The four guys at the bar were paying attention, waiting to see the show. They were young, and they looked hungry for action. I suspected they'd jump in when it was the right time.

Lula pulled a gun out of her tiger print stretch pants and leveled it at Rodriguez. And from the doorway there was the unmistakable ratchet of a sawed-off shotgun. I didn't recognize the guy in black, filling the doorway, but I knew he'd come from the SUV. Not hard to spot one of Ranger's men. Big muscles, no neck, big gun, not much small talk.

"You want to drop the knife," I said to Rodriguez.

Rodriguez narrowed his eyes. "Make me."

Ranger's man blasted a three-foot hole in the ceiling over Rodriguez and plaster flew everywhere.

"Hey," Lula said to Ranger's man. "You want to watch it? I just had my hair done. I don't need no plaster in it. Next time just shoot a hole in this punk-ass loser, will you?"

Ranger's man smiled at her.

Minutes later, we had Rodriguez in the backseat of the Cayenne, cuffed and shackled, and we were on our way to the police station.

"Did you see that hunk of burning love smile at me?" Lula said. "Was he hot, or what? Did you see the size of his gun? I'm telling you, I'm getting a flash. I could have a piece of that."

"How about a piece of this?" Rodriguez said.

"You watch your mouth," Lula said. "You're close to being roadkill. We could throw you out and run over you, and nobody'd know the difference."

I took Third to State and headed south. I went one block, stopped for a light, and when the light changed, Harold Pancek passed me going in the opposite direction in his blue Honda Civic.

"Holy cow," Lula said. "Did you see him? That was Harold Pancek. I'd know him anywhere with his yellow square head."

I was already in motion, making an illegal U-turn. I did some aggressive driving and got myself directly behind Pancek. Ranger's guys had been caught by surprise and were struggling to catch up, two cars back. We stopped for another light, and Lula jumped out of the Porsche and ran for Pancek. She had her hand on the passenger-side door when he looked around and saw her. The light changed, and Pancek took off. Lula climbed back into the Porsche, and I closed the gap. I was riding close on his bumper, hoping he'd get demoralized and stop. He was checking his rear mirrors, weaving around traffic, taking side streets in an attempt to lose me.

"He don't know where he's going," Lula said. "He's just trying to get away from you. I bet he's never been in this neighborhood before."

That was my guess, too. We were in a poor section of Trenton, heading toward an even worse section of Trenton. Pancek drove like a bat out of hell down four blocks on Sixth Street.

I hit the brakes when Pancek crossed Lime. Comstock was one block away. Comstock was Slayerland. I wasn't following Pancek into Slayerland.

"Do we have a cell phone number for Pancek?" I asked Lula. "Can we warn him he's in Slayerland?"

"We never got a cell for him," Lula said. "And anyway, it's too late. He's turned up Comstock."

I slowly cruised a couple blocks on Lime, hoping Pancek would pop out of Slayerland. No luck. So I turned around and pointed the Porsche in the direction of North Clinton.

When we got to the station, I left Lula with the Cayenne, and I marched Rodriguez in through the front door. I know it was moronic, but I wanted the guys to see I could capture a man with all his clothes on.

It was close to five and Morelli was gone for the day. Thank God for small favors. I didn't know what to do about Morelli. Thanks to Ranger's stupid shower gel, face-to-face meetings with Morelli were now beyond uncomfortable. Okay, let's be honest. It was more than the shower gel. It was Ranger. The man was deadly sexy.

And he was walking around without underwear. I couldn't stop thinking about it. I gave myself a mental face slap. Get a grip, I told myself. You don't really know for sure. Just because you didn't *find* any underwear, doesn't mean he doesn't own any. Maybe they were all in the laundry. All right, so this was a little improbable. I was going to go with it anyway, because the thought of standing next to Ranger when he was commando had me in a state.

Connie had closed up shop by the time I got back to the bonds office, so I dropped Lula at her car, and I returned to the RangeMan building. The black SUV followed me into the garage and parked in one of the side slots. Two of the four slots reserved for Ranger were occupied. The Mercedes and Turbo were in place. The truck was missing. I parked the Cayenne next to the Turbo, walked over to the SUV, and knocked on the passenger-side window.

"Thanks for the help," I said.

The guy in the passenger seat nodded acknowledgment. Neither said anything. I gave them something between a smile and a grimace, and I scurried off to the elevator.

I let myself into the apartment and dropped the keys in the dish on the sideboard. The sideboard also held a bowl of fresh fruit and a silver tray filled with unopened mail.

I was in the process of selecting a piece of fruit when I heard the lock tumble on the front door. I slipped the bolt back and opened the door to Ranger.

He tossed his keys into the dish and rifled through the mail, not opening any. "How was your day?" he asked.

"Good. You were right about Rodriguez. He was open for business at the bar on Third and Laramie." I didn't have to say more. I was sure Ranger had already gotten a full report.

"Who's getting married?"

"Valerie."

There was a knock at the door, and Ella came in with a food tray.

"Would you like me to set the table?" she asked.

"Not necessary," Ranger said. "You can just leave the tray in the kitchen."

Ella swept past us, deposited the food, and returned to the front foyer.

"Is there anything else?" she asked.

"No," Ranger said. "We're good for the night. Thank you."

I couldn't believe the big bad Special Forces survival nut lived like this. Clothes washed and ironed, bed made, gourmet food delivered daily.

Ranger locked the door after Ella and followed me into the kitchen. "This is ruining my image, isn't it?" Ranger said.

"All this time, I thought you were so tough. I imagined you sleeping on a dirt floor somewhere."

He uncovered one of the dishes. "There were years like that."

Ella'd brought us roasted vegetables, wild rice, and chicken in a lemon sauce. We filled plates and ate at the counter, sitting on bar stools.

I finished my chicken and looked over at the silver tray. "No dessert?"

Ranger pushed back from the counter. "Sorry, I don't eat dessert. Where are you keeping your Slayer?"

"Vinnie's house in Point Pleasant."

"Who knows about this?"

"Connie, Lula, and me."

He reached across, unzipped my sweatshirt, and released the Velcro tabs on the vest. "This isn't going to help you, Babe," he said. "Junkman shot his last two victims in the head."

I removed the sweatshirt and the vest and put the sweatshirt back on. It had stopped raining, but it had gotten cooler.

Ranger dialed Ella and told her we were leaving. He got a utility belt and sweatshirt from the dressing room. The black nylon web belt carried a gun, a stun gun, pepper spray, cuffs, and a Maglite, plus ammo. We left the apartment, locked up, and took the elevator. There were two men waiting in the garage. I knew them both. Tank and Hal. They took a black Ford Explorer, and Ranger and I took the Porsche Turbo. Ranger was wearing the sweatshirt. The belt was in the back.

We rolled out of the garage and cut over to Broad. It was a dark, moonless night. The cloud cover was low, threatening more rain. The SUV's headlights stayed constant behind us. Ranger was silent, driving relaxed, his sweatshirt sleeves pushed halfway up his forearms, his watch catching the occasional light from overhead streetlights.

I wasn't nearly so relaxed. I was worried that Anton Ward might have escaped. And I was worried that he might still be there. "You aren't going to hurt him, are you?" I asked Ranger.

Ranger flicked a glance at me via the rearview mirror. "Babe," he said.

"I know he probably killed a couple people," I said. "But I'm sort of responsible for his safety."

"You want to explain that?"

I told Ranger how we bonded Ward out and then kidnapped him.

"Nice," Ranger said.

Vinnie's street was totally black, not a single light burning. Ranger tucked the Porsche into the driveway, and Tank pulled the SUV in behind him.

"I can leave you in the car with Hal," Ranger said, getting the belt from the back. "Would you feel more comfortable with that?"

"No. I'm coming in."

The house was quiet, but I could feel Ward's sullen presence. He was in the bathroom, just as we left him, shackled to the toilet and sink pipe. He didn't look happy to see Ranger.

"Do you know who I am?" Ranger asked him quietly.

Ward nodded his head, checking out the belt with the gun and the Maglite. "Yeah, I know who you are."

"I'm going to ask you some questions," Ranger said. "And you need to give me the right answers."

Ward's eyes darted from me to Ranger and beyond Ranger to Tank.

"If you don't give me the right answers, I'm going to leave you alone in the house with Tank and Hal," Ranger said. "Do you understand?"

"Yeah, I understand."

"Tell me about Junkman."

"Nothing to tell. He's from out of town. L.A. Nobody even knows his name. Just Junkman."

"Where does he live?"

"Moves around, livin' with the bitches. Always got a new bitch. We're not exactly best friends, you know? Like I don't know his bitches."

"What's the deal with the killing? What's the list about?"

"Hey, man, I can't talk to you about these things. I'm a brother."

Ranger whacked Ward in the knee with the Maglite, and Ward went down like a sack of sand.

"Anybody finds out I talked to you, I'm a dead man," Ward said, holding his knee.

"You don't talk to me and you're going to wish you were dead," Ranger said.

"It's about being Five Star General. Junkman was a lieutenant in the organization out in L.A. He got sent here to take over on account of Trenton's had some leadership problems. Power vacuum after our OG Moody Black got taken out. Only thing, Junkman gotta impress the members first. He gotta eat some serious food, you know. Like he has to make some kills that count. He already took out a Second Crown of the Kings and an enforcer. What he's got left is a cop and sweetie pie, here."

"Why Stephanie?"

"She's a bounty hunter. She collected a bunch of the brothers. And it's not good to get collected by snatch. It's not got a high prestige factor. So for Junkman's last proof of worthiness the council decided he had to give the members some bounty hunter. The plan is he catches the snatch and passes it around to the members before he does her. She's part of the coronation."

My vision got cobwebby, and there was a loud clanging in my head. I staggered out of the bathroom and collapsed on the couch in the living room. My mother and Morelli were right. I needed a new job.

I heard the door to the bathroom close, and Ranger came over and squatted beside me.

"Are you okay?" he asked.

"I'm fine. It was getting boring, so I thought I'd take a nap."

This got me the almost smile. "We're done with Anton Ward. Do you have plans for him?"

"I was going to revoke his bond and put him back in jail."

"And the reason for this?"

"He agreed to wear a PTU and then refused when we got him released, escaping out the bonds office bathroom window before we could install the unit."

"I'll have Tank take care of it. We'll hold him over until tomorrow morning, so we can get the paperwork straight. Did you bring him in blindfolded?"

"He was wrapped in a blanket. It was dark and I doubt he saw much."

It took forty minutes to get back to Trenton and neither of us spoke. Normal for Ranger. Not normal for me. I had a lot of thoughts in my head, but almost none of them were thoughts I wanted to say out loud. Ranger parked the car, and we got out together. When we got in the elevator, he touched the number four button.

"What's on the fourth floor?" I asked.

"Studio apartments that are available to RangeMan employees. I moved one of the men out so you could have your own place until it's safe for you to leave." The doors opened to the fourth floor and Ranger wrapped my hand around a key. "Don't expect me to always be this civilized."

"I'm undone. I don't know what to say."

Ranger took the key back, crossed the hall, and opened the door to 4B. He flipped the light on, gave me the key, and shoved me inside.

"Lock the door before I change my mind," he said. "Hit seven if you need me."

I closed and locked the door and looked around. Kitchenette against one wall. Queen-size bed in an alcove. Writing desk and chair. Comfy-looking leather couch. Coffee table and television. All done in earth tones. Clean and tasteful. The bed was made with fresh sheets. The bathroom had clean towels and a basket of toiletries.

My clothes were freshly washed and folded in a wicker basket at the edge of the sleeping alcove.

I took a shower and got dressed in a clean T-shirt and boxer shorts. The boxers weren't black and silky and sexy like Ranger's. They were soft cotton. Pink with little yellow daisies. Seemed just right for spending an evening alone, pretending life was safe and happy.

It was a couple minutes after ten, so I called Morelli at home. No answer. Painful contraction around my heart, resulting from irrational stab of jealous insecurity. If I was having a hard time keeping my hands off Ranger, Morelli could be having a similar problem. Women followed him down the street and committed crimes, hoping to meet him. Morelli wouldn't have a problem finding a sympathetic body to sleep beside.

Morelli with another woman wasn't an appealing thought, so I sunk into the couch and did some channel surfing, looking for a diversion. I settled on a West Coast ball game. I watched for ten minutes but couldn't get involved. I channel-surfed some more. I looked up at the ceiling. Ranger was three floors above me. It was more comfortable to think about Ranger than to think about Morelli. Thinking about Ranger got me overheated and frustrated. Thinking about Morelli got me sad.

I shut the television off, crawled into bed, and ordered myself to go to sleep. A half hour later I was still awake. The little room felt sterile. It was safe, but it gave no comfort. The pillow didn't smell like Ranger. And Anton Ward's words kept cycling through my brain. A tear slid out of my eye. Jeez. What was the deal with the tears! It wasn't even that time of the month. Maybe it was my diet. Not enough Tastykakes. Too many vegetables.

I got out of bed, grabbed all my keys, and took the elevator to the seventh floor. I marched across the foyer and rang Ranger's bell. I was ready to ring it a second time when he opened the door. He was still dressed in the black T-shirt and cargo pants. I was thankful for this. I thought I could manage to keep from ripping the cargo pants off him. I wasn't sure about the black silk boxers.

"It's lonely on the fourth floor," I said. "And your sheets are nicer than mine."

"Ordinarily I'd take that as a sexual invitation, but after this morning I'm going to guess you just want my sheets."

"Actually, I was hoping I could sleep on your couch."

Ranger pulled me into his apartment and locked the door. "You can sleep anywhere you want, but I'm not going to be responsible for my actions if you fondle me again when I'm sleeping."

"I didn't fondle you!"

We were at the breakfast table, and Ranger was watching me eat a croissant.

"Tell me the truth," Ranger said. "Were you really freaked out last night? Or did you just want my sheets and my shower gel and my food?"

I smiled at him while I chewed. "Does it matter?"

Ranger thought about it for a long moment. "Only minimally."

I'd slept on his couch, wrapped in a down comforter, my head on one of his pillows with the wonderful smooth pillowcase. It wasn't as comfy as his bed, but it had been guilt-free.

"I got some bad news while you were in the shower this morning," Ranger said. "Junkman tagged his cop."

My heart stuttered. "Anyone I know?"

"No. He was a member of the State Police Street Gang Unit. He was working locally, but he was based out of north Jersey."

I was next up.

"Junkman will get taken out," Ranger said. "There are a lot of people looking for him. In the meantime, I want you to stay in the building. If I don't have to worry about you, I can have two extra men on the street tracking Junkman."

Fine by me. I wasn't anxious to be part of Junkman's coronation ceremony. And staying in Ranger's apartment wasn't a hardship.

I poured more coffee into my mug. "You have a lot of overhead here. How can you afford to have men following me around and looking for Junkman?"

"Junkman just killed a state cop. There's a big enough reward for Junkman to justify assigning some manpower to search for him. There's no monetary way to justify a security detail to watch over you. I bleed money every time you need protection."

I didn't know how to respond. I'd never really thought about Ranger as a businessman. He'd always seemed more like a superhero, recruiting men and cars from a parallel galaxy. Or at the very least, from the mob.

"Jeez," I said. "I'm sorry."

Ranger finished his coffee and stood. "I said there was no *monetary* way to justify your security. The truth is, you're a line item in my budget."

I followed him into the bedroom and watched while he got his gun, checked it out, and attached it to his belt.

"I have you listed under entertainment," Ranger said, sliding money and credit cards into his pants pocket. "This is a high-stress business, and you're comedy relief for my entire team. Plus, I get a tax break."

My eyes opened wide and my eyebrows shot up an inch into my forehead. This didn't sound flattering. "Comedy relief?"

Ranger gave me one of his rare full-on smiles. "I like you. We *all* like you." He grabbed me by the front of my shirt, lifted me two inches off the ground, and kissed me. "The truth is, I love you . . . in my own way." He set me back down and turned to go. "Have a nice day. And remember, you're on camera the instant you leave this apartment. I've given orders to stun-gun you if you try to leave the building."

And Ranger was gone.

I was totally flummoxed. I had no idea when Ranger was serious and when he was kidding. There was no doubt in my mind that I amused him. In the past, the amusement always felt affectionate, never malicious. Being a line item under entertainment was pushing it. And what the heck was I supposed to think about the *I love you* that was qualified by *in my own way*? I was supposed to think it was nice, I decided. I loved *him* in my own way, too.

The front bell chimed, and I opened the door to Ella. She had the basket of clean clothes I'd left in the fourth-floor room.

"Ranger asked me to bring these up to you," Ella said. "And your phone is in the basket, too. It was on the night table." She collected the breakfast tray and turned to leave. "When would be a good time for me to come in to clean?" she asked.

"Whenever it's convenient for you."

"I can tidy up right now," she said. "I won't be long. There isn't much to do today."

Not counting my mother, no one had ever cleaned or cooked for me. I wasn't in the income bracket to have a housekeeper. I didn't know anyone, other than Ranger, who had help. It was a luxury I'd always wanted, but it was uncharted territory for me right now, and it felt weird. It was one thing for Ella to come in and make Ranger's life easier while he was out catching desperadoes. It was totally different to have her cleaning up my mess while I sat around watching television.

Chapter FIFTEEN

I solved the Ella problem by helping her make the bed and straighten the apartment. She wouldn't allow me to touch the laundry, not wanting to be held responsible should I mix Ranger's blacks with his whites. Although, from what I could see, he didn't have any whites, other than sheets. We'd moved from the bedroom to the bathroom. Ella was setting out fresh towels, and I was smelling the soap.

"I love this soap," I said.

"My sister works on the cosmetic floor of a department store, and she gave me a sample of the Bulgari. It's very expensive, but it suits Ranger. Not that Ranger would notice. All he thinks about is work. Such a nice handsome young man and no girlfriend. Until you."

"I'm not exactly a girlfriend."

Ella stood straight and did a sharp inhale, focusing her snapping bird eyes on me. "He isn't paying you, is he? Like the way Richard Gere was paying Julia Roberts in *Pretty Woman*?"

"No. Ranger and I work together. I'm a bounty hunter."

"Maybe you'll *become* a girlfriend," she said hopefully.

"Maybe." But doubtful. In this case, I didn't think

love and sex equated to boyfriend. "Do you take care of all his properties?" I asked Ella.

"Just this building. I take care of the apartments on the fourth floor and Ranger. My husband, Louis, takes care of everything else."

Rats. I was hoping to get a lead on the Bat Cave.

Ella gathered the day's laundry and turned to go. "Would you like me to bring lunch?" she asked. "Ranger is never at home for lunch, but I'd be happy to make you a sandwich and a nice salad."

"Not necessary," I said. "I have some sandwich things here. But thank you for offering."

I let Ella out and my cell phone rang.

"Everybody's been trying to get you," Grandma said. "You haven't been answering your phone."

"I misplaced it."

"Your sister's driving us nuts. Ever since that fitting she's been impossible. I swear, I never saw anybody with such wedding jitters. I don't want to think what's going to happen if Valerie backs out. Your mother's hitting the sauce, as is. Not that I blame her. I take a nip now and then, too, what with all the googie bear and oogiewoogie snuggy sweetie stuff. Anyway, I just called to see if you wanted to go to the shower with Sally and me. Your mother's bringing Valerie."

"Thanks," I said, "but I'll get myself to the shower." Silent groan. The shower was Friday, and I didn't have a present. If Junkman was going to kill me, let it be today, I thought. At least I'd get out of the shower.

I disconnected and dialed Morelli.

"What?" he answered. Not happy.

"It's me," I said. "Have you been trying to call me?"

"Yeah. I worked a double shift yesterday, running down leads on Junkman. It was after eleven before I got home and checked my phone. Next time leave a message, so I know you're okay. Seeing your number pop up on my caller ID and then not being able to reach you doesn't do a lot for my acid reflux."

"Sorry. I wasn't calling for anything special. And then I misplaced my phone."

"Junkman got his cop."

"I just heard."

"I'd feel better if I knew where you were."

"No you wouldn't," I said. "But you'd worry less."

"I can read between the lines on that one," Morelli said. "Be careful."

No ranting and raving. No jealous accusations. Just an affectionate *Be careful.*

"You trust me," I said.

"Yeah."

"That's really rotten."

"I know. Live with it."

I could sense the smile. I was entertainment for Morelli, too.

I disconnected and called Valerie.

"What's going on?" I asked her. "Grandma says you're having a meltdown."

"I saw myself in the gown, and I had a total panic attack. It wasn't just that I was fat, either. It was everything. All the fuss. I know it's my own fault. I wanted a wedding, but it's gotten really scary. And now I have to get through a shower! Seventy-eight women in the VFW hall. Good thing there isn't a gun in the house because I'd shoot myself."

"The shower is supposed to be a secret."

"*I planned it!* What was I thinking? And what if this marriage doesn't work out? I thought my first marriage was perfect. I was clueless!"

"Albert's a nice guy. You're not going to find him in the coat closet with the baby-sitter. You'll have a nice comfortable life with Albert."

And that couldn't be said for the two men in my life, I thought. They were volatile domineering alpha males. Life wouldn't be dull with either of them, but it also wouldn't be easy.

"Maybe you should elope," I told Valerie. "Just go off and quietly get married and get on with your life."

"I couldn't do that to Mom."

"She might be relieved."

Okay, I have to admit this was self-serving, because I really didn't want to wear the eggplant gown. Still, I thought it was decent advice.

"I'll think about it," Valerie said.

"Just don't tell anyone I gave you the idea."

I hung up and went into the kitchen to say hello to Rex. I dropped a couple Frosted Flakes into his cage; he rushed out of his soup can, whiskers twitching, shoved the cereal into his cheek, and rushed back to the soup can.

Okay, that was fun, but now what? What do people do all day when they have nothing to do?

I flipped the television on and surfed through about forty channels, finding nothing. How could there be so little on so many channels?

I called the office.

"What's going on?" I asked Connie.

"Ranger was in. He's looking for Junkman. He's got a lot of company. Every bounty hunter and every cop in the state is looking for Junkman. You heard about the latest killing?"

"I heard."

"Did you also hear about Pancek? He was shot in the head last night, at the corner of Comstock and Seventh. Somehow he drove four more blocks before he lost consciousness and crashed his car. He's at St. Francis. It looks like he's going to make it."

"My fault," I said. "I chased him into Slayerland."

"Wrong," Connie said. "You followed him to Slay-erland. Since you're not here, I'm assuming you're hid-ing?"

"That's the plan, but it's getting old."

"Yeah, you've been at it for what, three or four hours?"

I got off the phone with Connie and shuffled into the bedroom to take a nap. I stood at the edge of the bed and couldn't bring myself to get in and wrinkle the perfectly ironed sheets. I looked to the bathroom. I'd already taken a shower. I went back to the kitchen and shook Rex's aquarium.

"Get up, you stupid hamster," I said. "I'm bored."

There was a slight rustling in the soup can as Rex hunkered in deeper.

I could explore the building, but that would involve interaction with Ranger's men. I wasn't sure I was ready for that. Especially since they might be stun-gun ready should I make a break for freedom.

I called Ranger on his cell phone.

Ranger answered with a soft, "Yo."

"Yo, yourself," I said. "I'm going nuts here. What am I supposed to do? There's nothing good on televi-sion. There are no books or magazines. No cross-stitch, needlepoint, knitting. And don't suggest I go to the gym. It's not going to happen."

Ranger disconnected.

I punched his number in again. "What was that?" I said. "You disconnected me!"

"Babe," Ranger said.

I did a sigh and hung up.

Ranger walked through the door a few minutes after six. He tossed his keys into the dish and did a cursory shuf-fle of the mail Ella had brought up earlier. He looked up from the mail and locked eyes with me. "You're looking a little crazy, Babe."

I was coming off five hours of television and two hours of hall pacing. "I'm leaving now," I said. "I'm going to the mall, and I just waited around so I could say thank you. I appreciate the use of your apartment, and I'm going to miss the shower gel big-time, but I have to go. So it would be good if you made sure no one stungunned me."

Ranger returned the letters to the silver tray. "No."

"No?"

"Junkman is still out there."

"Have you made any progress?"

"We have a name," Ranger said. "Norman Carver."

"Norman's not going to be at the mall. And excuse me, you're blocking the door."

"Give it a rest," Ranger said.

"Give it a rest, yourself," I said, giving him a shot to the shoulder. "Get out of my way."

All day long the car keys had been sitting in the dish. And truth is, I didn't actually believe Ranger told his guys to stun-gun me. I'd stayed in the apartment because I didn't want to die. And I still didn't want to die, but I was resenting the passive role I was forced to play. I was antsy, and I was unhappy. I wanted my life to be different. I wanted to be Ranger. He was good at being a tough guy. I was crappy at it. I was also finding it ironic that I'd walked out on Morelli only to find myself in the same position with Ranger.

I gave Ranger another shove, and he shoved back, pinning me to the wall with his body.

"I've had a long, unsatisfying day," Ranger said. "I'm low on patience. Don't push me."

He was effortlessly leaning into me, holding me there with his weight, and I was immobilized. Not only was I immobilized, I was starting to get turned on.

"This really pisses me off," I said.

He'd been out all day, and he still smelled wonderful. His warmth was oozing into me, his cheek was resting against the side of my head, his hands were flat against the wall, framing my shoulders. Without thinking, I snuggled into him and brushed my lips across his neck in a light kiss.

"No fair," he said.

I shifted under him and felt him stir against me.

"I've got the weight and the muscle," he said. "But I'm starting to think you've got the power."

"Do I have enough power to persuade you to take me shopping?"

"God doesn't have that much power. Did Ella bring dinner up?"

"About ten minutes ago. It's in the kitchen."

He pushed away from me, ruffled my hair, and went to the kitchen in search of food. The door was left unattended. The car keys were in the dish.

"Arrogant bastard," I yelled after him.

He turned and flashed me the full-on smile.

I was still at the breakfast table when Ranger came out of the bedroom wearing a fully loaded utility belt and an unzipped flak jacket. "Try not to get too crazy today," he said, heading for the door.

"Yeah," I said. "And you should try not to get shot."

It was a disturbing good-bye because we both meant what we said.

At five o'clock Lula called on my cell phone. "They got him," she said. "Connie and me have been listening to the police channel, and we just heard that they got Junkman."

"Any details?"

"Not much. It sounded to us like he got stopped for running a red, and when they checked him out they got lucky."

"No one was hurt?"

"No call went out."

I felt weak with relief. It was over. "Thanks," I said. "I'll see you tomorrow."

"Have fun," Lula said.

If I hurried, I could pick something up for Valerie and make the shower. I left a note to Ranger, grabbed the keys to the Turbo, and took the elevator to the garage.

The elevator doors opened at garage level, and Hal burst out of the stairwell door. "Excuse me," he said, "Ranger would prefer that you stay in the building."

"It's okay," I told him. "Code red is over, and I'm going shopping."

"I'm afraid I can't let you do that."

So, Ranger hadn't been yanking my chain. He'd actually given orders to keep me here.

"Men!" I said. "You're all a bunch of chauvinist morons."

Hal didn't have anything to say to that.

"Get out of my way," I said to him.

"I can't let you leave the building," he said.

"And how are you going to stop me?"

He shifted uncomfortably from foot to foot. He had a stun gun in his hand.

"Well?" I asked.

"I'm supposed to stun you, if I have to."

"Okay, let me get this straight. You're going to stun-gun the woman who's been living with Ranger?"

Hal's face was red, leaning toward purple. "Don't give me a hard time," he said. "I like this job, and I'll lose it if I screw up with you."

"You touch me with that stun gun and I'll have you arrested for assault. You won't have to worry about this job."

"Jeez," Hal said.

"Wait a minute," I said. "Let me see the gun for just a second."

Hal held the stun gun out to me. I took it, pressed it to his arm, and he went down like a ton of bricks. Hal wasn't a bad guy, but he was dumb as a box of rocks.

I leaned over him to make sure he was breathing, gave him his gun back, got into the Turbo, and motored out of the garage. I knew the control room would see me on the screen, and someone would check on Hal. I hated to stun him, but I was a woman on a mission. I needed a shower gift.

Ordinarily I'd go to the mall off Route 1, but I didn't have a lot of time, and I was worried about traffic. So I stopped at an electronics store on the way across town and bought Valerie a picture cell phone and a year's service. It wasn't a real bridey present, but I knew she needed a phone and couldn't afford to buy one for herself. I swung into a pharmacy and got a card and a gift bag, and I was in business. I could have been a little more dressed. Sneakers and jeans, a white stretchy T-shirt, and denim jacket weren't standard fare for a Burg shower, but it was the best I could do without making another stop.

The lot was filled when I got to the hall. The big yellow school bus was parked at the edge. My mother had hired Sally and his band to entertain. JoAnne Waleski was catering. When we did a shower in the Burg, we really did a shower.

I was in the lot when my cell phone rang.

"Babe," Ranger said. "What are you doing at the VFW?"

"Valerie's shower. Is Hal okay?"

"Yeah. You were caught on camera again. The men in the control room were laughing so hard when you stunned Hal they couldn't get down the stairs fast enough to stop you from leaving the garage."

"I heard they caught Junkman, so I thought it was okay to leave."

"I heard that, too, but I haven't been able to confirm the capture. I've got a man on you. Try not to destroy him."

Disconnect.

I went into the hall and looked for Grandma. Sally was on stage, doing rap in a red cocktail dress and red sequined heels. The rest of the band was in gargantuan T-shirts and baggy-ass pants.

It was too noisy to hear my phone ring, but I felt the vibration.

"Stephanie," my mother said, "is your sister with you? She was supposed to be here an hour ago."

"Did you call the apartment?"

"Yes. I talked to Albert. He said Valerie wasn't there. He said she took off in the Buick. I thought maybe she got confused and went to the shower without me. She's been getting confused a lot lately."

"Valerie doesn't have a Buick."

"She was having problems with her car, so she borrowed Uncle Sandor's Buick yesterday."

I got a sick feeling in my stomach. "I'll get back to you."

I located Grandma and asked if she'd seen Valerie.

"Nope," Grandma said. "But she better show up soon. The natives are restless."

I went out to the lot, got the gun Ranger always kept under the seat, and put it in my denim jacket pocket. Somewhere in the lot was a black SUV with Ranger's man in it. I thought that was a good thing. And my sister was somewhere in the powder blue Buick. That was a bad thing. I was associated with the powder blue Buick. That's why I wasn't driving it. I'd thought it was safely locked up in my parents' garage. Out of sight, out of the Slayers' minds. Not to panic, I told myself. Junkman was in jail, and probably Valerie was in a bar trying to get numb enough to survive the shower. I just hoped she didn't pass out before she got to the hall.

I called Morelli.

"You've got Junkman locked up in jail, right?" I asked him.

"We've got someone locked up in jail. We're not sure who he is. He's telling us he's Junkman, but he's not checking out. He was driving a car with California plates belonging to Norman Carver, and Gang Intelligence tells us Junkman's name is Norman Carver."

"So, what's the problem?"

"He's too short. According to California DMV, Carver's a big guy. And we got a little guy."

"No ID on him?"

"None."

"Tattoos?"

"None."

"That's not good."

"Tell me about it," Morelli said. "Where are you?"

"Valerie's shower."

"I'm assuming Ranger's got a man on you?"

"That's what he tells me."

"Poor dumb bastard," Morelli said. And he hung up.

I wasn't sure what to do next. Part of me wanted to run back to the safety of Ranger's building. Part of me wanted to go inside the hall and fill my plate with meatballs. And part of me worried about Valerie. The worrying about Valerie part was at the front of the line. Problem was, I hadn't a clue where to look for her.

I saw my mother pull into the lot and park. She hurried out of the car, and I met her before she got to the door.

"I left your father at home to wait for Valerie," she said. "I can't imagine what's happened to her. I hope she hasn't been in a car crash. Do you think I should call the hospital?"

I was mentally gnawing on my fingernails. I wasn't worried about a car crash. I was worried that Valerie had been spotted by a Slayer. I was worried that they sometimes staked out places I was known to frequent. Like my apartment. Not a thought I wanted to share with my mother. I had my phone in my hand, and I was about to call Morelli back when I heard a familiar rumble. It was the sound of gas getting sucked into an internal combustion engine at an astonishing rate. It was the Buick.

Valerie swung Big Blue into the lot and parked in handicapped parking a couple feet from my mother and me. Neither of us said anything because we both thought Val qualified.

"I got lost," she said. "I left the apartment, and I had so much on my mind I guess I was on autopilot. Anyway, next thing I knew I was on the other side of town by Helene Fuld Hospital."

I got a head-to-toe chill. She'd been way too close to Slayerland. In fact, she probably passed over Comstock. Thank goodness, luck had been with her, and she'd found her way to the VFW unharmed.

Grandma appeared at the front door to the hall.

"There you are!" she said. "Hurry up inside. The band ran out of steam and had to go outside to smoke some weed. I don't know why anybody'd want to smoke weeds, but that's what they said. And worse than that, we're gonna run out of food if we don't get this crowd to sit down soon."

I still didn't feel comfortable with the Buick being out on the streets. And I especially didn't want Valerie driving it home to my apartment. "Give me your key," I said to Valerie. "I'll move the car out of the handicapped spot." Way out. All the way to my parents' garage.

Val gave me the keys, and everyone went inside. I got into the Buick and started it up. I backed out of the parking slot, and I cruised the length of the lot to the exit. I'd spotted Ranger's man parked across the street. It was a smart spot that gave him full view of the entrance to the lot and the front door to the hall. Unfortunately, he didn't have a good view of the exit, so I made a left turn out of the lot to circle the block and come alongside him. He could follow me to my parents' house, and then he could give me a ride back to the hall. Val could go home with either my mother or me.

I'd barely made the turn out of the lot when the black Hummer came out of nowhere, swerved around me and pulled in front, forcing me into a parked car. I leaned on the horn and reached for Ranger's gun, but I had two guys on me before I got the gun in my hand. I did all the things I knew I was supposed to do. Put up a fight. Make noise. And it didn't matter. In a matter of seconds, I was yanked from behind the wheel and dragged around to the back of the Buick. The trunk was opened, and I was shoved in. The trunk slammed shut, and that was it. The world went black.

Chapter

SIXTEEN

I remember seeing a nature show on television where a ground squirrel was hiding in an underground den, and a wolverine reached in and grabbed the ground squirrel. It happened so fast it was a blur on the screen. That's the way it is with disaster. In an instant your future can disappear. And nothing can adequately prepare you for the moment. There's a millisecond of surprise and then a heaviness of heart when finality is recognized.

I didn't have the gun. It had fallen out of my pocket in the scramble. And I didn't have my cell phone. My phone was in my purse, and my purse was inside the car. I'd made some noise, so there was the possibility that Ranger's man might have heard me. I didn't think the possibility was good. There might have been a way to open the trunk from the inside, but I was at a loss. It was an old car, designed before safety features like interior-opening trunk lids. I felt around the lock area, trying to pry the lid up with my nails, trying to trip a catch that I couldn't see.

I was twisted into a fetal position, wrapped around and on top of a spare tire. I knew there had to be a tire iron in the trunk. If I found the tire iron I might be able to force the trunk open. Or I might be able to do some damage when one of the Slayers opened the trunk. Enough to give me a chance to run.

The air was thick with the smell of tire, and the total blackness was smothering. Still, the smothering blackness was better than what awaited me when the trunk was opened. More irony, I thought. I drove Anton Ward to the shore like this. And here I am being driven to my fate under the same frightening, painful conditions. The Catholic in me rose to the surface. What goes around, comes around.

I gave up searching for the tire iron. Probably it was under the tire. And try as I might, I couldn't get myself into a position to get under the tire. So, I concentrated my energies on kicking at the trunk and yelling. The car was stopping for lights and pausing at intersections. Maybe someone would hear me.

I was so absorbed in kicking and yelling that I missed the moment when the engine cut off. I was in midscream when the trunk was opened, and I looked up into the faces of the men who'd abducted me. After all my recoveries, I was on the other side.

I'd always thought in a situation like this the major emotion I'd feel would be terror, but my major emotion was anger. I'd been taken away from my sister's shower. How freaking rude is that? And on top of it, I was still dieting, and I was cranky as hell. There'd been meatballs at the shower. And sheet cake. I'd been steadily working myself into a frenzy while I was in the trunk, thinking about the sheet cake. I glared out at the faces of the degenerate losers who'd kidnapped me, and I wanted to get close enough to them to sink my thumbs into their eye sockets. I wanted to draw blood with my nails.

I was hauled out of the trunk, in full rant, and dragged across the street to a bleak vest-pocket playground. The playground equipment was skeletal, covered with gang graffiti. The ground was littered with bottles and cans and fast food wrappers. The lighting was eerie. Dark shadows and an unearthly green wash from an overhead streetlight.

The playground was surrounded by four-story brick apartment buildings. Windows were tightly shut and shades drawn on the park exposure. No one wanted to see or hear what transpired here. This was the middle of the seven hundred block of Comstock Street. This was Slayerland.

Someone had painted a large white circle onto the cracked blacktop. I was shoved into the circle, and the members gathered around, careful not to step inside. Most of them were young. In their teens or early twenties. Hard to say how many there were. Could be ten. Could be fifty. I was still in a blind rage, too crazed to count.

A big guy stepped forward, his face lost in the shadow of his hooded sweatshirt. Junkman.

"This is the circle where we try the enemy," he said. "If you're not a member, you're the enemy. We already disposed of three of the enemy. This is your night. Are you the enemy?"

I didn't say anything. His fist swung out and caught me on the side of my face. The impact cracked like a rifle shot inside my head, my teeth cut into my bottom lip, and I staggered back. A roar went up from the group and hands grabbed at me, holding fast to my jacket, tearing my T-shirt. I lurched away, sacrificing the jacket to the grabbing men, going down to one knee.

This is the game, I thought, crawling to the relative safety of the center of the circle. They can't put a foot inside the ring. Only Junkman was inside the ring. And Junkman would continue to hit me until I was dragged out of the circle by the grabbing hands. And once I was out of the circle I guessed I was at the mercy of the gang, and they would do whatever it was that crazed depraved mobs did to women.

Junkman pulled me to my feet and hit me with another roundhouse swing, the force of the blow sending me to the circle's edge. I tried to escape to the center, but one of the men had a handful of T-shirt and another had me by the hair. I was yanked over the line and hand-passed deep into the mob. And brought face to face with Eugene Brown.

"Remember me?" Eugene asked. "You ran over me. Now I'm gonna be the first to run over you."

My nose was running, and my vision was blurred by tears. Hard to say if the tears were from fright or from roiling, flaming fury. I didn't think I had a lot to lose by getting in one last kick, so I swung from the knee with as much power as I could find, and I caught Brown square in the crotch with my toe. He doubled over and went to the ground. I'd probably get raped by every other member of the gang, but I had the satisfaction of depriving Eugene Brown of the honor. I'd shoved Brown's nuts halfway up his throat. Brown wasn't going to be raping anyone for a while.

A murmur rippled through the men behind me. I was ready to kick out again, but the mob's attention had shifted to the street. Several blocks south, a single set of headlights could be seen moving forward down Comstock. There'd been no traffic on the street prior to this. Probably there were Slayer sentries redirecting cars. Or maybe no one dared to travel the street after dark. I prayed that it was Joe or Ranger or Ranger's man in the SUV. No red light flashing. Hard to tell what sort of vehicle was attached to the headlights.

Everyone was watching the approaching vehicle. No one spoke. Guns were drawn.

The vehicle was a block away.

"What the . . ." one of the men said.

It was a big yellow school bus.

The disappointment was crushing. I knew who drove the bus, and it was unlikely he could pull off a rescue. His intentions were undoubtedly heroic, but I worried that not only couldn't he save me . . . he probably was rushing to his own death.

The bus was barreling down the street at an alarming speed, bouncing and swaying, barely under control. It was surreal. It was riveting. And the mob watched in stupefied silence.

The bus went into a skid as it came abreast of the playground. It jumped the curb and plowed into the stunned gang members, brakes squealing, gang members yelling and scrambling to get out of the way.

The bus lurched to a smoking stop in the middle of the circle. The door to the bus opened with a *whoosh*, and Sally wobbled out, all long, gangly, hairy legs and knobby knees, in his red chiffon cocktail dress and four-inch red sequined heels. His hair was Wild Man of Borneo. His eyes were dilated to the size of quarters.

I had a split second of mind-numbing terror for Sally. And then I saw that he was two-handing an Uzi.

"Rock and roll," Sally said.

A bullet zinged past him and bounced off the bus. I dropped flat to the ground, and Sally squeezed off what sounded to me like about seven hundred rounds. When the dust settled, there were several bloody bodies writhing in pain on the blacktop. Some had been run over, and some had been shot. Fortunately, I wasn't one of them.

Junkman had been one of those run over, his feet sticking out from under the bus like the Wicked Witch in *The Wizard of Oz*. The rest of the Slayers had scattered like cockroaches when the light goes on.

"F-F-F-Fudge," Sally said. "Freaking fucking fudge."

"Guess you were scared, hunh?"

"Mother freaking fucking fudge," he said. "I almost pissed myself."

I was surprisingly calm. My life had taken on a feature film quality. I was living *Die Hard* in Trenton. And Bruce Willis was in drag. And I wasn't dead. I wasn't raped. I was almost completely dressed. I was beyond calm. I was euphoric. The anger was gone.

Sirens and lights were flashing in the distance. Lots of headlights. It looked like everything but the Marines were on their way to the playground.

There were a bunch of dropped guns on the blacktop. I kicked them around to make sure all of the guys Sally'd nailed had a gun by him, not within reach, but close enough to believe they'd first drawn on Sally.

Two heads popped out of the bus door. The rest of the band.

"Holy shit," one guy said. And they both retreated back into the bus and closed the door.

"We were taking a break out back, and I saw them grab you," Sally said. "I couldn't get across the parking lot fast enough to stop them, so I ran and got the bus. By the time I got it started up and out of the lot you were gone, but I got to thinking about this spot. I drive by here all the time on my route, and the kids talk about it, and how this is where the beatings and killings happen."

The first car to arrive was a Trenton PD blue-and-white. It slid to a stop behind the bus and Robin Russell got out, gun drawn, eyes wide. "Holy Toledo," she said.

"I called everyone I could think of while I was driving," Sally said. "Including the fire department."

No shit. I was going to have a seizure from the flashing lights.

Ranger pulled to a stop behind Russell's blue-and-white, and Morelli was behind Ranger. Morelli had his portable *Kojak* light, flashing red, stuck to the roof of his SUV. I knew he had to have flown through town to get here this fast.

Morelli and Ranger hit the ground running. They slowed when they saw Sally and me standing in the middle of the massacre, the Uzi dangling from Sally's trigger finger.

I smiled at Morelli and Ranger and gave them a small wave.

"My heroes," I said to Sally. "Upstaged by a guy in a red dress and heels."

"Freakin' humbling," Sally said.

Robin Russell was already securing the crime scene with tape. Ranger and Morelli slipped under the tape and picked their way around the bodies.

"Hi," I said to them. "What's up?"

"Not a lot," Morelli said. "What's up with you?"

"Same old, same old."

"Yeah, I can see that," Morelli said.

"You remember Sally Sweet," I said.

Ranger and Sally shook hands. And Joe and Sally shook hands.

"Sally mowed all these Slayers," I said.

"I made sort of a mess," Sally said. "I didn't mean to run over them like this. I tried to stop, but the brakes aren't what they used to be on old Betsy. And it's friggin' hard to, you know, brake in heels. But what the hell, it turned out okay, right? All's well that ends well."

Morelli and Ranger were both trying hard not to smile too wide.

"There's a nice reward being offered on Junkman," Morelli said to Sally. "Ten big ones."

Ranger looked at the gun Sally was holding. "Do you always carry an Uzi?"

"I keep it in the bus," Sally said. "Gotta protect the

little dudes. I tried an AK-47, but it wouldn't fit under my seat. I like the Uzi better, anyway. It looks better with the dress. The AK seems too casual to me."

"It's important to accessorize properly," I said.

"Fudgin' A," Sally said.

ELEVEN
ON TOP

This book is a Jan-Jen production, brought to life through the extraordinary powers of SuperEditor Jen Enderlin

Thanks to Shanna Littlejohn
for suggesting the title for this book.

ONE

My name is Stephanie Plum. When I was eighteen, I got a job working a hot dog stand on the boardwalk on the Jersey shore. I worked the last shift at Dave's Dogs, and I was supposed to start shutting down a half hour before closing so I could clean up for the day crew. We did chili dogs, cheese dogs, kraut dogs, and bean-topped barking dogs. We grilled them on a big grill with rotating rods. Round and round the rods went all day long, turning the dogs.

Dave Loogie owned the dog stand and came by every night to lock the stand down. He checked the garbage to make sure nothing good was thrown away, and he counted the dogs that were left on the grill.

"You gotta plan ahead," Dave told me every night. "You got more than five dogs left on the grill when we close, I'm gonna fire your ass and hire someone with bigger tits."

So every night, fifteen minutes before closing, before Dave showed up, I ate hot dogs. Not a good way to go when you're working at the shore nights and on the beach in a skimpy bathing suit by day. One night I ate fourteen hot dogs. Okay, maybe it was only nine, but it felt like fourteen. Anyway, it was *too many* hot dogs. Well hell, I needed the job.

For years Dave's Dogs took the number-one slot on my list of all-time crappy jobs held. This morning, I decided my present position had finally won the honor of replacing Dave's Dogs. I'm a bounty hunter. A bond enforcement agent, if you want to make me sound more legitimate. I work for my cousin Vinnie in his bail bonds office in the Chambersburg section of Trenton. At least I used to work for my cousin Vinnie. Thirty seconds ago, I quit. I handed in the phony badge I bought off the Net. I gave back my cuffs. And I dropped my remaining open files on Connie's desk.

Vinnie writes the bonds. Connie shuffles the paperwork. My sidekick, Lula, files when the mood strikes her. And an incredibly sexy, incredibly handsome badass named Ranger and I hunt down the morons who don't show up for trial. Until today. As of thirty seconds ago, all the morons got transferred to Ranger's list.

"Give me a break," Connie said. "You can't quit. I've got a stack of open files."

"Give them to Ranger."

"Ranger doesn't do the low bonds. He only takes the high-risk cases."

"Give them to Lula."

Lula was standing hand on hip, watching me spar with Connie. Lula's a size-sixteen black woman squashed into size-ten leopard print spandex. And the weird thing is, in her own way, Lula looks pretty good in the animal spandex.

"Hell yeah," Lula said. "I could catch them sonsabitches. I could hunt down their asses good. Only I'm gonna miss you," she said to me. "What are you gonna do if you don't work here? And what brought this on?"

"Look at me!" I said. "What do you see?"

"I see a mess," Lula said. "You should take better care of yourself."

"I went after Sam Sporky this morning."

"Melon-head Sporky?"

"Yeah. Melon-head. I chased him through three yards. A dog tore a hole in my jeans. Some crazy old lady shot at me. And I finally tackled Sporky behind the Tip Top Cafe."

"Looks like it was garbage day," Lula said. "You don't smell too good. And you got something looks like mustard all over your ass. Least I hope that's mustard."

"There were a bunch of garbage bags at the curb and Melon-head rolled me into them. We made sort of a mess. And then when I finally got him in cuffs, he spit on me!"

"I imagine that's the glob of something stuck in your hair?"

"No. He spit on my shoe. Is there something in my hair?"

Lula gave an involuntary shiver.

"Sounds like a normal day," Connie said. "Hard to believe you're quitting because of Melon-head."

Truth is, I don't exactly know why I was quitting. My stomach feels icky when I get up in the morning. And I go to bed at night wondering where my life is heading. I've been working as a bounty hunter for a while now and I'm not the world's best. I barely make enough money to cover my rent each month. I've been stalked by crazed killers, taunted by naked fat men, firebombed, shot at, spat at, cussed at, chased by humping dogs, attacked by a flock of Canadian honkers, rolled in garbage, and my cars get destroyed at an alarming rate.

And maybe the two men in my life add to the icky feeling in my stomach. They're both Mr. Right. And they're both Mr. Wrong. They're both a little scary. I wasn't sure if I wanted a relationship with either of them. And I hadn't a clue how to choose between them.

One wanted to marry me, sometimes. His name was Joe Morelli and he was a Trenton cop. Ranger was the other guy, and I wasn't sure what he wanted to do with me beyond get me naked and put a smile on my face.

Plus, there was the note that got slipped under my door two days ago. I'M BACK. What the heck did that mean? And the follow-up note tacked to my windshield. DID YOU THINK I WAS DEAD?

My life is too weird. It's time for a change. Time to get a more sensible job and sort out my future.

Connie and Lula shifted their attention from me to the front door. The bonds office is located on Hamilton Avenue. It's a small two-room storefront setup with a cluttered storage area in the back, behind a bank of file cabinets. I didn't hear the door open. And I didn't hear footsteps. So either Connie and Lula were hallucinating or else Ranger was in the room.

Ranger is the mystery man. He's a half head taller than me, moves like a cat, kicks ass all day long, only wears black, smells warm and sexy, and is 100 percent pure perfectly toned muscle. He gets his dark complexion and liquid brown eyes from Cuban ancestors. He was Special Forces, and that's about all anyone knows about Ranger. Well hell, when you smell *that* good and look *that* good, who cares about anything else, anyway?

I can usually feel Ranger standing behind me. Ranger doesn't ordinarily leave any space between us. Today, Ranger was keeping his distance. He reached around me and dropped a file and a body receipt on Connie's desk.

"I brought Angel Robbie in last night," he said to Connie. "You can mail the check to RangeMan."

RangeMan is Ranger's company. It's located in an office building in center city and specializes in security systems and fugitive apprehension.

"I got big news," Lula said to Ranger. "I've been promoted to bounty hunter on account of Stephanie just quit."

Ranger picked a couple strands of sauerkraut off my shirt and pitched them into Connie's wastebasket. "Is that true?"

"Yes," I said. "I quit. I'm done fighting crime. I've rolled in garbage for the last time."

"Hard to believe," Ranger said.

"I'm thinking of getting a job at the button factory," I told him. "I hear they're hiring."

"I don't have a lot of domestic instincts," Ranger said to me, his attention fixing on the unidentifiable glob of goo in my hair, "but I have a real strong urge to take you home and hose you down."

I went dry mouthed. Connie bit into her lower lip, and Lula fanned herself with a file.

"I appreciate the offer," I told him. "Maybe some other time."

"Babe," Ranger said on a smile. He nodded to Lula and Connie and left the office.

No one said anything until he drove off in his shiny black Porsche Turbo.

"I think I wet my pants," Lula said. "Was that one of them double entendres?"

I drove back to my apartment, took a shower all by myself, and got dressed up in a stretchy white tank top and a tailored black suit with a short skirt. I stepped into four-inch black heels, fluffed up my almost shoulder-length curly brown hair, and added one last layer to my mascara and lipstick.

I'd taken a couple minutes to print out a résumé on my computer. It was pathetically short. Graduated with mediocre grades from Douglass College. Worked as a lingerie buyer for a cheap department store for a bunch of years. Got fired. Tracked down scumbags for my cousin Vinnie. Seeking management position in a classy company. Of course, this was Jersey and classy here might not be the national standard.

I grabbed my big black leather shoulder bag and yelled good-bye to my roomie, Rex-the-hamster. Rex lives in a glass aquarium on the kitchen counter. Rex is pretty much nocturnal so we're sort of like ships passing in the night. As an extra treat, once in a while I drop a Cheez Doodle into his cage and he emerges from his soup can home to retrieve the Doodle. That's about as complicated as our relationship gets.

I live on the second floor of a blocky, no-frills, three-story apartment building. My apartment looks out over the parking lot, which is fine by me. Most of the residents in my building are seniors. They're home in front of their televisions before the sun goes down, so the lot side is quiet at night.

I exited my apartment and locked up behind myself. I took the elevator to the small ground-floor lobby, pushed through the double glass doors, and crossed the lot to my car. I was driving a dark green Saturn SL2. The Saturn had been the special of the day at Generous George's Used Car Emporium. I'd actually wanted a Lexus SC 430, but Generous George thought the Saturn was more in line with my budget constraints.

I slid behind the wheel and cranked the engine over. I was heading off to apply for a job at the button factory and I was feeling down about it. I was telling myself it was a new beginning, but truth is, it felt more like a sad ending. I turned onto Hamilton and drove a couple blocks to Tasty Pastry Bakery, thinking a doughnut would be just the thing to brighten my mood.

Five minutes later, I was on the sidewalk in front of the bakery, doughnut bag in hand, and I was face-to-face with Morelli. He was wearing jeans and scuffed boots and a black V-neck sweater over a black T-shirt. Morelli is six feet of lean, hard muscle and hot Italian libido. He's Jersey guy smart, and he's not a man you'd want to annoy . . . unless you're me. I've been annoying Morelli all my life.

"I was driving by and saw you go in," Morelli said. He was standing close, smiling down at me, eyeing the bakery bag. "Boston creams?" he asked, already knowing the answer.

"I needed happy food."

"You should have called me," he said, hooking his finger into the neckline of my white tank, pulling the neck out to take a look inside. "I have just the thing to make you happy."

I've cohabitated with Morelli from time to time and I knew this to be true. "I have stuff to do this afternoon and doughnuts take less time."

"Cupcake, I haven't seen you in weeks. I could set a new land speed record for getting happy."

"Yeah, but that would be *your* happiness," I said, opening the bag, sharing the doughnuts with Morelli. "What about mine?"

"Your happiness would be top priority."

I took a bite of doughnut. "Tempting, but no. I have a job interview at the button factory. I'm done with bond enforcement."

"When did this happen?"

"About an hour ago," I said. "Okay, I don't actually have an interview *appointment,* but Karen Slobodsky works in the personnel office, and she said I should look her up if I ever wanted a job."

"I could give you a job," Morelli said. "The pay wouldn't be great but the benefits would be pretty decent."

"Gee," I said, "that's the second scariest offer I've had today."

"And the scariest offer would be?"

I didn't think it was smart to tell Morelli about Ranger's offer of a hosing down. Morelli was wearing a gun on his hip, and Ranger wore guns on multiple parts of his body. Seemed like a bad idea to say something that might ratchet up the competition between them.

I leaned into Morelli and kissed him lightly on the mouth. "It's too scary to share," I told him. He felt nice against me, and he tasted like doughnut. I ran the tip of my tongue along his lower lip. "Yum," I said.

Morelli's fingers curled into the back of my jacket. "*Yum* is a little mild for what I'm feeling. And what I'm feeling shouldn't be happening on the sidewalk in front of the bakery. Maybe we could get together tonight."

"For pizza?"

"Yeah, that too."

I'd been taking a time-out from Morelli and Ranger, hoping to get a better grip on my feelings, but I wasn't making much progress. It was like choosing between birthday cake and a big-boy margarita. How could I possibly decide? And probably I'd be better off without either, but jeez, that wouldn't be any fun.

"Okay," I said. "I'll meet you at Pino's."

"I was thinking my house. The Mets are playing and Bob misses you."

Bob is Morelli's dog. Bob is a big, orange, incredibly huggable shaggy-haired monster with an eating disorder. Bob eats *everything*.

"No fair," I said. "You're using Bob to lure me to your house."

"Yeah," Morelli said. "So?"

I blew out a sigh. "I'll be over around six."

I drove a couple blocks down Hamilton and left-turned onto Olden. The button factory is just beyond the city limits of north Trenton. At four in the morning, it's a ten-minute drive from my apartment. At all other hours, the drive time is unpredictable. I stopped for a red light at the corner of Olden and State and just as the light flashed green I heard the pop of gunshot behind me and the *zing, zing, zing* of three rounds tearing into metal and fiberglass. I was pretty sure it was *my* metal and fiberglass, so I floored the Saturn and sailed across the intersection. I crossed North Clinton and kept going, checking my rearview mirror. Hard to tell in traffic, but I didn't think anyone was following me. My heart was racing, and I was telling myself to chill. No reason to believe this was anything more than a random shooting. Probably just some gang guy having fun, practicing his sniping. You've got to practice somewhere, right?

I fished my cell phone out of my purse and called Morelli. "Someone's taking potshots at cars on the corner of Olden and State," I told him. "You might want to send someone over to check things out."

"Are you okay?"

"I'd be better if I had that second doughnut." Okay, so this was my best try at bravado. My hands were white- knuckled gripping the wheel and my foot was shaking on the gas pedal. I sucked in some air and told myself I was just a little excited. Not panicked. Not terrified. Just a little excited. All I had to do was calm down and take a couple more deep breaths and I'd be fine.

Ten minutes later, I pulled the Saturn into the button factory parking lot. The entire factory was housed in a mammoth three-story redbrick building. The bricks were dark with age, the old-fashioned double-hung windows were grimy, and the landscaping was lunar. Dickens would have loved it. I wasn't so sure it was my thing. But then, *my thing* wasn't clearly defined anymore.

I got out and walked to the rear of the car, hoping I'd been wrong about the gunshot. I felt another dump of adrenaline when I saw the damage. I'd taken three hits. Two rounds were embedded in the back panel and one had destroyed a rear light.

No one had followed me into the lot, and I didn't see any cars lingering on the road. Wrong place, wrong time, I told myself. And I would have believed it entirely if it hadn't been for my lousy previous job and the two notes. As it was, I had to back-burner some paranoia so as not to be in a terror-induced cold sweat while trying to talk some guy into hiring me.

I crossed the lot to the large glass double doors leading to the offices, and I sashayed through the doors into the lobby. The lobby was small with a chipped tile floor and seasick green walls. Somewhere, not far off, I could hear machines stamping out buttons. Phones rang in another part of the building. I approached the reception desk and asked for Karen Slobodsky.

"Sorry," the woman said. "You're two hours too late. She just quit. Stormed out of here like hurricane Slobodsky, yelling something about sexual harassment."

"So there's a job opening?" I asked, thinking my day was finally turning lucky.

"Sure looks that way. I'll buzz her boss, Jimmy Alizzi."

Ten minutes later, I was in Alizzi's office, sitting across from him. He was at his desk and his slight frame was dwarfed by his massive furniture. He looked to be in his late thirties to early forties. He had slicked-back black hair and an accent and skin tone that had me thinking Indian.

"I will tell you now that I am not Indian," Alizzi said. "Everyone thinks I am Indian, but that is a false assumption. I come from a very small island country off the coast of India."

"Sri Lanka?"

"No, no, no," he said, wagging his bony finger at me. "Not Sri Lanka. My country is even smaller. We are a very proud people, so you must be careful not to make ethnic slurs."

"Sure. You want to tell me the name of this country?"

"Latorran."

"Never heard of it."

"You see, already you are treading in very dangerous waters."

I squelched a grimace.

"So, you were a bounty hunter," he said, skimming over my résumé, eyebrows raised. "That is a quite exciting job. Why would you want to quit such a job?"

"I'm looking for something that has more potential for advancement."

"Oh dear, that would be *my* job you would eventually be seeking."

"Yes, well I'm sure it would take years, and then who knows . . . you might be president of the company by then."

"You are an outrageous flatterer," he said. "I like that. And what would you do if I were to ask you for sexual favors? Would you threaten to sue me?"

"No. I guess I'd ignore you. Unless you got physical. Then I'd have to kick you in a place that hurt a lot and you probably wouldn't be able to father any children."

"That sounds fair," he said. "It happens that I have an immediate position to fill, so you're hired. You can start tomorrow, promptly at eight o'clock. Do not be late."

Wonderful. I have a real job in a nice clean office where no one will shoot at me. I should be happy, yes? This was what I wanted, wasn't it? Then why do I feel so depressed?

I dragged myself down the stairs to the lobby and out to the parking lot. I found my car and the depression deepened. I hated my car. Not that it was a bad car. It just wasn't the *right* car. Not to mention, it would be great to have a car that didn't have three bullet holes in it.

Maybe I needed another doughnut.

A half hour later, I was back in my apartment. I'd stopped in at Tasty Pastry and left with a day-old birthday cake. The cake said HAPPY BIRTHDAY LARRY. I don't know how Larry celebrated his birthday, but apparently it was without cake. Larry's loss was my gain. If you want to get happy, birthday cake is the way to go. This was a yellow cake with thick, disgusting white frosting made with lard and artificial butter and artificial vanilla and a truckload of sugar. It was decorated with big gunky roses made out of pink and yellow and purple frosting. It was three layers thick with lemon cream between the layers. And it was designed to serve eight people, so it was just the right size.

I dropped my clothes on the floor and dug into the cake. I gave a chunk of cake to Rex, and I worked on the rest. I ate all the pieces with the big pink roses. I was starting to feel nauseous, but I pressed on. I ate all the pieces with the big yellow roses. I had a purple rose and a couple roseless pieces left. I couldn't do it. I couldn't eat any more cake. I staggered into my bedroom. I needed a nap.

I dropped a T-shirt over my head and pulled on a pair of Scooby-Doo boxers with an elastic waist. God, don't you love clothes with elastic? I had one knee on the bed when I saw the note pinned to my pillowcase. BE AFRAID. BE VERY AFRAID. NEXT TIME I'LL AIM HIGHER.

I thought I'd be more afraid if I hadn't just eaten

five pieces of birthday cake. As it was, I was mostly afraid of throwing up. I looked under the bed, behind the shower curtain, and in all the closets. No knuckle-dragging monsters anywhere. I slid the bolt home on the front door and shuffled back to the bedroom.

Now, here's the thing. This isn't the first time some-one's broken into my apartment. In fact, people regu-larly break in. Ranger slides in like smoke. Morelli has a key. And various bad guys and psychos have man-aged to breach the three locks I keep on the door. Some have even left threatening messages. So I wasn't as freaked out as I might have been prior to my career in bounty huntering. My immediate feelings ran more toward numb despair. I wanted all the scary things to go away. I was tired of scary. I'd quit my scary job, and now I wanted the scary people out of my life. I didn't want to be kidnapped ever again. I didn't want to be held at knifepoint or gunpoint. I didn't want to be threatened, stalked, or run off the road by a homicidal maniac.

I crawled under the covers and pulled the quilt over my head. I was almost asleep when the quilt was yanked back. I let out a shriek and stared up at Ranger.

"What the heck are you doing?" I yelled at him, grabbing at the quilt.

"Visiting, Babe."

"Did you ever think about ringing a doorbell?"

Ranger smiled down at me. "That would take all the fun out of it."

"I didn't know you were interested in fun."

He sat on the side of the bed and the smile widened. "You smell good enough to eat," Ranger said. "You smell like a party."

"It's birthday cake breath. And are we looking at an-other double entendre?"

"Yeah," Ranger said, "but it's not going anywhere.

I have to get back to work. Tank's waiting for me with the motor running. I just wanted to find out if you're serious about quitting."

"I got a job at the button factory. I start tomorrow."

He reached across and removed the note from the pillowcase next to me. "New boyfriend?"

"Someone broke in while I was out. And I guess he shot at me this afternoon."

Ranger stood. "You should discourage people from doing that. Do you need help?"

"Not yet."

"Babe," Ranger said. And he left.

I listened carefully, but I didn't hear the front door open or close. I got up and tiptoed through the apartment. No Ranger. All the locks were locked and the bolt was in place. I suppose he could have gone out the living room window, but he would have had to climb down the side of the building like Spider-Man.

The phone rang, and I waited to see the number pop up on my caller ID. It was Lula. "Yo," I said.

"Yo, your ass. You got some nerve sticking me with this job."

"You volunteered."

"I must've had sunstroke. A person has to be nuts to want this job."

"Something go wrong?"

"Hell, yes. *Everything's* wrong. I could use some assistance here. I'm trying to snag Willie Martin, and he's not cooperating."

"How uncooperative is he?"

"He hauled his nasty ass out of his apartment and left me handcuffed to his big stupid bed."

"That's pretty uncooperative."

"Yeah, and it gets worse. I sort of don't have any clothes on."

"Omigod! Did he attack you?"

"It's a little more complicated than that. He was in the shower when I busted in. You ever see Willie Martin naked? He is *fine*. He used to play pro ball until he made a mess of his knee and had to turn to boosting cars."

"Un hunh."

"Well, one thing led to another and here I am chained to his hunk-of-junk bed. Hell, it's not like I get it regular, you know. I'm real picky about my men. And besides, anybody would've jumped those bones. He's got muscles on muscles and a butt you want to sink your teeth into."

The mental image had me considering turning vegetarian.

Willie Martin lived in a third-floor loft in a graffiti-riddled warehouse that contained a ground-floor chop shop. It was located on the seven-hundred block of Stark Street, an area of urban decay that rivaled Iraqi bomb sites.

I parked behind Lula's red Firebird and transferred my five-shot Smith & Wesson from my purse to my jacket pocket. I'm not much of a gun person and almost never carry one, but I was sufficiently creeped out by the shooting and the notes that I didn't want to venture onto Stark Street unarmed. I locked the car, bypassed the rickety open-cage service elevator on the ground floor, and trudged up two flights of stairs. The stairwell opened to a small grimy foyer and a door with a size-nine high-heeled boot print on it. I guess Willie hadn't answered on the first knock and Lula got impatient.

I tried the doorknob, and the door swung open. Thank God for small favors because I'd never had any success at kicking in a door. I tentatively stuck my head in and called "Hello."

"Hello, yourself," Lula said. "And don't say no more. I'm not in a good mood. Just unlock these piece-of-crap

handcuffs and stand back because I need fries. I need
a whole *shitload* of fries. I'm having a fast-food emergency."

Lula was across the room, wrapped in a sheet, one
hand cuffed to the iron headboard of the bed, the other
hand holding the sheet together.

I pulled the universal handcuff key out of my pocket
and looked around the room. "Where are your clothes?"

"He took them. Do you believe that? Said he was going to teach me a lesson not to go after him. I tell you,
you can't trust a man. They get what they want and then
next thing they got their tighty whities in their pocket
and they're out the door. I don't know what he was so
upset about, anyway. I was just doing my job. He said,
'Was that good for you?' And I said, 'Oh yeah, baby,
it was real good.' And then I tried to cuff him. Hell,
truth is it wasn't all that good, and besides, I'm a professional bounty hunter now. Bring 'em back dead or
alive, with or without their pants, right? I had an obligation to cuff him."

"Yeah, well next time put your clothes on *before* you
try to cuff a guy."

Lula unlocked the cuffs and tied a knot in the sheet
to hold it closed. "That's good advice. I'm gonna remember that. That's the kind of advice I need to be a
first-class bounty hunter. At least he forgot to take my
purse. I'd be really annoyed if he'd taken my purse."
She went to a chest on the far wall, pulled out one of
Willie's T-shirts and a pair of gym shorts, and put them
on. Then she scooped the rest of the clothes out of the
chest, carried them to the window, and threw them out.

"Okay," Lula said, "I'm starting to feel better now.
Thanks for coming here to help me. And good news, it
looks like no one's stolen your car. I saw it still sitting
at the curb." Lula went to the closet and scooped up
more clothes. Suits, shoes, and jackets. All went out the

window. "I'm on a roll now," she said, looking around the loft. "What else we got that can go out the window? You think we can fit his big-ass TV out the window? Hey, how about some kitchen appliances? Go get me his toaster." She crossed the room, grabbed a table lamp, and brought it to the window. "Hey!" she yelled, head out the window, eyes focused on the street. "Get away from that car. Willie, is that you? What the hell are you doing?"

I ran to the window and looked out. Willie Martin was whaling away at my car with a sledgehammer.

"I'll show you to throw my clothes outta the window," he said, taking a swing at the right rear quarter panel.

"You dumb premature ejaculator," Lula shouted at him. "You dumb-ass moron! That's not my car."

"Oh. Oops," Willie said. "Which one's *your* car?"

Lula hauled a Glock out of her purse, squeezed off two rounds in Willie's direction, and Willie left the scene. One of the rounds pinged off my car roof. And the other round made a small hole in my windshield.

"Must be something wrong with the sight on this gun," Lula said to me. "Sorry about that."

I trudged down the stairs and stood on the sidewalk examining my car. Deep scratch in roof from misplaced bullet. Hole in windshield plus embedded bullet in passenger seat. Bashed-in right rear quarter panel and right passenger-side door from sledgehammer. Previous damage from creepy gun attack by insane stalker. And someone had spray painted EAT ME on the driver's side door.

"Your car's a mess," Lula said. "I don't know what it is with you and cars."

TWO

Morelli drives an SUV. He used to own a 4×4 truck, but he traded it in so Bob could ride around with him and be more comfortable. This isn't normal behavior for Morelli men. Morelli men are known for being charming but worthless drunks who rarely care about the comfort of their wife and kids, much less the dog. How Joe escaped the Morelli Man syndrome is a mystery. For a while he seemed destined to follow in his father's footsteps, but somewhere in his late twenties, Joe stopped chasing women and fighting in bars and started working at being a good cop. He inherited his house from his Aunt Rose. He adopted Bob. And he decided, after years of hit-and-run sex, he was in love with me. Go figure that. Joseph Morelli with a house, a dog, a steady job, and an SUV. And on *odd* days of the month he woke up wanting to marry me. It turns out I only want to marry him on *even* days of the month, so to date we've been spared commitment.

When I arrived at Morelli's house, his SUV was parked curbside and Morelli and Bob were sitting on Morelli's tiny front porch. Usually Bob goes gonzo when he sees me, jumping around all smiley face. Today Bob was sitting there drooling, looking sad.

"What's with Bob?" I asked Morelli.

"I don't think he feels good. He was like this when I came home."

Bob stood and hunched. *"Gak,"* Bob said. And he hacked up a sock and a lot of Bob slime. He looked down at the sock. And then he looked up at me. And then he got happy. He jumped around, doing his goofy dance. I gave him a hug and he wandered off, tail wagging, into the house.

"Guess we can go in now," Morelli said. He got to his feet, slid his arm around my shoulders, and hugged me to him for a friendly kiss. He broke from the kiss and his eyes strayed to my car. "I don't suppose you'd want to tell me about the body damage?"

"Sledgehammer."

"Of course."

"You're pretty calm about all this," I said to him.

"I'm a calm kind of guy."

"No, you're not. You go nuts over this stuff. You always yell when people go after me with a sledgehammer."

"Yeah, but in the past you haven't liked that. I'm thinking if I start yelling it might screw up my chances of getting you naked. And I'm desperate. I really need to get you naked. Besides, you quit the bonds office, right? Maybe your life will settle down now. How'd the interview go?"

"I got the job. I start tomorrow."

I was wearing a T-shirt and jeans. Morelli grinned down at me and slid his hands under my T-shirt. "We should celebrate."

His hands felt nice against my skin, but I was starving and I didn't want to encourage any further celebrating until I got my pizza. He pulled me close and kissed his way up my neck. His lips moved to my ear and my temple and by the time he got to my mouth I was thinking the pizza could wait.

And then we heard it . . . the pizza delivery car coming down the street, stopping at the curb.

Morelli cut his eyes to the kid getting out of the car. "Maybe if we ignore him he'll go away."

The steaming extra-large, extra cheese, green peppers, pepperoni pizza smell oozed from the box the kid was carrying. The smell rushed over the porch and into the house. Bob's toenails clattered on the polished wood hall floor as he took off from the kitchen and galloped for all he was worth at the kid.

Morelli stepped back from me and snagged Bob by the collar just as he was about to catapult himself off the porch.

"Ulk," Bob said, stopping abruptly, tongue out, eyes bugged, feet off the ground.

"Minor setback with the celebration plan," Morelli said.

"No rush," I told him. "We have all night."

Morelli's eyes got soft and dark and dreamy. Sort of the way Bob's eyes got when he ate Tastykake Butterscotch Krimpets and then someone rubbed his belly. "All right," Morelli said. "I like the way that sounds."

Two minutes later, we were on the couch in Morelli's living room, watching the pregame show, eating pizza, and drinking beer.

"I heard you were working on the Barroni case," I said to Morelli. "Having any luck with it?"

Morelli took a second piece of pizza. "I have a lot out on it. So far nothing's come in."

Michael Barroni mysteriously disappeared eight days ago. He was sixty-two years old and in good health when he vanished. He owned a nice house in the heart of the Burg on Roebling and a hardware store on the corner of Rudd and Liberty Street. He left behind a wife, two dogs, and three adult sons. One of the

Barroni boys graduated with me, and one graduated two years earlier with Morelli.

There aren't a lot of secrets in the Burg and according to Burg gossip Michael Barroni didn't have a girlfriend, didn't play the numbers, and didn't have mob ties. His hardware store was running in the black. He didn't suffer from depression. He didn't do a lot of drinking, and he wasn't hooked on Levitra.

Barroni was last seen closing and locking the back door to the hardware store at the end of the day. He got into his car, drove away . . . and *poof*. No more Michael Barroni.

"Did you ever find Barroni's car?" I asked Morelli.

"No. No car. No body. No sign of struggle. He was alone when Sol Rosen saw him lock up and take off. Sol said he was putting out trash from his diner and he saw Barroni leave. He said Barroni looked normal. Maybe distracted. Sol said Barroni waved but didn't say anything."

"Do you think it's a random crime? Barroni was in the wrong place at the wrong time?"

"No. Barroni lived four blocks from his store. Every day he went straight home from work. Four blocks through the Burg. If something had gone down on Barroni's usual route home, someone would have heard or seen something. The day Barroni disappeared he went someplace else. He didn't take his usual route home."

"Maybe he just got tired of it all. Maybe he started driving west and didn't stop until he got to Flagstaff."

Morelli fed his pizza crust to Bob. "I'm going to tell you something that's just between us. We've had two other guys disappear on the exact same day as Barroni. They were both from Stark Street, and a missing person on Stark Street isn't big news, so no one's paid much attention. I ran across them when I checked Barroni's missing-person status.

"Both these guys owned their own businesses. They both locked up at the end of the day and were never seen again. One of the men was real stable. He had a wife and kids. He went to church. He ran a bar on Stark Street, but he was clean. The other guy, Benny Gorman, owned a garage. Probably a chump-change chop shop. He'd done time for armed robbery and grand theft auto. And two months ago he was charged with assault with a deadly weapon. Took a tire iron to a guy and almost killed him. He was supposed to go to trial last week but failed to appear. Ordinarily I'd say he skipped because of the charge but I'm not so sure on this one."

"Did Vinnie bond Gorman out?"

"Yeah. I talked to Connie. She handed Gorman off to Ranger."

"And you think the three guys are connected?"

A commercial came on and Morelli channel-surfed through a bunch of stations. "Don't know. I just have a feeling. It's too strong a coincidence."

I gave Bob the last piece of pizza and snuggled closer to Morelli.

"I have feelings about other things, too," Morelli said, sliding an arm around my shoulders, his fingertips skimming along my neck and down my arm. "Would you like me to tell you about my other feelings?"

My toes curled in my shoes and I got warm in a bunch of private places. And that was the last we saw of the game.

Morelli is an early riser in many ways. I had a memory of him kissing my bare shoulder, whispering an obscene suggestion, and leaving the bed. He returned a short time later with his hair still damp from the shower. He kissed me again and wished me luck with my new job. And then he was gone . . . off on his mission to rid Trenton of bad guys.

It was still dark in Morelli's bedroom. The bed was warm and comfy. Bob was sprawled on Morelli's side of the bed, snuffling into Morelli's pillow. I burrowed under the quilt, and when I reawakened the sunlight was pouring into the room through a break in the curtain. I had a moment of absolute delicious satisfaction immediately followed by panic. According to the bedside clock it was nine o'clock. I was massively late for my first day at the button factory!

I scrambled out of bed, gathered my clothes up off the floor, and tugged them on. I didn't bother with makeup or hair. No time. I took the stairs at a run, grabbed my purse and my car keys, and bolted out of the house.

I skirted traffic as best I could, pulled into the button factory parking lot on two wheels, parked, jumped out of the car, and hit the pavement running. The time was nine-thirty. I was an hour and a half late.

I took the stairs to save time and I was sweating by the time I skidded to a stop in Alizzi's office.

"You are late," Alizzi said.

"Yes, but . . ."

He wagged his finger at me. "This is not a good thing. I told you that you must be on time. And look at you. You are in a T-shirt. If you are going to be late you should at least wear something that is revealing and shows me your breasts. You are fired. Go away."

"No! Give me another chance. Just one more chance. If you give me another chance I'll wear something revealing tomorrow."

"Will you perform a lewd act?"

"What kind of lewd act?"

"Something very, very, very lewd. There would have to be nakedness and body fluids."

"*Ick*. No!"

"Well then, you are still fired."

"That's horrible. I'm going to report you for sexual harassment."

"It will only serve to enhance my reputation."

Unh. Mental head slap.

"Okay. Fine," I said. "I didn't want this job anyway."

I turned on my heel and flounced out of Alizzi's office, down the stairs, through the lobby, and crossed the lot to my bashed-in, bullet-riddled, spray-painted car. I gave the door a vicious kick, wrenched it open, and slid behind the wheel. I punched Metallica into the sound system, cranked it up until the fillings in my teeth were vibrating, and motored across town.

By the time I got to Hamilton I was feeling pretty decent. I had the whole day to myself. True, I wasn't making any money, but there was always tomorrow, right? I stopped at Tasty Pastry, bought a bag of doughnuts, and drove three blocks into the Burg to Mary Lou Stankovic's house. Mary Lou was my best friend all through school. She's married now and has a bunch of kids. We're still friends but our paths don't cross as much as they used to.

I walked an obstacle course from my car to Mary Lou's front door, around bikes, dismembered action figures, soccer balls, remote-control cars, beheaded Barbie dolls, and plastic guns that looked frighteningly real.

"Omigod," Mary Lou said when she opened the door. "It's the angel of mercy. Are those doughnuts?"

"Do you need some?"

"I need a new life, but I'll make do with doughnuts."

I handed the doughnuts off to Mary Lou and followed her into the kitchen. "You have a good life. You like your life."

"Not today. I have three kids home sick with colds. The dog has diarrhea. And I think there was a hole in the condom we used last night."

"Aren't you on the pill?"

"Gives me water retention."

I could hear the kids in the living room, coughing at the television, whining at each other. Mary Lou's kids were cute when they were asleep and for the first fifteen minutes after they'd had a bath. All other times the kids were a screaming advertisement for birth control. It wasn't that they were bad kids. Okay, so they dismembered every doll that came through the door, but they hadn't yet barbecued the dog. That was a good sign, right? It was more that Mary Lou's kids had an excess of energy. Mary Lou said it came from the Stankovic side of the family. I thought it might be coming from the bakery. That's where I got *my* energy.

Mary Lou opened the doughnut bag and the kids came rushing into the kitchen.

"They can hear a bakery bag crinkle a mile away," Mary Lou said.

I'd brought four doughnuts so we gave one to each kid and Mary Lou and I shared a doughnut over coffee.

"What's new?" Mary Lou wanted to know.

"I quit my job at the bonds office."

"Any special reason?"

"No. My reasoning was sort of vague. I got a job at the button factory, but I spent the night with Joe to celebrate and then I overslept this morning and was late for my first day and got fired."

Mary Lou took a sip of coffee and waggled her eyebrows at me. "Was it worth it?"

I took a moment to consider. "Yeah."

Mary Lou gave her head a small shake. "He's been making trouble worthwhile for you since you were six years old. I don't know why you don't marry him."

My reasoning was sort of vague on that one, too.

It was late morning when I left Mary Lou. I cut over two blocks to High Street and parked in front of my parents' house. It was a small house on a small lot. It had three bedrooms and bath up and a living room, dining room, kitchen down. It shared a common wall with a mirror image owned by Mabel Markowitz. Mabel was old beyond imagining. Her husband had passed on and her kids were off on their own, so she lived alone in the house, baking coffee cakes and watching television. Her half of the house is painted lime green because the paint had been on clearance when she'd needed it. My parents' house is painted Gulden mustard yellow and dark brown. I'm not sure which house is worse. In the fall my mom puts pumpkins on the front porch and it all seems to work. In the spring the paint scheme is depressing as hell.

Since it was the end of September, the pumpkins were on display and a cardboard witch on a broomstick was stuck to the front door. Halloween was just four weeks away, and the Burg is big on holidays.

Grandma Mazur was at the front door when I set foot on the porch. Grandma moved in with my parents when my Grandpa Mazur got a hot pass to heaven compliments of more than a half century of bacon fat and butter cookies.

"We heard you quit your job," Grandma said. "We've been calling and calling, but you haven't been answering your phone. I need to know the details. I got a beauty parlor appointment this afternoon and I gotta get the story straight."

"Not much of a story," I said, following Grandma into the hallway foyer. "I just thought it was time for a change."

"That's it? Time for a change? I can't tell people that story. It's boring. I need something better. How about we tell them you're pregnant? Or maybe we could say you got a rare blood disease. Or there was a big contract put on your head unless you gave up being a bounty hunter."

"Sorry," I said. "None of those things are true."

"Yeah, but that don't matter. Everybody knows you can't believe everything you hear."

My mother was at the dining room table with a bunch of round pieces of paper spread out in front of her. My sister, Valerie, was getting married in a week, and my mother was still working on the seating arrangements.

"I can't make this work," my mother said. "These round tables don't hold the right number of people. I'm going to have to seat the Krugers at two different tables. And no one gets along with old Mrs. Kruger."

"You should do away with the seating chart," Grandma said. "Just open the doors to the hall and let them fight for their seats."

I love my sister, but I'd deport her to Bosnia if I thought I could get away with it and it'd get me out of her wedding. I'm supposed to be her maid of honor and somehow through my lack of participation and a fabric swatch inaccuracy I've been ordered a gown that makes me look like a giant eggplant.

"We heard you quit your job," my mother said to me. "Thank goodness. I can finally sleep at night knowing you're not running around the worst parts of town chasing after criminals. And I understand you have a wonderful job at the button factory. Marjorie Kuzak called yesterday and told us all about it. Her daughter works in the employment office."

"Actually, I sort of got fired from that job," I said.

"Already? How could you possibly get fired on your first day?"

"It's complicated. I don't suppose you know anybody who's hiring?"

"What kind of job are you looking for?" Grandma asked.

"Professional. Something with career advancement potential."

"I saw a sign up at the cleaners," Grandma said. "I don't know about career advancement, but they do a lot of professional pressing. I see a lot of people taking their business suits there."

"I was hoping for something a little more challenging."

"Dry cleaning's challenging," Grandma said. "It's not easy getting all them spots out. And you gotta have people skills. I heard them talking behind the counter about how hard it was to find someone with people skills."

"And no one would shoot at you," my mother said. "No one ever robs a dry cleaner."

I had to admit, that part appealed to me. It would be nice not to have to worry about getting shot. Maybe working at the dry cleaners would be an okay temporary job until the right thing came along.

I got myself a cup of coffee and poked through the refrigerator, searching for food. I settled on a piece of apple pie and carted the coffee and pie back to the dining room, where my mom was still arranging the paper tables.

"What's going on in the Burg?" I asked her.

"Harry Farstein died yesterday. Heart attack. He's at Stiva's."

"He's gonna have a viewing tonight," Grandma said. "It's gonna be a good one, too. His lodge will be there. And Lydia Farstein is the drama queen of the Burg. She'll be carrying on something awful. If you haven't got anything better to do, you should come to the viewing with me. I could use a ride."

Grandma loved going to viewings. Stiva's Funeral Home was the social center of the Burg. I thought having my thumb amputated would be a preferred activity.

"And everyone's going to be talking about the

Barroni thing," Grandma said. "I can't believe he hasn't turned up. It's like he was abducted by Martians."

Okay, now this interested me. Morelli was working on the Barroni disappearance. And Ranger was working on the Gorman disappearance, which might be connected to the Barroni disappearance. I was glad I wasn't working on either of those cases, but on the other hand, I felt a smidgeon left out. So sue me, I'm nosy.

"Sure," I said. "I'll pick you up at seven o'clock."

"Your father got gravy on his gray slacks," my mother said. "If you're going to apply for a job at the cleaner, would you mind taking the slacks with you? It would save me a trip."

A half hour later, I had a job with Kan Klean. The hours were seven to three. They were open seven days a week, and I agreed to work weekends. The pay wasn't great, but I could wear jeans and a T-shirt to work, and they confirmed my mother's suspicion that they'd never been held up and that to date none of their employees had been shot while on the job. I handed over the gravy-stained slacks and agreed to show up at seven the next morning.

I didn't feel quite as nauseated as I had after getting the button factory job. So I was making progress, right?

I drove three blocks down Hamilton and stopped at the bonds office to say hello.

"Look what the wind blew in," Lula said when she saw me. "I heard you got the job at the button factory. How come you're not working?"

"I spent the night with Morelli and overslept. So I was late rolling in to work."

"And?"

"And I got fired."

"That was fast," Lula said. "You're good. It takes most people a couple days to get fired."

"Maybe it all worked out for the best. I got another job already at Kan Klean."

"Do you get a discount?" Lula wanted to know. "I got some dry cleaning to send out. You could pick it up tomorrow here at the office on your way to work."

"Sure," I said. "Why not." I shuffled through the small stack of files on Connie's desk. "Anything fun come in?"

"Yeah, it's all fun," Connie said. "We got a rapist. We got a guy who beat up his girlfriend. We got a couple pushers."

"I'm doing the DV this afternoon," Lula said.

"DV?"

"Domestic violence. My time's real valuable now that I'm a bounty hunter. I gotta use abbreviations. Like I'm doing the DV in the PM."

I heard Vinnie growl from his inner office. "Jesus H. Christmas," he said. "Who would have thought my life would come to this?"

"Hey, Vinnie," I yelled to him. "How's it going?"

Vinnie poked his head out his door. "I gave you a job when you needed one and now you desert me. Where's the gratitude?"

Vinnie is a couple inches taller than me and has the slim, boneless body of a ferret. His coloring is Mediterranean. His hair looks like it's slicked back with olive oil. He wears pointy-toed shoes and a lot of gold. He's the family pervert. He's married to Harry-the-Hammer's daughter. And in spite of his personality shortcomings (or maybe because of them) he's an okay bail bondsman. Vinnie understands the criminal mind.

"You didn't *give* me the job," I said to Vinnie. "I blackmailed you into it. And I got good numbers when I was working for you. My apprehension rate was close to ninety percent."

"You were lucky," Vinnie said.

This was true.

Lula took her big black leather purse from the bottom file drawer and stuffed it under her arm. "I'm going out. I'm gonna get that DV and I'm gonna kick his ass all the way back to jail."

"No!" Vinnie said. "You're *not* gonna kick his ass *anywhere*. Ass kicking is not entirely legal. You will introduce yourself and you will cuff him. And then you will escort him to the station in a civilized manner."

"Sure," Lula said. "I knew that."

"Maybe you want to go with her," Vinnie said to me. "Since it looks like you don't have anything better to do."

"I start a new job tomorrow. I got a job at Kan Klean."

Vinnie's eyes lit up. "Do you get a discount? I got a shitload of dry cleaning."

"I wouldn't mind if you rode along," Lula said. "This guy's gonna be slam bam, thank you, ma'am. And then we drop his sorry behind off at the police station and go get some burgers."

"I don't want to get involved," I told her.

"You can stay in the Firebird. It'll only take me a minute to cuff this guy and drag . . . I mean, *escort* him out to the car."

"Okay," I said, "but I *really* don't want to get involved."

A half hour later we were at the public housing project on the other side of town and Lula was motoring the Firebird down Carter Street, looking for 2475A.

"Here's the plan," Lula said. "You just sit tight and I'll go get this guy. I got pepper spray, a stun gun, a head-bashing flashlight, two pairs of cuffs, and the BP in my purse."

"BP?"

"Big Persuader. That's what I call my Glock." She pulled to the curb and jerked her thumb at the apartment building. "This here's the building. I'll be back in a minute."

"Try to keep your clothes on," I said to her.

"Hunh," Lula said. "Funny."

Lula walked to the door and knocked. The door opened. Lula disappeared inside the house and the door closed behind her. I looked at my watch and decided I'd give her ten minutes. After ten minutes I'd do something, but I wasn't sure what it would be. I could call the police. I could call Vinnie. I could run around the outside of the building yelling *fire!* Or I could do the least appealing of all the options—I could go in after her.

I didn't have to make the decision because the front door opened after just two minutes. Lula tumbled out the door, rolled off the stoop, landed on a patch of hard packed dirt that would have been lawn in a more prosperous neighborhood, and the door slammed shut behind her. Lula scrambled to her feet, tugged her spandex lime green miniskirt back down over her ass, and marched up to the door.

"Open this door!" she yelled. "You open this door right now or there's gonna be big trouble." She tried the doorknob. She rang the bell. She kicked the door with her Via Spigas. The door didn't open. Lula turned and looked over at me. "Don't worry," she said. "This here's just a minor setback. They don't understand the severity of the situation."

I slid lower in my seat and became engrossed in the mechanics of my seat belt.

"I'm giving you one more chance to open this door and then I'm going to take action," Lula yelled at the house.

The door didn't open.

"Hunh," Lula said. She backed off from the door and cut over to a front window. Curtains had been drawn across the window, but the flicker of a television screen could faintly be seen through the sheers. Lula stood on tiptoes and tried to open the window, but the window wouldn't budge. "I'm starting to get annoyed now," Lula said. "You know what I think? I think this here's an accident waiting to happen."

Lula pulled her big Maglite out of her purse, set her purse on the ground, and smashed the window with the Maglite. She bent to retrieve her purse, and what remained of the window was blown out with a shotgun blast from inside. If Lula hadn't bent down to get her purse, the surgeon of the day at St. Francis would have spent the rest of his afternoon picking pellets out of her.

"What the F!" Lula said. And Lula did a fast sprint to the car. She wrenched the driver's-side door open, crammed herself behind the wheel, and there was a second shotgun blast through the apartment window. "That dumb son of a bitch shot at me!" Lula said.

"Yeah," I said. "I saw. I was impressed you could run like that in those heels."

"I wasn't expecting him to shoot at me. He had no call to do that."

"You broke his window."

"It was an accident."

"It wasn't an accident. I saw you do it with the Maglite."

"That guy's nuts," Lula said, taking off from the curb, leaving a couple inches of rubber on the road. "He should be reported to somebody. He should be arrested."

"*You* were supposed to arrest him."

"I was supposed to *escort* him. Vinnie made that real clear. *Escort him.* And I could escort the hell out of him except I'm hungry. I gotta get something to eat," Lula said. "I work better on a happy stomach. I could take that woman-beating moron in anytime I want, so what's the rush, right? Might as well get a burger first, that's what I think. And anyway, he might be more Ranger's speed. I wouldn't want to step on Ranger's toes. You know how Ranger likes all that shooting stuff."

"I thought you liked the shooting stuff."

"I don't want to hog it."

"Considerate of you."

"Yeah, I'm real considerate," Lula said, turning into a Cluck-in-a-Bucket drive-thru. "I'm seriously thinking of giving this case to Ranger."

"What if Ranger doesn't want it?"

"You think he'd turn down a good case like this?"

"Yeah."

"Hunh," Lula said. "Wouldn't that be a bitch?"

She got a Cluck Burger with cheese, a large side of fries, a chocolate shake, and an Apple Clucky Pie. I wasn't in a Cluck-in-a-Bucket mood so I passed. Lula finished off the last piece of the pie and looked at her watch. "I'd go back and root out that nutso loser, but it's getting late. Don't you think it's late?"

"Almost three o'clock."

"Practically quitting time."

Especially for me, since I quit yesterday.

THREE

I'm not the world's best cook, but I have some specialties, and almost all of them include peanut butter. You can't go wrong with peanut butter. Today I was having a peanut butter and olive and potato chip sandwich for dinner. Very efficient since it combines legumes and vegetables plus some worthless white bread carbohydrates all in one tidy package. I was standing in the kitchen, washing the sandwich down with a cold Corona, and Morelli called.

"What are you doing?" he asked.

"Eating."

"Why aren't you eating in my house?"

"I don't live in your house."

"You were living in my house last night."

"I was *visiting* your house last night. That's different from living. Living involves commitment and closet allocation."

"We don't seem to be all that good at commitment, but I'd be happy to give up a couple closets in exchange for wild gorilla sex at least five days out of seven."

"Good grief."

"Okay, four days out of seven, but that's my best offer. How's the new job at the button factory going?"

"Got fired. And it was your fault. I was late for work on my first day."

I could feel Morelli smile at the other end of the line. "Am I good, or what?"

"I got a job at Kan Klean. I start tomorrow."

"We should celebrate."

"No celebrating! That's what lost me the button factory job. Don't you want to ask me if I can get you discount cleaning?"

"I don't clean my clothes. I wear them until they fall apart and then I throw them away."

I finished the sandwich and chugged the beer. "I've got to go," I told Morelli. "I told Grandma I'd pick her up at seven. We're going to Harry Farstein's viewing at Stiva's."

"I can't compete with that," Morelli said.

Grandma was waiting at the door when I drove up. She was dressed in powder blue slacks, a matching floral-print blouse, a white cotton cardigan, and white tennis shoes. She had her big black patent-leather purse in the crook of her arm. Her gray hair was freshly set in tight little baloney curls that marched across her pink skull. Her nails were newly manicured and painted fire-engine red. Her lipstick matched her nails.

"I'm ready to go," she said, hurrying over to the car. "We don't get a move on, we're not gonna get a good seat. There's gonna be a crowd tonight and ever since Spiro took off, Stiva hasn't been all that good with organization. Spiro was a nasty little cockroach but he could organize a crowd like no one else."

Spiro was Constantine Stiva's kid. I went to school with Spiro and near the end I guess I inadvertently helped him disappear. He was a miserable excuse for a human being, involved in running guns and God knows what else. He tried to kill Grandma and me, there was a shoot-out and a spectacular fire at the funeral home, and somehow, in the confusion, Spiro vanished into thin air.

When I got the notes saying I'M BACK and DID YOU THINK I WAS DEAD? Spiro was one of the potential psychos who came to mind. Sad to say, he was just one name among many. And he wasn't the most likely candidate. Spiro had been a lot of things . . . dumb wasn't one of them. Plus I couldn't see Spiro being obsessed with revenge. Spiro had wanted money and power.

The funeral home was on Hamilton, a couple blocks down from the bail bonds office. It had been rebuilt after the fire and was now a jumble of new brick construction and old Victorian mansion. The two-story front half of the house was white aluminum siding with black shutters. A large porch wrapped around the front and south side of the house. Some of the viewing rooms and all of the embalming rooms were located in the new brick addition at the rear. The preferred viewing rooms were in the front and Stiva had given them names: the Blue Salon, the Rest in Peace Salon, and the Executive Slumber Salon.

It was a five-minute drive from my parents' house to Stiva's. I dropped Grandma at the door and found street parking half a block away. When I got to the funeral home Grandma was waiting for me at the entrance to the Executive Slumber Salon.

"I don't know why they call this the Executive Salon," she said. "It's not like Stiva's laying a lot of executives to rest. Think it's just a big phony-baloney name."

The Executive Slumber Salon was the largest of the viewing rooms and was already packed with people. Lydia Farstein was at the far end, one hand dramatically touching the open casket. She was in her seventies and looked surprisingly happy for a woman who had just lost her husband of fifty-odd years.

"Looks like Lydia's been hitting the sauce," Grandma said. "Last time I saw her that happy was . . . never. I'm going back to give her my condolences and take a look at Harry."

Looking at dead people wasn't high on my list of favorite activities, so I separated from Grandma and wandered to the far side of the entrance hall, where complimentary cookies had been set out.

I scarfed down a couple sugar cookies and a couple spice cookies and I felt a prickling sensation at the back of my neck. I turned and looked across the room and saw Morelli's Grandma Bella glaring at me. Grandma Bella is a white-haired old lady who dresses in black and looks like an extra out of a *Godfather* flashback. She has visions, and she puts spells on people. And she scares the crap out of me.

Bitsy Mullen was standing next to me at the cookie table. "Omigod," Bitsy said. "I hope she's glaring at you and not me. Last week she put the eye on Francine Blainey, and Francine got a bunch of big herpes sores all over her face."

The eye is like Grandma Bella voodoo. She puts her finger to her eye and she mumbles something and whatever calamity happens to you after that you can pin on the eye. I guess it's a little like believing in hell. You hope it's bogus, but you never really know for sure, do you?

"I'm betting Francine got herpes from her worthless boyfriend," I said to Bitsy.

"I'm not taking any chances," Bitsy said. "I'm going to hide in the ladies' room until the viewing is over. Oh no! Omigod. Here she comes. What should I do? I can't breathe. I'm gonna faint."

"Probably she just wants a cookie," I said to Bitsy. Not that I believed it. Grandma Bella had her beady eyes fixed on me. I'd seen the look before and it wasn't good.

"You!" Grandma Bella said, pointing her finger at me. "You broke my Joseph's heart."

"No way," I said. "Swear to God."

"Is there a ring on your finger?"

"N-N-No."

"It's a scandal," she said. "You've brought disgrace to my house. A respectable woman would be married and have children by now. You go to his house and tempt him with your body and then you leave. Shame on you. Shame. Shame. I should put the eye on you. Make your teeth fall out of your head. Turn your hair gray. Cause your female parts to shrink away until there's nothing left of them."

Grandma Mazur elbowed her way through the crush of people around the cookie table. "What's going on here?" she asked. "What'd I miss about female parts?"

"Your granddaughter is a Jezebel," Grandma Bella said. "Jumping in and out of my Joseph's bed."

"Half the women in the Burg have been in and out of his bed," Grandma Mazur said. "Heck, half the women in the state . . ."

"Not lately," I said. "He's different now."

"I'm going to put the eye on her," Grandma Bella said. "I'm going to make her female parts turn to dust."

"Over my dead body," Grandma Mazur said.

Bella scrunched up her face. "That could be arranged."

"You better watch it, sister," Grandma Mazur said. "You don't want to get me mad. I'm a holy terror when I'm mad."

"Hah, you don't scare me," Bella said. "Stand back. I'm going to give the eye."

Grandma Mazur pulled a .45 long barrel out of

her big black patent-leather purse and pointed it at
Bella. "You put your finger to your eye and I'll put a
hole in your head that's so big you could push a potato
through it."

Bella's eyes rolled around in her head. "I'm having a
vision. I'm having a vision."

I grabbed the gun from Grandma and shoved it back
into her bag. "No shooting! She's just a crazy old lady."

Bella snapped to attention. "Crazy old lady? Crazy
old lady? I'll show you crazy old lady. I'll give you a
thrashing. Someone get me a stick. I'll put the eye on
everyone if someone doesn't give me a stick."

"No one thrashes my granddaughter," Grandma
Mazur said. "And besides, look around. Do you see
any sticks? It's not like you're in the woods. You know
what your problem is? You gotta learn how to chill."

Bella grabbed Grandma Mazur by the nose. She was
so fast Grandma never saw it coming. "You're a demon
woman!" Bella shouted.

Grandma Mazur clocked Bella on the side of the
head with the big patent-leather purse, but Bella had
a death grip on Grandma Mazur. Grandma hit her a
second time and Bella hunkered in. Bella scrunched up
her face and held tight to the nose.

I was in the mix, trying to wrestle Bella away.
Grandma accidentally caught me with a roundhouse
swing of the purse that knocked me off my feet.

Bitsy Mullen was jumping around, wringing her
hands and shrieking. "Help! Stop! Someone do something!"

Mrs. Lubchek was behind Bitsy, at the cookie table,
watching the whole thing. "Oh, for the love of God,"
Mrs. Lubchek said with an eyeroll. And Mrs. Lubchek
grabbed the pitcher of iced tea off the cookie table and
dumped it on Grandma Bella and Grandma Mazur.

Grandma Bella released Grandma Mazur's nose and looked down at herself. "I'm wet. What is this?"

"Iced tea," Mrs. Lubchek said. "I poured iced tea on you."

"I'll turn you into an artichoke."

"You need to take a pill," Mrs. Lubchek said. "You're nutsy cuckoo."

Stiva hurried across the room with Joe's mother close on his heels.

"We're out of iced tea," Mrs. Lubchek said to Stiva.

"I'm having a vision," Grandma Bella said, her eyes rolling around in her head. "I see fire. A terrible fire. I see rats escaping, running from the fire. Big, ugly, sick rats. And one of the rats has come back." Bella's eyes snapped open and focused on me. "He's come back to get *you*."

"Omigod," Bitsy said. "Omigod. Omigod!"

"I need to lay down now. I always get tired after I have a vision," Bella said.

"Wait," I said to her. "What kind of a vision is that? A rat? Are you sure about this vision thing?"

"Yeah, and what do you mean the rat's sick?" Grandma Mazur wanted to know. "Does it have rabies?"

"That's all I'm going to say," Bella said. "It's a vision. A vision is a vision. I'm going home."

Bella whirled on her heel and walked to the door with her back ramrod straight and Joe's mom behind her, scurrying to keep up.

Grandma Mazur turned to the cookie tray and picked through the cookies, looking for a chocolate chip. "I tell you a person's gotta get here early or there's only leftovers."

We were both dripping iced tea. And Grandma Mazur's nose was red and swollen.

"We should go home," I said to Grandma Mazur. "I have to get out of this shirt."

"Yeah," Grandma Mazur said. "I guess I could go. I paid my respects to the deceased and this cookie tray's a big disappointment."

"Did you hear anything about Michael Barroni?"

Grandma dabbed at her shirt with a napkin. "Only that he's still missing. The boys are running the store, but Emma Wilson tells me they're not getting along. Emma works there part-time. She said the young one is a trial."

"Anthony."

"That's the one. He was always a troublemaker. Remember there was that business with Mary Jane Roman."

"Date rape."

"Nothing ever came of that," Grandma said. "But I never doubted Mary Jane. There was always something off about Anthony."

We'd walked out of the funeral home and down the street to the car. I looked inside the car and saw a note on the driver's seat.

"How'd that get in there?" Grandma wanted to know. "Don't you lock your car?"

"I stopped locking it. I'm hoping someone will steal it."

Grandma took a good look at the car. "That makes sense."

We both got in and I read the note. YOUR TURN TO BURN, BITCH.

"Such language," Grandma said. "I tell you, the world's going to heck in a handbasket."

Grandma was upset about the language. I was upset about the threat. I wasn't exactly sure what it meant, but it didn't feel good. It was crazy and scary. Who *was* this person, anyway?

I pulled away from the curb and headed for my parents' house.

"I can't get that dumb note out of my head," Grandma said when we were half a block from home. "I could swear I even smell smoke."

Now that she mentioned it . . .

I glanced in the rearview mirror and saw flames licking up the backseat. I raced the half block to my parents' house, careened into the driveway, and jerked to a stop.

"Get out," I yelled. "The backseat's on fire."

Grandma turned and looked. "Danged if it isn't."

I ran into the house, told my mother to call the fire department, grabbed the fire extinguisher that was kept in the kitchen under the sink, and ran back to the car. I broke the seal on the extinguisher and sprayed the flaming backseat. My father appeared with the garden hose and between the two of us we got the fire under control.

A half hour later, the backseat of the Saturn was pronounced dead and flame free by the fire department. The fire truck rumbled away down the street, and the crowd of curious neighbors dispersed. The sun had set, but the Saturn could be seen in the ambient light from the house. Water dripped from the undercarriage and pooled on the cement driveway in grease-slicked puddles. The stench of cooked upholstery hung in the air.

Morelli had arrived seconds behind the fire truck. He was now standing in my parents' front yard with his hands in his pockets, wearing his unreadable cop face.

"So," I said to him. "What's up?"

"Where's the note?"

"What note?"

His eyes narrowed ever so slightly.

"How do you know there was a note?" I asked.

"Just another one of those feelings."

I took the note from my pocket and handed it over.

"Do you think this has something to do with the rat?" Grandma asked me. "Remember how Bella had that vision about the fire and the rat? And she said the rat was gonna get you. Well, I bet it was the rat that wrote the note and started the fire."

"Rats can't write," I said.

"What about human rats?" Grandma wanted to know. "What about big mutant human rats?"

Morelli cut his eyes to me. "Do I want to know about this vision?"

"No," I told him. "And you also don't want to know about the fight in the funeral home between Bella and Grandma Mazur when Grandma tried to stop Bella from putting a curse on me for breaking your heart."

Morelli smiled. "I've always been her favorite."

"I didn't break your heart."

"Cupcake, you've been breaking my heart for as long as I've known you."

"How did you know about the fire?" I asked Morelli.

"Dispatch called me. They always call me when your car explodes or goes up in flames."

"I'm surprised Ranger isn't here."

"He got me on my cell. I told him you were okay."

I moved closer to the Saturn and peered inside. Most of the water and fire damage was confined to the backseat.

Morelli had his hand at the nape of my neck. "You're not thinking of driving this, are you?"

"It doesn't look so bad. It probably runs fine."

"The backseat is completely gutted and there's a big hole in the floorboard."

"Yeah, but other than that it's okay, right?"

Morelli looked at me for a couple beats. Probably trying to decide if this was worth a fight.

"It's too dark to get a really good assessment of the damage," he finally said. "Why don't we go home and come back in the morning and take another look? You don't want to drive it tonight anyway. You want to open the windows and let it air out."

He was right about the airing out part. The car reeked. And I knew he was also right about looking at the car when the light was better. Problem was, this was the only car I had. The only thing worse than driving this car would be borrowing the '53 Buick Grandma Mazur inherited from my Great Uncle Sandor. Been there, done that, don't want to do it again.

And the danger involved in driving this car seemed to me to be hardly worth mentioning compared to the threat I was facing from the criminally insane stalker who set the fire.

"I'm more worried about the arsonist than I am about the car," I said to Morelli.

"I haven't got a grip on the arsonist," Morelli said. "I don't know what to do about him. The car I have some control over. Let me give you a ride home."

Five minutes later we were parked in front of Morelli's house.

"Let me guess," I said to Morelli. "Bob still misses me."

Morelli ran a finger along the line of my jaw. "Bob could care less. I'm the one who misses you. And I miss you bad."

"How bad?"

Morelli kissed me. "Painfully bad."

At six-fifteen I dragged myself out of Morelli's bed and into the shower. I'd thrown my clothes in the washer and dryer the night before, and Morelli had them in the bathroom, waiting for me. I did a half-assed job of drying my hair, swiped some mascara on my lashes, and followed my nose to the kitchen, where Morelli had coffee brewing.

Both of the men in my life looked great in the morning. They woke up clear-eyed and alert, ready to save the world. I was a befuddled mess in the morning, stumbling around until I got my caffeine fix.

"We're running late," Morelli said, handing me a travel mug of coffee and a toasted bagel. "I'll drop you off at the cleaner. You can check the car out after work."

"No. I have time. This will only take a minute. I'm sure the car is fine."

"I'm sure the car *isn't* fine," Morelli said, nudging me out of the kitchen and down the hall to the front door. He locked the door behind us and beeped his SUV open with the remote.

Minutes later we were at my parents' house, arguing on the front lawn.

"You're not driving this car," Morelli said.

"Excuse me? Did I hear you give me an order?"

"Cut me some slack here. You and I both know this car isn't drivable."

"I don't know any such thing. Okay, it's got some problems, but they're all cosmetic. I'm sure the engine is fine." I slid behind the wheel and proved my point by rolling the engine over. "See?" I said.

"Get out of this wreck and let me drive you to work."

"No."

"In twenty seconds I'm going to *drag* you out and reignite the fire until there's nothing left of this death trap but a smoking cinder."

"I hate when you do the macho-man thing."

"I hate when you're stubborn."

I hit the door locks and automatic windows, put the car into reverse, and screeched out of the driveway into the road. I changed gears and roared away, gagging on the odor of wet barbecued car. He was right, of course. The car was a death trap, and I was being stubborn. Problem was, I couldn't help myself. Morelli brought out the stubborn in me.

Kan Klean was a small mom-and-pop dry cleaners that had been operating in the Burg for as long as I can remember. The Macaroni family owned Kan Klean. Mama Macaroni, Mario Macaroni, and Gina Macaroni were the principals, and a bunch of miscellaneous Macaronis helped out when needed.

Mama Macaroni was a contemporary of Grandma Bella and Grandma Mazur. Mama Macaroni's fierce raptor eyes took the world in under drooping folds of parchment-thin skin. Her shrunken body, wrapped in layers of black, curved over her cane and conjured up images of mummified larvae. She had a boulder of a mole set into the roadmap of her face somewhere in the vicinity of Atlanta. Three hairs grew out of the mole. The mole was horrifying and compelling. It was the dermatological equivalent of a seven-car crash with blood and guts spread all over the highway.

I'd never been to Kan Klean when Mama Macaroni wasn't sitting on a stool behind the counter. Mama nodded to customers but seldom spoke. Mama only spoke when there was a problem. Mama Macaroni was the problem solver. Her son Mario supervised the day-to-day operation. Her daughter-in-law, Gina, kept the books and ran day care for the hordes of grandchildren produced by her four daughters and two sons.

"It's not difficult," Gina said to me. "You'll be working the register. You take the clothes from the customer and you do a count. Then you fill out the order form and give a copy to the customer. You put a copy in the bag with the clothes and you put the third copy in the box by the register. Then you put the bag in one of the rolling bins. One bin is laundry and one bin is dry cleaning. That's the way we do it. When a customer comes in to pick up his cleaned clothes, you search for the clothes by the number on the top of his receipt. Make sure you always take a count so the customer gets all his clothes."

Mama Macaroni mumbled something in Italian and slid her dentures around in her mouth.

"Mama says you should be careful. She says she's keeping her eye on you," Gina said.

I smiled at Mama Macaroni and gave her a thumbs-up. Mama Macaroni responded with a death glare.

"When you have time between customers you can tag the clothes," Gina said. "Every single garment must get tagged. We have a machine that you use, and you have to make sure that the number on the tag is the same as the number on the customer's receipt."

By noon I'd completely lost the use of my right thumb from using the tagging machine.

"You got to go faster," Mama Macaroni said to me from her stool. "I see you slow down. You think we pay for nothing?"

A man hurried through the front door and approached the counter. He was mid-forties and dressed in a suit and tie. "I picked my dry cleaning up yesterday," he said, "and all the buttons are broken off my shirt."

Mama Macaroni got off her stool and caned her way to the counter. "What?" she said.

"The buttons are broken."

She shook her head. "I no understand."

He showed her the shirt. "The buttons are all broken."

"Yes," Mama Macaroni said.

"You broke them."

"No," Mama said. "Impossible."

"The buttons were fine when I brought the shirt in. I picked the shirt up and the buttons were all broken."

"I no understand."

"What don't you understand?"

"English. My English no good."

The man looked at me. "Do you speak English?"

"What?" I said.

The man whipped the shirt off the counter and left the store.

"Maybe you not so slow," Mama Macaroni said to me. "But don't get any ideas about taking it easy. We don't pay you good money to stand around doing nothing."

I started watching the clock at one o'clock. By three o'clock I was sure I'd been tagging clothes for at least five days without a break. My thumb was throbbing, my feet ached from standing for eight hours, and I had a nervous twitch in my eye from Mama Macaroni's constant scrutiny.

I took my bag from under the counter and I looked over at Mama Macaroni. "See you tomorrow."

"What you mean, *See you tomorrow*? Where you think you going?"

"Home. It's three o'clock. My shift is over."

"Look at little miss clock watcher here. Three o'clock on the dot. *Bing*. The bell rings and you out the door." She threw her parchment hands into the air. "Go! Go home. Who needs you? And don't be late tomorrow. Sunday is big day. We the only cleaner open on Sunday."

"Okay," I said. "And have a nice mole." *Shit!* Did I just say that? "Have a nice *day!*" I yelled. Crap.

I'd parked the Saturn in the small lot adjacent to Kan Klean. I left the building and circled the car. I didn't see any notes. I didn't smell anything burning. No one shot at me. Guess my stalker was taking a day off.

I got into the car, turned my cell phone on, and scrolled to messages.

First message. "Stephanie." That was the whole message. It was from Morelli at seven-ten this morning. It sounded like it had been said through clenched teeth.

Second message. Morelli breathing at seven-thirty.

Third message. "Call me when you turn your phone on." Morelli again.

Fourth message. "It's two-thirty and we just found Barroni's car. Call me."

Barroni's car! I dialed in Joe's cell number.

"It's me," I said. "I just got off work. I had to turn my phone off because Mama Macaroni said it was giving her brain cancer. Not that it would matter."

"Where are you?"

"I'm on the road. I'm going home to take a nap. I'm all done in."

"The car . . ."

"The car is okay," I told Morelli.

"The car is *not* okay."

"Give up on the car. What about Barroni?"

"I lied about Barroni. I figured that was the only way you'd call."

I put my finger to my eye to stop the twitching, disconnected Morelli, and cruised into my lot.

Old Mr. Ginzler was walking to his Buick when I pulled in. "That's some lookin' car you got there, chicky," Mr. Ginzler said. "And it stinks."

"I paid extra for the smell," I told Mr. Ginzler.

"Smart-ass kid," Mr. Ginzler said. But he smiled when he said it. Mr. Ginzler liked me. I was almost sure of it.

Rex was snoozing in his soup can when I let myself into my apartment. There were no messages on my machine. Most people called my cell these days. Even my mother called my cell. I shuffled into the bedroom, kicked my shoes off, and crawled under the covers. The best I could say about today was that it was marginally better than yesterday. At least I hadn't gotten fired. Problem was, it was hard to tell if not getting fired from Kan Klean was a good thing or a bad thing. I closed my eyes and willed myself to sleep, telling myself when I woke up my life would be great. Okay, it was sort of a fib, but it kept me from bursting into tears or smashing all my dishes.

A couple hours later I was still awake and I was thinking less about breaking something and more about eating something. I strolled out to the kitchen and took stock. I could construct another peanut butter sandwich. I could mooch dinner off my mother. I could take myself off to search for fast food. The last two choices meant I'd have to get back into the Saturn. Not an appealing prospect, but still better than another peanut butter sandwich.

I laced up my sneakers, ran a brush through my hair, and applied lip gloss. The natural look. Acceptable in Jersey only if you've had your boobs enhanced to the point where no one looked beyond them. I hadn't had my boobs enhanced, and most people found it easy to look beyond them, but I didn't care a whole lot today.

I took the stairs debating the merits of a chicken quesadilla against the satisfaction of a dozen doughnuts. I was still undecided when I pushed through the lobby door and crossed the lot to my car. Turns out it wasn't a decision I needed to make because my car was wearing a police boot.

I ripped my cell phone out of my bag and punched in Morelli's number.

"There's a police boot on my car," I said to him. "Did you put it on?"

"Not personally."

"I want it off."

"I'm crimes against persons. I'm not traffic."

"Fine. I want to report a crime against a person. Some jerk booted my car."

Morelli blew out a sigh and disconnected.

I dialed Ranger. "I have a problem," I said to Ranger.

"And?"

"I was hoping you could solve it."

"Give me a hint."

"My car's been booted."

"And?"

"I need to get the boot off."

"Anything else?"

"I could use some doughnuts. I haven't had dinner."

"Where are you?"

"My apartment."

"Babe," Ranger said, and the connection went dead.

Ten minutes later, Ranger's Porsche rolled to a stop next to the Saturn. Ranger got out and handed me a bag. Ranger was in his usual black. Black T-shirt that looked like it was painted onto his biceps and clung to his washboard stomach. Black cargo pants that had lots of pockets for Ranger's goodies, although clearly not all his goodies were relegated to the pockets. His hair was medium cut and silky straight, falling across his forehead.

"Doughnuts?" I asked.

"Turkey club. Doughnuts will kill you."

"And?"

Ranger almost smiled at me. "If I had to drive this Saturn I'd want to die, too."

FOUR

"Can you get the boot off?" I asked Ranger.

Ranger toed the big chunk of metal that was wrapped around my tire. "Tank's on his way with the equipment. How'd you manage to get booted in the lot?"

"Morelli. He thinks the car's unsafe."

"And?"

"Okay, so it's got some cosmetic problems."

"Babe, it's got a twelve-inch hole in the floor."

"Yeah, but the hole's in the back and I can't even see it when I'm in the front. And if I leave the back windows open the fumes get sucked out before they get to me."

"Good to know you've thought this through."

"Are you laughing at me?"

"Do I look like I'm laughing?"

"I thought I saw your mouth twitch."

"How'd this happen?"

I took the turkey club out of the bag and unwrapped it. "It was the note guy. I took Grandma to a viewing at Stiva's, and when we left, there was a note in the car. It said it was my turn to burn . . . and then the back-seat caught fire on the way to my parents' house." I took a bite of the sandwich. "I have a feeling about the note guy. I think the note guy is Stiva's kid. Spiro. Joe's

Grandma Bella told me she had a vision about rats running away from a fire. And one of the rats was sick and it came back to get me."

"And you think that rat is Spiro?"

"Do you remember Spiro? Beady rat eyes. No chin. Bad overbite. Mousy brown hair."

"Bella's a little crazy, Babe."

I finished the turkey club. "A guy named Michael Barroni disappeared ten days ago. Sixty-two years old. Upstanding citizen. Had a house on Roebling. Owned the hardware store on Rudd and Liberty. Locked the store up at the end of the day and disappeared off the face of the earth. Morelli punched Barroni into missing persons and found there were two other similar cases. Benny Gorman and Louis Lazar. Connie said you're looking for Gorman."

"Yeah, and he feels like a dead end."

"Maybe it's a dead end because he's dead."

"It's crossed my mind."

I crumpled the sandwich bag and tossed it into the back of the Saturn. It bounced off the charred backseat and fell through the hole in the floor, onto the pavement, under the car.

Ranger gave a single, barely visible shake to his head. Hard to tell if he was amused or if he was appalled.

"Did you know Barroni?" Ranger asked me.

"I went to school with his youngest son, Anthony. Here's the thing about Michael Barroni. There's no obvious reason why he disappeared. No gambling debts. No drinking or drug problems. No health problems. No secret sex life. He just locked up the store, got into his car, and drove off into the sunset. He did this on the same day and at the same time Lazar and Gorman drove off into the sunset. It was like they were all going to a meeting."

"I made the Lazar connection," Ranger said. "I didn't know there was a third."

"That's because you're the Stark Street expert and I'm the Burg expert."

"You handed your cuffs and fake badge over to Connie," Ranger said. "Why the interest in Barroni and Lazar and Gorman?"

"In the beginning, Barroni was just Burg gossip and cop talk. Now I'm thinking Spiro's gone psycho and he's back in town and stalking me. And Barroni might be connected to Spiro. I know that sounds like a stretch, but Spiro makes bad things happen. And he drags his friends into the muck with him. All through school, Spiro hung out with Anthony Barroni. Suppose Spiro's back and he's got something bad going on. Suppose Anthony's involved and somehow his dad got in the way."

"That's a lot of supposing. Have you talked to Morelli about this?"

"No. I'm not talking to Morelli about *anything*. He booted my car. I'm doing all my talking to you."

"His loss is my gain?"

"This is your lucky day," I said to Ranger.

Ranger curled his fingers into the front of my jean jacket and pulled me close. "How much luck are we talking about?"

"Not that much luck."

Ranger brushed a light kiss over my lips. "Someday," he said.

And he was probably right. Ranger and I have a strange relationship. He's my mentor and protector and friend. He's also hot and mysterious and oozes testosterone. A while ago, he was my lover for a single spectacular night. We both walked away wanting more, but to date, my practical Burg upbringing plus strong survival instincts have kept Ranger out of my bed. This is in direct contrast to Ranger's instincts. His instincts run more to keeping his eye on the prize while he enjoys the chase and waits for his chance to move in for the kill. He is, after all, a hunter of men . . . and women.

Ranger released my jacket. "I'm going to take a look at Barroni's house and store. Do you want to ride along?"

"Okay, but it's just to keep you company. It's not like I'm involved. I'm done with all that fugitive apprehension stuff."

"Still my lucky day," Ranger said.

My apartment is only a couple miles from the store, but it was after six by the time we got to Rudd and Liberty, and the store was closed. We cruised past the front, turned the corner, and took the service road at the rear. Ranger drove the Porsche down the road and paused at Barroni's back door. There was a black Corvette parked in the small lot.

"Someone's working late," Ranger said. "Do you know the car?"

"No, but I'm guessing it belongs to Anthony. His two older brothers are married and have kids, and I can't see them finding money for a toy like this."

Ranger continued on, turned the corner, and pulled to the curb. There'd been heavy cloud cover all day and now it was drizzling. Streetlights stood out in the gloom and red brake lights traced across Ranger's rain-streaked windshield.

After five minutes, the Corvette rolled past us with Anthony driving. Ranger put the Porsche in gear and followed Anthony at a distance. Anthony wandered through the Burg and stopped at Pino's Pizza. He was inside Pino's for a couple minutes and returned to his car carrying two large pizza boxes. He found his way to Hamilton Avenue, crossed Hamilton, and after two blocks he pulled into a driveway that belonged to a two-story town house. The town house had an attached garage, but Anthony didn't use it. Anthony parked in the driveway and hustled to the small front porch. He fumbled with his keys, got the door open, and rushed inside.

"That's a lot of pizza for a single guy," Ranger said. "And he has something occupying space in his garage. It's raining, and he has his hands full of pizza boxes, and he parked in the driveway."

"Maybe Spiro's in there. Maybe he's got his car parked in Anthony's garage."

"I can see that possibility turns you on," Ranger said.

"It would be nice to find Spiro and put an end to the harassment."

Shades were drawn on all the windows. Ranger idled for a few minutes in front of the town house and moved on. He retraced the route to the hardware store and had me take him from the store to Michael Barroni's house on Roebling.

It was a large house by Burg standards. Maybe two thousand square feet. Upstairs and downstairs. Detached garage. The front of the house was gray fake stone. The other three sides were white vinyl siding. It had a full front porch and a postage-stamp front yard. There was a plaster statue of the Virgin Mary in the front yard. A small basket of plastic flowers had been placed at her feet. Shades were up in the Barroni house and it was easy to look from one end to the other. A lone woman moved in the house. Carla Barroni, Michael Barroni's wife. She settled herself in front of the television in the living room and lost herself to the evening news.

I was spellbound, watching Carla. "It must be awful not to know," I said to Ranger. "To have someone you love disappear. Not to know if he was murdered and buried in a shallow grave, or if you drove him away, or if he was sick and couldn't find his way home. It makes my problems seem trivial."

"Being on the receiving end of threatening letters isn't trivial," Ranger said.

Everything's relative, I thought. The threatening letters weren't nearly as frightening as the prospect of spending another eight hours with Mama-the-Mole Macaroni. And the problems I was thinking about were personal. My life had no clear direction. My goals were small and immediate. Pay the rent. Get a better car. Make a dinner decision. I didn't have a career. I didn't have a husband. I didn't have any special talents. I didn't have a consuming passion. I didn't have a hobby. Even my pet was small . . . a hamster. I liked Rex a lot, but he didn't exactly make a big statement.

Ranger broke into my moment. "Babe, I get the feeling you're standing on a ledge, looking down."

"Just thinking."

Ranger put the Porsche into gear and headed across town. We checked out Louis Lazar's house and bar. Then we went four blocks north on Stark and parked in front of Gorman's garage. The garage was dark. No sign of life inside. A CLOSED sign hung on the office door.

"Gorman's manager kept the garage going for a week on his own and then cut out," Ranger said. "Gorman isn't married. He was living with a woman, but she has no claim to his property. He has a pack of kids, all with different mothers. The kids are too young to run the business. The rest of Gorman's relatives are in South Carolina. I did a South Carolina search, and it came back negative. From what I can tell the business was operating in the black. Gorman had a mean streak, but he wasn't stupid. He would have made arrangements to keep the garage running if he was going FTA. I can't see him just walking away. Usually I pick up a vibe from someone . . . mother, girlfriend, coworker. I'm not getting anything on this."

We cut back two blocks and parked in front of a run-down apartment building.

"This was Gorman's last known address," Ranger said. "His girlfriend didn't wait as long as his manager. The girlfriend had a new guy hanging his clothes in her closet on day five. If she knew Gorman's location, she'd have given him up for a pass to the multiplex."

"No one saw him after he drove away from the garage?"

Ranger watched the building. "No. All I know is he drove north on Stark. Consistent with Lazar."

North on Stark didn't mean much. Stark Street deteriorated as it went north. Eventually Stark got so bad even the gangs abandoned it. At the very edge of the city line Stark was a deserted war zone of fire-gutted brick buildings with boarded-up windows. It was a graveyard for stolen, stripped-down cars and used-up heroin addicts. It was a do-it-yourself garbage dump. North on Stark also led to Route 1 and Route 1 led to the entire rest of the country.

Ranger's pager buzzed, he checked the message, and pulled away from the curb, into the stream of traffic. Ranger is hot, but he has a few personality quirks that drive me nuts. He doesn't eat dessert, he has an overdeveloped sense of secret, and unless he's trying to seduce me or instruct me in the finer points of bounty hunting, conversation can be nonexistent.

"Hey," I finally said, "Man of Mystery . . . what's with the pager?"

"Business."

"And?"

Ranger slid a glance my way.

"It's no wonder you aren't married," I said to him. "You have a lot to learn about social skills."

Ranger smiled at me. Ranger thought I was amusing.

"That was my office," Ranger said. "Elroy Dish went FTA two days ago. I've been waiting for him to show up at Blue Fish, and he just walked in."

Vinnie's bonded out three generations of Dishes. Elroy is the youngest. His specialties are armed robbery and domestic violence, but Elroy is capable of most anything. When Elroy's drunk or drugged he's fearless and wicked crazy. When he's clean and sober he's just plain mean.

Blue Fish is a bar on lower Stark, dead center in Dish country. No point to breaking down a door and attempting to drag a Dish out of his rat-trap apartment when you can just wait for him to waltz into Blue Fish for a cold one.

Ranger brought the Porsche to the curb two doors from Blue Fish, cut the motor and the lights. Three minutes later, a black SUV rolled down the street and parked in front of us. Tank and Hal, dressed in RangeMan black, got out of the SUV and strapped on utility belts. Tank is Ranger's shadow. He watches Ranger's back, and he's second in the line of command at RangeMan. His name is self-explanatory. Hal is newer to the game. He's not the sharpest tack on the corkboard, but he tries hard. He's just slightly smaller than Tank and reminds me of a big lumbering dinosaur. He's a Halosaurus.

Ranger reached behind him and grabbed a flak vest from the small backseat. "Stay here," he said. "This will only take a couple minutes and then I'll drive you home."

Ranger angled out of the Porsche, nodded to Tank and Hal, and the three of them disappeared inside Blue Fish. I checked my watch, and I stared at the door to the bar. Ranger didn't waste time when he made an apprehension. He identified his quarry, clapped the cuffs on, and turned the guy over to Tank and Hal for the forced march to the SUV.

I was feeling a little left out, but I was telling myself it was much better this way. No more danger. No more mess. No more embarrassing screw-ups. I was focused on the door to the bar, not paying a lot of attention to the street, and suddenly the driver's-side door to the Porsche was wrenched open and a guy slid in next to me. He was in his twenties, wearing a ball cap sideways and about sixty pounds of gold chains around his neck. He had a diamond chip implanted into his front tooth and the two teeth next to the chip were missing. He smiled at me and pressed the barrel of a gleaming silver-plated monster gun into my temple.

"Yo, bitch," he said. "How about you get your ass out of my car."

In my mind I saw myself out of the car and running, but the reality of the situation was that all systems were down. I couldn't breathe. I couldn't move. I couldn't speak. I stared openmouthed and glassy-eyed at the guy with the diamond dental chip. Somewhere deep in my brain the word *carjack* was struggling to rise to the surface.

Diamond dental chip turned the key in the Porsche's ignition and revved the engine. "Out of the car," he yelled, pushing the gun barrel against my head. "I'm giving you one second and then I'm gonna blow your brains all over this motherfucker. Now get your *fat ass* out of the car."

The mind works in weird ways, and it's strange how something dumb can push a button. I was willing to overlook the use of the MF word, but getting called a fat ass really pissed me off.

"Fat ass?" I said, feeling my eyes narrow. "Excuse me? Fat ass?"

"I haven't got time for this shit," he said. And he rammed the car into gear, mashed the gas to the floor, and the Porsche jumped away from the curb.

He was driving with his left hand and holding the gun and shifting with his right. There was light traffic on Stark, and he was weaving around cars and running lights. He came up fast behind a Lincoln Navigator and hit the brake hard. He moved to shift, and I knocked the gun out of his hand. The gun hit the console and fell to the floor on the driver's side.

"Fuck," he said. "Fucking fuck. Fucking bitch."

He leaned forward and reached for the gun, and I punched him in the ear as hard as I could. His head bounced off the wheel, the wheel jerked hard to the left, and we cut across oncoming traffic. The Porsche jumped the curb, plowed through a stack of black plastic garbage bags, and crashed through the plate glass window of a small delicatessen that was closed for the night.

The front airbags inflated with a *bang,* and I was momentarily stunned. I fought my way through the bag, somehow got the door open, and rolled out onto the deli floor. I was on my hands and knees in the dark, and it was wet under my hand. Blood, I thought. Get outside and get help.

A leg came into my field of vision. Black cargo pants, black boots. Hands under my armpits, lifting me to my feet. And then I was face-to-face with Ranger.

"Are you okay?" he asked.

"I must be bleeding. The floor was wet and sticky."

He looked at my hand. "I don't see any blood on you." He put my hand to his mouth and touched his tongue to my palm, giving me a rush that went from my toes to the roots of my hair. "Dill," he said. He looked beyond me, to the crumpled hood of the Porsche. "You crashed into the counter and smashed the pickle barrel."

"I'm sorry about your Porsche."

"I can replace the Porsche. I can't replace you. You need to be more careful."

"I was just sitting in your car!"

"Babe, you're a magnet for disaster."

Tank had the carjacker in cuffs. He shoved him across the floor to the door, the carjacker slid in the pickle juice and went down to one knee, and I heard Tank's boot connect with solid body. "Accident," Tank said. "Didn't see you down there in the dark." And then he yanked the carjacker to his feet and threw him into a wall. "Another accident," Tank said, grabbing the carjacker, jerking him to his feet again.

Ranger cut his eyes to Tank. "Stop playing with him."

Tank grinned at Ranger and dragged the carjacker out to the SUV.

We followed Tank out, and Ranger looked at me under the streetlight. "You're a mess," he said, picking noodles and wilted lettuce out of my hair. "You're covered in garbage again."

"We hit the bags on the curb on the way into the store. And I guess we dragged some of it with us. I probably rolled in it when I fell out of the car."

A smile hung at the corners of Ranger's mouth. "I can always count on you to brighten my day."

A shiny black Ford truck angled to a stop in front of us, and one of Ranger's men got out and handed Ranger the keys. I could see a police car turn onto Stark, two blocks away.

"Tank and Hal and Woody can take care of this," Ranger said. "We can leave."

"You have a guy named Woody?"

Ranger opened the passenger-side door to the truck for me. "Do you want me to explain it?"

"Not necessary."

I was in the Saturn, parked next to Kan Klean. It was Sunday. It was the start of a new day, it was one minute to seven, and Morelli was on my cell.

"I'm in your lot," he said. "I stopped by to take you to work. Where are you? And where's your car?"

"I'm at Kan Klean. I drove."

"What happened to the boot?"

"I don't know. It disappeared."

There was a full sixty seconds of silence while I knew Morelli was doing deep breathing, working at not getting nuts. I looked at my watch, and my stomach clenched.

Mama Macaroni appeared at car side and stuck her face in my open window, her monster mole just inches from my face, her demon eyes narrowed, her thin lips drawn tight against her dentures.

"What you doing out here?" Mama yelled. "You think we pay for talking on the phone? We got work to do. You kids . . . you think you get money for doing nothing."

"Jesus," Morelli said. "What the hell is that?"

"Mama Macaroni."

"She has a voice like fingernails on a chalkboard."

I needed a pill really bad. It was noon and I had a fireball behind my right eye and Mama Macaroni screeching into my left ear.

"The pink tag's for dry cleaning and the green tag's for laundry," Mama shrieked at me. "You mixing them up. You make a mess of everything. You ruin our business. We gonna be out on the street."

The tinkle bell attached to the front door jangled, and I looked up to see Lula walk in.

"Hey, girlfriend," Lula said to me. "What's shakin'? What's hangin'? What's the word?"

Lula's hair was gold today and styled in ringlets, like Shirley Temple at age five. Lula was wearing black high-heeled ankle boots, a tight orange spandex skirt that came to about three inches below her ass, and a matching orange top that was stretched tight across her boobs and belly. And Lula's belly was about as big as her boobs.

"What word?" Mama Macaroni asked. "Wadda you mean word? Who is this big orange person?"

"This is my friend Lula," I said.

"You friend? No. No friends. Wadda you think, this is a party?"

"Hey, chill," Lula said to Mama. "I came to pick up my dry cleaning. I'm a legitimate customer."

I had the merry-go-round in motion, looking for Lula's cleaning. The motor whirred, and plastic-sleeved, hangered orders swished by me, carried along on an overhead system of tracks.

"I'll take Vinnie's and Connie's too," Lula said.

Mama was off her stool. "You no take anything until I say so. Let me see the slip. Where's the slip?"

I had Lula's cleaning in hand and Mama stepped in front of me. "What's this on the slip? What's this discount?"

"You said I got a discount," I told her, trying hard not to stare at the mole, not having a lot of luck at it.

"*You* get a discount. This big pumpkin don't get no discount."

"Hey, hold on here," Lula said, lower lip stuck out, hands on hips. "Who you calling a pumpkin?"

"I'm calling *you* a pumpkin," Mama Macaroni said. "Look at you. You a big fat pumpkin. And you don't get no pumpkin discount." Mama turned on me. "You try to pull a fast one. Give everybody a discount. Like we run a charity here. A charity for pumpkins. Maybe you get the kickback. You think you make some money on the side."

"I don't like to disrespect old people," Lula said. "And you're about as old as they get. You're as old as dirt, but that don't mean you can insult my friend. I don't put up with that. I don't take that bus. You see what I'm saying?"

The pain was radiating out from my eye into all parts of my head, and little men in pointy hats and spiky shoes were running around in my stomach. I had to get Lula out of the store. If Mama Macaroni called Lula a pumpkin one more time, Lula was going to squash Mama Macaroni, and Mama Macaroni was going to be Mama Pancake.

I shoved Lula's clothes at her, but Mama got to them first. "Gimme those clothes," Mama said. "She can't have them until she pays full price. Maybe I don't give them to her at all. Maybe I keep them for evidence that you steal from us."

"I need that red sweater," Lula said. "That's my most flattering sweater."

"Too bad for you," Mama said. "You should think of this before you steal from us."

"That does it," Lula said. "I didn't steal from you. And I don't like your attitude. And I'm a bounty hunter now, and I don't got time for this like when I was a file clerk."

Lula got a knee up on the counter and lunged for Mama Macaroni and the dry cleaning.

"Help! Police!" Mama shrieked.

"Police, my patoot," Lula said. And she was over the counter, going for Mama Macaroni.

Mama jumped away and scrambled around a clothes bin, hugging the dry cleaning to her chest. Gina Macaroni and three other women, all shouting in Italian, came running from the back room.

Gina was wielding a broom like a baseball bat. "What's going on?" Gina wanted to know.

"Thieves. Robbers," Mama said. "They trying to steal from us. Hit them with the broom. Hit them good. Knock their heads off."

"This old woman's nuts," Lula said. "I just want my

dry cleaning. I'd've paid for it fair and square." Lula pulled her Glock out of her handbag, and all the women shrieked and dropped to the floor. Except for Mama Macaroni. Mama Macaroni flipped Lula the bird.

"You should give her the dry cleaning," I said to Mama Macaroni. "She's real dangerous. She's shot a lot of people." That was sort of a fib. Lula's shot *at* a lot of people. I don't know that she's ever connected.

"She don't scare me," Mama said. And Mama reached underneath her long black skirt, pulled out a semiautomatic, and started shooting. She was shooting wild, taking out light fixtures and chunks of plaster from the ceiling, but that didn't make it any less terrifying . . . or for that matter, any less dangerous.

Lula and I dove for the front of the store, rolled out the door, and scrambled to the Firebird. Lula jumped behind the wheel, and we roared off.

"Do you frickin' believe that?" Lula yelled. "That crazy old lady shot at us! She could have killed us. You know what she needs?"

I looked expectantly at Lula.

"A dermatologist," Lula said. "Did you see that mole? It should be illegal to have a mole like that. That was a mutant mole. I didn't even bring it up in the conversation either. I was being real polite. Even when she was a meanie, I was still polite."

"You told her she was as old as dirt."

Lula pulled into the Cluck-in-a-Bucket lot. "Yeah, but that was a fact. You can't count a fact. How long do you get for lunch? We might as well have lunch as long as we're out."

"I don't think lunch is an issue. My employer just called me a thief and shot at me. That would lead me to believe I'm unemployed."

"I wouldn't be so sure of that. It's hard to get good help these days. That dry cleaner's lucky to have you.

And I didn't hear anybody fire you. The old lady wasn't shooting at you and saying *you're fired*. The old lady was just Anna Banana probably on account of she has that mole."

We went inside, placed our order, and waited for our food to be assembled.

"Well okay, now that I think about it, probably you're fired," Lula said. "It was a nasty job anyway. You had to look at that mole all day. And I'm sorry, that's no normal mole."

"It's the mole from hell."

"Friggin' A," Lula said. "And you shouldn't worry about getting another job. You could get a better job than that. You could even get a job here. Look at the sign by the register. It says they're hiring. And there'd be advantages to working here. I bet you get free chicken and fries." Lula went back to the counter. "We want to see the manager," she said. "My friend's interested in having a job here. I'm not interested myself because I'm a kick-ass bounty hunter, but Stephanie over there just got unemployed."

I had Lula by the arm, and I was trying to drag her away from the counter. "No!" I whispered to Lula. "I don't want to work here. I'd have to wear one of those awful uniforms."

"Yeah, but you wouldn't ruin any of your real clothes that way," Lula said. "Probably you get a lot of grease stains here. And I don't think the uniform's so bad. Besides, your skinny little ass makes everything look good."

"The *hat*!"

"Okay, I see what you're saying about the hat. Suppose the hat had an accident? Suppose the hat fell into the french fry machine first thing? I bet it would take days to get a new hat."

A little guy came up behind me. He was half a head shorter than me, and he looked like a chubby pink pig in pants. His cheeks were round and pink. His hands were pink sausages. His belly jiggled when he moved. His mouth was round and his lips were pink . . . and best not to think about the pig part the mouth most resembled, but it could be found under the curly pig tail.

"I'm the manager," he said. "Milton Mann."

"This here's Stephanie Plum," Lula said. "She's looking for a job."

"Minimum wage," Mann said. "We need someone for the three-to-eleven shift."

"How about food?" Lula wanted to know. "Does she eat free? And what about takeout?"

"There's no eating on the job, but she can eat for free on her dinner break. Takeout gets a twenty percent discount."

"That sounds fair," Lula said. "She'll take the job."

"Come in a half hour early tomorrow," Mann said to me. "I'll give you your uniform and you can fill out the paperwork."

"Look at that," Lula said, claiming her tray of food, steering me back to the table. "See how easy it is to get a job? There's jobs everywhere."

"Yeah, but I don't want this job. I don't want to work here."

"Twenty percent off on takeout," Lula said. "You can't beat that. You can feed your family . . . *and friends.*"

I took a piece of fried chicken from the bucket on the tray. "My car is back at the dry cleaner."

"And I didn't get my sweater. That was my favorite sweater, too. It was just the right shade of red to flatter my skin tone."

I finished my piece of chicken. "Are you going back to get your sweater?"

"Damn skippy I'm going back. Only thing is I'm waiting until they're closed and it's nice and dark out." Lula looked over my shoulder and her eyes focused on the front door. "Uh oh," Lula said. "Here comes Officer Hottie, and he don't look happy."

Morelli moved behind me and curled his fingers into the back of my jacket collar. "I need to talk to you . . . outside."

"I wouldn't go if I was you," Lula said to me. "He's wearing his mad cop face. At least you should make him leave his gun here."

Morelli shot Lula a look, and she buried her head in the chicken bucket.

When we got outside Morelli dragged me to the far side of the building, away from the big plate glass windows. He still had a grip on my jacket, and he still had the don't-mess-with-me cop face. He held tight to my jacket, and he stared at his shoes, head down.

"Practicing anger management?" I asked.

He shook his head and bit into his lower lip. "No," he said. "I'm trying not to laugh. That crazy old lady shot at you and I don't want to trivialize it, but I totally lost it at Kan Klean. And I wasn't the only one. I was there with three uniforms who responded to the call, and we all had to go around to the back of the building to compose ourselves. Your friend Eddie Gazarra was laughing so hard he wet his uniform. Was there really a shoot-out between the old lady and Lula?"

"Yeah, but Mama Macaroni did all the shooting. She trashed the place. Lula and I were lucky to get out alive. How'd you know where to find me?"

"I did a drive-by on all the doughnut shops and fast-food places in the area. And by the way, Mama Macaroni said to tell you that you're fired." Morelli leaned into me and nuzzled my neck. "We should celebrate."

"You wanted to celebrate when I got the job. Now you want to celebrate because I've lost the job?"

"I like to celebrate."

Sometimes I had a hard time keeping up with Morelli's libido. "I'm not talking to you," I told Morelli.

"Yeah, but we could still celebrate, right?"

"Wrong. And I need to get back inside before Lula eats all the food."

Morelli pulled me to him and kissed me with a lot of tongue. "I *really* need to celebrate," he said. And he was gone, off to file a report on my shoot-out.

Lula was finishing her half gallon of soda when I returned to the table. "How'd that go?" she wanted to know.

"Average." I looked in the chicken bucket. One wing left.

"I'm in a real mean mood after that whole cleaning incident," Lula said. "I figure I might as well make the most of it and go after my DV. When I was a file clerk I didn't usually work on Sunday, unless I was helping you. But now that I'm a bounty hunter I'm on the job twenty-four/seven. You see what I'm saying? And I know how you're missing being a bounty hunter and all, so I'm gonna let you ride with me again."

"I don't miss being a bounty hunter. And I don't want to ride with you."

"Please?" Lula said. "Pretty please with sugar on it? I'm your friend, right? And we do things together, right? Like, look at how we just shared lunch together."

"You ate all the chicken."

"Not *all* the chicken. I left you a wing. 'Course, it's true I don't particularly like wings, but that's not the point. Anyways, I kept you from putting a lot of ugly fat on your skinny ass. You aren't gonna be getting any from Officer Hottie if you get all fat and dimply. And I know you need to be getting some on a regular basis because I remember when you weren't getting *any* and you were a real cranky pants."

"Stop!" I said. "I'll go with you."

FIVE

It took us a half hour to get to the public housing projects and work our way through the grid of streets that led to Emanuel Lowe, also known as the DV. Lula had the Firebird parked across the street from Lowe's apartment, and we were both watching the apartment door, and we were both wishing we were at Macy's shopping for shoes.

"We need a better plan this time," Lula said. "Last time, I did the direct approach and that didn't work out. We gotta be sneaky this time. And we can't use me on account of everybody here knows me now. So I'm thinking it's going to have to be you to go snatch the DV."

"Not in a million years."

"Yeah, but they don't know you. And there's hardly anybody sneakier than you. I'd even cut you in. I'd give you ten bucks if you collected him for me."

I did raised eyebrows at Lula. "Ten dollars? I used to pay you fifty and up."

"I figure it goes by the pound and a little bitty thing like you isn't worth as much as a full-figured woman like me." Lula took a couple beats. "Well okay, I guess that don't fly. It was worth a try though, right?"

"Maybe you should just sit here and wait for him to come out and then you can run over him with your Firebird."

"That's sarcasm, isn't it? I know sarcasm when I hear it. And it's not attractive on you. You don't usually do sarcasm. You got some Jersey attitude going, don't you?"

I slumped lower in my seat. "I'm depressed."

"You know what would get you out of that depression? An apprehension. You need to kick some butt. You need to get yourself empowered. I bet you'd feel real good if you snagged yourself an Emanuel Lowe."

"*Fine.* Okay. I'll get Lowe for you. The day's already in the toilet. Might as well finish it off right." I unbuckled my seat belt. "Give me your gun and your cuffs."

"You haven't got your own gun?"

"I didn't think I needed to carry a gun because I didn't think I was going to be doing this anymore. When I left the house this morning I thought I was going to be working at the dry cleaners."

Lula handed me her gun and a pair of cuffs. "You always gotta have a gun. It's like wearing undies. You wouldn't go out of the house without undies, would you? Same thing with a gun. Boy, for being a bounty hunter all that time, you sure don't know much."

I grabbed the gun from Lula and marched up to Lowe's front door. I knocked twice, Lowe opened the door, and I pointed the gun at him. "On the ground," I said. "*Now.*"

Lowe gave a bark of laughter. "You not gonna shoot me. I'm a unarmed man. You get twenty years for shooting me."

I aimed high, squeezed a round off, and took out a ceiling fixture.

"Crazy bitch," he said. "This here's public housing. You costing the taxpayer money. I got a mind to report you."

"I'm not in a good mood," I said to Lowe.

"I can see that. How you like me to improve your mood? Maybe you need a man to make you feel special."

Emanuel Lowe was five foot nine and rail thin. He had no ass, no teeth, and I was guessing no deodorant, no shower, no mouthwash. He was wearing a wife-beater T-shirt that had yellowed with age, and baggy homeboy-style brown pants precariously perched on his bony hips. And he was offering himself up to me. This was the state of my life. Maybe I should just shoot *myself.*

I leveled the barrel at his head. "On the floor, on your stomach, hands behind your back."

"Tell you what. I'll get on the floor if you show me some pussy. It gotta be good pussy, too. The full show. You aren't bald down there, are you? I don't know what white bitches thinking of, waxing all the bush off. Gives me the willies. It's like bonin' supermarket chicken."

So I shot him. I did it for women worldwide. It was a public service.

"Yow!" he said. "What the fuck you do that for? We just talking, having some fun."

"*I* wasn't having any fun," I said.

I'd shot him in the foot, and now he was hopping around, howling, dripping blood. From what I could see, I'd nicked him somewhere in the vicinity of the little toe.

"If you aren't down on the floor, hands behind your back, in three seconds, I'm going to shoot you again," I said.

Lowe dropped to the floor. "I'm dying. I'm gonna bleed to death."

I cuffed him and stood back. "I just tagged your toe. You'll be fine."

Lula poked her head in. "What's going on? Was that gunshot?" She walked over to Lowe and stood hands on hips, staring down at Lowe's foot. "Damn," Lula said. "I hate when I have to take bleeders in my Fire-bird. I just got new floor mats, too."

"How bad is it?" Lowe wanted to know. "It feels real bad."

"She just ripped a chunk out of the side of your foot," Lula said. "Looks to me like you got all your toes and everything."

I ran to the kitchen and got a kitchen towel and a plastic garbage bag. I wrapped Lowe's foot in the towel and pulled the plastic bag over the foot and the towel and tied it at the ankle. "That's the best I can do," I said to Lula. "You're going to have to deal with it."

We got him to the curb, and Lula looked down at Lowe's foot. "Hold on here," she said. "We ripped a hole in the Baggie when we dragged him out here, and he's bleeding through the towel. He's gonna have to hang his leg out the window."

"I'm not hanging my leg outta the window," Lowe said. "How's that gonna look?"

"It's gonna look like you're on the way to the hospital," Lula said. "How else you think you're gonna get to the hospital and get that foot stitched up? You gonna sit here and wait for an ambulance? You think they're gonna rush to come get *your* sorry behind?"

"You got a point," Lowe said. "Just hurry up. I'm not feeling all that good. It wasn't right of her to shoot me. She had no call to do that."

"The hell she didn't," Lula said. "You gotta learn to cooperate with women. My opinion is she should have shot higher and rearranged your nasty."

Lula rolled the rear side window down, and Lowe got in and hung his legs out the window.

"I feel like a damn fool," Lowe said. "And this here's uncomfortable. My foot's throbbing like a bitch."

Lula walked around to the driver's side. "I saw a picture of what he did to his girlfriend," Lula said. "She had a broken nose and two cracked ribs, and she was in the hospital for three days. My thinking is he deserves some pain, so I'm gonna drive real slow, and I might even get lost on the way to the emergency room."

"Don't get too lost. Wouldn't want him to bleed to death since I was the one who shot him."

"I didn't see you shoot him," Lula said. "I especially didn't see you shoot him with my gun that might not be registered on account of I got it from a guy on a street corner at one in the morning. Anyways, I figured Lowe was running away and tore himself up on a broken bottle of hooch. You know how these guys always have broken bottles of hooch laying around." Lula muscled herself behind the wheel. "You coming with me or you staying behind to tidy up?"

I gave Lula her gun. "I'm staying behind."

"Later," Lula said. And she drove off with Lowe's legs hanging out her rear side window, the plastic bag rattling in the breeze.

I went into Lowe's apartment and prowled through the kitchen. I found a screwdriver and a mostly empty bottle of Gordon's gin. I used the screwdriver to dig the bullet out of Lowe's floor. I pocketed the round and the casing. Then I dropped the bottle of gin on the bloodiest part of the floor and smashed it with the screwdriver. I went back to the kitchen and washed the screwdriver, washed my hands, and threw the screwdriver into a pile of garbage that had collected in the corner of the kitchen. Discarded pizza boxes, empty soda bottles, fast-food bags, crumpled beer cans, and stuff I preferred not to identify.

"I hate this," I said to the empty apartment. I pulled my cell phone out of my bag and called my dad. A couple years ago my dad retired from his job at the post office, and now he drives a cab part-time.

"Hey," I said when he answered. "It's me. I need a cab."

I locked the doors and secured the windows while I waited for my dad. Not that there was much to steal from Lowe's apartment. Most of the furniture looked like Lowe had shopped at the local Dumpster. Still, it was his and I felt an obligation to be a professional. Probably should have thought about my professional obligation before shooting Lowe in the foot.

I called Ranger. "I just shot a guy in the foot," I told him.

"Did he deserve it?"

"That's sort of a tough moral question. I thought so at the time, but now I'm not so sure."

"Did you destroy the evidence? Were there witnesses? Did you come up with a good lie?"

"Yes. No. Yes."

"Move on," Ranger said. "Anything else?"

"No. That's about it."

"One last word of advice. Stay away from the doughnuts." And he disconnected.

Great.

Twenty minutes later, my father rolled to a stop at curbside. "I thought you were working at the button factory," he said.

My father's body showed up at the dinner table every evening. His mind was usually somewhere else. I suppose that was the secret to my parents' marital success. That plus the deal that my father made money and my mother made meatloaf and the division of labor was clear and never challenged. In some ways, life was simple in the Burg.

"The button factory job didn't work out," I told my father. "I helped Lula with an apprehension today and ended up here."

"You're like your Uncle Peppy. Went from one job to the next. Wasn't that he was dumb, either. Was just that he didn't have a direction. He didn't have a passion, you know? It didn't look like he had any special talent. Like take me. I was good at sorting mail. Now, I know that doesn't seem like a big deal, but it was something I was good at. Of course, I got replaced by a machine. But that doesn't take away that I was good at something. Your Uncle Peppy was forty-two before he found out he could do latch hook rugs."

"Uncle Peppy's doing time at Rahway for arson."

"Yeah, but he's doing latch hook there. When he gets out he can make a good living with rugs. You should see some of his rugs. He made a rug that had a tiger head in it. You ask me, he's better hooking rugs than arson. He never got the hang of arson. Okay, so he set a couple good fires, but he didn't have the touch like Sol Razzi. Sol could set a fire and no one ever knew how it started. Now, *that's* arson."

Jersey's one of the few places where arson is a profession.

"Where are we going?" my father wanted to know.

"What's Mom making for supper?"

"Meatballs with spaghetti. And I saw a chocolate cake in the kitchen."

"I'll go home with you."

There were two cars parked in front of my parents' house. One belonged to my sister. And one belonged to a friend of mine who was helping my mom plan my sister's wedding. My father paused at the driveway entrance and stared at the cars with his eyes narrowed.

"If you smash into them your insurance will go up," I said.

My father gave a sigh, pulled forward, and parked. When my father blew out the candles on his birthday cake I suspect he wished my grandmother would go far away. He'd wish my sister into another state, and my friend Sally Sweet, a.k.a. the Wedding Planner, into another universe. I'm not sure what he wanted to do with me. Maybe ride along on a bust. Don't get me wrong. My dad isn't a mean guy. He wouldn't want my grandmother to suffer, but I think he wouldn't be too upset if she suddenly died in her sleep. Personally, I think Grandma's a hoot. Of course, I don't have to live with her.

All through school my sister, Valerie, looked like the Virgin Mary. Brown hair simply styled, skin like alabaster, beatific smile. And she had a personality to match. Serene. Smooth. Little Miss Perfect. The exact opposite of her sister, Stephanie, who was Miss Disaster. Valerie graduated college in the top 10 percent of her class and married a perfectly nice guy. They followed his job to L.A. They had two girls. Valerie morphed into Meg Ryan. And one day the perfectly nice guy ran off to Tahiti with the baby-sitter. No reflection on Meg. It was just that time in his life. So Valerie moved back home with her girls. Angie is the firstborn and a near perfect clone of Valerie the Virgin. Mary Alice is two years behind Angie. And Mary Alice thinks she's a horse.

It's a little over a year now since Valerie returned, and she's since gained sixty pounds, had a baby out of wedlock, and gotten engaged to her boss, Albert Kloughn, who also happens to be the baby's father. The baby's name is Lisa, but most often she's called The Baby. We're not sure who The Baby is yet, but from the amount of gas she produces I think she's got a lot of Kloughn in her.

Valerie and Sally were huddled at the dining room table, studying the seating chart for the wedding reception.

"Hey, girlfriend," Sally said to me. "Long time no see."

Sally drove a school bus during the week, and weekends he played in a band in full drag. He was six foot five inches tall, had roses tattooed on his biceps, hair everywhere, a large hook nose, and he was lanky in a guitar-playing-maniac kind of way. Today Sally was wearing a big wooden cross on a chain and six strands of love beads over a black Metallica T-shirt, black hightop Chucks, and washed-out baggy jeans.

Okay, not your average wedding planner, but he'd sort of adopted us, and he was free. He'd become one of the family with my mom and grandma and they endured his eccentricities with the same eyerolling tolerance that they endured mine. I guess a pothead wedding planner seems respectable when you have a daughter who shoots people.

Angie was doing her homework across from Valerie. The Baby was in a sling attached to Valerie's chest, and Mary Alice was galloping around the table, whinnying. My father went straight to his chair in the living room and remoted the television. I went to the kitchen.

My mother was at the stove, stirring the red sauce. "Emily Restler's daughter got a pin for ten years' service at the bank," my mother said. "Ten years and she was never once in a shoot-out. I have a daughter who works one day at a dry cleaners and turns it into the gunfight at the O.K. Corral. And on a Sunday, too. The Lord's Day."

"It wasn't me. I didn't even have a gun. It was Mama Macaroni. And she wouldn't give Lula her dry cleaning."

Grandma was at the small kitchen table. "I hate to think you couldn't take down Mama Macaroni. If I'd been there you would have got the dry cleaning. In fact, I got a mind to go over there and get it for you."

"*No,*" my mother and I said in unison.

I got a soda from the fridge and eyed the cake on the counter.

"It's for supper," my mother said. "No snitching. It's got to be nice. The wedding planner is eating with us."

Sally is one of my favorite people, but Sally didn't care a lot about what went in his mouth unless it was inhaled from a bong or rolled in wacky tobacky paper.

"Sally wouldn't notice if there were roaches in the icing," I told my mom.

"It has nothing to do with Sally," my mom said. "My water glasses don't have spots. There's no dust on the furniture. And I don't serve guests half-eaten cake at my dinner table."

I didn't serve guests half-eaten cake either. To begin with, I never had guests, unless it was Joe or Ranger. And neither of them was interested in my cake. Okay, maybe Joe would want cake . . . but it wouldn't be the first thing on his mind, and he wouldn't care if it was half-eaten.

I grated parmesan for my mother, and I sliced some cucumbers and tomatoes. In the dining room, Valerie and Sally were yelling at each other, competing with the television and the galloping horse.

"Is there any news about Michael Barroni?" I asked.

"Still missing," Grandma said. "And they haven't found his car, either. I hear he only had it for a day. It was brand-new right out of the showroom."

"I saw Anthony yesterday. He was driving a Corvette that looked new."

Grandma got dishes from the cupboard. "Mabel Such says Anthony's spending money like water. She don't know where he's getting it from. She says he doesn't make all that much at the store. She says he was on a salary just like everybody else. Michael Barroni came up the hard way, and he wasn't a man to give money away. Not even to his sons."

I got silverware and napkins, and Grandma and I set the table around Valerie and Sally and Angie.

"You can stare at that seating chart all you want," Grandma said to Valerie. "It's never gonna get perfect. Nobody wants to sit next to Biddie Schmidt. Everybody wants to sit next to Peggy Linehart. And nobody's going to be happy sitting at table number six, next to the restrooms."

My mother brought the meatballs and sauce to the table and went back for the spaghetti. My father moved from his living room chair to his dining room chair and helped himself to the first meatball. Everyone sat except Mary Alice. Mary Alice was still galloping.

"Horses got to eat," Grandma said. "You better sit down."

"There's no hay," Mary Alice said.

"Sure there is," Grandma said. "See that big bowl of spaghetti? It's people hay, but horses can eat it, too."

Mary Alice plunged her face into the spaghetti and snarfed it up.

"That's disgusting," Grandma said.

"It's the way horses eat," Mary Alice told her. "They stick their whole face in the feed bag. I saw it on television."

The front door opened and Albert Kloughn walked in. "Am I late? I'm sorry I'm late. I didn't mean to be late. I had a client."

Everyone stopped what they were doing and looked at Kloughn. Kloughn didn't get a lot of clients. He's a lawyer and his business has been slow to take off. Partly the problem is that he's a sweetie-pie guy . . . and who wants a sweetie-pie lawyer? In Jersey you want a lawyer who's a shark, a sonuvabitch, a first-class jerk. And partly the problem is Kloughn's appearance. Kloughn looks like a soft, chubby, not-entirely-with-the-program fourteen-year-old boy.

"What kind of client?" Grandma asked.

Kloughn took his place at the table. "It was a woman from the Laundromat next to my office. She was doing her whites, and she saw my sign and the light on in my office. I went in to do some filing, but I was actually playing poker on my computer. Anyway, she came over for advice." Kloughn helped himself to spaghetti. "Her husband took off on her, and she didn't know what to do. Sounded like she didn't mind him leaving. She said they'd been having problems. It was that he took their car, and she was stuck with the payments. It was a brand-new car, too."

I felt the skin prickle at the nape of my neck. "When did this guy disappear?"

"A couple weeks ago." Kloughn scooped a meatball onto the big serving spoon. The meatball rolled off the spoon, slid down Kloughn's shirt, and ski jumped off his belly into his lap. "I knew that was going to happen," Kloughn said. "This always happens with meatballs. Does it happen with chicken? Does it happen with ham? Okay, sometimes it happens with chicken and ham, but not as much as meatballs. If it was me, I wouldn't make meatballs round. Round things roll, right? Am I right? What if you made meatballs square? Did anybody think of that?"

"That would be meat*loaf*," Grandma said.

"Did this woman report her missing husband to the police?" I asked Kloughn.

"No. It was just one of those personal things. She said she knew he was going to leave her. I guess he was fooling around on the side and things weren't working out for them." Kloughn retrieved the meatball and set it on top of his spaghetti. He dabbed at his shirt with his napkin, but the smear of red sauce only got worse. "I felt sorry for her with the car payment and all, but boy, can you imagine being that dumb? Here she is living with this guy and all of a sudden he just up and leaves her. And it turns out she has nothing but bills. They had two mortgages that she didn't even know about. The bank account was empty. What a dope."

My mother, father, and Grandma and I all sucked in some air and slid our eyes to Valerie. This was exactly what happened to Valerie. This was like calling *Valerie* a dope.

"You think this woman is a dope because her husband managed to swindle her out of everything?" Valerie asked Kloughn.

"Well yeah. I mean, duh. She was probably too lazy to keep track of things and got what she deserved."

The color rose from Valerie's neck clear to the roots of her hair. I swear I could see her scalp glowing like hot coals.

"Oh boy," Grandma said.

Sally inched his chair away from Valerie.

Kloughn was working at the stain on his shirt and not looking at Valerie, and I was guessing he hadn't a clue what he'd just said. Somehow the words got put together into sentences and fell out of his mouth. This happened a lot with Kloughn. Kloughn looked up from his shirt to dead silence. Only a slight sizzle where Valerie's scalp was steaming.

"What?" Kloughn said. He searched the faces in the room. Something was wrong, and he'd missed it. He focused on Valerie, and you could see his mind working backward. And then it hit him. *Kaboom.*

"You were different," he said to Valerie. "I mean, you had a reason for being a dope. Well, not a dope actually. I don't mean to say you were a dope. Okay, you might have been a little dop*ey*. No, wait, I don't mean that either. Not dopey or dope or any of those things. Okay, okay, just a teensy bit dopey, but in a good way, right? Dopey can be good. Like dumb blond dopey. No, I don't mean that either. I don't know where that came from. Did I say that? I didn't say that, did I?"

Kloughn stopped talking because Valerie had gotten to her feet with the fourteen-inch bread knife in her hand.

"You don't want to do anything silly here," I said to Val. "You aren't thinking of stabbing him, are you? Stabbing is messy."

"Fine. Give me your gun, and I'll shoot him."

"It's not good to shoot people," I said. "The police don't like it."

"You shoot people all the time."

"Not *all* the time."

"I'll give you my gun," Grandma said.

My mother glared at my grandmother. "You told me you got rid of that gun."

"I meant I'd give her my gun if I had one," Grandma said.

"Great," Valerie said, flapping her arms, her voice up an octave. "Now I'm dopey. I'm fat, and I'm dopey. I'm a big fat dope."

"I didn't say you were fat," Kloughn said. "You're not fat. You're just . . . chubby, like me."

Valerie went wild-eyed. "*Chubby?* Chubby is awful! I used to be perfect. I used to be serene. And now look at me! I'm a wreck. I'm a big, fat, dopey, chubby wreck. And I look like a white whale in my stupid wedding gown. A big, huge *white whale!*" She narrowed her eyes and leaned across the table at Kloughn. "You think I'm dopey and lazy and chubby, and that I got what I deserved from my philandering husband!"

"No. I swear. I was under stress," Kloughn said. "It was the meatball. I never think. You know I never think."

"I never want to see you again," Valerie said. "The wedding is off." And Valerie gathered up her three kids, her diaper bag, her sling thing, her kids' backpacks, and the collapsible stroller. She went to the kitchen and took the chocolate cake. And she left.

"Dudes," Sally said. "I did the best I could with the dress."

"We're not blaming you," Grandma said. "But she *does* look like a white whale."

Kloughn turned to me. "What happened?"

I looked over at him. "She took the cake."

I caught a ride home with Sally, and I was parked in front of my television when my doorbell rang at nine o'clock. It was Lula, and she was dressed in black from head to toe, including a black ski mask.

"Are you ready?" Lula wanted to know.

"Ready for what?"

"To get my cleaning. What do you think?"

"I think we should give up on the cleaning and send out for a pizza. Aren't you hot in that ski mask?"

"That Mama Macaroni got my favorite sweater. I need that sweater. And on top of that it's the principle of the thing. It's just not right. I was a hundred percent in the right. I'm surprised at you wanting to let this go. Where's your crusading spirit? I bet Ranger wouldn't let it go. And you got to get your car, anyway. How're you gonna get over there to get your car if you don't go with me?"

My car. Mental head slap. I'd forgotten about the car.

Ten minutes later, we were idling across the street from Kan Klean. "It's nice and dark tonight," Lula said. "We got some cloud cover. Not a star in the sky and it looks like someone already took out the street-light."

I looked at Lula and grimaced.

"Hey, don't give me that grimace. I expected you'd compliment me on my shooting. I actually hit that freaking lightbulb!"

"How many shots did it take?"

"I emptied a whole clip at it." Lula cut the engine and pulled her ski mask back over her head. "Come on. Time to rock and roll."

Oh boy.

We got out of the Firebird and waited for an SUV to pass before crossing the street. The SUV driver caught a glance at Lula in the ski mask and almost jumped the curb.

"If you can't drive, you shouldn't be on the road," Lula yelled after him.

"It was the mask," I said. "You scared the crap out of him."

"Hunh," Lula said.

We got to the store and Lula tried the front door. Locked. "How many other doors are there?" she asked.

"Just one. It's in back. But it's a fire door. You'll never get through it. There aren't any windows back there either. Just a couple big exhaust fans."

"Then we got to go in through the front," Lula said. "And I don't mind doing it because I'm justified. This here's a righteous cause. It's not every day I can find a sweater like that." She turned to me. "You go ahead and pick the lock."

"I don't know how to pick a lock."

"Hell, you were the big bounty hunter. How could you be the big bounty hunter without knowing how to pick a lock? How'd you ever get in anywhere?" She stood back and looked at the store. "Ordinarily I'd just break a window, but they got one big-ass window here. It's just about the whole front of the place. It might look suspicious if I broke the window."

Lula ran across the street to the Firebird and came back with a tire iron. "Maybe we can pry the door open." She put the tire iron to the doorjamb and another car drove by. The car slowed as it passed us and then took off.

"Maybe we should try the back door," Lula said.

SIX

We went around to the back and Lula tried to wedge the tire iron under the bolt. "Don't fit," she said. "This door's sealed up tight." Lula gave the door a whack with the tire iron and the door swung open. "Will you look at this," Lula said. "Have we got some luck, or what?"

"I don't like it. They always lock up and set the alarm."

"They must have just forgot. It was a traumatic day."

"I think we should leave. This doesn't feel right."

"I'm not leaving without my sweater. I'm close now. I can hear my sweater calling to me. Soon's we get inside I'll switch on my Maglite, and you can work that gizmo that makes the clothes go around, and before you know it we'll be outta here."

We both took two steps forward, the door closed behind us, and Lula hit the button on the Maglite. We cautiously walked past the commercial washers and dryers and the large canvas bins that held the clothes. We stopped and listened for sirens, for someone else breathing, for the beeping of an alarm system ready to activate.

"Feels okay to me," Lula said.

It didn't feel okay to me. All the little hairs on my

arm were standing at attention, and my heart was thumping in my chest.

"We got the counter right in front of us," Lula said. "You switch on the whirly clothes thing."

I reached for the switch and every light in the store suddenly went on. It was as bright as day. And there was Mama Macaroni, perched on her chair, a hideous crone dressed in a black shroud, sighting us down the barrel of a gun, her mole hairs glinting under the fluorescent light.

"Holy crap," Lula said. "Holy Jesus. Holy cow."

Mama Macaroni held the gun in one hand and Lula's dry cleaning in the other. "I knew you'd be back," she said. "Your kind has no honor. All you know is stealing and whoring."

"I quit whoring," Lula said. "Okay, maybe I do a little recreational whoring once in a while . . ."

"Trash," Mama Macaroni said. "Cheap trash. Both of you." She turned to me. "I never want to hire you. I tell them anything that come from your family is bad. Hungarians!" And she spat on the floor. "That's what I think of Hungarians."

"I'm not Hungarian," Lula said. "How about giving me my dry cleaning?"

"When hell freezes. And that's where you should be," Mama Macaroni said. "I put a curse on you. I send you to hell."

Lula looked at me. "She can't do that, can she?"

"You never get this sweater," Mama Macaroni said. "*Never*. I take this sweater to the grave with me."

Lula looked at me like she wouldn't mind arranging that to happen.

"It'd be expensive," I said to Lula. "Be cheaper just to buy a new sweater."

"And *you*," Mama Macaroni said to me. "You never gonna see that car again. That *my* car now. You leave it in my lot and that make it mine." She squinted down the barrel at me, leveling it at forehead level. "Give me the key."

"You don't suppose she'd actually shoot you, do you?" Lula asked.

There was no doubt in my mind. Mama Macaroni would shoot me, and I'd be dead, dead, dead. I pulled the car key out of my pocket and gingerly handed it over to Mama.

"I'm gonna leave now," Mama said. "I got a TV show I like to watch. And you gonna stay here." She backed away from us, past the washers and dryers to the rear door. She set the alarm and scuttled through the fire door. The door closed after her, and I could hear her throw the bolt.

I immediately went to the front of the store and stood behind the counter so I could look out the window. "We'll wait until we see her drive away, and then we'll leave," I said to Lula. "We'll trip the alarm when we open the door, but we'll be long gone before the police get here."

I heard the Saturn engine catch, and then there was an explosion that rocked the building. The explosion blew the fire door off its hinges, shattered the big front window, and knocked Lula and me to our knees.

"Fudge!" Lula said.

My instinct was to leave the building. I didn't know what caused the explosion, but I wanted to get out before it happened again. And I didn't know if the building was structurally sound. I grabbed Lula and got her to her feet and pulled her to the front door. We were walking carefully, crunching over glass shards. Lucky we'd been behind the counter when the explosion occurred. The door had been blown open, and Lula and I picked our way through the debris, onto the sidewalk.

Kan Klean was in a mixed neighborhood of small

businesses and small homes, and people were coming out of their houses, looking around for the source of the explosion.

"What the heck was that?" Lula said. "And why's there a tire in the middle of the sidewalk?"

I looked at Lula and Lula looked at me, and we knew why there was a tire in the middle of the sidewalk.

"Car bomb," Lula said.

We ran around to the parking lot on the side of the building and stopped short. The Saturn was a blackened skeleton of smoking, twisted metal. Difficult to see details in the dark. Chunks of shredded fiberglass body, upholstered cushion, and odds and ends of car parts were scattered over the lot.

Lula had her flashlight out, playing it across the disaster. She momentarily held the light on a segment of steering wheel. Part of a hand still gripped the wheel. A ragged shred of black cloth was attached to the hand.

"Uh oh," Lula said. "It don't look good for my dry cleaning."

I felt a wave of nausea slide through my stomach. "We should secure this area until the police get here."

Fifteen minutes later, the entire block was cordoned. Yellow police tape stretched everywhere and fire trucks and emergency vehicles were angled between police cars, lights flashing. Banks of portable lights were going up to better see the scene. Macaronis from all parts of the Burg were gathered in a knot to one side of the lot.

Morelli arrived shortly after the first blue-and-white, and he immediately whisked me away, lest I be torn limb from limb by Macaronis. He got the story, and then he stuffed me into his SUV with police escort. Forty-five minutes later, he returned and slid behind the wheel.

"Tell me again how this happened," Morelli said.

"Lula and I were driving by and I saw the light on, so I thought I'd go in and try to get Lula's dry cleaning. Mama Macaroni was alone in the store, she pulled a gun on me, demanded the keys to the Saturn, and left through the back door. Moments later, I heard the explosion."

"Good," Morelli said. "Now tell me what really happened."

"Lula and I broke in through the back door so we could steal her dry cleaning. Mama Macaroni was waiting for us, and the rest of the story is the same."

"Definitely go with the first version," Morelli said.

"Did they find the rest of Mama Macaroni?"

"Most of her. They're still looking through the bushes. Mama Macaroni covered a lot of ground." Morelli turned the key in the ignition. "Do you want to go home with me?"

"Yeah. I'm a little creeped out."

"I was hoping you'd want to go home with me because I'm smart and sexy and fun."

"That, too. And I like your dog."

"That car bomb was meant for you," Morelli said.

"I thought my life would get better if I stopped chasing after bad guys."

"You've made some enemies."

"It's Spiro," I told him.

Morelli stopped for a light and looked at me. "Spiro Stiva? Constantine's kid? Do you know this for sure?"

"No. It's just a gut feeling. The notes sound like him. And he was friends with Anthony Barroni. And now Barroni's dad is missing, and people say Anthony is spending money he shouldn't have."

"So you think something's going on with Anthony Barroni and Spiro Stiva?"

"Maybe. And maybe Spiro's whacko and decided I ruined his life and now he's going to end mine."

Morelli thought about it for a moment and shrugged. "It's not much, but it's as good as anything I've got. How do the other two disappearances fit in?"

"I don't know, but I think there might be one more." And I told him about Kloughn's client. "And there's something else. Kloughn's client's husband disappeared in their brand-new car. Michael Barroni also disappeared in a brand-new car."

Morelli slid a sideways look at me.

"Okay, so I know lots of people have new cars. Still, it's something they had in common."

"Barroni, Gorman, and Lazar were the same age within two years, and they all owned small businesses. Does Kloughn's client fit that profile?"

"I don't know."

Morelli turned a corner, drove two blocks, and parked in front of his house. "You'd think someone would have seen Spiro if he was back. The Burg's not good at keeping a secret."

"Maybe he's hiding."

My mother called on my cell phone. "People are saying you blew up Mama Macaroni."

"She was in my car, and she accidentally blew herself up. *I* did not blow her up."

"How can someone accidentally blow herself up? Are you okay?"

"I'm fine. I'm going home with Joe."

It was early morning, and I was sitting on the side of the bed, watching Morelli get dressed. He was wearing black jeans, cool black shoes with a thick Vibram sole, and a long-sleeved blue button-down shirt. He looked like a movie star playing an Italian cop.

"Very sexy," I said to Morelli.

He strapped his watch on and looked over at me. "Say it again and the clothes come off."

"You'll be late."

Morelli's eyes darkened, and I knew he was weighing pleasure against responsibility. There was a time in Morelli's life when pleasure would have won, no contest. I'd been attracted to that Morelli, but I hadn't especially liked him. The moment passed and Morelli's eyes regained focus. The guy part was under control. Not to give him more credit than he deserved, I suspected this was made possible by the two orgasms he'd had last night and the one he'd had about a half hour ago.

"I can't be late today. I have an early meeting, and I'm way behind on my paperwork." He kissed the top of my head. "Will you be here when I come home tonight?"

"No. I'm working the three-to-eleven shift at Cluckin-a-Bucket."

"You're kidding."

"It was one of those impulse things."

Morelli grinned down at me. "You must need money real bad."

"Bad enough."

I followed him down the stairs and closed the door after him. "Just you and me," I said to Bob.

Bob had already eaten his breakfast and gone for a walk, so Bob was feeling mellow. He wandered away, into the living room where bars of sunshine were slanting through the window onto the carpet. Bob turned three times and flopped down onto the sun spot.

I shuffled out to the kitchen, got a mug of coffee, and took it upstairs to Morelli's office. The room was small and cluttered with boxes of income tax files, a red plastic milk carton filled with old tennis balls collected during dog walks in the park, a baseball bat, a stack of phone books, gloves and wraps for a speed bag, a giant blue denim dog bed, a well-oiled baseball glove, a power screwdriver, roles of duct tape, a dead plant in a clay pot, and a plastic watering can that had obviously never been used. He had a computer and a desktop printer on a big wood desk that had been bought used. And he had a phone.

I sat at the desk, and I took a pen and a yellow legal pad from the top drawer. I had the morning free, and I was going to use it to do some sleuthing. Someone wanted me dead, and I didn't feel comfortable sitting around doing nothing, waiting for it to happen.

First on my list was a call to Kloughn.

"She wouldn't let me in the house," he said. "I had to sleep here in the office. It wasn't so bad since I have a couch, and the Laundromat is next door. I got up early and did some laundry. What should I do? Should I call? Should I go over there? I had this terrible nightmare last night. Valerie was floating over top of me in the wedding gown except she was a whale. I bet it was because she kept saying how she was a whale in the wedding gown. Anyway, there she was in my dream . . . a big huge whale all dressed up in the white wedding gown. And then all of a sudden she dropped out of the sky, and I was squashed under her, and I couldn't breathe. Good thing I woke up, hunh?"

"Good thing. I need to know your client's name," I told him. "The one with the missing husband."

"Terry Runion. Her husband's name is Jimmy Runion."

"Do you know what kind of car he just bought?"

"Ford Taurus. He got it at that big dealership on Route One. Shiller Ford."

"His age?"

"I don't know his exact age, but his wife looks like she's late fifties."

"What about his job? Did he quit his job when he disappeared?"

"He didn't have a job. He used to work for some computer company, but he took early retirement. About Valerie . . ."

"I'll talk to Valerie for you," I said. And I hung up.

Valerie answered on the second ring. "Yuh," she said.

"I just talked to Albert. He said he slept in his office."

"He said I was fat."

"He said you were chubby."

"Do you think I'm chubby?" Val asked.

"No," I told her. "I think you're fat."

"Oh God," Valerie wailed. "*Oh God!* How did this happen? How did I get *fat*?"

"You ate everything. And you ate it with gravy."

"I did it for the baby."

"Well, something went wrong because only seven pounds went to the baby, and you got the rest."

"I don't know how to get rid of it. I've never been fat before."

"You should talk to Lula. She's good at losing weight."

"If she's so good at losing weight, why is she so big?"

"She's also good at *gaining* weight. She gains it. She loses it. She gains it. She loses it."

"The wedding is on Saturday. If I really worked at it, do you think I could lose sixty pounds between now and Saturday?"

"I guess you could have it sucked out, but I hear that's real painful and you get a lot of bruising."

"I hate my life," Val said.

"Really?"

"No. I just hate being fat."

"That doesn't mean you should hate Albert. He didn't make you fat."

"I know. I've been awful to him, and he's such an adorable oogie woogams."

"I think it's great that you're in love, Val. And I'm

happy for you . . . I really am. But the baby talk cuddle umpkins oogie woogams thing is making me a
little barfy warfy. What about the Virgin Mary, Val?
Remember when everyone said you were just like the
Virgin Mary? You were cool and serene like the Virgin
Mary, like a big pink plaster statue of the Virgin. Would
the Virgin refer to God as her cuddle umpkins? I don't
think so."

The next call was to my cousin Linda at the DMV. "I
need some information," I said to Linda. "Benny Gorman, Michael Barroni, Louis Lazar. I want to know if
they got a new car in the last three months and what
kind?"

"I heard you quit working for Vinnie. So what's up
with the names?"

"Part-time job. Routine credit check for CBNJ." I
had no idea what CBNJ stood for, but it sounded good,
right?

I could hear Linda type the names into her computer. "Here's Barroni," she said. "He bought a Honda
Accord two weeks ago. Nothing on Gorman. And
nothing's coming up on Lazar."

"Thanks. I appreciate it."

"Boy, the wedding's almost here. I guess everyone's
real excited."

"Yeah. Valerie's a wreck."

"That's the way it is with weddings," Linda said.

I disconnected and took a moment to enjoy my coffee. I liked sitting in Morelli's office. It wasn't especially pretty, but it felt nice because it was filled with
all the bits and pieces of Morelli's life. I didn't have an
office in my apartment. And maybe that was a good
thing because I was afraid if I had an office it might be
empty. I didn't have a hobby. I didn't play sports. I had
a family, but I never got around to framing pictures. I

wasn't learning a foreign language, or learning to play the cello, or learning to be a gourmet cook.

Well hell, I thought. I could just pick one of those things. There's no reason why I can't be interesting and have an office filled with stuff. I can collect tennis balls in the park. And I can get a plant and let it die. And I can play the damn cello. In fact, I could probably be a terrific cello player.

I took my coffee mug downstairs and put it in the dishwasher. I grabbed my bag and my jacket. I yelled good-bye to Bob as I was going out the door. And I set off on foot for my parents' house. I was going to borrow Uncle Sandor's Buick. Again. I had no other option. I needed a car. Good thing it was a long walk to my parents' house and I was getting all this exercise because I was going to need a doughnut after taking possession of the Buick.

Grandma was at the door when I strolled down the street. "It's Stephanie!" Grandma yelled to my mother.

Grandma loved when I blew up cars. Blowing up Mama Macaroni would be icing on the cake for Grandma. My mother didn't share Grandma's enthusiasm for death and disaster. My mother longed for normalcy. Dollars to doughnuts, my mother was in the kitchen ironing. Some people popped pills when things turned sour. Some hit the bottle. My mother's drug of choice was ironing. My mother ironed away life's frustrations.

Grandma opened the door for me, and I stepped into the house and dropped my bag on the hall table.

"Is she ironing?" I asked Grandma Mazur.

"Yep," Grandma said. "She's been ironing since first thing this morning. Probably would have started last night but she couldn't get off the phone. I swear, half the Burg called about you last night. Finally we disconnected the phone."

I went to the kitchen and poured myself a cup of coffee. I sat down at the little kitchen table and looked over at my mother's ironing basket. It was empty. "How many times have you ironed that shirt you've got on the board?" I asked my mother.

"Seven times," my mother said.

"Usually you calm down by the time the basket's empty."

"Somebody blew up Mama Macaroni," my mother said. "That doesn't bother me. She had it coming. What bothers me is that it was supposed to be you. It was your car."

"I'm being careful. And it's not certain that it was a bomb. It could have been an accident. You know how it is with my cars. They catch on fire, and they explode."

My mother made a strangled sound in her throat, and her eyes sort of glazed over. "That's true," she said. "Hideously true."

"Marilyn Rugach said Stiva's got most of Mama Macaroni at the funeral parlor," Grandma said. "Marilyn works there part-time doing bookkeeping. I talked to Marilyn this morning, and she said they brought the deceased to the home in a zippered bag. She said there was still some parts missing, but she wouldn't say if they found the mole. Do you think there's any chance that they'll have an open casket at the viewing? Stiva's pretty good at patching people up, and I sure would like to see what he'd do with that mole."

My mother made the sign of the cross, a hysterical giggle gurgled out of her, and she clapped a hand over her mouth.

"You should give up on the ironing and have a snort," Grandma said to my mother.

"I don't need a snort," my mother said. "I need some sanity in my life."

"You got a lot of sanity," Grandma said. "You got a

real stable lifestyle. You got this house and you got a husband . . . sort of. And you got daughters and grand-daughters. And you got the Church."

"I have a daughter who blows things up. Cars, trucks, funeral parlors, people."

"That only happens once in a while," I said. "I do lots of other things besides that."

My mother and grandmother looked at me. I had their full attention. They wanted to know what other things I did besides blowing up cars and trucks and funeral parlors and people.

I searched my mind and came up with nothing. I did a mental replay of yesterday. What did I do? I blew up a car and an old lady. Not personally but I was some-where in the mix. What else? I made love to Morelli. A lot. My mother wouldn't want to hear about that. I got fired. I shot a guy in the foot. She wouldn't want to hear that either.

"I can play the cello," I said. I don't know where it came from. It just flew out of my mouth.

My mother and grandmother stood frozen in open-mouthed shock.

"Don't that beat all," Grandma finally said. "Who would have thought you could play the cello?"

"I had no idea," my mother said. "You never men-tioned it before. Why didn't you tell us?"

"I was . . . shy. It's one of those personal hobbies. Personal cello playing."

"I bet you're real good," Grandma said.

My mother and grandmother looked at me expec-tantly. They wanted me to be good.

"Yep," I said. "I'm pretty good."

Stephanie, Stephanie, Stephanie, I said to myself. What are you doing? You are such a goofus. You don't even know what a cello looks like. Sure I do, I answered. It's a big violin, right?

"How long have you been taking lessons?" Grandma wanted to know.

"A while." I looked at my watch. "Gee, I'd like to stay, but I have things to do. I was hoping I could borrow Uncle Sandor's Buick."

Grandma took a set of keys out of a kitchen drawer. "Big Blue will be happy to see you," she said. "He doesn't get driven around too much."

Big Blue corners like a refrigerator on wheels. It has power brakes but no power steering. It guzzles gas. It's impossible to park. And it's powder blue. It has a shiny white top, powder blue body, silver-rimmed portholes, fat whitewall tires, and big gleaming chrome bumpers.

"I guess you need a big car like Blue so you can carry that cello around with you," Grandma said.

"It's a perfect fit for the backseat," I told her.

I took the keys and waved myself out of the house. I walked to the garage, opened the door, and there it was . . . Big Blue. I could feel the vibes coming off the car. The air hummed around me. Men loved Big Blue. It was a muscle car. It rode on a sweaty mix of high-octane gas and testosterone. Step on the gas and hear me roar, the car whispered. Not the growl of a Porsche. Not the *vroooom* of a Ferrari. This car was a bull walrus. This car had cojones that hung to its hubcaps.

Personally, I prefer cojones that sit a little higher, but hey, that's just me. I climbed aboard, rammed the key in, and cranked Blue over. The car came to life and vibrated under me. I took a deep breath, told myself I'd own a Lexus someday, and slowly backed out of the garage.

Grandma trotted over to the car with a brown grocery bag. "Your mother wants you to drop this off at Valerie's house. Valerie forgot to take it last night."

Valerie was renting a small house at the edge of the Burg, about a half mile away. Until yesterday, she was sharing the house with Albert Kloughn. And since she was back to calling him her oogie woogams, I suppose he was about to return.

I wound through a maze of streets, brought Big Blue to the curb in front of Val's house, and stared at the car parked in front of me. It was Lula's red Firebird. Two possibilities. One was that Valerie had skipped out on a bond. The other was that she'd taken my smart-mouth advice and called Lula for diet tips. I rolled out of the Buick and got on with the brown-bag delivery.

Val opened the door before I reached the porch. "Grandma called and said you were on your way."

"Looks like Lula's here. Are you FTA?"

"No. I'm F-A-T. So I called Lula like you suggested. And she came right over."

"I take other people's dieting seriously," Lula said to Valerie. "I'm gonna have you skinny in no time. This might even turn out to be a second career for me. Of course, now that I'm a bounty hunter I've got a lot of demands on my time. I've got a real nasty case that I'm working on. I should be out tracking this guy down right now, only I figured I could take a break from it and help you out."

"What kind of case is it?" Val asked.

"He's wanted for AR and PT," Lula said. "That's bounty hunter shorthand for armed robbery and public tinkling. He held up a liquor store and then took a leak in the domestic table wines section. I bet Stephanie here is gonna be so happy I'm helping you that she's gonna ride along and help out with the apprehension."

"Not likely," I said. "I have to be at work at three."

"Yeah, but at the rate you're going, you'll be fired by five," Lula said. "I just hope you last through dinner-time, because I was planning on coming in for a bucket of extra crispy."

"Is that on *my* diet?" Val asked.

"Hell no," Lula said. "Ain't nothing on your diet. You want to lose weight, you gotta starve. You gotta eat a bunch of plain-ass carrots and shit."

"What about that no-carb diet? I hear you can eat bacon and steak and lobster."

"You didn't tell me what kind of diet you wanted to do. I just figured you wanted the starvation diet on account of it's the easiest and the most economical. You don't have to weigh anything. And you don't have to cook anything. You just don't eat anything." Lula motored off to the kitchen. "Let's check out your cupboards and see if you got *good* food or *bad* food." Lula poked around. "Uh oh, this don't look like skinny food. You got chips in here. Boy, I sure would like some of these chips. I'm not gonna eat them, though, 'cause I got willpower."

"Me, too," Valerie said. "I'm not going to eat them either."

"I bet you eat them when we leave," Lula said.

Valerie bit into her lower lip. Of course she'd eat them. She was human, wasn't she? And this was Jersey. And the *Burg,* for crissake. We ate chips in the Burg. We ate *everything.*

"Maybe I should take those chips," Lula said. "It would be okay if *I* ate the chips later being that *I'm* currently not in my weight-losing mode. I'm currently in my weight-*gaining* mode."

Valerie pulled all the bags of chips out of the cupboard and dumped them into a big black plastic garbage bag. She threw boxes of cookies and bags of candy into the bag. She added the junk-sugar-loaded cereals, the toaster waffles, the salted nuts. She handed the bag over to Lula. "And I'm only going to eat one pork chop tonight. And I'm not going to smother it in gravy."

"Good for you," Lula said. "You're gonna be skinny in no time with an attitude like that."

Valerie turned to me. "Grandma was all excited when she called. She said they just found out you've been playing the cello all these years."

Lula's eyes bugged out. "Are you shitting me? I didn't know you played a musical instrument. And the cello! That's real fancy-pants. That's fuckin' classy. How come you never said anything?"

Small tendrils of panic curled through my stomach. This was getting out of control. "It's no big thing," I said. "I'm not very good. And I hardly ever play. In fact, I can't remember the last time I celloed."

"I don't ever remember seeing a cello in your apartment," Valerie said.

"I keep it in the closet," I told her. *I was such a good fibber!* It had been my one real usable talent as a bounty hunter. I made a show of checking my watch. "Boy, look at the time. I have to go."

"Me, too," Lula said. "I gotta go get that stupid AR." She wrapped her arms around the bag of junk food and lugged it out to her car. "It would be like old times if you rode with me on this one," Lula said to me. "It wouldn't take us long to round up Mr. Pisser, and then we could eat all this shit."

"I have to go home and take a shower and get dressed for work. And I have to feed Rex. And I don't want to do bond enforcement anymore."

"Okay," Lula said. "I guess I could understand all that."

Lula roared off in her Firebird. And I slowly accelerated in the Buick. The Buick was like a freight train. Takes a while to get a full head of steam, but once it gets going it'll plow through anything.

I stopped at Giovichinni's Meat Market on the way home. I idled in front of the store and looked through the large front window. Bonnie Sue Giovichinni was working the register. I dialed Bonnie Sue and asked her if there were any Macaronis in the store.

"Nope," Bonnie Sue said. "The coast is clear."

I scurried around, gathering the bare essentials. A loaf of bread, some sliced provolone, a half pound of sliced ham, a small tub of chocolate ice cream, a quart of skim milk, and a handful of fresh green beans for Rex. I added a couple Tastykakes to my basket and lined up behind Mrs. Krepler at the checkout.

"I just talked to Ruby Beck," Mrs. Krepler said. "Ruby tells me you've left the bonds office so you can play cello with a symphony orchestra. How exciting!"

I was speechless.

"And have you heard if they found the mole yet?" Mrs. Krepler asked.

I paid for my groceries and hurried out of the store. The cello-playing thing was going through the Burg like wildfire. You'd think with something as good as Mama Macaroni getting blown to bits there wouldn't be time to care about my cello playing. I swear, I can't catch a break here.

I drove home and docked the boat in a spot close to the back door. I figured the closer to the door, the less chance of a bomb getting planted. I wasn't sure the theory held water, but it made me feel better. I took the stairs and opened the door to my apartment cautiously. I stuck my head in and listened. Just the sound of Rex running on his wheel in his cage in the kitchen. I locked and bolted the door behind me and retrieved my gun from the cookie jar. The gun wasn't loaded because I'd forgotten to buy bullets, but I crept through the apartment, looking in closets and under the bed with the gun drawn anyway. I couldn't shoot anyone, but at least I looked like I could kick ass.

I took a shower and got dressed in jeans and a T-shirt. I didn't spend a lot of time on my hair since I'd be wearing the dorky Cluck hat. I lined my eyes and slathered on mascara to make up for the hair. I gave Rex a couple beans, and I made myself a ham and cheese sandwich. I glanced at my gun while I ate my sandwich. The gun was loaded. I went to the cookie jar and looked inside. There was a RangeMan business card in the bottom of the jar. A single word was handwritten on the card. BABE!

I had a momentary hot flash and briefly considered checking out my underwear drawer for more business cards. "He's trying to protect me," I said to Rex. "He does that a lot."

I got the tub of ice cream from the freezer and took it to the dining room table, along with a pad. I sat at the table and ate the ice cream and made notes for myself. I had four guys who were all about the same age. They all had a small business at one time or another. Two bought new cars. They all disappeared on the same day at about the same time. None of their cars was ever retrieved. That was all I knew.

My hunch about Anthony and Spiro didn't really amount to much. Probably I was trying to make a connection where none existed. One thing was certain. Someone was stalking me, trying to scare me. And now it looked like that person was trying to kill me. Not a happy thought.

I'd eaten about a third of the tub of ice cream. I put the lid on the tub and walked it back to the freezer. I put all the food away and wiped down the countertop. I wasn't much of a housekeeper, but I didn't want to be killed and have my mother discover my kitchen was a mess.

SEVEN

I left my apartment at two-ten and gingerly circled the Buick, looking for signs of tampering. I looked in the window. I crouched down and looked under the car. Finally I put the key in the lock, squinched my eyes closed, and opened the door. No explosion. I slid behind the wheel, took a deep breath, and turned the engine over. No explosion. I thought this was good news and bad news. If it had exploded I'd be dead, and that would be bad. On the other hand, I wouldn't have to wear the awful Cluck hat, and that would be very good.

Twenty minutes later, I was standing in front of Milton Mann, receiving instructions.

"We're going to start you off at the register," he said. "It's all computerized so it's super simple. You just punch in the order and the computer sends the order to the crew in the back and tells you how much to charge the customer. You have to be real friendly and polite. And when you give the customer their change you say, 'Thank you for visiting Cluck-in-a-Bucket. Have a clucky day.' And always remember to wear your hat. It's our special trademark."

The hat was egg-yolk yellow and rooster-comb red. It had a bill like a ball cap, except the bill was shaped like a beak, and the rest of the hat was a huge chicken head, topped off with the big floppy red comb. Red chicken legs with red chicken toes hung from either side of the bottom of the hat. The rest of the uniform consisted of an egg-yolk yellow short-sleeve shirt and elastic-waist pants that had the Cluck-in-a-Bucket chicken logo imprinted everywhere in red. The shirt and pants looked like pajamas designed for the criminally insane.

"You'll do a two-hour shift at the register and then we'll rotate you to the chicken fryer," Mann said.

If it was in the cards that the bomber was going to succeed in killing me, I prayed that it happened before I got to the chicken fryer.

It turns out the three-to-five shift at the register is light. Some after-school traffic and some construction workers.

A woman and her kid stepped up to the counter.

"Tell the chicken what you want," the woman said.

"It's not a chicken," the kid said. "It's a girl in a stupid chicken hat."

"Yes, but she can cluck like a chicken," the woman said. "Go ahead," she said to me. "Cluck like a chicken for Emily."

I looked at the woman.

"Last time we were here the chicken clucked," the woman said.

I looked down at Emily. "Cluck."

"She's no good," Emily said. "The other chicken was *way* better. The other chicken flapped her arms."

I took a deep breath, stuffed my fists under my armpits, and did some chicken-wing flapping. "Cluck, cluck, cluck, cluck, clu-u-u-u-ck," I said.

"I want french fries and a chocolate shake," Emily said.

The next guy in line weighed three hundred pounds and was wearing a torn T-shirt and a hard hat. "You gonna cluck for me?" he asked. "How about I want you to do something besides cluck?"

"How about I shove my foot so far up your ass your nuts get stuck in your throat?"

"Not my idea of a good time," he said. "Get me a bucket of extra crispy and a Diet Coke."

At five o'clock I was marched back to the fryer.

"It's a no-brainer," Mann said. "It's all automated. When the green light goes on the oil is right for frying, so you dump the chicken in."

Mann pulled a huge plastic tub of chicken parts out of the big commercial refrigerator. He took the lid off the tub, and I almost passed out at the site of slick pink muscle and naked flesh and cracked bone.

"As you can see, we have three stainless-steel tanks," Mann said. "One is the fryer and one is the drainer and one is the breader. It's the breader that sets us apart from all the other chicken places. We coat our chicken with the specially seasoned secret breading glop right here in the store." Mann dumped a load of chicken into a wire basket and lowered it into the breader. He swished the basket around, raised it, and gently set it into the hot oil. "When you put the chicken into the oil you push the Start button and the machine times the chicken. When the bell rings you take the chicken out and set the basket in the drainer. Easy, right?"

I could feel sweat prickle at my scalp under my hat. It was about two hundred degrees in front of the fryer, and the air was oil saturated. I could smell the hot oil. I could taste the hot oil. I could feel it soaking into my pores.

"How do I know how much chicken to fry?" I asked him.

"You just keep frying. This is our busy time of day. You go from one basket to the next and keep the hot chicken rolling out."

A half hour later, Eugene was yelling at me from the bagging table. "We need extra-spicy. All you're doing is extra-crispy. And there's all wings here. You gotta give us some backs and some thighs. People are bitchin' about the friggin' wings. If they wanted all wings, they'd order all wings."

At precisely seven o'clock, Mann appeared at my side. "You get a half-hour dinner break now, and then we're going to rotate you to the drive-thru window until closing time at eleven."

My muscles ached from lifting the chicken baskets. My uniform was blotched with grease stains. My hair felt like it had been soaked in oil. My arms were covered with splatter burns. I had thirty minutes to eat, but I didn't think I could gag down fried chicken. I shuffled off to the ladies' room and sat on the toilet with my head down. I think I fell asleep like that because next thing I knew, Mann was knocking on the ladies' room door, calling my name.

I followed Mann to the drive-thru window. The plan was that I remove my Cluck hat, put the headset on, and put the Cluck hat back over the headset. Problem was, after tending the fryer, my hair was slick with grease and the headset kept sliding off.

"Ordinarily I don't put people in the drive-thru after the fryer just for this problem," Mann said, "but Darlene went home sick and you're all I got." He disappeared into the storeroom and came back with a roll of black electrical tape. "Necessity is the mother of invention," he said, holding the headset to my head, wrapping my head with a couple loops of tape. "Now you can put your hat on and get clucky, and that headset isn't going anywhere."

"Welcome to Cluck-in-a-Bucket," I said to the first car.

"I wanna crchhtra skraapyy, two orders of fries, and a large crchhhk."

Mann was standing behind me. "That's extra crispy chicken, two fries, and a large Coke." He gave me a pat on the shoulder. "You'll get the hang of it after a couple cars. Anyway, all you have to do is ring them up, take their money, and give them their order. Fred is in back filling the order." And he left.

"Seven-fifty," I said. "Please drive up."

"What?"

"Seven-fifty. Please drive up."

"Speak English. I can't understand a friggin' thing you're saying."

"Seven-fifty!"

The car pulled to the window. I took money from the driver, and I handed him the bag. He looked into the bag and shook his head. "There's only one fries in here."

"Fred," I yelled into my mouthpiece, "you shorted them a fries."

Fred ran over with the fries. "Sorry, sir," he said to the guy in the car. "Have a clucky day."

Fred was a couple inches taller than me and a couple pounds lighter. He had pasty white skin that was splotched with grease burns, pale blue eyes, and red dreads that stuck out from his hat, making him look a little like the straw man in *The Wizard of Oz*. I put him at eighteen or nineteen.

"Cluck you," the guy said to Fred, and drove off.

"Thank you, sir," Fred yelled after him. "Have a nice day. Go cluck yourself." Fred turned to me. "You gotta go faster. We have about forty cars in line. They're getting nasty."

After a half hour I was hoarse from yelling into the microphone. "Seven-twenty," I croaked. "Please drive up."

"What?"

I took a sip of the gallon-size Coke I had next to my register. "Seven-twenty."

"What?"

"Seven fucking twenty."

An SUV pulled up to the window, I reached for the money, and I found myself staring into Spiro Stiva's glittering rat eyes. The lighting was bad, but I could see that his face had obviously been badly burned in the funeral home fire. I stood rooted to the spot, unable to move, unable to speak.

His mouth had become a small slash in the scarred face. The mouth smiled at me, but the smile was tight and joyless. He handed me a ten. His hand shook, and the skin on his hand was mottled and glazed from burn scars.

Fred gave me a bag, and I automatically passed it through to Spiro.

"Keep the change," Spiro said. And he tossed a medium-size box wrapped in Scooby-Doo paper and tied with a red ribbon through the drive-thru window. And he drove away.

The box bounced off the small service counter and landed on the floor between Fred and me. Fred picked the box up and examined it. "There's a gift tag attached. It says 'Time is ticking away.' What's that supposed to mean? Hey, and you know what else? I think this thing is ticking. Do you know that guy?"

"Yeah, I know him." I took the box and turned to throw it out the drive-thru window. No good. Another car had already pulled up.

"What's the deal?" Fred asked.

"I need to take this outside."

"No way. There are a bazillion cars lined up. Mann will have a cow." Fred reached for the box. "Give it to me. I'll put it in the back room for you."

"No! This might be a bomb. I want you to *very quietly* call the police while I take this outside."

"Are you shitting me?"

"Just call the police, okay?"

"Holy crap! You're serious. That guy gave you a bomb?"

"Maybe . . ."

"Put it under water," Fred said. "I saw a show on television and they put the bomb under water."

Fred ripped the box out of my hand and dumped it into the chicken fryer. The boiling oil bubbled up and spilled over the sides of the fryer. The oil slick carried to the grill, there was a sound like *phuunf,* and suddenly the grill was covered in blue flame.

Fred's eyes went wide. "Fire!" he shrieked. He grabbed a super-size cup and scooped water from the rinse sink.

"No!" I yelled. "Get the chemical extinguisher."

Too late. Fred threw the water at the grill fire, a whoosh of steam rose in the air, and fire raced up the wall to the ceiling.

I pushed Fred to the front of the store and went back to make sure no one was left in the kitchen area. Flames were running down the walls and along the counters and the overhead sprinkler system was shooting foam. When I was sure the prep area was empty I left through a side door.

Sirens were screaming in the distance and the flash of emergency-vehicle strobes could be seen blocks away. Black smoke billowed high in the sky and flames licked out windows and doors and climbed up the stucco exterior.

Customers and employees stood in the parking lot, gawking at the spectacle.

"It wasn't my fault," I said to no one in particular.

Carl Costanza was the first cop on the scene. He locked eyes with me and smiled wide. He said something to Dispatch on his two-way, and I knew Morelli would be getting a call. Fire trucks and EMT trucks roared into the parking lot. More cop cars. The crowd of spectators was growing. They spilled onto the street and clogged the sidewalk. The evening news van pulled up. I moved away from the building to stand by the Buick at the outermost perimeter of the lot. I would have driven home, but the keys were in my bag, and my bag was barbecued.

The flashing strobes and the glare of headlights made it difficult to see into the jumble of parked cars and emergency trucks. Fire hoses snaked across the lot and silhouettes of men moved against the glare. Two men walked toward me, away from the pack. The silhouettes were familiar. Morelli and Ranger. They had a strange alliance. They were two very different men with similar goals. They were teammates of a sort. And they were competitors. They were both smiling when they reached me. I'd like to think it was because they were happy to see me alive. But probably it was because I was my usual wreck. I was grease stained and smoke smudged. I still had the headset taped to my head. I was still wearing the awful chicken hat and Cluck pajamas. And globs of pink foam hung from the hat and clung to my shirt.

They both stood hands on hips when they reached me. They were smiling, but there was a grim set to their mouths.

Morelli reached over and swiped at the pink gunk on my hat.

"Fire extinguisher foam," I said. "It wasn't my fault."

"Costanza told me the fire was started with a bomb."

"I guess that might be true . . . indirectly. I was working the drive-thru window, and Spiro pulled up. He tossed a gift-wrapped box at me and drove away. The box was ticking, and Fred got all excited and dumped the box in the vat of boiling oil. The oil bubbled over onto the grill and next thing the place was toast."

"Are you sure it was Spiro?"

"Positive. His face and hands are scarred, but I'm sure it was him. The card on the box said 'Time is ticking away.'"

Morelli took a quarter from his pocket and flipped it into the air. "Call it," he said to Ranger.

"Heads."

Morelli caught the quarter and slapped it over. "Heads. You win. I guess I have to clean her up."

"Good luck," Ranger said. And he left.

I was too exhausted to get totally irate, but I managed to muster some half-assed outrage. I glared at Morelli. "I don't believe you tossed for me."

"Cupcake, you should be happy I lost. He would have put you through the car wash at the corner of Hamilton and Market." He took my hand and tugged me forward. "Let's go home."

"Will Big Blue be safe here?"

"Big Blue is safe *everywhere*. That car is indestructible."

Morelli was in the shower with me. "Okay," he said. "There's some bad news, and then there's some bad news. The bad news is that it would seem some clumps of hair got yanked out of your head when we ripped the electrician's tape off. The other bad news is that you still smell like fried chicken, and it's making me hungry. Why don't we towel you off and send out for food?"

I put my hand to my hair. "How bad is it?"

"Hard to tell with all that oil in it. It's sort of clumping together."

"I shampooed three times!"

"I don't think shampoo is going to cut it. Maybe you need something stronger . . . like paint stripper."

I grabbed a towel, stepped out of the shower, and

looked at myself in the mirror over the sink. He was right. Shampoo wasn't working, and I had bald spots at the side of my head where the tape had been bound to me.

"I'm not going to cry," I said to him.

"Thank God. I hate when you cry. It makes me feel really shitty."

A tear slid down my cheek.

"Oh crap," Morelli said.

I wiped my nose with the back of my hand. "It's been a long day."

"We'll figure this out tomorrow," Morelli said. He took the cap off a tube of aloe ointment and carefully dabbed the ointment on my chicken-fryer burns. "I bet if you go to that guy at the mall, Mr. Whatshisname . . ."

"Mr. Alexander."

"Yeah, he's the one. I bet he'll be able to fix your hair." Morelli recapped the tube and reached for his cell phone. "I'm calling Pino. What do you want to eat?"

"Anything but chicken."

I woke up thinking Morelli was licking me, but it turned out to be Bob. My face was wet with Bob slurpies, and he was gnawing on my hair. I made a sound that was halfway between laughing and crying, and Morelli opened an eye and batted Bob away.

"It's not his fault," Morelli said. "You still smell like fried chicken."

"Great."

"Could be worse," Morelli said. "You could still smell like cooked car."

I rolled out of bed and shuffled into the bathroom. I soaped myself in the shower until there was no more hot water. I got out and sniffed at my arm. Fried chicken. I returned to the bedroom and checked out the bed. Empty. Large grease stain on my pillowcase.

I borrowed some sweats from Morelli's closet and followed the coffee smell to the kitchen.

Bob was sprawled on the floor next to his empty food bowl. Morelli was at the table, reading the paper.

I poured out a mug of coffee and sat across from Morelli. "I'm not going to cry."

"Yeah, I've heard that before," Morelli said. He put the paper aside and slid a bakery bag over to me. "Bob and I went to the bakery while you were in the shower. We thought you might need happy food."

I looked inside the bag. Two Boston cream doughnuts. "That's so nice of you," I said. And I burst into tears.

Morelli looked pained.

"My emotions are a little close to the surface," I told him. I blew my nose in a paper napkin and took a doughnut. "Any word on the fire?"

"Yeah. First, some good news. Cluck-in-a-Bucket is closed indefinitely, so you don't have to go back to work there. Second, some mixed news. Big Blue is parked at the curb in front of my house. I'm assuming this is Ranger's handiwork. Unfortunately, unless you have an extra key you're not going to be driving it until you get a locksmith out here. And now for the interesting stuff. They were able to retrieve the gift box from the chicken fryer."

I pulled the second doughnut out of the bag. "And?"

"It was a clock. No evidence that it was a bomb."

"Is that for sure?"

"That's what the lab guys said. I also got a report back on the car bomb. It was detonated from an outside source."

"What does that mean?"

"It means it didn't go off when Mama Macaroni stepped on the gas or turned the key in the ignition. Someone pushed the button on Mama Macaroni when

they saw her get into the car. We'll assume it was Spiro
since he gave you the box. Hard to believe he'd mistake
Mama Macaroni for you, so I have to think he blew her
away for giggles."

"Yikes."

Bob lumbered over and sniffed at the empty doughnut bag. Morelli crumpled the bag and threw it across
the room, and Bob bounded after it and tore it to shreds.

"I'm guessing Spiro was waiting for you and when
Mama Macaroni showed up he couldn't resist blowing
her to smithereens. Hell, I'm not sure *I* could resist."
Morelli took a sip of my coffee. "Anyway, it looks like
he isn't trying to kill you . . . yet."

I drank a second cup of coffee. I called Mr. Alexander and made an appointment for eleven o'clock. I
stood to leave and realized I had nothing. No key to the
Buick. No key to my apartment. No credit cards. No
money. No shoes. No underwear. We'd thrown all my
clothes, including my shoes, into the trash last night.

"Help," I said to Morelli.

Morelli smiled at me. "Barefoot and desperate. Just
the way I like you."

"Unless you also like me with a greasy head you'd
better find a way to get me dressed and out to the mall."

"No problemo. I have a key to your apartment. And
I have the day off. I'm ready to roll anytime you are."

"How did this happen?" Mr. Alexander asked, studying
my hair. "No. On second thought, don't tell me. I'm sure
it's something awful. It's *always awful!*" He leaned over
me and sniffed. "Have you been eating fried chicken?"

Morelli was slouched in a chair, hiding behind a
copy of *GQ*. He was armed, he was hungry, and he was
hoping for a nooner. From time to time, women walked
in and checked Morelli out, starting with the hip work
boots, going to the long legs in professionally faded

jeans, pausing at the nicely packaged goods. He didn't have a ring on his left hand. He didn't have a diamond stud in his ear. He didn't look civilized enough to be gay. He also didn't return the interest. If he looked beyond the magazine, it was to assess the progress Mr. Alexander was making. If he locked eyes with an ogling woman, his message wasn't friendly and the woman hurried on her way. I suspected the unfriendly disinterest was more a reflection of Morelli's impatience than of his single-minded love for me.

"I'm done!" Mr. Alexander said, whipping the cape off me. "This is the best I can do to cover up the bald spots. And we've gotten all the oil out." He looked over at Morelli. "Do you want me to tame the barbarian?"

"Hey, Joe," I yelled to him. "Do you need a haircut?"

Morelli *always* needed a haircut. Ten minutes after he got a haircut he still needed a haircut.

"I just got a haircut," Morelli said, getting to his feet.

"It would look wonderful if we took a smidgeon more off the sides," Mr. Alexander said to Morelli. "And we could put the tiniest bit of gel in the top."

Morelli stood hands on hips, his jacket flared, his gun obvious on his hip.

"But then maybe not," Mr. Alexander said. "Maybe it's perfect just as it is."

Morelli's cell phone rang. He answered the phone and passed it over to me. "Your mother."

"I've been calling and calling you," my mother said. "Why don't you answer your cell phone?"

"My phone was in my bag and my bag was in Cluck-in-a-Bucket when it burned down."

"Omigod, it's true! People have been calling night and day, and I thought they were joking. Since when do you work at Cluck-in-a-Bucket?"

"Actually, I don't work there anymore."

"Where are you? You're with Joseph. Are you in jail?"

"No. I'm at the mall."

"Four days to your sister's wedding and you're burning down the Burg. You have to stop exploding things and burning things. I need help. Someone has to check on the cake. Someone has to pick up the decorations for the cars. And the flowers for the church."

"Albert is in charge of the flowers."

"Have you seen Albert lately? Albert is drinking. Albert is locked away in his office having conversations with Walter Cronkite."

"I'll talk to him."

"No! No talking. It's better he's drunk. If he gets sober he might back out. And leave him in the office. The less time spent with Valerie the more likely he is to marry her."

I could see Morelli losing patience. He wasn't much of a mall person. He was more a bedroom and bar and playing-football-in-the-park person.

My grandmother was yelling in the background. "I gotta go to a viewing tonight. Stiva's laying out Mama Mac. I need a ride."

"Are you insane?" my mother said to my grandmother. "The place will be filled with Macaronis. They'll tear you to pieces."

Morelli parked the SUV in front of my parents' house and looked over at me. "Don't get any ideas about your powers of persuasion. I'm only doing this for the meatloaf."

"And later you're going to play detective with me."

"Maybe."

"You promised."

"The promise doesn't count. We were in bed. I would have promised *anything*."

"Spiro's going to make an appearance, one way or

another. I know it. He's going to have to see his handiwork. He's going to want to be part of the process."

"He won't see any of his handiwork tonight. The lid will be nailed down. I know Stiva's good, but trust me, all the king's horses and all the king's men couldn't put Mama Macaroni together again."

Morelli and I got out of the SUV and watched a car creep down the street toward us. It was a blue Honda Civic. It was Kloughn's car. Kloughn hit the curb and eased one tire over before coming to a complete stop. He looked through the windshield at us and waved with just the tips of his fingers.

"Snockered," I said to Morelli.

"I should arrest him," Morelli said.

"You can't arrest him. He's Valerie's cuddle umpkins."

Morelli closed the distance, opened the door for Kloughn, and Kloughn fell out of the car. Morelli dragged Kloughn to his feet and propped him against the Civic.

"You shouldn't be driving," Morelli said to Kloughn.

"I know," Kloughn said. "I tried walking, but I was too drunk. It's okay. I was driving very slooooowly and 'sponsibly."

Kloughn started to sink to the ground, and Morelli grabbed him by the back of his coat. "What do you want me to do with him?" Morelli asked.

Here's the thing. I like Albert Kloughn. I wouldn't marry him. And I wouldn't hire him to defend me if I was accused of murder. I might not even trust him to baby-sit Rex. Kloughn sort of falls into the Bob Dog category. Kloughn inspires maternal pet instincts in me.

"Bring him inside," I told Morelli. "We'll put him to bed and let him sleep it off."

Morelli carted Kloughn into the house and up the stairs with Grandma trotting behind.

"Put him in the third bedroom," Grandma said to Morelli. "And then let's get to the table. Dinner's almost ready, and I don't want to get a late start on the meatloaf. I gotta get to the viewing."

"Over my dead body," my mother yelled from the bottom of the stairs.

My father was already at the table. He had his fork in his hand, and he was watching the kitchen door, as if the food would come marching out to him without my mother's help.

A car pulled up outside. Car doors opened and slammed shut, and then there was chaos. Valerie, Angie, The Baby, and the horse were in the house, and the house suddenly got very small.

Grandma bustled down the stairs and took the diaper bag off Valerie's shoulder. "Everybody sit," Grandma said. "The meatloaf's done. We got meatloaf and gravy and mashed potatoes. And we got pineapple upside-down cake for dessert. And we put lots of whipped cream on the cake." Grandma eyed Mary Alice. "And only horses who sit at the table and eat their vegetables and meatloaf are gonna get any of the whipped cream and cake."

"Where's my oogie woogie bear?" Valerie wanted to know. "I saw his car on the curb."

"He's upstairs drunk as a skunk," Grandma said. "I just hope his liver don't explode before we get you married off. You should make sure he's got life insurance."

My mother brought the meatloaf and green beans to the table. Grandma brought the red cabbage and a bowl of mashed potatoes. I pushed my chair back and went to the kitchen to fetch the gravy and get milk for the girls.

Dinner at my parents' house is survival of the fastest. We all sit down at the table. We all put napkins on our laps. And that's where the civility ends and the action heats up. Food is passed, shoveled onto plates, and consumed at warp speed. To date, no one has been stabbed with a fork for taking the last dinner roll, but that's only because we all understand the rules. Get there first and fast. So we were all a little stunned when Valerie put five green beans on her big empty plate and angrily stabbed them with her fork. *Thunk, thunk, thunk.*

"What's with you?" Grandma said to Valerie.

"I'm on a diet. All I get to eat are these beans. Five boring hideous beans." The grip on her fork was white-knuckled, her lips were pressed tightly together, and her eyes glittered feverishly as she took in Joe's plate directly across from her. Joe had a mountain of creamy mashed potatoes and four thick slabs of meatloaf, all drenched in gravy.

"Maybe this isn't a good time to be on a diet, what with all the stress over the wedding and all," Grandma said.

"It's *because* of the wedding that I have to diet," Valerie said, teeth clenched.

Mary Alice forked up a piece of meatloaf. "Mommy's a blimp."

Valerie made a growling sound that had me worrying her head was going to start doing full rotations on her neck.

"Maybe I should check on Albert," Morelli said to me.

I narrowed my eyes and looked at him sideways. "You're going to sneak out, aren't you?"

"No way. Honest to God." He blew out a sigh. "Okay, yeah, I was going to sneak out."

"I had a good idea today," Grandma said, ignoring the possibility that Valerie might be possessed. "I thought it would be special if we could have Stephanie play the cello at Valerie's wedding. She could play it at the church while the people are coming in. Myra Sklar had a guitar player at her wedding, and it worked out real good."

My mother's face brightened. "That's a wonderful idea!"

Morelli turned to me. "You play the cello?"

"You bet she does," Grandma said. "She's good, too."

"No, really, I'm not that good. And I don't think it would work if I played at the church. I'm in the wedding party. I have to be with Valerie."

Valerie was momentarily distracted from her green-bean stabbing. "It would just be while the people are walking in," Valerie said. "And then you can put the cello aside and take your place in line."

Morelli was smiling. He knew I didn't play the cello. "I think you should do it," Morelli said. "You wouldn't want all those years of cello lessons to go to waste, would you?"

I shot him a warning look. "You are *so toast.*"

EIGHT

"This is going to be a humdinger of a wedding," Grandma said, returning her attention to her meatloaf and potatoes. "And it's going to be smooth sailing because we got a wedding planner."

Morelli and I exchanged glances. The Kloughn wedding was going to be a disaster of epic proportions.

We heard some scuffling and mumbling from the second floor. There was a moment of silence. And then Kloughn rolled down the stairs and landed at the bottom with a good solid thud. We all pushed back from the table and went to assess the damage.

Kloughn was spread-eagled on his back. His face was white and his eyes were wide. "I had the nightmare again," he said to me. "The one I told you about. It was awful. I couldn't breathe. I was suffocating. Every time I go to sleep I get the nightmare."

"What nightmare is he talking about?" Valerie wanted to know.

I didn't want to tell Valerie about the whale. It wasn't the sort of recurring dream a bride could get all gushy about. Especially since Val had almost gone into cardiac arrest when Mary Alice had called her a blimp. "It's a nightmare about an elevator," I said. "He's in this elevator, and all the air gets sucked out, and he can't breathe."

"All that white," Kloughn said, sweat popping out on his forehead. "It was all I could see. I could only see white. And then I couldn't breathe."

"It was a white elevator," I said to Valerie. "You know how dreams can get weird, right?"

Morelli had Kloughn on his feet, holding him up by the back of his jacket again. "Now what?" Morelli said. "Where do you want him this time?"

"We should lock him up someplace safe where he can't get away," Grandma said. "Someplace like jail. Maybe you should bust him."

"What's in his jacket pocket?" Valerie asked, patting the pocket. "It's a candy bar!" She ran her fingers over it. "It feels like a Snickers."

Some people can read Braille . . . my sister can feel up a candy bar in a pocket and identify it.

"I need that candy bar," Valerie said.

"It wouldn't be good for your diet," I told her.

"Yeah," Grandma said. "Go eat another green bean."

"I *need* that candy bar," Valerie said, eyes narrowed. "I *really need* it."

Kloughn pulled the candy bar out of his pocket, the candy bar slipped through his fingers, flew through the air, and bounced off Valerie's forehead.

Valerie blinked twice and burst into tears. "You hit me," she wailed.

"You're a nutso bride," Grandma said, retrieving the candy bar, tucking it into the zippered pocket of her warm-up suit jacket. "You're imagining things. Just look at Snoogie Boogie here. Does he look like he could hit someone? He don't know the time of day."

"I don't feel so good," Kloughn said. "I want to lie down."

"Put him on the couch," my mother said to Morelli. "He'll be safer there. He's lucky he didn't break his neck when he fell down the stairs."

We went back to the table and everybody dug in again.

"Maybe I don't want to get married," Valerie said.

"Of course you want to get married," Grandma told her. "How could you pass up Snogle Wogle out there? It'll be his job to take the garbage out on garbage day. And he'll get the oil changed in the car. You want to do those things all by yourself? And after we get you married off we gotta work on Stephanie." Grandma fixed an eye on Morelli. "How come you don't marry her?"

"Not my fault," Morelli said. "She won't marry *me*."

"Of course it's your fault," Grandma said. "You must be doing something wrong, if you know what I mean. Maybe you need to buy a book that tells you how to do it. I hear there are books out there with pictures and everything. I saw one in the store the other day. It was called *A Sex Guide for Dummies*."

Morelli paused with a chunk of meatloaf halfway to his mouth. No one had ever questioned his expertise in the sack before. His sexual history was legend in the Burg.

My sister gave a bark of laughter and quickly clapped a hand over her mouth. My mother went pale. And my father kept his head down, not wanting to lose the fork-to-mouth rhythm he had going.

Morelli sat frozen in his seat for a long moment and then obviously decided no answer was the way to go. He gave me a small tight smile and got on with his meal. Things quieted down after that until Grandma started checking her watch halfway through dessert.

"No," my mother said to her. "Don't even think it."

"Think what?" Grandma asked.

"You know what. You're not going to the viewing. It

would be in terrible taste. The Macaronis have suffered enough without us adding to their grief."

"The Macaronis are probably dancing in their socks," Grandma said. "Susan Mifflin saw them eating at Artie's Seafood House the day after the accident. She said they were going at the all-you-can-eat crab legs like it was a party."

When the only thing left of the pineapple upside-down cake was a smudge of whipped cream on the cake plate, I helped my mother clear the table. I promised I'd get the decorations for the cars. And I made a mental note that in the future I would avoid weddings, mine or anyone else's. And while I was making my never-again list, I might add never have another dinner at my parents' house . . . although it was pretty funny when Grandma suggested Morelli get a *Dummies'* guide to good sex.

Ten minutes later, Morelli and I were parked on Hamilton, across from the funeral home.

"Tell me again why we're doing this," Morelli said.

"The bad guy always returns to the scene of the crime. Everybody knows that."

"This isn't the scene of the crime."

"Work with me here, okay? It's close enough. Spiro seems like the kind of guy who would hate to be left out. I think he'd want to watch the spectacle."

We sat for a couple minutes in silence and Morelli turned to me. "You're smiling," Morelli said. "It's making me uneasy. Anyone in their right mind wouldn't be smiling after that dinner."

"I thought there were some good moments."

Morelli was dividing his attention between the people arriving for the viewing and me. "Like when your grandmother suggested I get a book?"

"That was the *best* moment."

It was deep twilight. Light pooled on the sidewalk

and road from overhead halogens, and Stiva's front porch was glowing. Stiva didn't want the old folks falling down the stairs after visiting with the deceased.

Morelli reached out to me in the darkened car. His fingertips traced along my hairline. "Do you want to throw out a comment here? Was your grandmother right? Is that why we're not married?"

"You're fishing for compliments."

That got Morelli smiling. "Busted."

Someone rapped on the driver's-side window, and we both flinched. Morelli rolled the window down a crack, and Grandma squinted in at us.

"I thought I recognized the car," Grandma said.

"What are you doing here?" I asked Grandma. "I thought it was settled that you'd stay away."

"I know your mother means well, but sometimes she can be a real pain in the patoot. This viewing will be the talk of the town. How can I go to the beauty parlor tomorrow if I don't know anything about the viewing? What will I say to people? I got a reputation to uphold. People expect me to know the dirt. So I sneaked out when your mother went to the bathroom. I was lucky to be able to hitch a ride with Mabel from next door."

"We can't let Grandma go to that viewing," I said to Morelli. "She'll be nothing but a grease spot on Stiva's carpet after the Macaronis get done with her."

"You really shouldn't go to the viewing," he said to Grandma. "Why don't you get in the car, and we'll go to a bar and get wasted?"

"Not a bad offer," Grandma said. "But no can do. I can't take a chance on them having the lid up."

"There's no chance they'll have the lid up," Morelli said. "I saw them collecting the pieces, and they're not going to fit together."

Grandma slid her dentures around in her mouth

while she weighed her choices. "Don't seem right not to pay my respects," she finally said.

"Here's the deal," Morelli said. "I'll go in and scope things out. If the lid is up I'll come get you. If the lid is down I'll drive you home."

"I guess that sounds reasonable," Grandma said. "I don't want to get torn limb from limb by the Macaronis for no good cause. I'll wait here."

"And ask Constantine if he's seen Spiro," I told Morelli.

Morelli got out, and Grandma took his place behind the wheel. We watched Morelli walk into the funeral home.

"He's a keeper," Grandma said. "He's turned into a real nice young man. And he's nice looking, too. Not as hot as that Ranger but pretty darn close."

Cars rolled past us on Hamilton. People parked in the lot next to Stiva's and made their way to the big front porch. A group of men stood just outside the door. They were smoking and talking and occasionally there'd be a bark of laughter.

"I guess you're unemployed again," Grandma said. "You have any ideas where you'll go next?"

"I hear they're hiring at the sanitary products plant."

"That might work out. That plant is way down Route One and they might not have heard about you yet."

The light changed at the end of the block and cars began moving again. An SUV slid by us going in the opposite direction . . . and Spiro was behind the wheel.

I started climbing over the console. "Get out of the car," I yelled. "I need to follow that SUV."

"No way. I'm not missing out on this. I can catch him," Grandma said. "Buckle your seat belt."

I opened my mouth to say no, but Grandma already had the car in gear. She shot back and rammed the car behind us, knocking him back a couple feet.

"That's better," Grandma said. "Now I got room to get out." She wheeled Morelli's SUV into traffic, stopped short, laid on the horn, and cut into the stream of oncoming cars.

Grandma learned to drive a couple years ago. She immediately racked up points for speeding and lost her license. She wasn't all that good a driver back then, and she wasn't any better now. I tightened my seat belt and started making deals with God. I'll be a better person, I told God. I swear I will. I'll even go to church. Okay, maybe that's not going to happen. I'll go to church on holidays. Just don't let Grandma kill us both.

"I'm coming up on him," Grandma said. "He's just two cars ahead of us."

"Keep the two cars between us," I told her. "I don't want him to see us."

The light changed at the corner. Spiro went through on the yellow, and we were stopped behind the two cars. Grandma yanked the wheel to the right, jumped the curb, and drove on the sidewalk to the intersection. She leaned on the horn, smashed her foot to the floor, and rocketed across two lanes of traffic. I had my feet braced against the dash and my eyes closed.

"I have a better idea," I said. "Why don't we go back to the funeral home? You wouldn't want to miss hearing that the lid was up. And maybe it would be a good idea to pull over and let me drive, since you don't have a license."

"I got him in my sights," Grandma said, hunched over the wheel, eyes narrowed.

Spiro turned right and Grandma raced to the corner and took it on two wheels. One block ahead of us we saw Spiro right-turn again. Grandma stuck with him, and two turns later we found ourselves back on Hamilton, heading for the funeral home. Spiro was going to make another pass.

"This is convenient," Grandma said. "We can see if Joseph is waiting for us."

"Not good," I said. "He won't be happy to see you behind the wheel. He's a cop, remember? He arrests people who drive without a license."

"He can't arrest me. I'm an old lady. I got rights. And besides, he's practically family."

Was that true? Was Morelli practically family? Had I become accidentally married?

My attention returned to Spiro, and I realized Grandma had closed the gap, and we were one car behind him. We sailed past the funeral home, past Morelli standing at the side of the road, hands on hips. He gave his head a small shake as we whizzed by. Probably best not to second-guess his thoughts . . . they didn't look happy.

"I know I should have stopped to find out about the viewing," Grandma said, "but I hate to lose this guy. I don't know why I'm following him, but I can't seem to quit."

Spiro drove three blocks and did another loop, taking himself back down Hamilton. We lost the single-car buffer, and Grandma got on Spiro's bumper just as he came up to the funeral home. Spiro flashed his right-turn signal and after that it was all horror and panic and life in slow motion, because Spiro jumped the curb and plowed into a group of men on the sidewalk. He hit two men I'd never seen before and Morelli. One of the men was knocked aside. One was pitched off the hood. And Morelli spiraled off the right front fender of Spiro's SUV and was thrown to the ground.

Probably I should have gone after Spiro, but I acted without thought. I was out of the car and running to Morelli before Grandma had come to a complete stop. He was on his back, his eyes open, his face white.

"Are you okay?" I asked, dropping to my knees.

"Do I look okay?"

"No. You look like you've just been run over by an SUV."

"Last time this happened I got to look up your skirt," he said. And then he passed out.

It was close to midnight when I was told Morelli was out of surgery. His leg had been broken in two places but aside from that he was fine. I'd taken Grandma home, and I was alone in the hospital. A bunch of cops had stopped by earlier. Eddie Gazarra and Carl Costanza had offered to stay with me, but I'd assured them it wasn't necessary. I'd already been informed Morelli's injuries weren't life threatening. The two other guys that were mowed down by Spiro were going to be okay, too. One had been sent home with scrapes and bruises. The other was being kept overnight with a concussion and broken collarbone.

I was allowed to see Morelli for a moment when he was brought up to his room. He was hooked to an IV drip, his leg was elevated on the bed, and he was still groggy. He was half a day beyond a five o'clock shadow. He had a bruise on his cheek. His eyes were partly closed, and his dark lashes shaded his eyes.

I brushed a light kiss across his lips. "You're okay," I told him.

"Good to know," he said. And then the drugs dragged him back into sleep.

I walked the short distance to the parking garage and found a blue-and-white parked next to Morelli's SUV. Gazarra was at the wheel.

"I had late shift and this is as good a place as any to hang," he said. "Lock the car in Morelli's garage tonight. I wouldn't want to see you in the room next to Mama Mac tomorrow."

I left the garage and followed Gazarra's instructions. It was a dark moonless night with a chill in the air that ordinarily would have me thinking about pumpkins and winter clothes and football games. As it was, I had a hard time pushing the anger and fear generated by Spiro into the background. Hard to think about anything other than the pain he'd caused Morelli.

Morelli's garage was detached from his house and at the rear of his property. Bob was waiting for me when I let myself into the house through the back door. He was sleepy-eyed and lethargic, resting his big shaggy orange head against my leg. I scratched him behind his ear and gave him a dog biscuit from the cookie jar on the counter.

"Do you have to tinkle?" I asked Bob.

Bob didn't look especially interested in tinkling.

"Maybe you should try," I told him. "I'm going to sleep late tomorrow."

I opened the back door, Bob picked his head up, his nose twitched, his eyes got wide, and he bolted through the door and took off into the night. Shit! I could hear Bob galloping two yards over, and then there was nothing but the sound of distant cars and the whir of Morelli's refrigerator in defrost cycle behind me.

Great job, Stephanie. Things aren't bad enough, now you've lost Morelli's dog. I got a flashlight, pocketed the house key, and locked up behind me. I crossed through two yards and stopped and listened. Nothing. I kept walking through yards, occasionally sweeping the area with the light. At the very end of the block I found Bob munching his way through a big black plastic garbage bag. He'd torn a hole in the bag and had pulled out chicken remains, wads of paper towels, empty soup cans, lunch-meat wrappers, and God knows what else.

I grabbed Bob by the collar and dragged him away from the mess. Probably I should clean up the garbage, but I was in no mood. With any luck, a herd of crows would descend on the carnage and cart everything off to Crowland.

I dragged Bob all the way home. When I got to the house, there was a piece of notebook paper tacked to the back door. A smiley face was drawn on the paper. ISN'T THIS FUN? was printed under the smiley face.

I got Bob inside and threw the bolt. And then as a double precaution I locked us into Morelli's bedroom.

It was a little after nine, and I had the phone cradled between my ear and shoulder as I scoured Morelli's kitchen floor, cleaning up the chicken bones Bob had hacked up.

"I can come home," Morelli said. "I need some shorts and a ride."

"I'll be there as soon as I finish cleaning the kitchen." I disconnected and looked over at Bob. "Are you done?"

Bob didn't say anything, but he didn't look happy. His eyes cut to the back door.

I hooked a leash to Bob and took him into the yard. Bob hunched over and pooped out a red lace thong. I was going to have to check upstairs to be sure, but I strongly suspected it was mine.

Morelli was on the couch with his foot propped up on a pillow on the coffee table. He had the television remote, a bowl of popcorn, his cell phone, a six-pack of soda, crutches, a week's supply of pills for pain, an Xbox remote, his iPod with headset, a box of dog biscuits, and a gun, all within reach. Bob was sprawled on the floor in front of the television.

"Is there anything else before I go?" I asked him.

"Do you have to go?"

"Yes! I promised my mother I'd get the decorations for the cars. I need to check in on Valerie. We have no food in the house. I used up all the paper towels cleaning up Bob barf. And I need to stop at the personal products plant and get a job application."

"I think you should stay home and play with me. I'll let you write dirty suggestions on my cast."

"Appealing, but no. Your mother and your grandmother are going to show up. They're going to need to see for themselves that you're okay. They're going to bring a casserole and a cake, because that's what they always do. And if I'm here they're going to grill us about getting married, because that's what they always do. And then Bella is going to have a vision that involves my uterus, because that's also a constant. Better to take the coward's way out and run errands." Plus, I wanted to drop in at the funeral home and talk to Constantine Stiva about his son.

"What if I fall and I can't get up?"

"Nice try, but I've got it covered. I've got a babysitter for you. Someone who will attend to your every need while I'm gone."

There was a sharp rap on the front door, and Lula barged in. "Here I am, ready to baby-sit your ass," she said to Morelli. "Don't you worry about a thing. Lula's here to take care of you."

Morelli looked over at me. "You're kidding."

"I wanted to make sure you were safe."

And that was true. I was worried about Spiro returning and setting the house on fire. Spiro was nuts.

Lula set her bag in the hall and walked to the curb with me. Big Blue was soaking up sun on the street, ready to spring into action. I had an extra car key from Grandma. I'd gotten an extra apartment key from my building super, Dillon Ruddick. I had Morelli's credit card for the food. I was ready to roll. It was early afternoon, and if I didn't hit too much traffic on Route 1 I'd be home to feed Morelli dinner.

"We'll be fine," Lula said. "I brought some videos

to watch. And I got the whole bag of tricks with me if anything nasty goes down. I even got a Taser. It's brand-new. Never been used. I bet I could give a guy the runs with that Taser."

"I should be back in a couple hours," I told her. I slid behind the wheel and turned the key in the ignition. Something under the car went *phunnnf*, and flames shot out on all sides and the car instantly died. I got out, and Lula and I got on our hands and knees and checked the undercarriage.

"Guess that was a bomb," Lula said.

Little black dots floated in front of my eyes, and there was a lot of clanging in my head. When the clanging stopped, I stood and brushed road gravel off my knees, using the activity to get myself under control. I was freaking out deep inside, and that wasn't a good thing. I needed to be brave. I needed to think clearly. I needed to be Ranger. Get a grip, I said to myself. Don't give in to the panic. Don't let this bastard run your life and make you afraid.

"You're starting to scare me," Lula said. "You look like you're having a whole conversation with someone and it isn't me."

"Giving myself a pep talk," I said. "Tell Morelli about the bomb. I'm taking his SUV."

"You're whiter than usual," Lula said.

"Yeah, but I didn't totally faint or throw up, so I'm doing good, right?"

I backed Morelli's car out of the garage and hit the first stop on my list. A party store on Route 33 in Hamilton Township. Valerie had, at last count, three bridesmaids, one maid of honor (me), and two flower girls (Angie and Mary Alice). We were riding in six cars. The party store had dolls in fancy gowns for the hood, bows for all the door handles, and streaming ribbons that got attached to the back of each car. Everything corresponded to the color of the gown inside the car. Mine was eggplant. Could it get any worse? I was going to look like the attendant to the dead.

"I'm here to pick up the car decorations for the Plum wedding," I said to the girl at the counter.

"We have them right here, ready to go," she said, "but there's a problem with one of them. I don't know what happened. The woman who makes these is always so careful. One of the dolls looks like . . . an eggplant."

"It's a vegetarian wedding," I told her. "New Age."

I lugged the six boxes out to the car and drove them to my parents' house. I left the SUV idling at the curb, ran in with the boxes, dumped them on the kitchen table, and turned to leave.

"Where are you going so fast?" Grandma wanted to know. "Don't you want a sandwich? We have olive loaf."

"No time. Lots of errands today. And I need to get back to Morelli." Also I didn't want to leave the car unattended long enough for Spiro to set another bomb.

My mother was at the stove, stirring a pot of vanilla pudding. "I hope Joseph is feeling better. That was a terrible thing last night."

"He's on the couch, watching television. His leg is achy, but he's going to be okay." I looked over at Grandma Mazur. "He said to tell you the lid was down, and rumor has it Mama Mac went to the hereafter without the mole. Morelli said the medical examiner thinks the mole is still in the parking lot somewhere, but there might not be a lot left of it due to all the foot traffic around the scene."

"I get a chill just thinking about it," Grandma said. "Someone could be walking around with Mama Mac's mole on the bottom of their shoe."

From the corner of my eye I saw my mother take a bottle out of a cupboard, pour two fingers of whisky into a juice glass, and knock it back. Guess the ironing wasn't doing it for her anymore.

"Gotta go," I said. "If you need me I'll be staying with Morelli. He needs help getting around."

"The organist at the church would like to know if you want her to accompany you when you play the cello," Grandma said. "I saw her at the market this morning."

I smacked my forehead with the heel of my hand. "With all the excitement I forgot to tell you. I don't have a cello anymore. I gave it away. It was taking up too much space in my closet. You know how it is when you live in an apartment. Never enough closet space."

"But you loved your cello," Grandma said.

I tried to plaster an appropriate expression of remorse on my face. "That's the way it goes. A girl has to have priorities."

"Who got the cello?"

"Who?" My mind was racing. Who got the cello? "My cello teacher," I said. "I gave it to my cello teacher."

"Do we know her?"

"Nope. She lived in New Hope. But she's moved. She moved to South Carolina. That's another reason I stopped playing. My cello teacher moved, and I didn't feel like finding a new cello teacher. So I gave the cello back to her. It was originally hers, anyway." Sometimes I was really impressed with my ability to come up with this shit. Once I got going, it just rolled out of me. I could compose a whole parallel universe for myself in a matter of seconds.

I glanced down at my watch. "Look at the time! I'm late."

I snatched a couple cookies off the plate on the kitchen table and ran through the house to the car. I jumped in the SUV and roared away. Next stop was Valerie. I didn't have any real reason to visit Valerie.

It was just that I was her sister and her maid of honor and Val wasn't entirely together these days. I thought it wouldn't hurt to check on her once in a while until she made it through the wedding.

The first thing I noticed when I got to her house was the absence of Kloughn's car. Not surprising since this was a workday. Sort of surprising that he was able to get himself up and out on the road with a raging hangover.

"What?" Val yelled when she opened the door to me.

"I just stopped by to say hello."

"Oh. Sorry I yelled at you. I'm having a problem with volume control. It turns out when you're starving to death you do a lot of yelling."

"Where's Albert? I thought he'd still be in bed with a hangover."

"He decided he was better off at the office. He couldn't stand the galloping and whinnying. You might want to see how he's doing. He left in his pajamas."

"You know, Val, not everyone's cut out to have a big wedding. Maybe you should reconsider the eloping option."

"I wish I'd never started this wedding thing," Val wailed. "What was I thinking?"

"It's not too late to bail."

"It is. And I'm too chicken. Everybody's made all these plans!"

"Yeah, but it's your wedding. It shouldn't be some horrible stressful thing. It should be something you enjoy." Not to mention, if Valerie eloped I wouldn't have to wear the hideous eggplant getup.

I left Valerie and drove to Kloughn's office. There was a CLOSED sign on his door and when I looked in the window I could see Kloughn was stretched out on the floor in his pajamas with a wet towel over his face. I didn't want to make him get up, so I tiptoed away and headed down Route 1 to the personal products plant. I parked in a visitor slot, ran in, and got a job application from the personnel office. I had no illusions of getting an office job here. I had no references and few skills. I'd be lucky if I could get a job on the line. I'd bring the application back tomorrow and wait for a phone call for an interview.

I slid to a stop in front of Giovichinni's Market and didn't bother to call to check on Macaronis. I figured I had bigger problems than Macaronis. I was being stalked by a homicidal maniac. Spiro was officially over the edge.

I ran through the store gathering together some basic foods. Bread, cheese, Tastykakes, peanut butter, cereal, milk, Tastykakes, eggs, frozen pizza, Tastykakes, orange juice, apples, lunch meat, and Tastykakes. I checked out and muscled my way through the door with bags in my arms.

Ranger was leaning against the SUV, waiting for me. He pushed off, took the bags, and put them in the car. "Looks like you're playing house," he said.

"More like nurse. Morelli needs some help."

"Is that your job application on the front seat?"

"Yep."

"Personal products plant?"

"It's halfway to New Brunswick. I'm hoping they won't have heard about me. That's Grandma's line, but it's true."

"Babe," Ranger said. He was smiling, but there was a quality to his voice that told me it wasn't actually funny. We both knew that my life wasn't going in the carefree direction I'd hoped for.

NINE

"**I have an** office position open," Ranger said. "Are you interested in working for RangeMan?"

"Oh great. A pity position."

"If I gave you a pity position, it wouldn't be in the office."

This got a burst of laughter out of me because I knew he was taking a zing at my sex life with Morelli. For the most part, Ranger had a consistent personality. He wasn't a guy who wasted a lot of unnecessary energy and effort. He moved and he spoke with an efficient ease that was more animal than human. And he didn't telegraph his emotions. Unless Ranger had his tongue in my mouth it was usually impossible to tell what he was thinking. But every now and then, Ranger would step out of the box, and like a little treat that was doled out on special occasions, he would make an entirely outrageous sexual statement. At least it would be outrageous coming from an ordinary guy . . . from Ranger it seemed on the mark.

"I didn't think you hired women," I said to him. "The only woman you have working for you is your housekeeper."

"I hire people who have the skills I need. Right now I could use someone in the building who can do phone work and paperwork. You'd be an easy hire. You already know the drill. Nine to five, five days a week. You can discuss salary with my business manager. You should consider it. The garage is secure. You wouldn't have to worry about getting blown up when you leave at the end of the day."

Ranger owns a small seven-story office building in downtown Trenton. The building is unspectacular on the outside. Well maintained but not architecturally interesting. The interior of the building is high tech and slick, equipped with a state-of-the-art control center, offices, a gym, studio apartments for some of Ranger's crew, plus an apartment for Ranger on the top floor. I'd stayed in Ranger's apartment for a short time on a nonconjugal basis not long ago. It had been equal parts pleasure and terror. Terror because it was Ranger's apartment and Ranger could sometimes be a scary guy. Pleasure because he lives well.

The job offer was tempting. My car would be safe. I'd be safe. I'd be able to pay my rent. And the chances of rolling in garbage were slim.

"Okay," I said. "I'll take the job."

"Use the intercom at the gate when you come in tomorrow. Dress in black. You'll be working on the fifth floor."

"Any leads on Benny Gorman?"

"No. That's one of the things I want you to do. I want you to see what you can turn up."

Ranger's pager buzzed, and he checked the readout. "Elroy Dish is back at Blue Fish. Do you want to ride along?"

"No thanks. Been there, done that."

"Be careful."

And he was gone.

I looked at my watch. Almost five. Perfect. Stiva would be between afternoon and evening viewings. I

drove the short distance up Hamilton and parked on the
street. I found Stiva in his office just off the large entrance foyer. I rapped on the doorjamb, and he looked
up from his computer.

"Stephanie," he said. "Always nice to see you."

I appreciated the greeting, but I knew it was a big fat
lie. Stiva was the consummate undertaker. He was an
island of professional calm in an ocean of chaos. And
he never alienated a future customer. The ugly truth is,
Stiva would rather shove a sharp stick in his eye than
see Grandma or me alive on his doorstep. Dead would
be something else.

"I hope this visit isn't due to bad news," Stiva said.

"I wanted to talk to you about Spiro. Have you seen
him since the fire?"

"No."

"Spoken to him?"

"No. Why do you ask?"

"He was driving the car that ran over Morelli."

Stiva went as still as stone, and his pale vanilla custard cheeks flushed pink. "Are you serious?"

"Unfortunately, yes. I'm sorry. I saw him clearly."

"How does he look?" Stiva asked.

I felt my heart constrict at his response. He was a
concerned parent, anxious to hear word of his missing
son. What on earth could I say to Stiva?

"I only saw him briefly," I said. "He seemed healthy.
Maybe some scars on his face from the fire."

"He must have been driving by and lost control of
his car," Stiva said. "At least I know he's alive. Thank
you for coming in to tell me."

"I thought you'd want to know."

No point to saying more. Stiva didn't have information to share, and I didn't want to tell him the whole
story. I left the funeral home and returned to the SUV.
I drove two blocks to Pino's and got two meatball subs,

a tub of coleslaw, and a tub of potato salad. Morelli was
going to be in a bad mood after spending the afternoon
with Lula. I figured I'd try to mellow him out with the
sub before I dropped the news about my new job. Morelli wasn't going to be happy to hear I was working for
Ranger.

I went out of my way on the trip home to drive by
Anthony Barroni's house. I had no real basis for believing he was involved with Spiro and the missing men.
Just a gut feeling. Maybe it was desperation. I wanted
to think I had a grip on the problem. The grip loosened
when I got to Barroni's house. No lights shining. Curtains drawn. Garage door closed. No car in driveway.

I turned at the corner and wound my way through
the Burg to Chambers Street. I crossed Chambers and
two blocks later I pulled the SUV into Morelli's garage.
Big Blue and Lula's Firebird were still at the curb. I
made sure the garage door was locked, and I carted the
bags in through the back door.

"Is that Stephanie Plum coming through the back
door?" Lula yelled. "'Cause if it's some maniac pervert
I'm gonna kick his ass."

"It's me," I yelled back. "Sorry you don't get to do
any ass kicking."

I put the bags on the counter and went into the living
room to see Lula and Morelli. Morelli was still on the
couch. Bob was still on the floor. And Lula was pack-
ing up.

"This wasn't so bad," Lula said. "We played poker
and I won three dollars and fifty-seven cents. I would
have won more, but your boyfriend fell asleep."

"It's the drugs," Morelli said. "You're a sucky poker
player. I would have won if I wasn't all drugged up.
You took advantage."

"I won fair and square," Lula said. "Anytime you

want to get even you let me know. I can always use extra cash."

"Any other fun things happen that I should know about?"

"Yeah," Lula said. "His mother and grandmother came over. And they're nuts. The old lady said she was putting the eye on me. I told her she better not pull any of that voodoo shit with me or I'll beat her like a piñata."

"I bet that went over big."

"They left after that. They brought a casserole, and I put it in the refrigerator. I didn't think it looked all that good."

"No cake?"

"Oh yeah, the cake. I ate the cake."

"All of it?"

"Bob had some. I would have given some to Morelli, but he was sleeping." She had her bag over her shoulder and her car keys in her hand. "I walked Bob about an hour ago, and he pooped twelve times, so he should be good for the night. I didn't feed him, but he ate one of Morelli's sneakers around three o'clock. You might want to go light on the dog crunchies until he horks the sneaker up."

Morelli waited until he heard Lula's car drive off before speaking again. "Another fifteen minutes and I would have shot her. I would have gone to jail for the rest of my life, and it would have been worth it."

I brought out the subs and the coleslaw and the potato salad. "Don't you want to know how my day went?"

He unwrapped his sub. "How did your day go?"

"I didn't get blown up."

"Speaking of getting blown up, the lab took a look at your Buick. The bomb was very similar to the bomb

that killed Mama Mac. The difference being that this
bomb was detonated when you turned the key in the
ignition, and it was much smaller. It wasn't intended
to kill."

"Spiro is still playing with me."

"You're sure it's Spiro?"

"Yes. I stopped in to see Stiva. He had no idea
Spiro was back. Said he hasn't heard from him since
the fire."

"You believed him?"

"Yeah."

"I talked to Ryan Laski today. He's been working the
Barroni case with me. I told him about Spiro, and I asked
him to keep an eye on Anthony Barroni. And I asked my
mother about Spiro. So far as I can tell, you're the only
one who's seen him. There's no gossip on Spiro circu-
lating in the Burg."

At ten o'clock Morelli and I were still on the couch. We'd
watched the news while we ate our subs. And then we
watched some sitcom reruns. And then we watched a
ball game. And now Morelli was getting *that look.*

"You have a cast on your leg, and you're full of painkillers," I said to him. "One would think it would slow
you down."

"What can I say . . . I'm Italian. And that part of me
isn't broken."

"There are some logistical things involved here. Can
you get up to the bedroom?"

"I might need motivation to get through the pain . . .
like, seeing you naked and gyrating at the top of the
stairs."

"And what about a shower?"

"Can't take a shower," Morelli said. "I'm going to have
to lie on the bed and let you wash me . . . everywhere."

"I can see you've given this some thought."

"Yeah. That's why it's not just my cast that's hard."

Okay, so this might not be so bad. I thought I could probably get into the naked gyrating and the washing. And it seemed to me I'd pick up some perks from the injury. Morelli wasn't going to be especially mobile with that heavy cast. Once I got him on his back he was going to stay there, and I'd have the top all to myself.

I'd set the alarm for 7:00 A.M. I didn't have to be at work until 9:00, but I had to shower and do the hair and makeup thing, walk and feed Bob, get Morelli set for the day, and make a fast trip back to my apartment in search of black clothes. And I needed to get Rex. He didn't require a lot of care, but I didn't like to leave him alone for more than a couple days.

Morelli threw an arm over me when the alarm went off. "Did you set it for sex?" he asked.

"No, I set it for *get up*."

"We don't have to get up early this morning."

I slipped out from under the arm and rolled out of bed. "*You* don't have to get up early. I have lots of things to do."

"Again? You're not going to bring Lula back, are you?"

"No. Based on your performance last night, I'd say you're not in the least impaired."

I didn't want to give details on the day's activities, so I hurried off to the bathroom. I showered, did the blow-dry thing, slathered on some makeup, and bumped into Morelli when I opened the bathroom door.

"Sorry," I said. "Are you waiting to use the bathroom?"

"No, I'm waiting to talk to you."

"Jeez, I'm in kind of a hurry. Maybe we can talk after I walk Bob."

Morelli pinned me to the wall. "Let's talk now. Where are you going today?"

"I need to go back to my apartment for clothes."

"And?"

"And I have a job."

"I hate to ask. Your jobs have been getting progressively worse. I can't imagine who would hire you after the Cluck-in-a-Bucket fiasco. Is it the personal products plant?"

"It's Ranger."

"That makes sense," Morelli said. "I should have guessed. I can hardly wait to hear your job description."

"It's a good job. I'm doing phone work from the office. Nothing in the field. And I get to park in the Range-Man garage, so my car will be secure. Is this where you start yelling?"

Morelli released me. "Hard to believe, but I'm actually relieved. I was afraid you were going to be out there trying to find Spiro today."

Go figure this. "You love me," I said to Morelli.

"Yeah. I love you." He looked at me expectantly. "And?"

"I . . . l-l-like you, too." *Shit.*

"Jesus," Morelli said.

I did a grimace. "I feel it. I just can't say it."

Bob padded out of the bedroom. *"Gak,"* Bob said, and he barfed out a slimy mess on the hall carpet.

"Guess that's what's left of my sneaker," Morelli said.

I parked Morelli's SUV in my lot and ran upstairs to change my clothes. I unlocked my apartment door, rushed inside, and almost stepped on a small, gift-wrapped box. Same wrapping paper Spiro had used for the clock. Same little ribbon bow.

I stared down at the box for a full minute without breathing. I didn't have a gun. I didn't have pepper spray. I didn't have a stun gun. My toys had all gone up in smoke at Cluck-in-a-Bucket.

"Anyone here?" I called out.

No one answered. I knew I should call Ranger and have him go through the apartment, but that felt wimpy. So I backed out, closed the door to my apartment, and called Lula.

Ten minutes later, Lula was standing alongside me in front of the door.

"Okay, open it," Lula said, gun in hand, Taser on her hip, pepper spray stuck into her pocket, bludgeoning flashlight shoved under the waistband of her rhinestone-studded spandex jeans, flak vest stretched to the max over her basketball boobs.

I opened the door and we both peeked inside.

"One of us should go through and check for bad guys," Lula said.

"You've got the gun."

"Yeah, but it's your apartment. I could check, but I don't want to be intrusive. It's not that I'm chicken or anything, I just don't want to deprive you of checking."

I rolled my eyes at her.

"Don't you roll eyes at me," Lula said. "I'm being considerate. I'm giving you the opportunity to get shot before me."

"Gee, thanks. Can I at least have the gun?"

"Damn skippy. It's loaded and everything."

I was 99 percent sure the apartment was empty. Still, why take a chance with the 1 percent, right? I crept through the apartment with Lula three steps behind me. We looked in closets, under the bed, behind the shower curtain. No spooky Spiro. We returned to the front door and stared down at the box.

"I guess you should open it," Lula said.

"Suppose it's a bomb?"

"Then I guess you should open it far away from me."

I cut a look to her.

"Well, if it's a bomb it's a little bitty one," Lula said. "Anyway, maybe it's not a bomb. Maybe it's a diamond bracelet."

"You think Spiro's sending me a diamond bracelet?"

"It would be a long shot," Lula said.

I blew out a sigh and gingerly picked the box up. It wasn't heavy. It wasn't ticking. I shook it. It didn't rattle. I carefully unwrapped the box. I lifted the lid and looked inside.

Lula looked over my shoulder. "What the hell is that?" Lula asked. "It's got hairs growing out of it. *Holy fuck!* Is that what I think it is?"

It was Mama Mac's mole. I dropped the box and ran into the bathroom and threw up. When I came out of the bathroom, Lula was on the couch, flipping through television channels.

"I scooped the mole up and put it back in the box," Lula said. "And then I put it in a plastic Baggie. It doesn't smell all that great. It's on the counter in the kitchen."

"I have to change clothes. I took a job working for Ranger, and I need to wear black."

"Does this job involve fancy underwear? Oral sex? Lap dancing?"

"No. It involves phone investigation."

Lula remoted the television off and stood to leave. "I bet it'll work its way around to one of those other things. You'd tell me, right?"

"You'll be the first to know."

I bolted the door after Lula and got dressed in black jeans, black Puma sneakers, and a stretchy black V-neck T-shirt. I took Mama's mole, shrugged into my denim jacket, and looked out the window at Morelli's SUV. No one lurking around, planting bombs. Hooray. I grabbed Rex's cage and vacated the apartment, locking up after me. Lot of good that did. Everybody and their brother broke into my apartment.

I drove the mole to Morelli's house, handed it over, and took Rex into the kitchen.

"This is disgusting," Morelli said, opening the box, checking the mole out. "This is sick."

"Yeah. You'd better call Grandma and let her come over to have a look before you turn it in. Grandma will never forgive you if you don't let her see the mole."

Morelli looked at the packet of painkillers on his coffee table. "I need more drugs," he said. "If I have to have your grandmother over here examining the mole I definitely need more drugs."

I gave him a fast kiss and ran back to the SUV. If I got all the lights right I might make work on time.

I parked in the underground garage and took the elevator to the fifth floor. I already knew most of the guys who worked for Ranger. No one looked surprised to see me when I came onto the floor of the control room. Everyone was dressed in black jeans or cargo pants and black T-shirts. Ranger and I were the only ones without RANGEMAN embroidered on the front of the shirt. Ranger had been slouched in a chair, watching a monitor, when I stepped out of the elevator. He came to my side and walked me station to station.

"As you can see there are two banks of monitors," Ranger said. "Hal's watching the cameras in the building and listening to police scanners. He also watches the GPS screen that tracks RangeMan vehicles. Woody and Vince are monitoring private security systems. RangeMan provides personal, commercial and residential security to select clients. It's not a large operation in the world of security specialists, but the profit margin is good. I have similar operations in Boston, Miami, and Atlanta. I'm in the middle of a sellout to my Atlanta partner, and I'll probably sell Boston. I like being out on the street. I'm not crazy about running a national empire. Too difficult to control quality.

"I'm going to give you the cubby on the far side of the room. It's the area we set aside for investigation. Silvio has been doing this job, but he's transferring to the Miami office on Monday. He has family there. He'll sit with you today and make sure you know how to get into the search programs. Initially, I want you to concentrate on Benny Gorman. We've already run him through the system. Silvio will give you the file. I want you to read the file and then start over.

"The gym is open to you. Unfortunately, the locker room is men only. I'm sure they'd be happy to share, but I don't think it's a good idea. If you need to change clothes or shower you can use my apartment. Tank will issue you a key fob similar to mine. It'll get you into the building and into my apartment. My housekeeper, Ella, keeps food in the kitchen at the end of the hall. It's for staff use. There are always sandwiches, raw vegetables, and fruit. You're going to have to bring your own Cheez Doodles and Tastykakes. My business manager will stop by later this morning to discuss salary and benefits. I'll have Ella order some RangeMan shirts for you. If you decide to go back to Vinnie you can keep the shirts." Ranger almost smiled. "I like the idea of you wearing my name on your breast." He had his hand at the back of my waist, and he guided me into the cubby. "Make yourself comfortable. I'll send Silvio in to you. I'll be out of the office all day, but you can reach me on my cell if there's a problem. Are there any new disasters you want to share with me before I take off?"

"Spiro sent me Mama Mac's mole."

"Her mole?"

"Yeah, she had this horrible mutant mole on her face that the crime lab was never able to find. Spiro left it for me in my apartment. He had it all gift wrapped in a little box."

"Walk me through this."

"I went back to my apartment this morning to find something black to wear to work. I opened my locked door and the little gift-wrapped package was on the floor in the foyer. I was worried Spiro might still be in the apartment, so I called Lula and we went through together."

"Why didn't you call me?"

"It felt wimpy."

"Do you honestly think Lula would protect you against Spiro?"

"She had a gun."

There was an awkward pause while Ranger came to terms with the possibility that I didn't have my own gun.

"My gun melted down in the Cluck-in-a-Bucket fire," I told him. Not nearly so much of a loss as my lip gloss.

"Tank will also outfit you with a gun," Ranger said. "I expect you to carry it. And I expect it to be loaded. We have a practice range in the basement. Once a week I expect you to visit the practice range."

I snapped him a salute. "Aye, aye, sir!"

"Don't let the rest of the men see you being a smart-ass," Ranger said. "They're not allowed."

"I'm allowed?"

"I have no illusions over my ability to control you. Just try to keep the power play private, so you don't undermine my authority with my men."

"You're assuming we'll have private time?"

"It would be nice." The almost smile turned into a for-sure smile. "Are you flirting with me?"

"I don't think so. Did it feel like flirting?" Of course

I was flirting with him. I was a horrible person. Morelli
was home with a broken leg and a mutant mole, and I
was flirting with Ranger. God, I was such a slut.

"Finish walking me through your latest disaster."

"Okay, so Lula and I went through the apartment
and there was no Spiro. So we went back to the box,
and I opened it."

"You weren't worried that it was a bomb?"

"It would have been a little bomb."

Ranger looked like he was trying hard not to grimace. "What happened after you opened it?"

"I threw up."

"Babe," Ranger said.

"Anyway, I gave the mole to Morelli. I figured he'd
know what to do with it."

"Good thinking. Anything else you want to share?"

"Maybe later."

"You're flirting again," Ranger said.

And he left.

I saw him stop to talk to Tank on his way out. Tank
nodded and looked my way. I gave Tank a little finger
wave and both men smiled.

The cubby walls were corkboard. Good for deaden-
ing sound, and also good for posting notes. I could see
holes where Silvio had tacked messages and whatever,
but the messages had all been removed, and only the
pushpins remained. I had a workstation desk, a comfy-
looking leather desk chair, a computer that could probably e-mail Mars, a phone that had too many buttons, a
headset to go with the phone, file cabinets, in/out baskets that were empty, a second chair for guests, and a
printer.

I sat in my chair and swiveled around. If I leaned
back I could see out of the cubby, into the control
room. The computer was different from the one I had
at home. I hadn't a clue how to work the darn thing.

Ditto the multiline phone. Maybe I shouldn't throw the personal products plant application away. Maybe overseeing the boxing machine was more my speed. I looked in the desk drawers. Pens, sticky-note pads, tape, stapler, lined pads, Advil. The Advil might not be a good sign. I was dying to go to the kitchen for coffee, but I didn't want to leave my cubby. It felt safe in the cubby. I didn't have to make eye contact with any of the guys. Some of Ranger's men looked like they should be wearing orange jumpsuits and ankle monitors.

Five minutes after Ranger left, Tank came into my cubicle with a small box. He set the box on my desk and removed the contents. Key fob for the garage and Ranger's apartment, Sig Sauer 9 with extra mag, stun gun, cell phone, laminated photo ID on a neck chain identifying me as a RangeMan employee. I hadn't posed for the photo and decided not to ask how it was obtained.

"I don't know how to work this kind of gun," I told Tank. "I use a revolver."

"Ranger has practice time reserved for you tomorrow at ten A.M. You're required to carry the gun, the phone, and the ID with you at all times. You don't have to wear the ID. It's for fieldwork. It's a good idea to keep it on you in case you're questioned about the gun."

Silvio arrived with a cup of coffee, and Tank disappeared. "I brought you cream, no sugar," he said, setting the coffee on the desk in front of me. "If you want sugar there are some packets in the left-hand drawer." He pulled the extra chair next to mine. "Okay," he said. "Let's see what you know about computers."

Oh boy.

By noon I had the phone figured out, and I could navigate the Net. I was already familiar with most of the search programs used by RangeMan. I'd used them from time to time on Connie's computer. Beyond the standard search programs that Connie used, RangeMan had a few extra that were frighteningly invasive. Just for the heck of it, I typed my name in on one of the super searchers and blanched at what appeared on my screen. I had no secrets. The file stopped just short of a Webcam view of my last gyn exam.

I followed Silvio to the kitchen and took a food survey. Fresh fruit and vegetables, cut and washed. Turkey, roast beef, tuna sandwiches on seven-grain bread. Low-fat yogurt. Energy bars. Juice. Skim milk. Bottles of water.

"No Tastykakes," I said to Silvio.

"Ella used to set out trays of cookies and brownie bars, but we started to get fat, so Ranger banned them."

"He's a hard man."

"Tell me about it," Silvio said. "He scares the crap out of me."

I took a turkey sandwich and a bottle of water and returned to my cubicle. Hal, Woody, and Vince were watching their screens. Silvio went off to clean out his locker. So I was now officially Miz Computer Wiz. Three requests for security searches were sitting in my in-box. Mental note. Never leave cubby. Work appears when cubby is left unattended. I looked at the name requesting the search requests. Frederick Rodriguez. Didn't know him. Didn't see him out and about in the control room. There was another floor of offices. I guessed Frederick Rodriguez was in one of those offices.

I called my mom on my new cell phone and gave her the number. I could hear my grandmother yelling in the background.

"Is that Stephanie?" Grandma Mazur hollered. "Tell her the Macaroni funeral is tomorrow morning, and I need a ride."

"You're not going to the funeral," my mother said to Grandma Mazur.

"It's gonna be the big event of the year," Grandma said. "I have to go."

"Joseph let you see the mole before he gave it over to the police," my mother said. "You're going to have to be satisfied with that." My mother's attention swung back to me. "If you take her to that funeral there's no more pineapple upside-down cake for the rest of your life."

I disconnected from my mother, ate my sandwich, and ran the first name. It was close to three by the time I was done running the second name. I set the third request aside and paged through the Gorman file. Then I did as Ranger suggested and ran Gorman through all the searches again. I called Morelli to make sure he was okay and to tell him I might be late. There was a stretch of silence while he wrestled with trust, and then he put in a request for a six-pack of Bud and two chili dogs.

"And by the way," Morelli said. "The lab guy called and told me the mole was made out of mortician's putty."

"Don't tell Grandma," I said. "It'll ruin everything for her."

TEN

I printed the Gorman search, and then I searched Louis Lazar. Both men yielded volumes of information. Date of birth, medical history, history of employment, military history, credit history, history of residence, class standings through high school. Neither man attended college. Personal history included photos, wives, kids, assorted relatives.

I printed Lazar and moved to Michael Barroni. Most of this information I already knew. Some was new and felt embarrassingly intrusive. His wife had miscarried two children. He'd gotten psychiatric counseling a year ago for anxiety. He'd had a hernia operation when he was thirty-six. He'd been asked to repeat the third grade.

I'd just started a credit check on Barroni when my cell rang.

"I'm hungry," Morelli said. "It's seven o'clock. When are you coming home?"

"Sorry. I lost track of the time."

"Bob is standing by the door."

"*Okay!* I'll be right there."

I put the Barroni search on hold and dropped the Lazar file and the Gorman file into my top desk drawer. I grabbed my bag and my jacket and dashed out of my cubby. There was an entirely new crew in the control room. Ranger ran the control room in eight-hour shifts around the clock. A guy named Ram was at one of the monitor banks. Two other men were at large.

I crossed the room at a run, barreled through the door to take the stairs, and crashed into Ranger. We lost balance and rolled tangled together to the fourth-floor landing. We lay there for a moment, stunned and breathless. Ranger was flat on his back, and I was on top of him.

"Oh my God," I said. "I'm so sorry! Are you okay?"

"Yeah, but next time it's my turn to have the top."

The door opened above us and Ram stuck his head out. "I heard a crash . . . oh, excuse me," he said. And he pulled his head back and closed the door.

"I wish this was as bad as it looks," Ranger said. He got to his feet, scooping me up with him. He held me at arm's length and looked me over. "You're a wreck. Did I do all this damage?"

I had some scratches on my arm, the knee had gotten torn on my jeans, and there was a rip in my T-shirt. Ranger was perfect. Ranger was like Big Blue. Nothing ever touched Ranger.

"Don't worry about it," I said. "I'm fine. I'm late. Gotta go." And I took off, down the rest of the stairs and out the door to the garage.

I crossed town and stopped at Mike the Greek's deli for the hot dogs and beer. Five minutes later, I had the SUV locked up in Morelli's garage. I took his back porch steps two at a time, opened the back door, and Bob rushed past me and tinkled in the middle of Morelli's backyard.

The instant the last drop hit grass, Bob bolted off into the night. I rustled the hot dog bag, pulled out a hot dog, and waved it in Bob's direction. I heard Bob stop galloping two houses down, there was a moment of silence, and then he came thundering back. Bob can smell a hot dog a mile away.

I lured him into the house with the hot dog and locked up. Morelli was still on the couch with his foot on the coffee table. The room was trashed around him. Empty soda cans, newspapers, a crumpled fast-food bag, a half-empty potato chip bag, an empty dough-nut box, a sock (probably Bob ate the mate), assorted sports and girlie magazines.

"This room is a Dumpster," I said to him. "Where'd all this stuff come from?"

"Some of the guys visited me."

I doled out the hot dogs. Two to Morelli, two to Bob, two to me. Morelli and I got a Bud. Bob got a bowl of water. I kicked through the clutter, brushed potato chip crumbs off a chair, and sat down. "You need to clean up."

"I can't clean up. I'm supposed to stay off my leg."

"You weren't worrying about your leg last night."

"That was different. That was an emergency. And anyway, I wasn't on my leg. I was on my back. And what's with the scratches on your arm and the torn clothes? What the hell were you doing? I thought you were supposed to be working in the office."

"I fell down the stairs."

"At RangeMan?"

"Yep. Do you want another beer? Ice cream?"

"I want to know how you managed to fall down the stairs."

"I was rushing to leave, and I sort of crashed into Ranger, and we fell down the stairs."

Morelli stared at me with his unreadable cop face. I was ready for him to morph into the jealous Italian boyfriend with a lot of arm flapping and yelling, but he gave his head a small shake and took another pull on his Bud. "Poor dumb bastard," he said. "I hope he's got insurance on that building."

I was pretty sure I'd just been insulted, but I thought it was best to let it slide.

Morelli leaned back into the couch and smiled at me. "And before I forget, your cello is in the front hall."

"My cello?"

"Yeah, every great cello player needs a cello, right?"

I ran to the hall and gaped at the big bulbous black case leaning against the wall. I dragged the case into the living room and opened it. There was a large violin sort of thing in it. I supposed it was a cello.

"How did this get here?" I asked Morelli.

"Your mother rented it for you. She said you gave yours away, and she knew how much you were looking forward to playing at Valerie's wedding, so she rented a cello for you. I swear to God, those were her exact words."

I guess the panic showed on my face because Morelli stopped smiling.

"Maybe you should fill me in on your musical accomplishments," Morelli said.

I plunked down on the couch beside him. "I don't have any musical accomplishments. I don't have any accomplishments of any kind. I'm stupid and boring. I don't have any hobbies. I don't play sports. I don't write poetry. I don't travel to interesting places. I don't even have a good job."

"That doesn't make you stupid and boring," Morelli said.

"Well, I *feel* stupid and boring. And I wanted to feel interesting. And somehow, someone told my mother and grandmother that I played the cello. I guess it was me . . . only it was like some foreign entity took possession of my body. I heard the words coming out of my mouth, but I'm sure they originated in some other brain. And it was so simple at first. One small mention. And then it took on a life of its own. And next thing, *everyone* knew."

"And you can't play the cello."

"I'm not even sure this *is* a cello."

Morelli went back to smiling. "And you think you're boring? No way, Cupcake."

"What about the stupid part?"

Morelli threw his arm around me. "Sometimes that's a tough call."

"My mother expects me to play at Valerie's wedding."

"You can fake it," Morelli said. "How hard can it be? You just make a couple passes with the bow and then you faint or pretend you broke your finger or something."

"That might work," I said. "I'm good at faking it."

This led to a couple moments of uncomfortable silence from both of us.

"You didn't mean . . . ?" Morelli asked.

"No. Of course not."

"Never?"

"Maybe once."

His eyes narrowed. "Once?"

"It's all that comes to mind. It was the time we were late for your Uncle Spud's birthday party."

"I remember that. That was great. You're telling me you faked it?"

"We were late! I couldn't concentrate. It seemed like the best way to go."

Morelli took his arm away and started flipping through channels with the remote.

"You're mad," I said.

"I'm working on it. Don't push me."

I got up and closed the cello case and kicked it to the side of the room. "Men!"

"At least we don't fake it."

"Listen, it was *your* uncle. And we were *late,*

remember? So I made the sacrifice and got us there in time for dessert. You should be thanking me."

Morelli's mouth was open slightly and his face was registering a mixture of astonished disbelief and wounded, pissed-off male pride.

Okay, it wasn't that much of a sacrifice at the time, and I knew he shouldn't be thanking me, but give me a break here . . . this wasn't famine in Ethiopia. And it wasn't as if I hadn't *tried* to have an orgasm. And it wasn't as if we didn't fib to each other from time to time.

"I should be thanking you," Morelli repeated, sounding like he was making a gigantic but futile effort to understand the female mind.

"All right, I'll concede the *thanking* thing. How about if you're just happy I got you to the party in time for dessert?"

Morelli cut me a sideways look. He wasn't having any of it. He returned his attention to the television and settled on a ball game.

This is the reason I live with a hamster, I thought.

Morelli was still on the couch watching television when I went downstairs to take Bob for his morning walk. I was wearing sweats that I'd found in Morelli's dresser, and I'd borrowed his Mets hat. I clipped the leash on Bob, and Morelli glanced over at me. "What's with the clothes? Trying to fake being me?"

"Get a grip," I said to Morelli.

Bob was dancing around, looking desperate, so I hurried him out the front door. He took a big tinkle on Morelli's sidewalk and then he got all smiley and ready to walk. I like walking Bob at night when it's dark and no one can see where he poops. At night Bob and I are the phantom poopers, leaving it where it falls. By day, I have to carry plastic pooper bags. I don't actually mind scooping the poop. It's carrying it around for the rest of the walk that I hate. It's hard to look hot when you're carrying a bag of dog poop.

I walked Bob for almost an hour. We returned to the house. I fed Bob. I made coffee. I brought Morelli coffee, juice, his paper, and a bowl of raisin bran. I ran upstairs, took a shower, did some makeup and hair magic, got dressed in my black clothes, and came downstairs ready for work.

"Is there anything you need before I leave?" I asked Morelli.

Morelli gave me a full body scan. "Dressing sexy for Ranger?"

I was wearing black jeans, black Chucks, and a stretchy V-neck black T-shirt that didn't show any cleavage. "Is that sarcasm?" I asked.

"No. It's an observation."

"This is *not* sexy."

"That shirt is too skimpy."

"I've worn this shirt a million times. You've never objected to it before."

"That's because it was worn for me. You need to change that shirt."

"Okay," I said, arms in air, nostrils flaring. "You want me to change my shirt. I'll change my shirt." And I stomped up the stairs and stripped off all my clothes. I'd brought every piece of black I owned to Morelli's house, so I pawed through my wardrobe and came up with skintight black spandex workout pants that rode low and were worn commando. I changed my shoes to black Pumas. And I wriggled into a black spandex wrap shirt that didn't quite meet the top of the work-out pants and showed *a lot* of cleavage . . . at least as much as I could manage without implants. I stomped back down the stairs and paraded into the living room to show Morelli.

"Is this better?" I asked.

Morelli narrowed his eyes and reached for me, but he couldn't move far without his crutches. I beat him to the crutches and ran to the kitchen with them. I hustled out of the house, backed Morelli's SUV out of the garage, and motored off to work.

I used my new key fob to get into the underground garage and parked in the area reserved for noncompany cars. I took the elevator to the fifth floor, stepped into the control room, and six sets of eyes looked up from the screens and locked onto me. Halfway to work, I'd pulled Morelli's sweatshirt out of my shoulder bag and put it on over my little stretchy top. It was a nice, big shapeless thing that came well below my ass and gave me a safe unisex look. I smiled at the six men on deck. They all smiled back and returned to their work.

I was a half hour early and for the first time in a long time I was excited to get to work. I wanted to finish the Barroni search, and then I wanted to move on to Jimmy Runion. I still had one file left to search for Frederick Rodriguez. I decided to do it first and get it off my desk. I was still working on the Rodriguez file when Ranger appeared in my cubby entrance.

"We have a date," Ranger said. "You're scheduled for ten o'clock practice downstairs."

Here's the thing about guns. I hate them. I don't even like them when they're not loaded. "I'm in the middle of something," I said. "Maybe we could reschedule for some other time." Like never.

"We're doing this now," Ranger said. "This is important. And I don't want to find your gun in your desk drawer when you leave. If you work for me, you carry a gun."

"I don't have permission to carry concealed."

Ranger shoved my chair with his foot and rolled me back from the computer. "Then you carry exposed."

"I can't do that. I'll feel like Annie Oakley."

Ranger pulled me out of the chair. "You'll figure it out. Get your gun. We have the range for an hour."

I took the gun out of the desk drawer, shoved it into my sweatshirt pocket, and followed Ranger to the elevator. We exited into the garage and walked to the rear. Ranger unlocked the door to the range and switched the light on. The room was windowless and appeared to stretch the length of the building. There were two lanes for shooters. Remote-controlled targets at the far end. Shelves and a thick bulletproof glass partition that separated the shooters at the head of each lane.

"With a little effort you could turn this into a bowling alley," I said to Ranger.

"This is more fun," Ranger said. "And I'm having a hard time seeing you in bowling shoes."

"It's not fun. I don't like guns."

"You don't have to like them, but if you work for me you have to feel comfortable with them and know how to use them and be safe."

Ranger took two headsets and a box of ammo and put them on my shelf. "We'll start with basics. You have a nine-millimeter Sig Sauer. It's a semiautomatic." Ranger removed the magazine, showed it to me, and shoved it back into the gun. "Now you do it," he said.

I removed the magazine and reloaded. I did it ten times. Ranger did a step-by-step demonstration on firing. He gave the gun back to me, and I went through the process ten times. I was nervous, and it felt stuffy in the narrow room, and I was starting to sweat. I put the gun on the shelf, and I took off Morelli's sweatshirt.

"Babe," Ranger said. And he pulled his key fob out of his pocket and hit a button.

"What did you just do?" I asked him.

"I scrambled the security camera in this room. Hal

will fall out of his seat upstairs if he sees you in this outfit."

"You don't want to know the long story, but the short story is I wore it to annoy Morelli."

"I'm in favor of anything that annoys Morelli," Ranger said. He moved in close and looked down at me. "This wouldn't be my first choice as a work uniform, but I like it." He ran a finger across the slash of stomach not covered by clothing, and I felt heat rush into private places. He splayed his hand at my hip and turned his interest to my workout pants. "I especially like these pants. What do you wear under them?"

And here's where I made my mistake. I was hot and flustered and a flip answer seemed in order. Problem was, the answer that popped out of my mouth was a tad flirty.

"There are some things a man should find out for himself," I said.

Ranger reached for the waistband on the spandex pants, and I shrieked and jumped back.

"Babe," Ranger said, smiling. I was amusing him, again.

I glanced at my watch. "Actually, I need to leave the building for a while."

"Looking for another job?"

"No. This is personal."

Ranger pushed the button to unscramble the surveillance camera. "Wear the sweatshirt when you're on deck in the control room."

"Deal."

A half hour later, I was idling across the street from Stiva's. The hearse and the flower cars were in place at the side entrance. Three black Town Cars lined up behind the flower cars. I sat and watched the casket come out. Macaronis followed. The flower cars were already

loaded. The cars slowly moved out and drove the short
distance to the church. I saw no sign of Spiro. I followed
at a distance and parked half a block from the church.
I had a clear view of the parking lot and the front of
the church. I settled back to wait. This would take a
while. The Macaronis would want Mass. The parking
lot was full and the surrounding streets were bumper-
to-bumper cars. The entire Burg had turned out.

An hour later, I was worrying about my cubicle sitting empty. I was getting paid to do computer searches,
not hang out at funerals. And then, just as I was thinking about leaving and returning to work, the doors to
the church opened and people began to file out. I caught
a glimpse of the casket being rolled out a side door to
the waiting hearse. Engines caught up and down the
street. Stiva's assistants were out, lining up cars, at-
taching flags to antennae. I was intently watching the
crowd at the church and jumped when Ranger rapped
on my side window.

"Have you seen Spiro?"

"No."

"I'm right behind you. Lock up and we'll take my car."

Ranger was driving a black Porsche Cayenne. I slid
onto the passenger seat and buckled up. "How did you
find me?"

"Woody picked you up on the screen, realized you
were following the funeral, and told me."

"It'll be ugly if Morelli finds out you're tracking his
SUV."

"I'll remove the transponder when you stop using
the car."

"I don't suppose there's any way I can get you to
stop tracking *me*?"

"You don't want me to stop tracking you, Babe. I'm
keeping you safe."

He was right. And I was sufficiently freaked out by Spiro to tolerate the intrusion.

"This isn't personal leave time," Ranger said. "This is work. You should have run it by me. We had to scramble to coordinate this."

"Sorry. It was a last-minute decision . . . as you can see from my clothes. My mother will need a pill after she starts getting the reports back on my cemetery appearance."

"We're wearing black," Ranger said. "We're in the ballpark. Just keep your sweatshirt zipped, so the men don't accidentally fall into the grave."

Cars were moving around in front of the church, jockeying for position. The hearse pulled into the street and the procession followed, single file, lights on. Ranger waited for the last car to go by before he fell into line. There'd been no sign of Spiro, but then I hadn't expected him to show up at church, shaking hands and chatting. I'd expected him to do another drive-by or maybe hang in a shadow somewhere. Or maybe he'd be hidden at some distance, waiting for the graveside ceremony, using binoculars to see the results of his insanity.

"Tank's already at the cemetery," Ranger said. "He's watching the perimeter. He's got Slick and Eddie working with him."

It was a slow drive to Mama Mac's final resting place. Ranger wasn't famous for making small talk, so it was also a quiet drive. We parked and got out of the Cayenne. The sky was overcast, and the air was unusually cool for the time of year. I was happy to have the sweatshirt. We'd been the last to arrive, and that meant we had the longest walk. By the time we made it to the grave site, the principals were seated and the large crowd had closed around them. This was perfect for our purpose. We were able to stand at a distance and keep watch.

Ranger and I were shoulder to shoulder. Two professionals, doing a job. Problem was, one of the professionals didn't do well at funerals. I was a funeral basket case. Possibly the only thing I hated more than a gun was a funeral. They made me sad. *Really sad*. And the sadness had nothing to do with the deceased. I got weepy over perfect strangers.

The priest stood and repeated the Lord's Prayer and I felt my eyes well with tears. I concentrated on counting blades of grass at my feet, but the words intruded. I blinked the tears back and swung my thoughts to Bob. I tried to envision Bob hunching. He was going to hork up a sock. The tears ran down my cheeks. It was no good. Bob thoughts couldn't compete with the smell of fresh-turned earth and funeral flowers. "Shit," I whispered. And I sniffed back some snot.

Ranger turned to me. His brown eyes were curious and the corners of his mouth were tipped up ever so slightly. "Are you okay?" he asked.

I found a tissue in one of the sweatshirt pockets, and I blew my nose. "I'm fine. I just have this reaction to funerals!"

Several people on the outermost ring of mourners glanced our way.

Ranger put his arm around me. "You didn't like Mama Mac. You hardly knew her."

"It doesn't m-m-matter," I sobbed.

Ranger drew me closer. "Babe, we're starting to attract a lot of attention. Could you drop the sobbing down a level?"

"Ashes to ashes . . ." the priest said.

And I totally lost it. I slumped against Ranger and cried. He was wearing a windbreaker, and he wrapped me in the open windbreaker, hugging me in to him, his face pressed to the side of my head, shielding me as best he could from people turning to see the sobbing idiot. I was burrowed into him, trying to muffle the sobs, and I could feel him shaking with silent laughter.

"You're despicable," I hissed, giving him a punch in the chest. "Stop laughing. This is s-s-s-sad."

Several people turned and shushed me.

"It's okay," Ranger said, still silently laughing, arms wrapped tight around me. "Don't pay any attention to them. Just let it all out."

I hiccupped back a couple small sobs, and I wiped my nose with my sleeve. "This is nothing. You should see me at a parade when the drums and the flag go by."

Ranger cradled my face in his hands, using his thumbs to wipe the tears from my eyes. "The ceremony is over. Can you make it back to the car?"

I nodded. "I'm okay now. Am I red and blotchy from crying?"

"Yes," Ranger said, brushing a kiss across my forehead. "I love you anyway."

"There's all kinds of love," I said.

Ranger took me by the hand and led me back to the SUV. "This is the kind that doesn't call for a ring. But a condom might come in handy."

"That's not love," I told him. "That's lust."

He was scanning the crowd as we walked and talked, watching for Spiro, watching for anything unusual. "In this case, there's some of both."

"Just not the marrying type?"

We'd reached the car, and Ranger remoted it open. "Look at me, Babe. I'm carrying two guns and a knife. At this point in my life, I'm not exactly family material."

"Do you think that will change?"

Ranger opened the door for me. "Not anytime soon."

No surprise there. Still, it was a teeny, tiny bit of a downer. How scary is that?

"And there are things you don't know about me," Ranger said.

"What kind of things?"

"Things you don't *want* to know." Ranger rolled the engine over and called Tank. "We're heading back," he said. "Anything on your end?"

The answer was obviously negative because Ranger disconnected and pulled into the stream of traffic. "Tank didn't see any bad guys, but it wasn't a total wash," Ranger said, handing his cell phone over to me. "I managed to take a picture for you while you were tucked into my jacket."

Ranger had a picture phone, exactly like the one I'd been issued. I went to the album option and brought up four photos of Anthony Barroni. The images were small. I chose one and waited while it filled the screen. Anthony appeared to be talking on his phone. Hold on, he wasn't talking . . . he was taking a picture. "Anthony's taking photos with his phone," I said. "Omigod, that's so creepy."

"Yeah," Ranger said. "Either Anthony's really into dead people or else he's sending photos to someone not fortunate enough to have a front-row seat."

"Spiro." Maybe.

Most of the cars left the cemetery and turned toward the Burg. The wake at Gina Macaroni's house would be packed. Anthony Barroni peeled away from the herd at Chambers Street. Ranger stuck to him, and we followed him to the store. He parked his Vette in the rear and sauntered inside.

"You should go talk to him," Ranger said. "Ask him if he had a good time."

"You're serious."

"Time to stir things up," Ranger said. "Let's raise the stakes for Anthony. Let him know he's blown his cover. See if anything happens."

I chewed on my lower lip. I didn't want to face Anthony. I didn't want to do this stuff anymore. "I'm an office worker," I said. "I think *you* should talk to him."

Ranger parked the SUV in front of the store. "We'll both talk to Anthony. Last time I left you alone in my car someone stole you."

It was early afternoon on a weekday, and there wasn't a lot of activity in the store. There was an old guy behind the counter, waiting on a woman who was buying a sponge mop. No other customers. Two of the Barroni brothers were working together, labeling a carton of nails in aisle four. Anthony was on his cell phone to the rear of the store. He was shuffling around, nodding his head and laughing.

I always enjoy watching Ranger stalk prey. He moves with single-minded purpose, his body relaxed, his gait even, his eyes unswerving and fixed on his quarry. The eye of the tiger.

I was one step behind Ranger, and I was thinking this wasn't a good idea. We could be wrong and look like idiots. Ranger never worried about that, but I worried about it constantly. Or we could be right, and we could set Anthony and Spiro off on a killing spree.

Anthony saw us approaching. He closed his phone and slipped it into his pants pocket. He looked to Ranger and then to me.

"Stephanie," he said, grinning. "Man, you were really bawling at the cemetery. Guess you got real broken up having Mama Melanoma blown to bits in your car."

"It was a touching ceremony," I said.

"Yeah," Anthony said, snorting and laughing. "The Lord's Prayer always gets to me, too."

Ranger extended his hand. "Carlos Manoso," he said. "I don't believe we've met."

Anthony shook Ranger's hand. "Anthony Barroni. What can I do for you? Need a plunger?"

Ranger gave him a small cordial smile. "We thought we'd stop by to say hello and see if Spiro liked the pictures."

"Waddaya mean?"

"It's too bad he couldn't have been there in person," Ranger said. "So much is lost in a photograph."

"I don't know what you're talking about."

"Sure you do," Ranger said. "You made a bad choice. And you're going to die because of it. You might want to talk to someone while there's still time."

"Someone?"

"The police," Ranger said. "They might be able to cut you a deal."

"I don't need a deal," Anthony said.

"He'll turn on you," Ranger said. "You made a bad choice for a partner."

"You should talk. Look who you've got for a partner. Little Miss Cry-Her-Eyes-Out." Anthony rubbed his eyes like he was crying. "Boohoohoo."

"This is embarrassing," I said. "I *hate* when I cry at funerals."

"Boohoo-ooo."

"Stop. That's enough," I said. "It's not funny."

"Boohoo boohoo boohoo."

So I punched him. It was one of those bypass-the-brain impulse actions. And it was a real sucker punch. Anthony never saw it coming. He had his hands to his eyes doing the boohoo thing, and I guess I threw all my fear and frustration into the punch. I heard his face crunch under my fist, and blood spurted out of his nose. I was so horrified I froze on the spot.

Ranger gave a bark of laughter and dragged me away so I didn't get splattered.

Anthony's eyes were wide, his mouth open, his hands clapped over his nose.

Ranger shoved a business card into Anthony's shirt pocket. "Call me if you want to talk."

We left the store and buckled ourselves into the Cayenne. Ranger turned the engine over and slid a glance my way. "I usually spar with Tank. Maybe next time I should get in the ring with you."

"It was a lucky punch."

Ranger had the full-on smile and there were little laugh lines at the corners of his eyes. "You're a fun date."

"Do you really think Spiro and Anthony are partners?"

"I think it's unlikely."

ELEVEN

I left Ranger in the control room and hurried into my cubicle, anxious to finish running the check on Barroni. I came to a skidding stop when I saw my in-box. Seven new requests for computer background searches. All from Frederick Rodriguez.

I stuck my head out of my cubicle and yelled at Ranger. "Hey, who's this Frederick Rodriguez guy? He keeps filling up my in-box."

"He's in sales," Ranger said. "Let them sit. Work on Gorman."

I finished Barroni, printed his entire file, and dropped it into the drawer with Gorman and Lazar. I entered Jimmy Runion into the first search program and watched as information rushed onto my screen. I'd been scanning the searches as they appeared, taking notes, trying to find the one thing that bound them together in life and probably in death. So far, nothing had jumped out at me. There were a few things that were common to the men, but nothing significant. They were all approximately the same age. They had all owned small businesses. They were all married. When I finished Runion I'd take all the files and read through them more carefully.

I was halfway through Runion when my mom called on my cell.

"Where are you?" she wanted to know.

"I'm at work."

"It's five-thirty. We're supposed to be at the church for rehearsal. You were going to stop here first, and then we were all going over to the church. We've been waiting and waiting."

Crap! "I forgot."

"How could you forget? Your sister's getting married tomorrow. How could you forget?"

"I'm on my way. Give me twenty minutes."

"I'll take your grandmother with me. You can meet us at the church. You just bring Joseph and the cello."

"Joseph and the cello," I dumbly repeated.

"Everyone's waiting to hear you play."

"I might be late. There might not be time."

"We don't have to be at Marsillio's for the rehearsal dinner until seven-thirty. I'm sure there'll be time for you to practice your cello piece."

Crap. *Crap.* And *double crap!*

I grabbed my bag and took off, across the control room, down the stairs, into the garage. Ranger had just pulled in. He was getting out of his car as I ran to Morelli's SUV.

"I'm late!" I yelled to him. "I'm frigging late!"

"Of course you are," Ranger said, smiling.

It took me twelve minutes to get across town to the Burg and then into Morelli's neighborhood. I'd had to drive on the sidewalk once when there was traffic at a light. And I'd saved two blocks by using Mr. Fedorka's driveway and cutting through his backyard to the alley that led to Morelli's house.

I locked the SUV in the garage, ran into the house, into the living room.

"The wedding rehearsal is tonight," I yelled at Morelli. "The wedding rehearsal!"

Morelli was working his way through a bag of chips. "And?"

"And we have to be there. We're in the wedding party. It's my sister. I'm the maid of honor. You're the best man."

Morelli set the chips aside. "Tell me those aren't blood splatters on your shoes."

"I sort of punched Anthony Barroni in the nose."

"Anthony Barroni was at RangeMan?"

"It's a long story. I haven't time to go into it all. And you don't want to hear it anyway. It's . . . embarrassing." I had Bob clipped to his leash. "I'm taking Bob out, and then I'm going to help you get dressed." I dragged Bob out the back door and walked him around Morelli's yard. "Do you have to go, Bob?" I said. "Gotta tinkle? Gotta poop?"

Bob didn't want to tinkle or poop in Morelli's yard. Bob needed variety. Bob wanted to tinkle on Mrs. Rosario's hydrangea bush, two doors down.

"This is it!" I yelled at Bob. "You don't go here and you're holding it in until I get back from the stupid rehearsal dinner."

Bob wandered around a little and tinkled. I could tell he didn't have his heart in it, but it was good enough, so I dragged Bob inside, fed him some dog crunchies for dinner, and gave him some fresh water. I ran upstairs and got clothes for Morelli. Slacks, belt, button-down shirt. I ran back downstairs and shoved him into the shirt, and then realized he couldn't get the slacks over the cast. He was wearing gray sweatpants with one leg cut at thigh level.

"Okay," I said, "the sweats are good enough." I took a closer look. Pizza sauce on the long leg. Not good enough.

I ran upstairs and rummaged through Morelli's closet. Nothing I could use. I rifled his drawers. Nothing there.

I went through the dirty clothes basket, found a pair of khaki shorts, and ran downstairs with them.

"Ta-*dah!*" I announced. "Shorts. And they're almost clean." I had Morelli out of his sweatpants in one fast swoop. I tugged the shorts up and zipped them.

"Jeez," Morelli said. "I can zip my own shorts."

"You weren't fast enough!" I looked at my watch. It was almost six o'clock! *Yikes.* "Put your foot on the coffee table, and I'll get shoes on you."

Morelli put his foot on the coffee table, and I stared up his shorts at Mr. Happy.

"Omigod," I said. "You're wearing boxers. I can see up your shorts."

"Do you like what you see?"

"Yes, but I don't want the world seeing it!"

"Don't worry about it," Morelli said. "I'll be careful."

I pulled a sock on Morelli's casted foot, and I laced a sneaker on the other. I raced upstairs, and I changed into a skirt and short-sleeved sweater. I threw my jean jacket over the sweater, grabbed my bag, got Morelli up on his crutches, and maneuvered him to the kitchen door.

"I hate to bring this up," Morelli said. "But aren't you supposed to take the cello?"

The cello. I squinched my eyes closed, and I rapped my head on the wall. *Thunk, thunk, thunk.* I took a second to breathe. I can do this, I told myself. Probably I can play a little something. How hard can it be? You just do the bowing thing back and forth and sounds come out. I might even turn out to be good at it. Heck, maybe I should take some lessons. Maybe I'm a natural talent and I don't even *need* lessons. The more I thought about it, the more logical it sounded. Maybe I was always meant to play the cello, and I'd just gotten sidetracked, and this was God's way of turning me in the direction of my true calling.

"Wait here," I said to Morelli. "I'll put the cello in the car, and I'll come back to get you."

I ran into the living room and hefted the cello. I carted it into the kitchen, past Morelli, out the door, and crossed the yard with it. I opened the garage door, rammed the cello into the back of the SUV, dropped my purse onto the driver's seat, and returned to the kitchen for Morelli. I realized he was just wearing a cotton shirt. No sweater on him. No jacket. And it was cold out. I ran upstairs and got a jacket. I helped him into the jacket, stuffed the crutches back under his arms, and helped him navigate through the back door and down the stairs.

We started to cross the yard, and the garage exploded with enough force to rattle the windows in Morelli's house.

The garage was wood with an asbestos-shingle roof. It hadn't been in the best of shape, and Morelli seldom used it. I'd been using it to keep the SUV bomb-free, but I now saw the flaw in the plan. It was an old garage without an automatic door opener. So to make things easier, I'd left the garage open when not in use. Easy to pull in and park. Also easy to sneak in and plant a bomb.

Morelli and I stood there, dumbstruck. His garage had gone up like fireworks and had come down like confetti. Splintered boards, shingles, and assorted car parts fell out of the sky into Morelli's yard. It was Mama Mac all over again. Almost nothing was left of the garage. Morelli's SUV was a fireball. His yard was littered with smoldering junk.

"Omigod!" I said. "The cello was in your SUV." I pumped my fist into the air and did a little dance. "*Yes!* Way to go! *Woohoo!* There is a God and He loves me. It's good-bye cello."

Morelli gave his head a shake. "You're a very strange woman."

"You're just trying to flatter me."

"Honey, my garage just blew up, and I don't think it was insured. We're supposed to be upset."

"Sorry. I'll try to look serious now."

Morelli glanced over at me. "You're still smiling."

"I can't help it. I'm trying to be scared and depressed, but it's just not working. I'm just so frigging relieved to be rid of that cello."

There were sirens screaming from all directions, and the first of the cop cars parked in the alley behind Morelli's house. I borrowed Morelli's cell phone and called my mother.

"Bad news," I said. "We're going to be late. We're having car trouble."

"How late? What's wrong with the car?"

"Real late. There's a lot wrong with the car."

"I'll send your father for you."

"Not necessary," I said. "Have the rehearsal without me, and I'll meet you at Marsillio's."

"You're the maid of honor. You have to be at the rehearsal. How will you know what to do?"

"I'll figure it out. This isn't my first wedding. I know the drill."

"But the cello . . ."

"You don't have to worry about that either." I didn't have the heart to tell her about the cello.

Two fire trucks pulled up to the garage. Emergency-vehicle strobes flashed up and down the alley, and headlights glared into Morelli's yard. The garage had been blown to smithereens, and the remaining parts had rained down over a three-house area. Some parts had smoked but none had flamed. The SUV had burned brightly but not long. So the fire had almost entirely extinguished itself before the first hose was unwound.

Ryan Laski crossed the yard and found Morelli.

"I'm seeing a disturbing pattern here," Laski said. "Was anyone hurt . . . or vaporized?"

"Just property damage," Morelli said.

"I've sent some uniforms off to talk to neighbors. Hard to believe no one ever sees this guy. This isn't the sort of place where people mind their own business."

A mobile satellite truck for one of the local television stations cruised into the alley.

Laski cut his eyes to it. "This is going to be a big disappointment. I'm sure they're hoping for disintegrated bodies."

There's something hypnotic about a disaster scene, and time moves in its own frame of reference, lost in a blur of sound and color. When the first fire truck rumbled away I looked at my watch and realized I had ten minutes to get to Marsillio's.

"The rehearsal dinner!" I said to Morelli. "I forgot about the rehearsal dinner."

Morelli was blankly staring at the charred remains of his garage and the blackened carcass of his SUV. "Just when you think things can't get any worse . . ."

"The rehearsal dinner won't be that bad." This was a blatant lie, but it didn't count since we both knew it was a blatant lie. "We need a car," I said. "Where's Laski? We can use his car."

"That's a department car. You can't borrow a department car to go to a rehearsal dinner."

I looked at my watch. Nine minutes! *Shit.* I didn't want to call anyone in the wedding party. I'd rather they read about this in the paper tomorrow. I didn't think Joe would be excited about getting a lift from Ranger. There was Lula, but it would take her too long to get here. I searched the crowd of people still milling around in Morelli's yard. "Help me out here, will you?" I said to Morelli. "I'm running down roads of blind panic."

"Maybe I can get someone to drop us off," Morelli said.

And then it came to me. Big Blue. "Wait a minute! I just had a brain flash. The Buick is still sitting in front of the house."

"You mean the Buick that's been sitting there unprotected? The Buick that's very likely booby-trapped?"

"Yeah, that one."

Now Morelli was seriously looking around. "I'm *sure* I can find someone . . ."

I could hear time ticking away. I looked down at my watch. Seven minutes. "I have seven minutes," I said to him.

"This is an extreme circumstance," Morelli said. "It's not every day someone blows up my garage. I'm sure your family will understand."

"They won't understand. This is an everyday occurrence for me."

"Good point," Morelli said. "But I'm not getting in the Buick. And you're not getting in it either."

"I'll be careful," I said. And I ran through the house, locking up behind myself. I got to the Buick, and I hesitated. I wasn't crazy about my life, but I wasn't ready to die. I especially didn't like the idea that my parts could be distributed over half the county. Okay, so what was stronger . . . my fear of death or my fear of not showing up at the rehearsal dinner? This one was a no-brainer. I unlocked the Buick, jumped behind the wheel, and shoved the key into the ignition. No explosion. I drove around the block, turned into the alley, and parked as close as I could to Morelli. I left the motor running and ran to retrieve him.

"You're a nut," he said.

"I looked it all over. I swear."

"You didn't. I know you didn't. You didn't have time. You just took a deep breath, closed your eyes, and got in."

"Five minutes!" I shrieked. "I've got five friggin' minutes. Are you going with me or what?"

"You're unglued."

"And?"

Morelli blew out a sigh and hobbled over to the Buick. I put the crutches in the trunk and loaded Morelli into the car with his back to the door, his casted leg stretched flat on the backseat.

"I guess you're not that unglued," Morelli said. "You just spared a few seconds to look up my pants leg again."

He was right. I'd taken a few seconds to look up his pants leg. I couldn't help myself. I liked the view.

I got behind the wheel and put my foot to the floor. When I reached the corner the Buick was rolling full-steam-ahead and I didn't want any unnecessary slow-downs, so I simply jumped the curb and cut across Mr. Jankowski's lawn. This was the hypotenuse is shorter than the sum of two sides school of driving, and the only thing I remember from high school trigonometry.

Morelli fell off the backseat when I jumped the curb, and a lot of creative cursing followed.

"Sorry," I yelled to Morelli. "We're late."

"You keep driving like this and we're going to be *dead*."

I got there with no minutes to spare. And there were no parking places. It was Friday night, and Marsillio's was packed.

"I'm dropping you off," I said.

"No."

"Yes! I'm going to have to park a mile away, and you can't walk with that cast." I double-parked, jumped out, and hauled Morelli out of the backseat. I gave him his crutches, and I left him standing on the curb while I ran inside and got Bobby V. and Alan. "Get him up the stairs and into the back room," I told them. "I'll be there in a minute."

I roared away, circling blocks, looking in vain for a place to park. I looked for five minutes and decided parking wasn't going to happen. So I parked in front of a fire hydrant. It was very close to Marsillio's, and if there was a fire I'd run out and move the car. Problem solved.

I rolled into the back room just as the antipasto was set on the table. I took my seat beside Morelli and shook out my napkin. I smiled at my mother. I smiled at Valerie. No one smiled back. I looked down the line at Kloughn. Kloughn smiled at me and waved. Kloughn was wasted. Drunk as a skunk. Grandma didn't look far behind.

Morelli leaned over and whispered in my ear. "Your ass is grass. Your mother's going to cut you off from pineapple upside-down cake."

"This is the big day," Morelli said.

I was slumped in a kitchen chair, staring at my mug of coffee. It was almost eight o'clock, and I wasn't looking forward to what lay in front of me. I was going to have to call my mom and tell her about the cello. Then I was going to have to give her the fire details. Then I was going to dress up like an eggplant and walk down the aisle in front of Valerie.

"Your big day, too," I said. "You're Albert's best man."

"Yeah, but I don't have to be a vegetable."

"You have to make sure he gets to the church."

"That could be a problem," Morelli said. "He wasn't looking good last night. I hate to be the bearer of bad news, but I don't think he's hot on marriage."

"He's confused. And he keeps having this nightmare about Valerie smothering him with her wedding gown."

Morelli was looking beyond me, out the back window to the place where he used to have a garage.

"Sorry about your garage," I said. "And your SUV."

"Tell you the truth, it wasn't much of a loss. The garage was falling apart. And the SUV was boring. Bob and I need something more fun. Maybe I'll buy a Hummer."

I couldn't see Morelli in a Hummer. I thought Morelli was more suited to his Duc. But of course, Bob couldn't ride on the Duc. "Your Ducati wasn't in the garage," I said. "Where's the Ducati?"

"Getting new pipes and custom paint. No rush now. By the time I get the cast off it'll be too cold to ride."

The phone rang and I froze. "Don't answer it."

Morelli looked at the caller ID and handed the phone over to me. "Guess who."

"Stephanie," my mother said. "I have terrible news. It's about your sister. She's gone."

"Gone? Gone where?"

"Disney World."

I covered the phone with my hand. "My mother's been drinking," I whispered to Morelli.

"I heard that," my mother said. "I haven't been drinking. For goodness sakes, it's eight o'clock in the morning."

"You have too been drinking," Grandma yelled from the background. "I saw you take a nip from the bottle in the cupboard."

"It was either that or kill myself," my mother said. "Your sister just called from the airport. She said they were all on a plane . . . Valerie, the three girls, and cuddle umpkins. And they were going to Disney World, and she had to disconnect because they were about to take off. I could hear the announcements over the phone. I sent your father over to her house, and it's all locked up."

"So there's no wedding?"

"No. She said she didn't lose enough weight. She said she was sixty pounds short. And then she said something about cuddle umpkins having an asthma attack from her wedding gown. I couldn't figure out what that was about."

"What about the reception? Is there a reception?"

"No."

"Never?"

"Never. She said if they liked Disney World they were going to live there and never return to Jersey."

"We should get the cake," I said. "Be a shame to waste the cake."

"At a time like this, you're thinking of cake? And what's wrong with your new cell phone?" my mother asked. "I tried to call you, and it's not working."

"It got blown up in Joe's garage."

"Be sure to give me your new number when you replace your phone," my mother said. "I'm sorry you didn't get to play the cello for everyone."

"Yeah, that would have been fun."

I disconnected and looked across the table at Morelli. "Valerie's going to Disney World."

"Good for her," Morelli said. "Guess that leaves the rest of the day open. It'll give you a chance to look up my pants leg again."

Here's a basic difference between Morelli and me. My first thought was always of cake. His first thought was always of sex. Don't get me wrong. I like sex . . . a lot. But it's never going to replace cake.

Morelli topped up our coffee. "What did your mother say when you told her about your cell phone?"

"She said I should tell her my new number when I got a new phone."

"That was it?"

"Pretty much. Guess your garage wasn't big news."

"Hard to top the Mama Macaroni explosion," Morelli said.

Last night, Morelli's garage had been cordoned off with crime-scene tape, and men were now carefully moving around inside the tape, gathering evidence, photographing the scene. A couple cop cars and crime-scene vans were parked in the alley. A few neighbors were standing, hands in pockets, watching at the edge of Morelli's yard.

I saw Laski cross the yard and come to the back door. Laski let himself in and put a white bakery bag on the table. "Doughnuts," he said. "You got coffee?"

Two uniforms followed Laski into the kitchen.

"Was that a bakery bag I saw come in here?" one of them asked.

I started a new pot of coffee going and excused myself. The house was going to be filled with cops today. Morelli wasn't going to need Nurse Stephanie. I took a shower, pulled my hair back into a half-assed ponytail, and dressed in black jeans, a black T-shirt, and the Pumas. I grabbed the jean jacket and the keys to the Buick and returned to the kitchen to give the good news to Morelli.

"I'm going to work," I told him. "I wasn't able to get through everything yesterday."

Our eyes held and I guess Morelli decided I was actually going in to work and not going in to boff Ranger. "Are you taking the Buick?"

"Yes."

"Let Ryan go over the car before you touch it."

That worked just fine for me. I wasn't in the mood to get exploded.

I had three complete files in front of me. Barroni, Gorman, and Lazar. I had Runion running on the first of the search programs. I had my pad half filled with notes, but so far, nothing had added up to anything resembling *a clue*.

I knew by the sudden silence that Ranger was in the control room. When the men were alone there was constant low-level chatter. When Ranger appeared there was silence. I rolled back so I could see into the room. Ranger was standing, quietly talking to Tank. He glanced my way and our eyes met. He finished his conversation with Tank, and he crossed the room to speak to me.

His hair was still damp from his shower, and when he entered my cubicle he brought the scent of warm Ranger and Bulgari shower gel with him. He leaned against my desk and looked down at me. "Aren't you supposed to be in a wedding?"

"Valerie took off for Disney World."

"Alone?"

"With Albert and the three kids. It's almost ten o'clock. Aren't you getting a late start? Have a late night?"

"I worked out this morning. I understand you had an interesting evening. You stopped sending signals abruptly at six-oh-four. We heard the fire and police request go out on the scanner at six-ten. Tank reported to me at six-twelve that there were no injuries. Next time call me, so I don't have to send a man out."

"Sorry. My phone went with the garage."

Ranger flipped my top drawer open. I'd left my gun and stun gun and pepper spray in the drawer overnight.

"I forgot to take them," I said.

"Forget them again, and you don't have a job."

"That's harsh."

"Yeah, but you can keep the key to my apartment."

TWELVE

Ranger took my pad and read through my notes. He looked over at the thick printouts on my desk. "Files on Barroni, Gorman, and Lazar?"

"Yes. I'm running Runion now. I think he fits the profile. If you haven't got anything better to do, you might go over the files for me. Maybe you'll see something I missed."

Ranger slouched in the chair next to me and started with Barroni.

I finished Runion a little after noon. I printed him out and pushed back from my station. Ranger looked over at me. He was on the third file.

"How long are you staying?" Ranger asked.

"As long as it takes. I'm going to the kitchen for a sandwich."

"Bring something back for me. I want to keep reading."

"Something?"

"Anything."

"You don't mean that. You have all these rules about eating. No fat. No sugar. No white bread."

"Babe, I don't keep things in my kitchen that I don't eat."

"You want tuna?"

"No. I don't want tuna."

"You see!"

Ranger put the file aside and stood. He crooked an arm around my neck, kissed the top of my head, and dragged me off to the kitchen. We got chicken salad on wheat, bottles of water, and a couple apples and oranges.

"No chips," I said. "Where are the chips?"

"I have chips upstairs in my apartment," Ranger said.

"Are you trying to lure me to your apartment with chips?"

Ranger smiled.

"Okay, tell me the truth. Do you really have chips?"

"There are some things a woman should find out for herself," Ranger said.

I thought that was as far as I wanted to go under the present circumstances. Going upstairs with Ranger, chips or no chips, was a complication I didn't think I could manage right now. So I returned his smile and carted my food back to the cubicle.

I was almost done rereading Runion when it hit me. The one possible thing that would tie the four men to each other. I looked over at Ranger and saw that he was watching me. Ranger had seen it, too. He was a step ahead of me.

"I haven't read Runion yet," Ranger said. "Tell me he was in the army."

"He was in the army."

"Thirty-six years ago he was stationed at Fort Dix."

"Bingo."

"A lot of people pass through Fort Dix," Ranger said. "But it feels good."

I agreed. It felt good. "I'm tired of sitting," I told him. "I think we need a field trip."

"Babe, you're not going to make me go to the mall, are you?"

"I was thinking more along the lines of doing some B and E on Anthony's house."

"I thought you were out of the B and E business."

"Here's the thing, someone keeps blowing up my cars, and it's getting old."

Ranger's cell rang. He answered it and passed it over to me. "It's Morelli," he said.

"I see you're working very closely with the boss," Morelli said.

"Don't start."

"I heard from the crime lab. The bomb was inside the garage, next to a wall, halfway to the rear. It was manually detonated."

"Like the Mama Macaroni bomb."

"Exactly. They found another interesting piece of equipment. Did you know you were being tracked?"

"Yes."

"And last but not least, your mother called and said she was having meatballs and wedding cake for dinner."

"I'll pick you up at six."

"It's amazing what you'll do for a piece of cake," Morelli said.

I gave the phone back to Ranger. "He could have killed me, but he didn't."

"Morelli?"

"The bomber. The bomb was detonated manually, like the bomb that killed Mama Macaroni."

"So this guy is still taking risks to play with you."

"I guess I can sort of understand his motivation. If he thinks I ruined his life, his face, maybe he wants to torment me."

"The notes felt real. The sniping felt real. The first car bomb made sense to me. They were all consistent with increasing harassment and intimidation. After the Mama Macaroni bombing he loses me."

"What's your theory?"

"I don't have a theory. I just think it feels off."

"Do you think there's a copy cat?"

"Possible, but you'd think the crime lab would have noticed differences in the bomb construction." Ranger slid the files into my file cabinet. "Let's roll. If we're going to break into Anthony's house, we want to do it before the store closes and he comes home."

I grabbed my jean jacket and got halfway out of my cubby when I was yanked back by my ponytail.

"What did you forget?" Ranger asked.

"My orange?"

"Your gun."

I blew out a sigh, took the gun out of my desk drawer, and then didn't know what to do with it. If I carry a gun, I almost always carry it in my purse, but guess what, no purse. My purse was a cinder in what was left of Morelli's SUV.

Ranger took the gun, pulled me flat against him, and slid the gun under the waistband of my jeans, so that it was nestled at the small of my back.

"This is uncomfortable," I said. "It's going to give me a bruise."

Ranger reached around and removed the gun. And before I realized what he was doing, he had the gun tucked into the front of my jeans at my hipbone. "Is this better?"

"No, but I can't imagine where you'll put it next, so let's just leave it where it is and forget about it."

We rode the elevator to the garage, and Ranger confiscated one of the black Explorers normally set aside for his crew. "Less memorable than a Porsche," he said. "In case we set off an alarm."

We got into the Explorer, and I couldn't sit with the gun rammed into my pants. "I can't do this," I said to Ranger. "This dumb gun is too big. It's poking me."

Ranger closed his eyes and rested his forehead against the wheel. "I can't believe I hired you."

"Hey, it's not my fault. You picked out a bad gun."

"Okay," he said, swiveling to face me. "Where's it poking you?"

"It's poking me in my . . . you know."

"No. I don't know."

"My pubic area."

"Your pubic area?"

I could tell he was struggling with some sort of emotion. Either he was trying hard not to laugh or else he was trying hard not to choke me.

"Give me the gun," Ranger said.

I extracted the gun from my pants and handed it over.

Ranger held the gun in the palm of his hand and smiled. "It's warm," he said. He put the gun in the glove compartment and plugged the key into the ignition.

"Am I fired?"

"No. Any woman who can heat up a gun like that is worth keeping around."

In twenty minutes we were parked across the street and two houses down from Anthony. Ranger cut the engine and dialed Anthony's home number. No answer.

"Try the door," he said to me. "If someone opens it tell them you're selling Girl Scout cookies and keep them talking until I call you. I'm going in through the back. I'm parking one street over."

I swung out of the Explorer and watched Ranger drive away. I waited a couple minutes and then I crossed the street, marched up to Anthony's front door, and rang the bell. Nothing. I rang again and listened. I didn't hear any activity inside. No television. No footsteps. No dog barking. I was about to ring a third time when the door opened, and Ranger motioned me in. I followed him to the second floor, and we methodically worked our way through all three levels.

"I don't see any evidence of a second person living here," Ranger said when we reached the basement.

"This is a real bummer," I said. "No books on how to build a bomb. No sniper rifles. No dirty underwear with 'Spiro' embroidered on it."

We were in the kitchen and only the garage remained. We knew there was something in the garage because Anthony never parked his fancy new Vette there. Ranger drew his gun and opened the door that led to the garage, and we both looked in at wall-to-wall boxes. Never-been-opened cartons containing toaster ovens, ceiling fans, nails, duct tape, grout guns, electric screwdrivers.

"I think the little jerk is stealing from his brothers," I said to Ranger.

"I think you're right. There'd be larger quantities of single items if he was hijacking trucks or legally storing inventory. This looks like he randomly fills his trunk every night when he leaves."

We backed out and closed the garage door.

Ranger looked at his watch. "We have a little time. Let's see what he's got on his computer."

Anthony had a small office on the first floor. Cherry built-ins lined the walls, but Anthony hadn't yet filled them with books or objets d'art. The cherry desk was large and masculine. The cushy desk chair was black leather. The desktop held a phone, a computer and keyboard, and small printer.

Ranger sat in the chair and turned the computer on. A strip of icons appeared on the screen. Ranger hit one of the icons and Anthony's e-mail program opened. Ranger scrolled through new mail and sent mail and deleted mail. Not much there. Anthony didn't do a lot of e-mailing. Ranger opened Anthony's address book.

No Spiro listed. Ranger closed the program and tried another icon.

"Let's see what he surfs," Ranger said. He went to the bookmarked sites. They were all porn.

Ranger closed the program and returned his attention to the icon strip. He hit iPhoto and worked his way through the photo library. There were a couple pictures of Anthony's Vette. A couple pictures of the front of his town house. And three photos from the Macaroni funeral. The quality wasn't great since they were downloaded from his phone, but the subject matter was clear. He'd been taking pictures of Carol Zambelli's hooters. Zambelli had just purchased the set, and couldn't get her coat closed at the graveside.

Ranger shut the computer down. "Time to get out of here."

We left through the back door and followed a bike path through common ground to the street. Ranger remoted the SUV open, we buckled ourselves in, and Ranger hung a U-turn and headed back to the office.

"This trip doesn't take Anthony Barroni out of the picture," Ranger said, "but it definitely back-burners him."

We pulled into the RangeMan garage at five-thirty. Ranger parked and walked me to the Buick. "You have a half hour to get to Morelli. Where are you taking him?"

"We're having dinner with my parents. They have wedding cake for two hundred."

"Isn't this nice," my mother said, glass in hand, amber liquid swirling to the rim, stopping just short of sloshing onto the white tablecloth. "It's so quiet. I hardly have a headache."

Two leaves had been taken out of the dining room table, and the small dining room seemed strangely spacious. The table had been set for five. My mother and father sat at either end, and Morelli and I sat side by side and across from Grandma, who was lost behind the massive three-tier wedding cake that had been placed in the middle of the table.

"I was looking forward to a party," Grandma said. "If it was me, I would have had the reception anyway. I bet nobody would even have noticed Valerie wasn't there. You could have just told everybody she was in the ladies' room."

Morelli and my father had their plates heaped with meatballs, but I went straight for the cake. My mother was going with a liquid diet, and I wasn't sure what Grandma was eating since I couldn't see her.

"Valerie called when they got off the plane in Orlando, and she said Albert was breathing better, and the panic attacks were not nearly as severe," my mother said.

My father smiled to himself and mumbled something that sounded like "friggin' genius."

"How'd Sally take the news?" I asked my mother. "He must have been upset."

"He was upset at first, but then he asked if he could have the wedding gown. He thought he could have it altered so he could wear it onstage. He thought it would give him a new look."

"You gotta credit him," Grandma said. "Sally's always thinking. He's a smart one."

I had the cake knife in hand. "Anyone want cake?"

"Yeah," Morelli said, shoving his plate forward. "Hit me."

"I heard your garage got blown up," Grandma said to Morelli. "Emma Rhinehart said it went up like a bottle rocket. She heard that from her son, Chester. Chester delivers pizza for that new place on Keene Street, and he was making a delivery a couple houses down from you. He said he was taking a shortcut through the alley, and all of a sudden the garage went up like a bottle rocket. Right in front of him. He said it was real scary because he almost hit this guy who was standing in the alley just past your house. He said the guy looked like his face had melted or something. Like some horror movie."

Morelli and I exchanged glances, and we were both thinking *Spiro*.

An hour later, I helped Morelli hobble down the porch stairs and cross the lawn. I'd parked the Buick in the driveway, and I'd bribed one of the neighborhood kids into baby-sitting the car. I loaded Morelli into the car, gave the kid five dollars, and ran back to the house for my share of the leftovers.

My mother had bagged some meatballs for me, and now she was standing in front of the cake. She had a cardboard box on the chair and a knife in her hand. "How much do you want?" she asked.

Grandma was standing beside my mother. "Maybe you should let me cut the cake," Grandma said. "You're tipsy."

"I'm not tipsy," my mother said, very carefully forming her words.

It was true. My mother wasn't tipsy. My mother was shit-faced.

"I tell you, we're lucky if we don't find ourselves talking to Dr. Phil one of these days," Grandma said.

"I like Dr. Phil," my mother said. "He's cute. I wouldn't mind spending some time with him, if you know what I mean."

"I know what you mean," Grandma said. "And it gives me the creeps."

"So how much of the cake do you want?" my mother asked me again. "You want the whole thing?"

"You don't want the whole thing," Grandma said to me. "You'll give yourself the diabetes. You and your mother got no control."

"Excuse me?" my mother said. "No control? Did you say I had no control? I am the queen of control. Look at this family. I have a daughter in Disney World with oogly woogly smoochikins. I have a granddaughter who thinks she's a horse. I have a mother who thinks she's a teenager." My mother turned to me. "And you! I don't know where to begin."

"I'm not so bad," I said. "I'm taking charge of my life. I'm making changes."

"You're a walking disaster," my mother said. "And you just ate seven pieces of cake."

"I didn't!"

"You did. You're a cakeaholic."

"I don't mind thinking I'm a teenager," Grandma said. "Better than thinking I'm an old lady. Maybe I should get a boob job, and then I could wear them sex-kitten clothes."

"Good God," my mother said. And she drained her glass.

"I'm not a cakeaholic," I said. "I only eat cake on special occasions." Like Monday, Tuesday, Wednesday, Thursday . . .

"You're one of them comfort eaters," Grandma said. "I saw a show about it on television. When your mother gets stressed, she irons and tipples. When you get stressed, you eat cake. You're a cake abuser. You need to join one of them help groups, like Cake Eaters Anonymous."

My mother sliced into the cake and carved off a chunk for herself. "Cake Eaters Anonymous," she said. "That's a good one." She took a big bite of the cake and got a smudge of icing on her nose.

"You got icing on your nose," Grandma said.

"Do not," my mother said.

"Do, too," Grandma Mazur said. "You're three sheets to the wind."

"Take that back," my mother said, swiping her finger through the frosting on the top tier and flicking a glob at Grandma Mazur. The glob hit Grandma in the forehead and slid halfway down her nose. "Now you've got icing on your nose, too," my mother said.

Grandma sucked in some air.

My mother flicked another glob at Grandma.

"That's it," Grandma said, narrowing her eyes. "Eat dirt and die!" And Grandma scooped up a wad of cake and icing and smushed it into my mother's face.

"I can't see!" my mother shrieked. "I'm blind." She was wobbling around, flailing her arms. She lost her balance and fell against the table and into the cake.

"I tell you it's pathetic," Grandma said. "I don't know how I raised a daughter that don't even know how to have a food fight. And look at this, she fell into a three-tiered wedding cake. This is gonna put a real crimp in the leftovers." She reached out to help my mother, and my mother latched on to Grandma and wrestled her onto the table.

"You're going down, old woman," my mother said to Grandma.

Grandma yelped and struggled to scramble away, but she couldn't get a grip. She was as slick as a greased pig, in lard icing up to her elbows.

"Maybe you should stop before someone falls and gets hurt," I told them.

"Maybe you should mind your own beeswax," Grandma said, mashing cake into my mother's hair.

"Hey, wait a minute," my mother said. "Stephanie didn't get her cake."

They both paused and looked over at me.

"How much cake did you want?" my mother asked. "This much?" And she threw a wad of cake at me.

I jumped to dodge the cake, but I wasn't quick enough, and it caught me in the middle of the chest. Grandma nailed me in the side of my head, and before I could move she got me a second time.

My father came in from the living room. "What the devil?" he said.

Splat, splat, splat. They got my father.

"Jesus Marie," he said. "What are you, friggin' nuts? That's good wedding cake. You know how much I paid for that cake?"

My mother threw one last piece of cake. It missed my father and hit the wall.

I had cake and icing in my hair, on my hands and arms, on my shirt, my face, my jeans. I looked over at the cake plate. It was empty. The aroma of sugar and butter and vanilla was enticing. I swiped at the cake sliding down the wall and stuck my finger in my mouth. If I'd been alone I probably would have licked the wall. My mother was right. I was a cakeaholic.

"Boy," my grandmother said to my mother. "You're fun when you've got a snootful."

My mother looked around the room. "Do you think that's how this happened?"

"Do you think you'd do this if you were sober?" Grandma asked. "I don't think so. You got a real stick up your ass when you're sober."

"That's it," my mother said. "I'm done tippling."

I caught myself licking cake off my arm. "And maybe I should cut back on the cake," I said. "I *do* feel a little addicted."

"We'll have a pact," my mother said. "No more tippling for me and no more cake for you."

We looked at Grandma.

"I'm not giving up nothing," Grandma said.

I took my bag of meatballs and went out to the car. I slid behind the wheel, turned the key in the ignition, and Morelli leaned over the seat at me.

"What the hell happened to you?" he asked.

"Food fight."

"Wedding cake?"

"Yep."

Morelli licked icing off my neck, and I accidentally jumped the driveway and backed out over my parents' front lawn.

"Okay, let me get this correct," Morelli said. "You're giving up sweets."

We were sitting at Morelli's kitchen table, having a late breakfast.

"If it's got sugar on it, I'm not eating it," I told Morelli.

"What about that cereal you've got in front of you?"

"Frosted Flakes. My favorite."

"Coated with sugar."

Shit. "Maybe I got carried away last night. Maybe I was overreacting to Valerie gaining all that weight, and then Kloughn dreaming about her smothering him. And my mother said I ate seven pieces of wedding cake, but I don't actually remember eating anything. I think she must have been exaggerating."

Morelli's phone rang. He answered and passed it to me. "Your grandmother."

"Boy, that was some mess we made last night," Grandma said. "We're gonna have to put up new paper in the dining room. It was worth it, though. Your mother got up this morning and cleaned the bottles out of the cupboard. 'Course, I still got one in my closet, but that's okay on account of I can handle my liquor. I'm not one of them anxiety-ridden drunks. I just drink because I like it. Anyway, your mother's not drinking so long as you're off the sugar. You're off the sugar, right?"

"Right. Absolutely. No sugar for me."

I gave the phone back to Morelli, and I went to look in the cupboard. "Do we have cereal that's not coated with sugar?"

"We have bagels and English muffins."

I popped a bagel into the toaster and drank coffee while I waited. "Ranger thinks some of the bombings feel off."

"I agree," Morelli said. "Laski's double-checking the crime-lab reports to make sure we don't have an opportunist at work. And I left a message for him to talk to Chester Rhinehart. So far Chester's the only other person besides you to see Spiro."

"So, what's up for today? How's your leg?"

"The leg is a lot better. No pain. My foot isn't swollen."

There was a lot of loud knocking on the front door. I grabbed my bagel and went to investigate.

It was Lula, dressed in a poison green tank and spandex jeans with rhinestones running down the side seam. "I heard about the wedding," Lula said. "I bet your mama had a cow. Imagine having to call all those people and tell them they're on their own for burgers tonight. But there's some good news in all this, right? You didn't have to go parading around like a freakin' eggplant."

"It all worked out for the best," I said.

"Damn skippy. Glad you feel that way. Wouldn't want you to be in a bad mood since I need a little help."

"Oh boy."

"It's just a little help. Moral support. But you can jump in on the physical stuff if you want. Not that I expect anyone's gonna shoot at us or anything."

"No. Whatever it is . . . I'm not doing it."

"You don't mean that. I can see you don't mean that. Where's Officer Hottie? He in the kitchen?" Lula swept past me and went in search of Morelli. "Hey," she said to him. "How's it shakin'? You don't mind if I borrow Stephanie today, do you?"

"He does," I said. "We were going to do something . . ."

"Actually, it's Guy Day," Morelli said to me. "I promised the guys we could hang out today."

"You hung out with the guys yesterday. And the day before."

"Those were cop guys. These are just guy guys. My brother Tony and my cousin Mooch. They're coming over to watch the game."

"Lucky for you I came along," Lula said to me. "You would have had to hide upstairs in your room so you didn't ruin Guy Day."

"You can stay and watch the game with us," Morelli said to me. "It's not like it's a stag party. It's just Tony and Mooch."

"Yeah," Lula said. "They probably be happy to have someone do the pizza run and open their beer bottles for them."

"Think I'll pass on Guy Day," I said to Morelli. "But thanks for inviting me." I grabbed my jacket and followed Lula out to the Firebird. "Who are we looking for?"

"I'm gonna take another shot at Willie Martin. I'm gonna keep my clothes on this time. I'm gonna nail his ass."

"He didn't leave town?"

"He's such an arrogant so-and-so. He thinks he's safe. He thinks no one can touch him. He's still in his cheap-ass apartment over the garage. My friend Lauralene made a business call on him last night. Do you believe it?"

In a former life, Lula was a 'ho, and she still has a lot of friends in the industry. "Is Lauralene still there?"

"No. Willie's too cheap to pay for a night. Willie's strictly pay by the job."

We crossed town, turned onto Stark, and Lula parked in front of the garage. We both looked up at Willie's apartment windows on the third floor.

"You got a gun?" Lula asked.

"No."

"Stun gun?"

"No."

"Cuffs?"

"Negative."

"I swear, I don't know why I brought you."

"To make sure you keep your clothes on," I said.

"Yeah, that would be it."

We got out of the Firebird and took the stairs. The air was foul, reeking of urine and stale fast-food burgers and fries. We got to the third-floor landing, and Lula started arranging her equipment. Gun shoved into the waistband of her jeans. Cuffs half out of her pocket. Stun gun rammed into her jeans at the small of her back. Pepper spray in hand.

"Where's the Taser?" I asked.

"It's in my purse." She rooted around in her big shoulder bag and found the Taser. "I haven't had a chance to test-drive this baby yet, but I think I could figure it out. How hard can it be, right?" She powered up and held on to the Taser. She motioned me to the door. "Go ahead and knock."

"Me?"

"He won't open the door if it's me. I'm gonna hide to the side, here. He see a skinny white girl like you standing at his door, he's gonna get all excited and open up."

"He'd better not get *too* excited."

"Hell, the more excited the better. Slow him down running. Make him do some pole vaulting."

I rapped on the door, and I stood where Martin could see me. The door opened, and he looked me over.

"I don't know what you're selling, but I might be willing to buy it," Willie said.

"Boy, that's real original," I said, walking into his apartment. "I bet you had a hard time coming up with that one."

"Wadda ya mean?"

I turned to face him. Was he really that dumb? I looked into his eyes and decided the answer was yes. And the frightening part is that he outsmarted Lula last time she tried to snag him. Best not to dwell on that realization. The door was still open, and I could see Lula creeping forward behind Willie Martin. She had pepper spray in one hand and the Taser in the other.

"I was actually looking for Andy Bartok," I said to Martin. "This is his apartment, right?"

"This is my apartment. There's no Andy here. Do you know who I am? You follow football?"

"No," I said, putting the couch between me and Martin. "I don't like violent sports."

"I like violent sports," Lula said. "I like the sport called kick Willie Martin in his big ugly blubber butt."

Martin turned to Lula. "You! Guess you didn't get enough of Will Martin, hunh? Guess you came back for more. And look at this here present you brought me . . . a candy-ass white woman."

"The only thing I brought you is a ticket to the lockup," Lula said. "I'm hauling your nasty blubber butt off to jail."

"I haven't got no blubber butt," Martin said. He turned again so he could moon Lula, and he dropped his drawers to prove his point.

I was standing in front of him so I got the pole-vaulting demonstration. Lula got the rear view, and whether it was intentional or just a jerk-action reflex was hard to say, but Lula shot Martin in the ass with the Taser.

Martin went down with his pants at half-mast and flopped around on the floor, twitching on the Taser line like a fresh-caught fish.

"Get your finger off the button," I yelled to Lula. "You're going to kill him!"

"Oops," Lula said. "Guess I should have read the instruction book."

Martin was facedown, doing shallow breathing. He was about six foot five and close to three hundred pounds. I had no idea how we were going to get him to the Firebird.

"I'll cuff him, and you pull his pants up," Lula said.

"Good try, but this is your party. I'm not doing pants wrangling."

"The bounty hunter assistant is supposed to take orders," Lula said.

I cut my eyes to her.

"Of course, that don't count for you," she said. "On account of you're not an official assistant. You're the . . ."

"The friend of the bounty hunter," I said.

"Yeah, that's it. The friend of the bounty hunter. How about you cuff him, and I'll get his pants up."

I took the cuffs from Lula. "Works for me."

I cuffed Martin's hands behind his back and stepped away, and Lula straddled him and yanked the Taser leads off. By the time she got his pants up, she was sweating.

"Usually I'm taking pants *off* a man," Lula said. "It's a lot more work getting them up than down."

Especially when you're wrestling them up the equivalent of a 280-pound sandbag.

Willie had one eye open, and he was making some low-level gurgling sounds.

"He's gonna be pissed off when he comes around," Lula said. "I'm thinking we want to get him into the car before that happens."

"I'd feel a lot better about this if you had ankle shackles," I said.

"I forgot ankle shackles."

I grabbed a foot and Lula grabbed a foot, and we threw our weight into dragging Martin to the door. We got him through the door and onto the cement landing and realized we were going to have to use the rickety freight elevator.

"It's probably okay," Lula said, pushing the button.

I closed and locked Martin's door. I repeated Lula's words. It's probably okay. It's probably okay.

The elevator made a lot of grinding, clanking noises, and we could see it shudder as it rose from the bottom floor.

"It's just three floors," Lula said, more to herself than to me. "Three floors isn't a whole lot, right? Probably you could jump from three floors if you had to. Remember when you fell off that fire escape? That was three floors, right?"

"Two floors by the time I actually started free falling." And it knocked me out and hurt like hell.

The open-air car came to a lurching stop three inches below floor level. Lula struggled with the grate and finally got it half open.

"You got the least weight," Lula said. "You go in first and see if it holds you."

I gingerly got into the cage. It swayed slightly but held. "Feels okay," I said.

Lula crept in. "See, this is gonna be fine," Lula said,

standing very still. "This is one sturdy-ass elevator. You give this elevator a coat of paint and it'll be like new."

The elevator groaned and dropped two inches.

"Just settling in," Lula said. "I'm sure it's fine. I could see this is a real safe elevator. Still, maybe we should get off and reconsider our options."

Lula took a step forward and the elevator went into a downslide, banging against the side of the building, groaning and screeching. It reached the second floor and the bottom dropped out from under us. Lula and I hit the ground level and lay there stunned, knocked breathless, with rust sifting down on us like fairy dust.

"Fuck," Lula said. "Take a look at me and tell me if anything's broken."

I got to my hands and knees and crawled out of the elevator. It was Sunday and the garage was closed, thank God. At least we didn't have an audience. And probably the guys who worked in the garage wouldn't be real helpful when it came to capturing Martin. Lula crawled out after me, and we slowly got to our feet.

"I feel like a truck rolled over me," Lula said. "That was a dumb idea to take the elevator. You're supposed to stop me from acting on those dumb ideas."

I tried to dust some of the rust and elevator grit off my jeans, but it was sticking like it was glued on. "I don't know how to break this to you," I said. "But your FTA is still on the third floor."

THIRTEEN

"We're just gonna have to carry Willie down the stairs," Lula said. "I got him cuffed. I'm not giving up now."

"We can't carry him. He's too heavy."

"Then we'll drag him. Okay, so he might get a little bruised, but we'll say we were walking him down and he slipped. That happens, right? People fall down the stairs all the time. Look at us, we just fell down an elevator, and are we complaining?"

We were standing next to a stack of tires that were loaded onto a hand truck. "Maybe we could use this hand truck," I said. "We could strap Martin on like a refrigerator. It'll be hard to get him down the two flights of stairs, but at least we won't crack his head open."

"That's a good idea," Lula said. "I was just going to think of that idea."

We off-loaded the tires and carted the truck up the stairs. Martin was still out. He was drooling and his expression was dazed, but his breathing had normalized, and he now had both eyes open. We laid the hand truck flat and rolled Martin onto it. I'd brought about thirty feet of strapping up with the hand truck, and we wrapped Martin onto the truck until he looked like a mummy. Then we pushed and pulled until we had Martin and the truck upright.

"Now we're going to ease him down, one step at a time," I said to Lula. "We're both going to get a grip on the truck, and between the two of us we should be able to do this."

By the time we got Martin to the second-floor landing we were soaked through. The air in the stairwell was hot and stagnant, and lowering Martin down the stairs one at a time was hard work. My hands were raw from gripping the strapping and my back ached. We stopped to catch our breath, and I saw Martin's fingers twitch. Not a good sign. I didn't want him struggling to get free on the next set of stairs.

"We have to get moving," I said to Lula. "He's coming around."

"I'm coming around, too," Lula said. "I'm having a heart attack. I think I gave myself a hernia. And look . . . I broke a nail. It was my best nail, too. It was the one with the stars and stripes decal."

We shifted the hand truck into position to take the first step, and Martin turned his head and looked me in the eye.

"What the . . ." he said. And then he went nuts, yelling and struggling against the strapping. He was crazy-eyed and a vein was popped out in his forehead. I was having a hard time hanging on to the hand truck, and I was watching the strapping around his chest go loose and show signs of unraveling.

"The stun gun," I yelled to Lula. "Give him a jolt with the stun gun. I can't hang on with him struggling like this."

Lula reached around back for the stun gun and came up empty. "Must have fallen out when the elevator crashed," she said.

"Do something! The strap is unraveling. Shoot him. Zap him. Kick him in the nuts. *Do something! Anything!*"

"I got my spray!" Lula said. "Stand back, and I'll spray the snot out of him."

"No!" I shrieked. "Don't spray in the stairwell!"

"It's okay, I got plenty," Lula said.

She hit the button, and I got a faceful of pepper spray. Martin gave an enraged bellow and wrenched the hand truck away from Lula and me. I was blinded and gagging, and I could hear the hand truck banging down the stairs like a toboggan. There was some scuffling at ground level, the door opened, and then it was quiet at the bottom of the stairs. At the top of the stairs, Lula and I were gasping for breath, feeling our way down, trying to get away from the droplets that were still hanging in the torpid air on the second-floor landing.

We stumbled over the hand truck when we got to the bottom. We pushed through the door and stood bent at the waist, waiting for the mucus production to slow, eyes closed and tearing, nose running.

"Guess pepper spray wasn't a good idea," Lula finally said.

I blew my nose in my T-shirt and tried to blink my eyes clear. I didn't want to touch them with my hand in case I still had some spray left on my skin. Martin was nowhere to be seen. The wrapping was in a heap on the sidewalk.

"You don't look too good," Lula said. "You're all red and blotchy. I'm probably red and blotchy, too, but I got superior skin tone. You got that pasty white stuff that only looks good after you get a facial and put on makeup."

We were squinting, not able to fully open our eyes, my throat burned like fire, and I was a mucus factory.

"I need to wash my hands and my face," I said. "I have to get this stuff off me."

We got into Lula's Firebird, and Lula crept down Stark to Olden. She turned on Olden and somehow the

Firebird found its way to a McDonald's. We parked and dragged ourselves into the ladies' room.

I stuck my entire head under the faucet. I washed my face and hair and hands as best I could, and I dried my hair under the hot-air hand dryer.

"You're a little scary," Lula said. "You got a white-woman-Afro thing going."

I didn't care. I shuffled out of the ladies' room and got a cheeseburger, fries, and a bottle of water.

Lula sat across from me. She had a mountain of food and a gallon of soda. "What's with you?" she wanted to know. "Where's your soda? Where's your pie? You gotta have a pie when you come here."

"No soda and no pie. I'm off sweets."

"What about cake? What about doughnuts?"

"No cake. No doughnuts."

"You can't do that. You need cake and doughnuts. That's your comfort food. That's your stress buster. You don't eat cake and doughnuts, and you'll get all clogged up."

"I made a deal with my mother. She's off the booze as long as I'm off the sugar."

"That's a bad deal. You're not good at that deprivation stuff. You're like a big jelly doughnut. You give it a squeeze and the jelly squishes out. You don't let it squish out where it wants and it's gotta find a new place to squish out. Remember when your love life was in the toilet and you weren't getting any? You were eating bags of candy bars. You're a compensator. Some people can hold their jelly in, but not you. Your jelly gotta squish out somewhere."

"You've got to stop talking about doughnuts. You're making me hungry."

"See, that's what I'm telling you. You're one of them hungry people. You deprive yourself of cake and you're gonna want to eat something else."

I shoved some fries into my mouth and crooked an eyebrow at Lula.

"You know what I'm saying," Lula said. "You better be careful, or you'll send Officer Hottie to the emergency room. And you're working for Ranger now. How're you gonna keep from taking a bite outta that? He's just one big hot sexy doughnut far as I'm concerned."

"What are you going to do about Willie Martin?"

"I don't know. I'm gonna have to think about it. Taking him down in his apartment doesn't seem to be working."

"Does he have a job?"

"Yeah, he works nights, stealing cars and hijacking trucks."

I drained my bottle of water and bundled my trash. "I need to go back to Morelli's house and get out of these clothes. Call me when you get a new plan for Martin."

"You mean you'd go out with me again?"

"Yeah." Go figure that. Truth is, it was getting pretty obvious that being a bounty hunter wasn't the problem. In fact, maybe being a bounty hunter was the solution. At least I'd acquired a few survival skills. When trouble followed me home I was able to cope. I was never going to be Ranger, but I wasn't Ms. Wimp either.

There were a bunch of cars parked in front of Morelli's house when Lula dropped me off.

"You sure you want to go in there?" Lula asked. "Looks like it's still Guy Day."

"I don't care what day it is. I'm beat. I want to take a shower, get into clean clothes, and turn into a couch potato."

I straggled into the house and found five guys slouched in front of the television. I knew them all. Mooch, Tony, Joe, Stanley Skulnik, and Ray Daily. There were pizza boxes, boxes of doughnuts, discarded candy bar wrappers, beer bottles, and chip bags on the coffee table. Bob was sound asleep on the floor by Morelli. He had orange Cheez Doodle dust on his nose, and a red jelly bean stuck in the fur on his ear. Everyone but Bob was eyes glued to the television. They all turned and stared at me when I walked into the room.

"How's it going?" Mooch said.

"Looking good," Stanley said.

"Yo," from Tony.

"Long time no see," Ray said.

And they turned back to the game.

I had hair from hell, I'd blown my nose in my shirt, I was covered with rust and crud, my jeans were torn, and I was holding a roll of toilet paper from McDonald's, and no one noticed. Not that I was surprised by this. After all, these guys were from the Burg, and a game was on television.

Morelli continued to stare after the others had turned away.

"Fell down an elevator shaft and got sprayed with pepper spray," I said to him. "Picked up the toilet paper at McDonald's."

"And you're okay?"

I nodded.

"Could you get me a cold one?"

I got into the shower and stood there until there was no more hot water. I got dressed in Morelli's sweats, blasted my hair with the dryer, and crawled into bed. It was close to seven when I woke up. The house was quiet. I shuffled into the bathroom, glanced in the mirror, and realized there was a note pinned to my sweatshirt.

WENT OUT TO EAT WITH MOOCH AND TONY. DIDN'T WANT TO WAKE YOU. CALL MY CELL IF YOU WANT ME

TO BRING SOMETHING HOME. THERE'S LEFTOVER PIZZA IN THE FRIDGE.

Apparently Guy Day continued into Guy Night. I shuffled downstairs and ate the leftover pizza. I washed it down with a Bud. I checked out the doughnut box. Three doughnuts left in the box. I blew out a sigh. I wanted a doughnut. I paced in the kitchen. I finished off a bag of chips. I drank another Bud. I couldn't stop thinking about the doughnuts. It's only been one friggin' day, I thought. Surely I can make it through one lousy day without a doughnut. I went to the living room and remoted the television. I flipped through the channels. I couldn't concentrate. I was haunted by the doughnuts. I stormed into the kitchen space, got the doughnuts, and threw them in the garbage. I paced around, and I got the doughnuts out of the garbage. I rammed them down the garbage disposal and ran the disposal. I stared into the sink at the empty drain. No doughnuts. I couldn't believe I had to disposal the doughnuts. I was pathetic.

I went back to the living room and tried television again. Nothing held my attention. I was restless. Big Blue was at the curb, but I had nowhere to go. It was Sunday night. The mall was closed. I wasn't up to a visit with my parents. Probably I shouldn't be driving Big Blue anyway. It was sitting out there unprotected.

A couple minutes after nine, Morelli swung in on his crutches. "You're looking better," he said. "You were out like a light when I left. I guess falling down an elevator shaft is exhausting. Did you get your man?"

"No. He ran away."

Morelli grinned. "You're not supposed to let them do that."

"Did I miss anything important?"

"Yeah. I just got a call from Laski. Four bodies were found in a shallow grave in a patch of woods off upper Stark this afternoon. Some kids stumbled across it. They said they were looking for their dog, but they were probably looking for a place to smoke weed." Morelli eased himself onto the couch. "Laski said the bodies were pretty decomposed, but there were rings and belt buckles. None of the bodies has been officially identified yet, but Laski's certain one of them is Barroni. He was wearing an initialed belt buckle when he disappeared, and the wedding ring matches the description his wife, Carla, gave when she filed missing persons."

I sat next to Morelli. "That's so sad. I always hoped they'd suddenly reappear. Did Laski know how they were killed?"

"Shot. Multiple times. All in the chest, as if they'd been standing together and someone sprayed them with bullets like in an old Al Capone movie."

"What about the cars?"

"Laski said there was a dirt road going in. Most likely used by kids looking for privacy for one reason or another. So cars could have driven in there. But no cars were found with the bodies."

"I have profiles on the four missing men. I've been trying to tie them together. And I had a feeling Anthony Barroni and Spiro Stiva were involved somehow. Now I'm not so sure. Maybe Spiro came back for the sole purpose of terrorizing me and eventually killing me. Maybe he's a lone gun out there and not hanging with anyone. That would partially explain why no one's seen him."

"There's a description out on him now. There's a corroborating witness that Spiro, or at least someone with a badly scarred face, was seen in the area when my garage went up. I don't know what to say about the men who were just found. It's pretty clear that someone called a meeting and executed them."

"They had to have known the gunman," I said. "I

can't see any of these men getting in his car and driving off to a meeting on upper Stark at the request of a stranger."

"I agree, but we don't know the relationship. It could have been something impersonal, like blackmail. And the blackmailer decided to terminate."

"Do you think that's it?"

"No," Morelli said. "I think they all knew each other, and there was a fifth member of the group who had his own agenda."

"They were all in the same unit at Fort Dix."

Morelli turned and looked at me. "You found that out?"

"Yeah."

"So, not only are you hot but you're smart, too?"

"You think I'm hot?"

Morelli had his hand up my shirt, tinkering with my bra. "Cupcake, I'm not sharing my house with you because you can cook."

I cut my eyes to him. "Are you telling me I'm here just for the sex?"

Morelli was concentrating on getting me undressed and not paying attention to the tone of my voice. "Yeah, the sex has been great."

"What about the companionship, the friendship, the relationship part of this?"

Morelli paused in his effort to release the clasp on my bra. "Uh oh, did I just say something stupid?"

"Yes. You said I was just here for the sex."

"I didn't mean that."

"Yes, you did! It's all you think about with me."

"Cut me some slack," Morelli said. "I have a broken leg. I sit here all day, eating jelly beans and thinking about you naked. It's what guys do when they have a broken leg."

"You did that *before* you broke your leg."

"Oh man," Morelli said. "This isn't going to turn into one of those issue discussions, is it? I hate those discussions."

"Suppose for some reason we couldn't have sex. Would you still love me?"

"Yeah, but not as much."

"What kind of an answer is that? That's not the right answer."

Okay, so I knew his answer wasn't serious, and I didn't really think my relationship with Morelli was entirely sexual, but I couldn't seem to stop myself from getting crazy. I was on my feet, flapping my arms and yelling. This was usually Morelli's role, and here I was, working myself into a frenzy, going down a one-way street to nowhere. And I suspected it was Lula's jelly doughnut. The doughnut was bursting with jelly, and the jelly was squishing out in all the wrong places. And if that wasn't frightening enough, I was turning myself on. All the while I was yelling about Morelli wanting nothing but sex, the truth is, I could think of nothing else.

"Can we finish this upstairs?" Morelli asked. "My leg wants to go to bed."

"Sure," I said. "There are parts of me that want to go to bed, too."

I was showered and dressed and ready to go to work. I'd had two mugs of coffee and an English muffin. It was 8:00 A.M., and Morelli was still in bed.

"Hey," I said. "What's up with you? You're always the early riser."

"Mmmmph," Morelli said, pillow over his face. "Tired."

"How could you be tired? It's eight o'clock. It's time to get up! I'm leaving. Don't you want to kiss me goodbye?"

Nothing. No answer. I whipped the sheet off him and left him lying there in all his glorious nakedness. Morelli still didn't move.

I sat on the bed next to him. "Joe?"

"I thought you were going to work."

"You're looking very sexy . . . except for Mr. Happy, who seems to be sleepy."

"He's not sleepy, Steph. He's in a coma. You woke him up every two hours and now he's dead."

"He's dead?"

"Okay, not dead, but he's not going to be up and dancing anytime soon. You might as well go to work. Did you walk Bob?"

"I walked Bob. I fed Bob. I cleaned the living room and the kitchen."

"Love you," Morelli said from under the pillow.

"I l-l-l-like you, too." *Shit.*

I went downstairs and stood at the front door, looking out at Big Blue. Probably perfectly safe, but I didn't feel comfortable taking the chance. Bob came to stand next to me. "I have no way to get to work," I said to Bob. "I could call Ranger, but lately it feels like I'm on a date when I'm in a car with Ranger, and it would be tacky to have a date pick me up here. Lula probably isn't up yet." I went to the kitchen and dialed my parents' number.

"I need a ride to work," I told my mom. "Can you or Dad take me?"

"Your father can pick you up," my mom said. "He's driving the cab today, anyway. Are you still off dessert?"

"Yes. How about you?"

"It's amazing. I don't even have the slightest need to tipple now that the wedding is behind us and Valerie's in Disney World."

Great. My mother doesn't need to tipple, and I'm so

strung out with doughnut cravings I put Mr. Happy into a coma.

My dad showed up ten minutes later. "What's wrong with the Buick?" he said.

"Broken."

"I figured you were worried it was booby-trapped."

"Yep. That, too."

Ranger was waiting for me when I arrived. He was in my cubby, slouched in the extra chair, reading through the files on Gorman, Lazar, Barroni, and Runion. There was a new cell phone on my desk, plus a new key fob, and my Sig. The Sig was in a holster that clipped to a belt.

"They found them," I said.

"I heard. How'd you get in to work?"

"My dad."

"I have a bike set aside for you downstairs. If you park it exposed, be sure to look it over before getting on. It's hard to hide a bomb on a bike, but you still need to be careful. The key is on your keychain.

"As far as RangeMan is concerned, Gorman is found, and the file is closed," Ranger said. "If you still think there's a connection between the murdered men and your stalker, and you want to use this office to continue searching, you have permission to do that."

I looked at my in-box and stifled a groan. It was packed with search requests.

Ranger followed my eyes. "You're going to have to divide your time and get through some of those files. They're not just from Rodriguez. You do the searches for everyone here, including me."

He stood and brushed against me, and I had a wave of desire rush into my chest and shoot south.

"What?" Ranger said.

"I didn't say anything."

"You moaned."

"I was thinking of Butterscotch Krimpets."

Our eyes locked for a long moment. "I'll be in my office the rest of the morning," Ranger said. "Let me know if you need anything."

Oh boy.

I sorted through the requests that had come in over the weekend. Three were from Ranger. I'd do them first. He was the boss. And he was hot. One was from some-one named Alvirez. The rest were from Rodriguez.

Ranger's files were all standard searches. Nothing unusual. I had them done by noon. My plan was to get a quick lunch, run the Alvirez and two for Rodriguez, and then see what I could turn up at Fort Dix. I prowled through the kitchen, not finding anything inspiring to eat. I settled on the turkey again and took it back to my cubicle with a bottle of water. I finished lunch, finished Alvirez and Rodriguez, and started surfing Fort Dix.

I called my mother, Morelli, Lula, and Valerie and told them I had a new cell phone. Valerie was in the Magic Kingdom and said she'd be home at the end of the week. They liked Florida, but the girls missed their friends, and Albert had broken out in hives when he was approached by a six-foot-tall, four-foot-wide Pooh Bear. Lula wasn't answering. I left a message. Morelli wasn't answering. I left a message. My mother invited me for dinner, and I declined.

It was midafternoon when Ranger returned to my cubby. I was pacing, unable to focus on anything be-yond my need for a cupcake.

"Babe," Ranger said. "You're looking a little strung out. Is there anything I should know?"

"I'm in sugar withdrawal. I've given up dessert, and it's all I can think about." That had been true five min-utes ago. Now that Ranger was standing in front of me I was thinking a cupcake wasn't what I actually wanted.

"Maybe I can help get your mind off doughnuts," Ranger said.

My mouth dropped open, and I think some drool might have dribbled out.

"Did Silvio show you how to search the newspapers?" Ranger asked.

"No."

"Sit down and I'll show you how to get into the programs. It's tedious work, but it accesses a lot of information. You want to go to the local paper and look for something bad that happened when the four men were at Dix. An unsolved murder, a high-stakes robbery, unsolved serial crimes like multiple burglaries."

"Morelli thinks there were five men involved. Originally, I thought Anthony Barroni was the fifth guy, but now I'm not sure. Is there a way to get a list of men who were in that unit at Dix?"

"I don't have access to those records. I could get someone to hack in but I'd rather not. It would be safer to have Morelli do it."

I was hearing the words, but they weren't sticking. My brain was clogged with naked and sweaty Ranger thoughts.

"Babe," Ranger said, smiling. "You just looked me up and down like I was lunch."

"I need a doughnut," I told him. "I *really* need a doughnut."

"That would have been my second guess."

"I'll feel better tomorrow. The sugar will be out of my system. The cravings will be gone." I sat down and faced the keyboard. "How do I do this?"

Ranger pulled a chair next to me. His leg pressed against mine and when he leaned forward to get to my keyboard we were shoulder to shoulder, his arm brushing the side of my breast when he typed. He was warm and he smelled delicious. I felt my eyes glaze over, and I worried I might start panting.

"You should take notes," Ranger said. "You're going to need to remember some passwords."

Get a grip, I said to myself. It wouldn't be good to jump on him here. You'd be on television. And you haven't got a door on your cubby. And then there was Morelli. I was living with Morelli. It wouldn't be right to live with Morelli and boink Ranger. And what was wrong with me, anyway, that I needed two men? Especially when the second man was Ranger. Ever since we'd had the discussion about marriage my imagination had been running wild dredging up possibilities for his deep dark secret. I knew it had nothing to do with killing people because that was no secret. I knew he wasn't gay. I'd seen that one firsthand. The memory brought a new rush of heat, and I resisted squirming in my seat. Was he scarred by a terrible childhood? Had his heart been so badly broken he was unable to recover?

"Earth to Babe," Ranger said.

I looked at him and unconsciously licked my lips.

"I'm going to have to disconnect your cubby's security camera," Ranger said. "I just heard everyone in the control room gasp when you licked your lips. I could have a hatchet murder taking place in full monitor view on one of my accounts, and I don't think anyone would notice as long as you're sitting in here." Ranger signed off the search he'd just pulled up. He took my pad and wrote out instructions for retrieving information from newspapers. He returned the pad to my desk and stood. "Let's go on a field trip," he said. "I want to see the area where the bodies were recovered."

I thought that sounded sufficiently grim to be a good doughnut diversion. I stood and clipped my new cell phone onto the waistband of my jeans. I pocketed the key fob. And I stared at the gun. The gun was in a holster that attached to a belt, and I wasn't wearing a belt.

"No belt," I said to Ranger.

"Ella has some clothes for you upstairs in my apartment. Try them on. I'm sure she's included a belt. I'll meet you in the garage. I need to talk to Tank."

I took the elevator to the top floor and stepped out into the small marble-floored foyer. I'd lived here for a brief time not long ago, so I was familiar with the apartment. I opened the locked door with the key he'd given me and stepped inside. His apartment always felt cool and serene. His furniture was comfortable, with clean lines and earth tones, and felt masculine without being overbearing. There were fresh flowers on the sideboard by the door. I doubted Ranger ever noticed the flowers, but Ella liked them. They were part of Ella's campaign to civilize Ranger and make his life nicer.

I dropped my keys in the silver dish beside the flowers. I walked through the apartment and found my clothes stacked on a black leather upholstered bench in Ranger's dressing room. Two black shirts, two black cargo pants, a black belt, a black windbreaker, a black sweatshirt, a black ball cap. I was going to look like a mini-Ranger. I stepped into the cargo pants. Perfect fit. Ella had remembered my size from the last time I'd stayed here. I belted the cargo pants, and I tugged the shirt over my head. It was a short-sleeved shirt, female cut with some spandex. It had a V-neck that was relatively high. RANGEMAN was embroidered on the left breast with black thread. The shirt was a good fit with the exception of being too short to tuck into the cargo pants. The shirt barely touched the top of the cargo pants waistband.

I called Ranger on his cell. "This shirt is short. I'm not sure you're going to like it on the control room floor."

"Put a jacket over it and come down to the garage."

I shrugged into the windbreaker. Black on black again, with RANGEMAN embroidered on the left breast of the jacket. I took my phone off my jeans and clipped it onto the cargo pants. I grabbed the black-on-black ball cap, and I left Ranger's apartment and rode the elevator to the garage.

Ranger was waiting by his truck. He was wearing a windbreaker exactly like mine, and the almost smile expression was fixed on his face.

"I feel like a miniature Ranger," I said to him.

Ranger unzipped the windbreaker and looked me over. "Nice, but you're no miniature Ranger." He took my Sig out of his jacket pocket and snapped it onto my belt just in front of my hip, his knuckles grazing bare skin. "There are some advantages to this short shirt," he said, sliding his hands under, fingertips stopping short of my bra.

"Okay, here's the deal," I said to him. "You know how when you squeeze a jelly doughnut and the jelly squirts out in the weakest spot of the doughnut? Well, if I'm a jelly doughnut then my weak spot is dessert. Every time I get stressed I head for the bakery. I'm trying to stop the dessert thing now, and so the jelly is squirting out someplace else."

"And?"

"And this place that it's squirting out . . . maybe squirting out isn't a good way to put this. Forget squirting out."

"You're trying to tell me something," Ranger said.

"Yes! And it would be a lot easier if you didn't have your hands under my shirt. It's hard for me to think when you've got your hands on me like this."

"Babe, has it occurred to you that you might be giving information to the enemy?"

"The thing is, I have all these excess hormones.

They used to be jelly-doughnut hormones, but somehow they got switched over to sex-drive hormones. Not that sex-drive hormones are bad, it's just that my life is so complicated right now. So I'm trying to control all these stupid hormones, to keep them locked up in the doughnut. And you're going to have to help."

"Why?"

"Because you're a good guy."

"I'm not that good," Ranger said.

"So I'm in trouble?"

"Big time."

"You told Ella to get me this short shirt, didn't you?"

Ranger's fingers were slowly creeping up my breast. "No. I told her to get you something that didn't look like it was made for Tank. She probably didn't realize it was cut off at the waist."

"The hand," I said. "You have to remove the hand. You're poaching."

Ranger smiled and kissed me. Light. No tongue. The appetizer on Ranger's dinner menu. "Don't count on my help with the overactive sex drive," he said. "You're on your own with this one."

I looked up at the security camera focused on us. "Do you think Hal will sell this tape to the evening news?"

"Not if he wants to live." Ranger took a step back and opened the passenger-side door to the truck for me.

"Ranger..."

FOURTEEN

Ranger took the wheel, drove out of the garage, and
headed for the patch of scrub woods east of center
city where the four men had been found. Neither of
us spoke. Understandable since there wasn't a lot to
say after I explained my jelly doughnut dilemma, and
Ranger'd declared open season on Stephanie. Still, it
was good to have cleared the air, and now if I accidentally ripped his clothes off he'd understand it was one
of those odd chemical things.

The crime-scene tape blocked the dirt road leading
back to the crime site and covered a couple acres along
the road and into the woods. Ranger parked the truck,
and we got out and scooted under the yellow tape. I
could see a van through the trees, and snatches of conversation carried to me. Men's voices. Two or three.

We walked the dirt road through the scrubby field
and into the woods. The graves weren't far in. There
was an area about the size of a two-car garage where
the vegetation had been trampled over the years, leaving hard-packed dirt and some hardscrabble grass. This
was the end of the road, the turnaround point. This was
the place where drug deals were made, sex was sold,
and kids got drunk, stoned, pregnant.

The van belonged to the state lab. The side door was open. One guy stood by the open door, writing on a pad. Two guys in shirtsleeves were working at the grave site. They were wearing disposable gloves and carrying evidence bags. They looked our way and nodded, recognizing Ranger.

"Your FTA's long gone," the guy at the van said.

"Just curious," Ranger told him. "Wanted to see what the scene looked like."

"Looks like you got a new partner. What happened to Tank?"

"It's Tank's day off," Ranger said.

"Hey, wait a minute," the guy said, smiling at me. "Aren't you Stephanie Plum?"

"Yes," I said. "And whatever you've heard . . . it isn't true."

"You two are kind of cute together," the guy said to Ranger. "I like the matching clothes. Does Celia know about this?"

"This is business," Ranger said. "Stephanie's working for RangeMan. Are you finding anything interesting?"

"Hard to say. There was a lot of trash here. Everything from left-behind panties to crack cookers. A lot of used condoms and needles. You want to watch where you walk. Be best if you stay on the road. The road's clean."

"How deep was the grave?"

"A couple feet. I'm surprised they weren't found sooner. It's on the far perimeter of the cleared area so maybe it wasn't noticed. Or maybe no one cared. From the way the ground's settled I'd say they were here for a while. Couple weeks at least. Looks to me like they were shot here. Won't know for sure until the lab tests come back."

"Did he leave the shells?"

"Took the shells."

Ranger nodded. "Later."

"Later. Give Celia a hug for me."

We got back to the truck and Ranger shielded his eyes from the low-angled sun and studied the road we'd just walked.

"There was just barely enough room back there for five cars," Ranger said. "We know two of them were SUVs. Probably they could at least partially be seen from the main road. And that probably ensured their privacy. We know when three of the men left work and got into their cars. If they came directly here they'd arrive around six-thirty, which meant there was still daylight."

"You'd think someone would have heard gunshots. This guy didn't just pop off a couple rounds."

"It's an isolated area. And if you were a passing motorist it might be hard to tell where the shots originated. Most likely you'd just get the hell out of here."

We climbed into the truck and buckled ourselves in.

"Who's Celia?" I asked Ranger.

"My sister. Marty Sanchez, the guy by the van, went to school with Celia. They dated for a while."

"Is she your only sister?"

"I have four sisters."

"Any brothers?"

"One."

"And you have a daughter," I said.

Ranger swung the truck onto the paved road. "Not many people know about my daughter."

"Understood. Do I get to ask more questions?"

"One."

"How old are you?"

"I'm two months older than you," Ranger said.

"You know my birthday?"

"I know lots of things about you. And that was two questions."

It was five o'clock when we pulled into the garage.

"How's Morelli doing?" Ranger asked.

"Good. He's going back to work tomorrow. The cast won't come off for a while, so he's limited. He's on crutches, and he can't drive, and he can't walk Bob. I'm going to stay until he's more self-sufficient. Then I'll go back to my apartment."

Ranger walked me to the bike. "I don't want you going back to your apartment until we get this guy."

"You don't have to worry about me," I said. "I've got a gun."

"Would you feel comfortable using it?"

"No, but I could hit someone over the head with it."

The bike was a black Ducati Monster. I'd driven Morelli's Duc, so I was on familiar ground. I took the black full-face helmet off the grip and handed it to Ranger. I took the key out of my pocket, and I swung my leg over the bike.

Ranger was watching me, smiling. "I like the way you straddle that," he said. "Someday . . ."

I revved the engine and cut off the rest of the sentence. I didn't have to read his lips to know where he was going. I put the helmet on, Ranger remoted the gate open for me, and I wheeled out of the garage.

It felt great to be on the bike. The air was cool, and traffic was light. It was just a few minutes short of rush hour. I took it slow, getting the feel of the machine. I cut to the alley and brought the bike in through Morelli's backyard. Morelli had an empty tool shed next to his house. The shed was locked with a combination lock, and I knew the combination. I spun the dial, opened the shed, and locked the bike away.

Morelli was waiting for me in the kitchen. "Let me guess," Morelli said. "He gave you a bike. A Duc."

"Yeah. It was terrific riding over here." I went to the fridge and studied the inside. Not a lot there. "I'll take Bob out, and you can dial supper," I said.

"What do you want?"

"Anything without sugar."

"You're still on the no-sugar thing?"

"Yeah. I hope you took a nap this afternoon."

Morelli poked me with his crutch. "Where are your clothes? You weren't wearing this when you left this morning."

"I left them at work. I didn't have a way to carry them on the bike. I could use a backpack." I still had the windbreaker zipped over the shirt. I thought it was best to delay the short-shirt confrontation until after we'd eaten. I clipped Bob to his leash and took off. I got back just as the Pino's delivery kid was leaving.

"I ordered roast beef subs," Morelli said. "Hope that's okay."

I took a sub and unwrapped it and gave it to Bob. I handed a sub to Morelli, and I unwrapped the third for myself. We were in the living room, on the couch, as always. We ate, and we watched the news.

"The news is always the same," I said. "Death, destruction, blah, blah, blah. There should be a news station that only does happy news."

I collected the wrappers when we were done eating and carted them off to the kitchen. Morelli followed after me on his crutches.

"Take your jacket off," Morelli said. "I want to see the rest of the uniform."

"Later."

"Now."

"I was thinking I might go back to work just for a couple hours. I started a search and didn't get to finish it."

Morelli had me backed into a corner. "I don't think so. I have plans for tonight. Let's see the shirt."

"I don't want to hear any yelling."

"It's that bad?"

It wasn't just the shirt. It was also the gun. Morelli was going to be unhappy that I was carrying. He knew I was a moron when it came to guns.

I took the jacket off and twirled for him. "What do you think?"

"I'm going to kill him. Don't worry. I'll make it look like an accident."

"He didn't pick out the shirt. His housekeeper picked out the shirt. She's short. It probably came to her knees."

"Who picked out the gun?"

"Ranger picked out the gun."

"Is it loaded?"

"I don't know. I didn't look."

"You aren't really going to keep working for him, are you? He's a nut. Plus half his workforce has graduated from Jersey Penal," Morelli said. "And what about not wanting a dangerous job?"

"The job isn't dangerous. It's boring. I sit at a computer all day."

I had Morelli up and dressed. I got him down the stairs and into the kitchen. I sat him at the table, put the coffee on, and left for a short walk with Bob. When I came back, Morelli was asleep with his head on the table. I put a mug of coffee in front of him, and he opened an eye.

"You have to open *both* eyes," I said. "You're going to work today. Laski's picking you up in five minutes."

"That gives me five minutes to sleep," Morelli said.

"No! Drink some coffee. Get some legal stimulants into your system." I danced in front of him. "Look at me. I'm wearing a gun! And look at the short shirt. Are you going to let me go to work like this?"

"Cupcake, I haven't got the energy to stop you. Anyway, maybe if you look slutty enough, Ranger will take up some of the slack in the bedroom before you make a permanent cripple out of me. Maybe you should wear that shirt with the neckline that lets your boobs hang out." Morelli squinted at me. "Why aren't you tired?"

"I don't know. I feel all energized. I always thought I couldn't keep up with you, but maybe you've just been slowing me down all these years."

"Stephanie, I'm begging you. Eat some doughnuts. I can't keep going like this."

I poured his coffee into a travel mug and got him to his feet. I shoved the crutches under his arms and pushed him to the front door. Laski was already at the curb. I helped Morelli hobble down the stairs and maneuver himself into the car. I threw his crutches onto the backseat and handed Morelli his mug of coffee.

"Have a nice day," I said. I gave him a kiss, closed the car door, and watched as Laski motored them away, down the street.

There was a chill to the air, so I went back to the house, ran upstairs, and borrowed Morelli's leather biker jacket. I tied the RangeMan windbreaker around my waist, I gave Bob a hug, and I let myself out through the back door. I unlocked the shed and rolled the bike out, and a half hour later, I was at my desk.

I went straight into the newspaper search. I limited the search to the last three months the men were at Dix. It seemed to me that was the most likely time frame for them to do something catastrophic. I began with a name search and came up empty. None of the men were mentioned in any of the local papers. My next search was front page. I was only reading headlines, but it was still a slow process.

I stopped the Fort Dix search at nine-thirty and switched to RangeMan business, working my way through the security check requests. By noon I was questioning my ability to do the job long-term. The words were swimming on the screen, and I felt creaky from sitting. I went to the kitchen and poked at the sandwiches. Turkey, tuna, grilled vegetables, roast beef, chicken salad. I dialed Ranger on my cell phone.

"Yo," Ranger said. "Is there a problem?"

"I don't like any of these sandwiches."

There was a moment of dead phone time before Ranger answered. "Go upstairs to my apartment. I think there's some peanut butter left from last time you stayed there."

"Where are you?"

"I'm with an account. I'm inspecting a new system."

"Are you coming home for lunch?"

"No," Ranger said. "I won't be back until three. Are you still off sugar?"

"Yes."

"Maybe I can get back sooner."

"No rush," I said. "I'm happy with peanut butter."

"I'm counting on that being a lie," Ranger said.

I let myself into Ranger's apartment and went straight to the kitchen. He still had the peanut butter in his fridge, and there was a loaf of bread on the granite countertop. I made myself a sandwich and washed it down with a beer. I was tempted to take a nap in Ranger's bed, but that felt too much like Goldilocks.

I was on my way out when I got a call from Lula. "I got him trapped," she yelled into the phone. "I got Willie Martin trapped in the deli at the corner of Twenty-fifth Street and Lowman Avenue. Only I'm gonna need help to bag him. If you're at RangeMan it's just around the corner."

"Are you sure you need my help?"

"Hurry!"

I took the elevator to the first floor and went out the front door. No point taking the bike. The deli was only a block away. I jogged to Lowman, and saw Lula standing in front of Fennick's Deli.

"He's in there eating," she said to me. "I just happened on him. I was going in for sandwiches for Connie and me and there he was. He's in the back where they have some tables."

"Did he see you?"

"I don't think so. I got out right away."

"So what do you need me for?"

"I thought you could be a diversion. You could go in there and get his attention, and then I'll sneak up and zap him with the stun gun."

"Didn't we already try the zapping thing?"

"Yeah, but we'd be better this time on account of we got some practice at it."

"Okay, but you'd better not screw up. If you screw up he's going to beat the crap out of me."

"Don't worry," Lula said. "The third time's a charm. This is going to work. You'll see. You go on up to him, and I'll sneak around from the side and get him from the back."

"Have you tested the stun gun? Does it work?"

We were standing next to a bus stop with a bench. Three elderly men were sitting on the bench. One was reading a paper, and the other two were zoned out, staring blankly into space. Lula reached out and pressed the stun gun to one of the men. He gave a twitch and slumped onto the man next to him.

"Yep," Lula said. "It works."

I was speechless. My mouth was open and my eyes were wide.

"What?" Lula said.

"You just zapped that poor old man."

"It's okay. I know him. That's Gimp Whiteside. He don't do nothing all day. Might as well help us hard-working bounty hunters. Anyway, he didn't feel any pain. He's just taking a snooze now." Lula looked me over and grinned. "Look at you! You look like Range-Man Barbie. You got a gun and everything."

"Yeah, and I have to get back to work, so let's do this. I'm going to talk to Willie and see if I can get him to surrender. Give me your cuffs, and don't use the stun gun until I tell you to use it."

Lula handed her cuffs over to me. "You're taking some of the fun out of it, but I guess I could do it that way."

I walked straight back to Willie Martin. He was sitting alone at a small bistro table. He'd finished his sandwich, and he was picking at a few remaining fries. There was a second chair at his table. I slid the chair over next to him and sat down. "Remember me?" I asked him.

Willie looked at me and laughed. It was a big open-mouthed, mashed-up-french-fries-and-ketchup laugh that sounded like *haw, haw, haw.* "Yeah, I remember you," he said. "You're the dumb white bitch who came with fat-ass Lula."

He dipped a french fry into a glob of ketchup with his right hand, and I clamped a cuff onto his left.

He looked down at the cuff and grinned. "I already got a pair of these. You giving me another?"

"I'm asking you nicely to return to the courthouse with me, so we can get you rescheduled."

"I don't think so."

"It's just a formality. We'll rebond you."

"Nope."

"I have a gun."

"You gonna use it?"

"I might."

"I don't think so," Willie said. "I'm unarmed. You

shoot me, and you'll do more time than I will. That's assault with a deadly weapon."

"Okay, how about this. If you don't let me cuff your other hand, and you don't quietly walk out with me and get in Lula's car, we're going to send enough electricity through you to make you mess your pants. And that's going to be an embarrassing experience. It'll probably make the papers—'Pro ball all-star Willie Martin messed his pants in Fennick's Deli yesterday . . .'"

"I didn't mess my pants last time."

"Do you want to risk it? We'd be happy to give you a few volts."

"You swear you'll rebond me?"

"I'll call Vinnie as soon as we get you into the car."

"Okay," Willie said. "I'm gonna stand and put my hands behind my back. And we'll do this real quiet so nobody notices."

Lula was a short distance away with the stun gun in hand, her eyes glued to Willie. I stood, and Willie stood, and next thing I knew I was flying through the air. He'd moved so fast and scooped me up so effortlessly, I never saw it coming. He threw me about fifteen feet, and I crash-landed on a table of four. The table gave way and I was on the floor with the burgers and shakes and soup of the day. I was flat on my back, the wind knocked out of me, dazed for a moment, the world swirling around me. I rolled to my hands and knees and crawled over smashed food and dishes to get to my feet.

Willie Martin was facedown on the floor just beyond the table debris. Lula was sitting on him, struggling with the second cuff. "Boy, you really know how to make a diversion," Lula said. "I zapped him good. He's out like a light. Only I can't get his second hand to cooperate."

I limped over and held Martin's hand behind his

back while she cuffed him. "Do you have shackles in the car?"

"Yeah. Maybe you should go get them while I baby-sit here."

I took the key to the Firebird, got the shackles, and brought them back to Lula. We got the shackles on Martin, and a squad car pulled up outside the deli. It was my pal Carl Costanza and his partner, Big Dog.

Costanza grinned when he saw me. "We got a call that two crazy fans were on Willie like white on rice."

"That would be Lula and me," I said. "Except we're not fans. He's FTA."

"Looks like you're wearing lunch."

"Willie threw me into the table. And then he decided to take a nap."

"We'd appreciate it if you could help us drag his sorry ass out of here," Lula said. "He weighs a ton."

Big Dog got Willie under the armpits, Carl took the feet, and we hauled Willie out of the deli and dumped him into the back of Lula's Firebird.

"We need to do a property damage report," Costanza said to me. "You're wearing RangeMan clothes. Are you hunting desperadoes for Vinnie or for Ranger?"

"Vinnie."

"Works for me," Costanza said. And they disappeared inside the deli.

Lula and I looked over at the bench by the bus stop. Two of the three men were gone from the bench. The guy Lula stun-gunned was still there.

"Looks like Gimp missed his bus," Lula said. "Guess he didn't come around fast enough. Hey, Gimp," she yelled. "You want a ride? Get your bony behind over here."

"You're a big softy," I said.

"Yeah, don't tell nobody."

I walked back to RangeMan and entered through

the front door. "Don't say anything," I told the guy at the desk. "I've just walked two blocks through town, and I've heard it all. And just in case you're wondering, those are noodles stuck in my hair, not worms."

I rode the elevator to the control room and had the full attention of everyone there as I crossed to my desk.

"I got tired of turkey so I went out for lunch," I told them.

I retrieved the key fob I'd left on my desk, got back into the elevator, and rode to Ranger's floor. I knocked on his door and didn't get an answer, so I let myself in. I took my shoes off in the hall and left them on the marble floor. I didn't want to trash Ranger's apartment, and the shoes were coated with chocolate milkshake and some smushed cheeseburger. I padded into Ranger's bathroom, locked the door, and dropped the rest of my clothes. I washed with his delicious shower gel and stood under the hot water until I was relaxed and no longer cared that just minutes before I'd had chicken noodle soup in my hair.

I wrapped myself in Ranger's luxuriously thick terry-cloth robe, unlocked the door, and stepped into his bedroom. Ranger was stretched out on the bed, ankles crossed, arms behind his head. He was fully clothed, and he was obviously waiting for me.

"I had a small mishap," I said.

"That's what they tell me. What happened?"

"I was helping Lula snag Willie Martin at Fennick's and next thing I knew I was airborne. He threw me about fifteen feet, into a table full of food and people."

"Are you okay?"

"Yeah, but my sneakers are history. They're covered with chocolate milkshake."

Ranger crooked a finger at me. "Come here."

"No way."

"What about the jelly-doughnut hormones and the sex-drive hormones?"

"Getting thrown across a room seems to have a calming effect on them."

"I could fix that," Ranger said.

I smiled at him. "There's no doubt in my mind, but I'd rather you didn't. I have a lot of things going on in my head right now, and you could make it a lot more confusing."

"That's promising," Ranger said. He got off the bed and crossed the room. He grabbed me by the big shawl collar on the robe and pulled me to him. "I like when you wear my robe."

"Because I'm cute in it?"

"No, because it's all you're wearing."

"You don't know that for sure," I said. "I could have clothes under this."

"Is this another one of those things I should find out for myself?"

I was skating on thin ice here. I had the jelly-doughnut hormone problem going on, and I didn't want it to get out of control. I'd spent a night with Ranger a while ago, and I knew what happened when he was encouraged. Ranger knew how to make a woman want him. Ranger was magic.

"Let's take a look at my life," I said to Ranger. "I keep rolling in garbage."

"Mind-boggling," Ranger said.

"And let's take a look at your life. You have a deep dark secret."

"Let it go," Ranger said.

"Are you sick?"

"No, I'm not sick. Not physically, anyway. I'm not

so sure sometimes about the mental, emotional, and sexual."

I locked myself in Ranger's dressing room and got dressed in the second RangeMan outfit. Short black T-shirt, black cargo pants, black socks. Ella hadn't provided underwear or shoes, so I sent my soda-and-ketchup-soaked underwear and my chocolate-shake-covered shoes off to the laundry with the first RangeMan outfit. I was feeling a little strange without underwear, but a girl's gotta do what a girl's gotta do, right?

I returned to my desk, and I ignored the search requests piling up in my in-box. I picked up where I left off with the Dix search, reading the front pages. By five o'clock I had a list of crimes that I thought had potential. Nothing sensational. Just good solid crimes like a rash of unsolved burglaries, an unsolved murder, an unsolved hijacking. None of the crimes really grabbed me, and I still had lots of front pages to read, so I decided to keep searching.

I called Morelli and told him I was working late.

"How late?" he said.

"I don't know. Does it matter?"

"Only if you come home with your underwear on backwards."

I could go him one better than that. How about no underwear at all?

"Dial yourself some food," I said. "And tie Bob out back. I need to finish this project. How was your day? Is your leg okay?"

"The leg is okay. The day was long. I don't like being stuck in the building."

"Anything on Barroni and the three other guys?"

"They've all been positively identified. You were right about all of them. They were killed on-site. That's it so far."

"No one's seen Spiro?"

"No, but the pizza kid gave a good description, and it matches yours."

I struggled up from a deep sleep and opened my eyes to Ranger.

"Babe," he said softly. "You need to wake up. You need to go home."

I had my arms crossed on my desk and my head on my arms. The screen saver was up on my computer. "What time is it?"

"It's a little after eleven. I just came back from a break-in on one of the RangeMan accounts and saw you were still here."

"I was looking for a crime."

"Did you call Morelli?"

"Earlier. He knows I'm working late."

Ranger looked down at my feet. "Have you heard anything about your shoes? Ella was going to wash them."

"Haven't heard anything."

Ranger punched Ella's extension on my phone. "Sorry to call so late," he said. "What's happening with Stephanie's shoes?"

Ranger smiled at Ella's answer. He disconnected and slung an arm around my shoulder. "Bad news on the shoes. They melted in the dryer. Looks like you're going home in your socks." He pulled me to my feet. "I'll drive you. You can't ride the bike like this."

FIFTEEN

We took the elevator to the garage, and Ranger went to the Porsche. Of all his cars, this was my favorite. I loved the sound of the engine, and I loved the way the seat cradled me. At night, the dash looked like controls on a jet, and the car felt intimate.

I was groggy from sleep and exhausted from the events of the day. And I suspected the last two nights were catching up with me. I closed my eyes and melted into the cushy leather seat. I felt Ranger reach across and buckle my seat belt. I heard the Porsche growl to life and move up the ramp to exit the garage. I dozed on the way home and came awake when the car stopped. I looked out at the darkened neighborhood. Not a lot of lights shining in windows at this time of the night. These were hardworking people who rose early and went to bed early. We were stopped half a block from Morelli's house.

"Why are we stopped here?" I asked Ranger.

"I have a working relationship with Morelli. I think he's a good cop, and he thinks I'm a loose cannon. Since we both carry guns, I try not to do things that would upset the balance in an insulting way. I wanted to give you a chance to wake up, so we didn't sit at the curb in front of his house like a couple teenagers adjusting their clothes." Ranger looked over at me. "You got the rest of your clothes from Ella, didn't you?"

Damn. "I forgot! I was working, and then I fell asleep. She's got my underwear."

Ranger laughed out loud, and when he looked back at me he was smiling the full-on Ranger smile. "I'm worrying about parking too long in front of Morelli's house, and I'm bringing his girlfriend home without her underwear. I'll have to put double security on the building tonight." He put the Porsche in gear, drove half a block, and parked. Lights were on in the downstairs rooms. "Are you going to be okay?" he asked.

"Morelli's a reasonable person. He'll understand." Plus he had a cast on his leg. He couldn't move fast. I'd head straight for the stairs, and I'd be changed before he could get to me.

Ranger locked eyes with me. "Just so you know, for future reference, *I* wouldn't understand. If you were living with me, and you came home without underwear, I'd go looking for the guy who had it. And it wouldn't be pretty when I found him."

"Something to remember," I said. And the truth is, Morelli wasn't so different from Ranger. And Morelli wasn't usually a reasonable person. Morelli was being uncharacteristically mellow. I wasn't sure why I was seeing the mellow, and I wasn't sure how long it would last. The main difference between Morelli and Ranger was that when Morelli got mad he got loud. And when Ranger got mad he got quiet. They were both equally scary.

I jumped out of the Porsche and ran to the house. I let myself in, called to Morelli, and ran up the stairs and into the bedroom to get clothes. I smacked into Morelli en route to the bathroom. He dropped a crutch and put an arm out to steady me.

"What are you doing up here?" I asked.

"Going to bed? I live here, remember?"

"I thought you were downstairs."

"You were wrong." He looked over at me. "Where's your bra?"

"What?"

"I know your body better than I know my own. And I know when you're not wearing a bra."

I slumped against the doorjamb. "It's in Ranger's dryer. You're not going to make a big deal about this, are you?"

"I don't know. I'm waiting to hear the whole story."

"I helped Lula capture Willie Martin this morning, and I sort of got thrown into a table filled with food and people."

"Costanza told me."

"Yeah, he responded to the call from Fennick's. Anyway, my clothes and my shoes were a mess, and I had chicken soup in my hair, so I used Ranger's shower to get cleaned up. And I put clean clothes on, except Ella hadn't gotten me any underwear or shoes." We both looked down at my feet. Black socks. No shoes. "So here I am, and I don't have any underwear."

"Was Ranger in the shower with you?"

"Nope. Just me."

"And you were actually working tonight?"

"Yep."

"If I had anyone else for a girlfriend I'd be out the door with a gun in my hand, looking for Ranger—but your life is so insane I'm willing to believe anything. Living with you is like being in one of the reality shows on television where people keep getting covered with bees and dropped off forty-story buildings into a vat of Vaseline."

"I admit it's been a little . . . hectic."

"Hectic is getting three kids to soccer practice on time. Your life is . . . there are no words for your life."

"That's what my mother says. Is this leading to something?"

"I don't know. I'm really tired right now. Let's talk about it tomorrow."

I picked Morelli's crutch up for him, and he moved toward the little guest room.

"Where are you going?" I asked him.

"I'm sleeping in the guest room, and I'm locking the door. I need a night of uninterrupted sleep. I'm running on empty. I was a mess at work. I couldn't keep my eyes open. And my guys feel like they've been run over by a truck. They need a day off."

"What about *my* guys?"

"Cupcake, you don't have guys."

"I have *something*."

"You do. And I love it. But you're on your own to-night. You're going to have to fly solo."

I rolled out of bed and crossed the hall to the little guest room. The door was open, and the room was empty. No Morelli in the bathroom or study, but Bob was sleeping in the bathtub. I crept down the stairs and walked through the house to the kitchen. There was hot coffee, and a note had been left by the coffeemaker.

SORRY ABOUT LAST NIGHT. THE GUYS MISSED YOU THIS MORNING. DON'T WORK LATE.

That sounded hopeful. I poured a mug of coffee, added milk, and took it upstairs. An hour later, I was dressed in black jeans and black T-shirt, and I was ready for work. I'd called my dad and mooched a ride. He was at the curb when I came down the stairs.

"You're doing pretty good on the new job," he said. "Almost a week. And nothing's caught fire or blown up at work."

It'd be a real challenge for Spiro to penetrate Range-Man. And that's probably the reason Morelli's garage got destroyed. Spiro went for what was available. Truth is I was beginning to be bothered by the lack of activity. The garage went five days ago and there hadn't been any threatening notes, snipings, or bombings since the Buick.

"They're holding a memorial service for Michael Barroni today," my father said. "Your mother said to tell you she's taking your grandmother. It's being held at Stiva's. Ordinarily they'd hold it at the church, but Stiva and Barroni were old friends, and I guess Stiva gave the Barronis a discount if they held the service in his chapel."

"I didn't realize Stiva and Barroni were that close."

"Yeah, me neither. I didn't see them spending a lot of time together. But then that happens when you got a big family and a business to run. You lose touch with your buddies."

I had a chill run up my spine to the roots of my hair, and my scalp was tingling like I was electric. "How'd Stiva and Barroni get to be friends?" I asked, holding my breath, my heart skipping beats.

"They were in the army together. They were both at Dix."

I might have the fifth man. I was so excited I was hyperventilating. Now here's the thing, *why was I so excited?* Ranger had his FTA, so the excitement didn't come from case closure. I barely knew Barroni and I didn't know the other three men at all, so there was nothing personal. My original long jump tying Anthony Barroni to Spiro and the missing men proved to be groundless. So why did I care? The four missing men seemed to be completely unrelated to anything I'd care about. And even if Spiro *did* turn out to have a tie to the four men, even if there *was* a crime involved, it really didn't matter to me, did it? Finding Spiro and stopping the harassment was really the only thing that mattered, right? Right. But stopping the harassment could be a problem. There were really only two ways the harassment would stop. Ranger could kill Spiro. Or Spiro could get convicted of a crime, like murdering Mama Macaroni, and get locked away. The latter was definitely the preferred. Okay, maybe I was excited about the fifth man because it might be Constantine Stiva. And if Con was involved, then Spiro might be involved. And if there wasn't evidence that convicted Spiro of the bombings, there might be evidence to convict him of the shallow grave homicides. So, was this why I couldn't wait to plug Con's name into the search program? I didn't think so. I suspected the hard reality was that it all just came down to tasteless curiosity. I was a product of the Burg. I had to know all the dirt.

My dad pulled up to the front of the building and I jumped out. "Thanks," I yelled, hitting the ground running.

I was supposed to sign in and sign out when I entered and left the building. And I was supposed to show my picture ID when I came through the first-floor lobby. I never remembered to sign in or out, and my picture ID was lost in the garage fire. Good thing everyone knew me. Being the only woman in an organization had its upside.

I waved to the guy at the desk and danced in place, waiting for the elevator. I barreled out of the elevator on the fifth floor and crossed to my cubby. I got my computer up and running and punched "Constantine Stiva" into the newspaper search program. A single article appeared. It was small and on page thirteen. I would have missed it on my front-page search.

Private First Class Constantine Stiva had been injured in his attempt to thwart a robbery. A government armored truck carrying payroll had been hijacked when it had stopped for a routine gate check at Fort

Dix. Stiva had been on guard duty, along with two other men. Stiva was the only guard to survive. He'd been shot in the leg. There'd been no mention of the amount of money involved. And there weren't a lot of details on the hijacking, other than a few brief sentences that the truck had been recovered. I searched papers for two weeks following the incident but came up empty. There'd only been the one article.

I called Ranger on his cell and got a message. I left my cubby and went to the console that monitored Rangeman cars. "Where's Ranger?" I asked Hal. "He's not answering his cell, and I don't see him on the board."

"He's on a plane," Hal said. "He had to bring an FTA up from Miami. He'll be back tonight. Manny was supposed to bring the guy up on a red-eye yesterday, but he had problems with security, so Ranger had to go down this morning." Hal tapped Ranger's number into his computer and a screen changed and brought Ranger's car up. Philadelphia airport. "He should be on the ground in three hours," Hal said. "His cell will come back on then."

I went back to my cubby and I called Morelli.

"I might know the fifth guy," I told him. "It might be Constantine Stiva. He was at Dix when Barroni was there. They were army buddies."

"I can't imagine Con in the army," Morelli said. "I can't imagine him ever being anything other than a funeral director."

"It gets even stranger. He was on guard duty, and he was shot during an armored car hijacking."

"How do you know all this?"

"I've been searching newspapers. I'm going to e-mail you the article on Con. I know it's stupid, but I just have this feeling everything fits somehow. Like maybe the four missing men were involved in the armored car hijacking and Con recognized them."

"Then it would seem to me Con should be the one in the shallow grave."

"Yes, but suppose Con told Spiro and Spiro came back and was extorting money from the four men? And then when he didn't think he could get any more he shot them."

"It's a lot of supposing," Morelli said.

"And here's something else that's interesting. There's been no activity since your garage got blown up. Five days without a note, a sniping, or a bombing. Don't you think that's odd?"

"I think it's all odd."

I sent the news article to Morelli, and then I went to the kitchen, got coffee with milk, no sugar, and went back to my desk and called my mother. "Are you tippling yet?" I asked her.

"No," she said.

Damn. "Dad said you and Grandma were going to the memorial service."

"Yes. It's at one o'clock. I feel so sorry for Carla and the three boys. What a terrible thing. I might have to tipple after the service. Do you think that would be bad?"

"Everybody tipples after a memorial service," I told her. I knew it was the wrong thing to say. God help me, I was a rotten daughter, but I really needed dessert!

I disconnected and started working my way through the search requests. I called Morelli at noon.

"How's it going?"

"I talked to Con."

"Just for the heck of it."

"Yeah. Just for the heck of it. He said the army tried to keep the armored truck robbery as quiet as possible. The two guards that Con was working with were shot and killed. Con said he was alive because he fainted when he got shot in the leg, and he supposed the hijackers thought he was dead. He couldn't identify any of the hijackers. They were all dressed in fatigues, wearing masks. For security purposes the army never released the entire death toll, but Con said it was rumored that there were three men in the truck who were killed."

"Did he say how much money was involved?"

"He didn't know."

"Did you ask him if he thought Barroni might have been involved in that hijacking?"

"Yeah. He looked at me like I was on drugs."

"Did Spiro know about the hijacking?"

"Spiro knew his dad was shot. Con said there was a time when Spiro was a kid, and he was sort of obsessed with it. Kept the newspaper article in a scrapbook."

"What does he have to say about the Spiro sightings?"

"Not much. He seemed confused more than anything else. He said he thought Spiro had perished in the fire. If he's telling the truth he's in a strange spot, not sure if he should be happy Spiro's alive or sad that Spiro blew up Mama Macaroni."

"Do you think he's telling the truth?"

"Don't know. He sounds convincing enough. The big problem for me isn't that Spiro came back to harass you. That I could easily believe, and you've actually seen him. My problem is I don't feel comfortable involving him in the Barroni murder."

"You don't think Spiro's a multitasker."

"Spiro's a rodent. You put a rodent in a maze, and he focuses on one thing, he goes for the piece of cheese."

"Then who killed Michael Barroni?"

"Don't know. If I was going on gut instinct, I'd have to say it feels like Spiro's got his finger in that pie, but there's absolutely no evidence. We don't know *why* Barroni was killed, and we have no reason to believe he was involved in the hijacking."

"Jeez, you're such a party pooper."

"Yeah, insisting on evidence is always a downer."

I hung up and went back to my searches, but I couldn't keep my mind on them. I was getting double vision from looking at the computer, and I was tired of sitting in the cubby. And even worse, I was feeling friendly. I was thinking Morelli's voice had sounded nice on the phone. I was wondering what he was wearing. And I was remembering what he looked like when he wasn't wearing anything. And I was thinking I might have to leave work early, so I could be naked by the time Morelli walked through the door at four o'clock.

I pushed away from my desk, stuffed myself into the windbreaker, and grabbed the key fob.

"I need to get some air," I told Hal. "I won't be gone long."

I rode the elevator to the garage and got on the bike. When I pushed away from my desk I didn't have a direction in mind. By the time I'd reached the garage I knew where I was going. I was going to the memorial service.

I got to Stiva's exactly at one o'clock. Latecomers were hunting parking places and hustling up to the big front porch. I zipped into the lot with the Duc and parked on a patch of grass separating the lot from the drive-thru lane for the hearse and the flower car. My mother's gray Buick was in the lot. From the location of her parking place I was guessing she'd gotten there early. Grandma always liked a seat up front.

Stiva had a chapel on the first floor to the rear of the building. When there was a large crowd he opened the doors and seated the overflow on folding chairs in the wide hallway. Today was standing room only. Since I was one of the last to arrive, I was far down the hall, catching the service over the speaker system.

I wandered away after fifteen minutes and peeked in some of the other rooms. Mr. Earls was in Slumber Salon number three. I thought he was sort of a sad sack in there all by himself while everyone else was at the service. It felt like poor Mr. Earls didn't get an invitation to the party. I snooped in the kitchen and spent a moment considering the cookie tray. I told myself they weren't that good. They were store-bought cookies, and there weren't any of my favorites on the tray. There were better things to nibble on, I told myself. Fresh doughnuts, homemade chocolate chip cookies . . . Ranger. I left the kitchen and tiptoed into Con's office. He'd left the door open. It was an announcement that he had nothing to hide. If you can't trust your undertaker, who *can* you trust, eh?

I don't ordinarily do recreational mortuary tours, and I'd absolutely believed Con when he said he hadn't seen Spiro, so I wasn't sure why I felt compelled to search the building. I guess it just wasn't adding up for me. I kept coming back to the mole. It had been made from mortician's putty. Stiva doesn't run the only funeral home in the greater Trenton area. And for that matter, you can probably order mortician's putty on the Net. Still, this was the easiest and most logical place for Spiro to get a chunk of the stuff. I had a feeling that if I opened enough doors here, I'd find Spiro or at least some evidence that Spiro had passed through.

I went upstairs and checked out the storage room and the two additional viewing rooms Con reserved for peak periods, like the week after Christmas. I returned to the ground level, exited the side door, and looked in the garage. Two slumber coaches, waiting for the call. Two flower cars that were somber, even when filled with flowers. Two Lincoln Town Cars. And Con's black Navigator, the vehicle of choice when someone inconveniently dies during a blizzard.

I returned to the main building through the back door. The chapel was straight ahead, at the end of a short corridor. The embalming rooms were in the new wing, to my left. These rooms were added after the fire. The new structure was cinder block and the equipment supposedly was state of the art, whatever that meant.

I took a deep breath and turned left. I'd gone this far, I should finish the search. I tested the door that led to the new wing. Locked. Gee, too bad. Guess God doesn't want me to see the embalming rooms.

The basement also remained unexplored. And that's the way it was going to stay. The furnaces and meat lockers are in the basement. This is where the fire started. I've been told the basement's all rebuilt and shiny and bright, but I'd rather not see for myself. I'm afraid the ghosts are still there . . . and the memories.

Con lived in a house that sat next to the mortuary. It was a good-size Victorian, not as big as the original mortuary house, but twice the size of my parents' house. Spiro had grown up in that house. I'd never been inside. Spiro hadn't been one of my friends. Spiro had been a kid who lived in shadows, scheming and spying on the rest of the world, occasionally sucking another kid into the darkness.

I went out through the back door and followed the walkway past the garages to Con's house. It was a pretty house, well maintained, the property professionally landscaped. It was painted white with black shutters, like the mortuary. I circled the house and stepped up onto the small back porch that sheltered the kitchen door. I looked in the windows. The kitchen was dark. I could see through to the dining room. It was also dark. Nothing out of place. No dirty dishes on the counter. No cereal boxes. No sweatshirt draped over a chair. I stood very still and listened. Nothing. Just the beating of my heart, which seemed frighteningly loud.

I tried the door. Locked. I worked my way around the side of the house. No open windows. I returned to the back of the house and looked up at the second floor. An open window. People felt safe leaving windows open on the second floor. And most of the time they were safe. But not this time. This window was over the little back porch, and I was good at climbing up back porches. When I was in high school my parents' back porch had been my main escape route when I was grounded. And I was grounded a lot.

Stephanie, Stephanie, Stephanie, I said to myself. This is insane. You're obsessed with this Spiro thing. There's no good reason to believe you'll find anything helpful in Con's house. What if you get caught? How embarrassing will that be? Then the stupid Stephanie spoke up. Yes, but I won't get caught, the stupid Stephanie said. Everyone's at the memorial service and it'll go on for another half hour at least. And no one can see this side of the house. It's blocked by the garage. The smart Stephanie didn't have an answer to that, so the stupid Stephanie shimmied up the porch railing and climbed through the second-story window and dropped into the bathroom.

The bathroom was white tile, white walls, white towels, white fixtures, white shower curtain, white toilet paper. It was blindingly antiseptic. The towels were perfectly folded and lined up on the towel bar. There was no scum in the soap dish. I took a quick peek in the medicine cabinet. Just the usual over-the-counter stuff you'd expect to find.

I walked through the three upstairs bedrooms, looking in closets and drawers and under beds. I went downstairs and walked through the living room, dining room, and den. The house was eerily unlived-in. No wrinkles on the pillowcases, and all the clothes hanging in the closet and folded in the chest were perfectly pressed. Just like Con, I thought. Lifeless and perfectly pressed.

I went to the kitchen. No food in the fridge. A bottle of water and a bottle of cranberry juice. The poor man was probably anemic from starvation. No wonder he was always so pale. His complexion frequently mirrored the deceased. Not flawed by death or disease but not quite human either. I thought it was by association, but Grandma said she thought Con dabbled in the makeup tray in the prep room.

Constantine Stiva was surrounded by grieving people every night, left alone with the dead by day, and went home to this sterile house after the evening viewings. And if we're to believe him, he has a son who came back to the Burg but never stopped by to say hello. Morelli thought Spiro was a single-minded rodent. I thought Spiro was a fungus. I thought Spiro fed off a host, and his host had always been Con.

I opened the door to the cellar, switched the light on, and cautiously crept down the stairs. *Eureka.* This was the room I'd been looking for. It was a windowless basement room that had been made into a do-it-yourself apartment. There was a couch covered by a rumpled sleeping bag and pillow. A television. A comfy chair that had seen better days. A scarred coffee table. A bookshelf that had been stocked with cans of soup and boxes of crackers. At the far end someone had installed a sink and a makeshift counter. There was a hotplate on the counter. And there was a small under-the-counter refrigerator. This was the perfect hiding hole for Spiro. There was a door next to the refrigerator. Bathroom, I thought.

I opened the door and looked around the room. I'd expected to find a small bathroom. What I had in front of me was a mortician's workroom. Two long tables covered with tubes of paint, artists' brushes, a couple large plastic containers of mortician's modeling clay, wigs and hairpieces, trays of cosmetics, jars of replacement teeth. And on a chair in the corner was a jacket and hat. Spiro's.

I had my cell phone clipped to my belt alongside my gun. I unclipped the phone and went to dial. No service in the basement. I was on my way through the door when a flash of color caught my eye. It was a rubbery blob that looked a lot like uncooked bacon. I moved closer and realized it was several pieces of the material morticians used for facial reconstruction. I didn't know a lot about the mechanics of preparing the dead for their last appearance, but I'd seen shows on movie makeup, and this looked similar. I knew it was possible to transform people into animals and aliens with this stuff. It was possible to make young actors look old, and it was possible to give the appearance of health and well-being to the newly departed. Stiva was a genius when it came to reconstructing the dead. He added fullness to the cheeks, smoothed over wrinkles, tucked away excess skin. He filled in bullet holes, added teeth, covered bruises, straightened noses when necessary.

Stiva was Burg comfort food. Burg residents knew their secrets and flaws were safe in Stiva's hands. At the end of the day, Stiva would make the fat look thin and the jaundiced look healthy. He wiped away time and alcoholism and self-indulgence. He chose the most flattering lipstick shade for the ladies. He hand-selected men's ties. Even fifty-two-year-old Mickey Branchek, who had a heart attack while laboring over Mrs. Branchek and died with an enormous erection that gave new meaning to the term stiffy, looked rested and respectable for his last hoohah. Best not to consider the process used to achieve that result.

Spiro had watched his father at work and would know the same techniques. So it wasn't shocking that the mole had been made from mortician's putty. The pieces of plastic that were lying on the table were more disturbing. They reminded me of Spiro's scars, and I realized Spiro would have the ability to change his appearance. A perfectly healthy Spiro could make himself horribly disfigured. He wouldn't fool anyone up close, but I'd only seen him at a distance, in a car. And Chester Rhinehart had seen him at night. If I was, in fact, looking at a disguise, it was pretty darn creepy.

I heard movement behind me, and I turned to find Con standing in the doorway.

"What are you doing? How'd you get in here?" he asked. "The doors to the house were closed and locked."

"The back door was open." When in a jam always go with a fib. "Is the service done?"

"No. I came back here because you tripped my alarm."

"I didn't hear it."

"It rings in my office. It monitors the cellar door, among others."

"You're hiding Spiro," I said. "I recognize the coat and hat on the chair. I'm sorry. This must be awful for you."

Con looked at me, his face composed, as always, his eyes completely devoid of emotion. "You're perfect," he said. "Stupid to the end. You haven't figured it out, have you? There's no Spiro. Spiro is dead. He died in the fire. There was nothing left of him but ashes and his school ring."

"I thought he was never found. There was never a service."

"He wasn't found. There wasn't anything left of him. Just the ring. I stumbled across it and never said anything. I didn't want a service. I wanted to move on, to rebuild my business. If he'd lived he would have ruined me, anyway. He was a moron."

This was the first I'd ever heard Con speak badly of

the dead. And it was of his son. I didn't know what to say. It was true. Spiro was a moron, but it was chilling to hear it from Con. And if Spiro was dead then who was tormenting me? Who blew up Mama Macaroni? I suspected the answer was standing two feet away, but I couldn't put it together. I couldn't imagine solicitous Constantine Stiva, Mr. No Personality, offing Mama Mac.

"So it wasn't Spiro who was leaving me notes and blowing up cars?"

"No."

"It was you."

"Hard to believe, isn't it?"

"Why? Why were you stalking me?"

"Why doesn't matter," Con said. "Let's just say you're serving a purpose. I guess it's just as well that you're here. I don't have to hunt you down."

I put my hand to the gun at my hip, but it was an unfamiliar act, and I was slow. Con was much faster with his weapon. He lunged forward, and I saw the glint of metal in his hand, and I barely registered *stun gun* before I went out.

I was in absolute blackness when I came around. My mind was working, but my body was slow to respond, and I couldn't see. I was cuffed and shackled, and I was blindfolded. No, I thought. Back up. I wasn't blindfolded. I could open and close my eyes. It was just very, very dark. And silent. And stuffy. I was disoriented in the dark, and I was having a hard time focusing. I rocked side to side. Not much room. I tried to sit but couldn't raise my head more than a couple inches. The space around me was minimal. The realization of confinement sent a shock of panic into my chest and burned in my throat. I was in a silk-lined container. God help me. Constantine Stiva had put me in one of his caskets. My heart was pounding and my mind was in free fall. This couldn't be real. Con was the heart and soul of the Burg. No one would ever suspect Con of bad things.

My hands ached from the cuffs, and I couldn't breathe. I was suffocating. I was buried alive. Hysteria came in waves and receded. Tears slid down my cheeks and soaked into the satin lining. I had no idea of time, but I didn't think much time had passed. Maybe a half hour. An hour at most. I had a moment of calm and realized I was breathing easier. Maybe I wasn't suffocating. Maybe I was just suffering a panic attack. I didn't smell dirt. I wasn't cold. Maybe I wasn't buried. Okay, hold that thought. Did I hear a siren far off in the distance? A dog barking?

My confinement stretched on with nothing to break the monotony. My muscles were cramping and my hands were numb. I no longer knew if it was day or night. What I knew with certainty was that Ranger would be looking for me. He'd return from Florida, and he'd do what he does best . . . he'd go into tracking mode. Ranger would find me. I just hoped he'd get to me in time.

I heard a door slam and an engine catch. The casket shifted. I was pretty sure I was being driven somewhere. I hoped it wasn't the cemetery. I strained to hear voices. If I heard voices I'd make noise. I seemed to have air, but I didn't want to chance depleting the oxygen if I didn't hear voices. We were stopping and starting and turning corners. We stopped, and a door opened and slammed shut, and then I was sliding and bumping along. I'd been to a lot of funerals with Grandma Mazur. I knew what this was. I was moving on the casket gurney. I was out of the hearse or the truck or whatever, and I was being taken somewhere. I was wheeled around corners, and then the motion stopped. Nothing happened for what seemed like years, and finally the lid was raised, and I blinked up at Con.

"Good," he said, "you're still alive. Didn't die of fright, eh?" He looked in at me. "Undertaker humor."

My first thought was that I wouldn't cry. I'd try to stay smart. I'd keep him talking. I'd look for an opportunity to escape. I'd stall for time. Time was my friend. If I had enough time, Ranger would find me.

"I need to get out of this casket," I said.

"I don't think that's a good idea."

"I need to use the bathroom . . . bad."

Con was fastidious to a fault, and he looked genuinely horrified at the possibility of a woman peeing in one of his silk-lined caskets. He cranked the gurney down to floor level and helped me wriggle myself out of the box.

"This is the way it will work," he said. "I don't want you making a mess all over everything, so I'm going to let you use the bathroom. I'm going to release one cuff, but I'll stun-gun you if you do anything dumb."

It took a moment to get my balance, and then I very carefully shuffled into the bathroom. When I shuffled out I felt a lot better. My hands were no longer numb and the cramps in my legs had subsided. We were in a house that looked like a small '70s ranch. It was sparsely furnished with mix-and-match hand-me-downs. The kitchen linoleum was old and the paint was faded. The counters were red Formica dotted with cigarette burns. The white ceramic sink was rust stained. Some of the over-the-counter kitchen cabinets were open and I could see they were empty. The casket was in the kitchen, and I was guessing it had been wheeled in from an attached garage.

"Is this in retaliation for Spiro's death or the fire in the funeral home?" I asked Con.

"Only tangentially. It's a bonus. Although it's a very nice bonus. There've been a couple nice bonuses to this charade. I got to kill Mama Macaroni. Who wouldn't love to do that? And then I got to bury her! Life doesn't get much better. The Macaronis bought the top-of-the-line slumber bed."

I cut my eyes to *my* slumber bed.

"Sorry," Con said. "Molded plastic. Not one of my better caskets. Lined with acetate. Still, it's good quality for people who haven't set aside funeral expenses. I'd like to put your grandmother in one of these. Her death should be declared a national holiday. What is this morbid obsession she has with the dead? I have to nail the lid down when there's a closed casket. And she's never happy with the cookies. Always wanting the kind with the icing in the middle. What does she think, cookies grow on trees?" Con smiled. "Maybe I'll nail your lid down just to annoy her. That would be fun."

"So, I guess that means you're not going to bury me alive?"

"No. If I buried you alive I'd have to put you back in the casket. And I have plans for the casket. Mary Aleski is on a table back at the mortuary, and she'll be on view in that casket tomorrow. And besides, do you have any idea how much digging is involved in burying someone in a casket? I have a better plan. I'm going to hack you up and leave you here on the kitchen floor. It's important to my plan that you're found in this house."

"Why?"

"This house belongs to Spiro. It's tied up in probate because he hasn't been pronounced dead. If Spiro killed you it would be in this house, don't you think?"

"You still haven't told me why you want to kill me."

"It's a long story."

"Are we in a rush?"

Con looked at his watch. "No. As a matter of fact, I'm ahead of schedule. I'm coordinating this with the last of the Spiro sightings. Spiro will be seen in his car around midnight, and then I'll come back here and kill you, and Spiro will disappear forever."

"I don't get the Spiro tie-in. I don't get anything."

"This is about a crime that happened a long time ago. Thirty-six years to be exact. I was stationed at Fort Dix, and I masterminded a hijacking. I had four friends who helped me. Michael Barroni, Louis Lazar, Ben Gorman, and Jim Runion."

"The four men who were found shot to death behind the farmers' market."

"Yes. An unfortunate necessity."

"I wouldn't have pegged you for a criminal mastermind."

"I have many unappreciated talents. For instance, I'm quite good as an actor. I play the role of the perfect undertaker each night. And as you know I'm a genius with makeup. All I needed was a hat and a jacket, some colored contacts and handmade scars, and I was able to fool you and that pizza delivery boy."

"You always seemed like you enjoyed being a funeral director."

"It has its moments. And I hold a certain prominence in the community. I like that."

Constantine Stiva has an ego, go figure. "So you masterminded a hijacking."

"I saw the trucks come through once a week, and I knew how easy it would be to take one of them down on that isolated back station. Lazar was a munitions expert. I learned everything I know about bombs from Lazar. Gorman had been stealing cars since he was nine. Gorman stole the tow truck we used to drag the armored truck away. Barroni had all kinds of connections to launder the money. Runion was the dumb muscle.

"Do you want to know how we did it? It was so simple. I was on guard duty with two other men. The armored truck pulled up. Runion and Lazar were directly behind it in a car. Lazar had already planted the bomb when the truck stopped for lunch. *Kaboom,* the bomb went off and disabled the truck. Runion killed the other two guards on duty and shot me in the leg. Then Gorman hooked the truck up to the tow truck and hauled it off about a quarter mile down the road into an abandoned barn. I wasn't there, of course, but they told me Lazar set a charge that opened the truck like he'd used a can opener. They killed the truck guards and in a matter of minutes were miles away and seven million dollars richer."

"And no one ever solved the crime."

"No. The army expended so much energy hushing it all up that there wasn't a lot of energy left to investigate. They didn't want anyone to know the extent of the loss. That was very big money back then."

"What happened to the money?"

"There were five of us. We each took two hundred thousand as seed money for start-up businesses when we got out. And we agreed that every ten years we'd take another two hundred thousand apiece until we hit the forty-year mark and then we'd divide up what was left."

"So?"

"We had a vault in the mortuary basement. We had a system that each of us had a number, and it took all of us to open the vault. No one knew, but over the years I'd figured out the numbers. So I borrowed from the vault from time to time. Then you and your grandmother burned my business down. The vault survived, but I didn't. I was underinsured. So I took what was left in the vault and used it to rebuild. Two months ago, Barroni found out he had colon cancer and asked for his share of the money. He wanted to make sure it went to his family. We set the meeting up in the field behind the farmers' market so we could take a vote. I knew they were going to give Barroni the money. And they were going to want their share early, too. We were all at that age. Colon cancer. Heart disease. Irritable bowel. Everyone wants to take a cruise. Live the good life. Buy a new car. They were going to go down to my basement, open the vault, find out I'd stolen the money, and then they would have killed me."

"So you killed them."

"Yes. Death isn't such a big deal when it's happening to someone else."

"How do I fit in?"

"You're my insurance policy."

"Just in case one of my comrades shared the secret with a wife and she came looking for me, maybe with the police, I would confess to telling Spiro about the crime. Of course, it would be my version of the crime and I'd be non-culpable. Easy to believe Spiro would return to extort money and then resort to mass murder. And easy to believe Spiro would be a little goofy and take to stalking you. And I'd be the poor grieving father of the little bastard."

"That's the dumbest thing I ever heard."

"*You* fell for it," Con said. "Actually my original plan was just to leave you a few notes. Then I realized you'd made so many enemies you might not consider Spiro as the stalker, so I had to get more elaborate. Probably I could have stopped after you identified me at Cluck-in-a-Bucket, but by that time I was addicted to the rush of the game. It's too bad I have to kill you. It would have been fun to blow up more cars. I really like blowing up cars. And it turns out I'm good at it."

He was crazy. He'd inhaled too much embalming fluid. "You won't get away with it," I told him.

"I think I will. Everyone loves me. Look at me. I'm above suspicion. I'm the social director of the Burg."

"You're insane. You blew up Mama Macaroni."

"I couldn't resist. Did you like my present to you? The mole? I thought that was a good touch."

"What about Joe? Why did you run him over?"

"It was an accident. I was trying to get home, and I couldn't get rid of you and your idiot grandmother. I hit the curb and lost control of the car. Too bad I didn't kill him. That was a slow week."

Shades were drawn in the house. I looked around for a clock.

"It's almost ten," Con said. "I need to have Spiro seen one last time, driving the car that will be found in this garage. Sadly, it will be my final Spiro performance. And your body will be found in the kitchen. Horribly mutilated, of course. It seems like Spiro's style. He had a flare for the dramatic. I suppose in some ways the apple didn't fall far from the tree." He held the stun gun up for me to see. "Do you want me to stun you before I put you away or will you cooperate?"

"What do you mean, put me away?"

"I want you to be freshly killed after Spiro is seen driving the car. So I'm going to have to put you on ice for a couple hours."

I cut my eyes to the casket. I really didn't want to go back in the casket.

"No," Con said. "Not the casket. I need to get that back to the mortuary. It was just an easy way to transport you." He was looking around. "I need to find something that will keep you out of sight. Something I can lock."

"Ranger will find me," I told him.

"Is that the Rambo bounty hunter? Not a chance. No one's going to find you until I point him in the right direction."

He turned and looked at me with his pale, pale eyes,

I saw his hand move, I heard something sizzle in my head, and everything was black.

My mouth was dry and my fingertips were tingling. The jerk had zapped me again and stuffed me into something. I was on my back, and I was curled up fetus style. No light. No room to stretch my legs. My arms were pinned under me and the cuffs were cutting into my wrists. No satin lining this time. I was pretty sure I was crammed into some sort of wooden box. I tried rocking side to side. No room to get any momentum and nothing gave. This wasn't as terrifying as being locked in the casket, but it was much more uncomfortable. I was taking shallow breaths against the pain in my back and arms, playing games to occupy my mind, imagining that I was a bird and could fly, that I was a fire-breathing dragon, that I could play the cello in spite of the fact that I wasn't sure what a cello sounded like.

And suddenly there was a very slim, faint sliver of light in my box. I went still and listened with every molecule in my body. Someone had turned a light on. Or maybe it was daylight. Or maybe I was going to heaven. There were muffled sounds and men's voices, and there was a lot of door banging. I opened my mouth to yell for help, but the box opened before I had the chance. I tumbled out, and fell into Ranger's arms.

He was as stunned as I was. He had a vise-like grip on my arms, holding me up. His eyes were dilated black, and the line of his mouth was tight. "I saw you folded up in there, and I thought you were dead," he said.

"I'm okay. Just cramped."

I'd been stuffed into one of the empty over-the-counter cabinets. How Con had gotten me up there was a mystery. I guess when you're motivated you find strength.

Ranger had come in with Tank and Hal. Tank was at my back with a handcuff key, and Hal was working on the shackles.

"It's not Spiro," I said. "It's Con, and he's coming back to kill me. If we hang around we can catch him."

Ranger raised my bruised and bloody wrist to his mouth and kissed it. "I'm sorry to have to do this to you, but there's no *we*. I've just had six really bad hours looking for you. I need to know you're safe. Sitting in this house waiting for a homicidal undertaker doesn't feel safe." And he clamped the handcuff back on my wrist. "You've had enough fun for one day," he said. And the other bracelet went on Tank's wrist.

"What the . . ." Tank said, caught by surprise.

"Take her back to the office and have Ella tend to her wrists and then take her to Morelli," Ranger told Tank.

I dug my heels in. "No way!"

Ranger looked at Tank. "I don't care how you do it. Pick her up. Drag her. Whatever. Just get her out of here and keep her safe. And I don't want those bracelets to come off either of you until you hand her over to Morelli."

I glared at Tank. "I'm staying."

Tank looked back at Ranger. Obviously trying to decide which of us was more to be feared.

Ranger locked eyes with me. "Please," he said.

Tank and Hal were goggle-eyed. They weren't used to "please." I wasn't used to it either. But I liked it.

"Okay," I said. "Be careful. He's insane."

Hal drove, and Tank and I sat in back in the Explorer. Tank was looking uncomfortable with me as an attachment, looking like he was searching for something to say but couldn't for the life of him come up with anything. I finally decided to come to his rescue.

"How did you find me?" I asked him.

"It was Ranger."

That was it. Three words. I knew he could talk. I saw him talking to Ranger all the time.

Hal jumped in from the front seat. "It was great. Ranger dragged some old lady out of bed to open the records office and hunt down real estate. He brought her in at gunpoint."

"Omigod."

"Boy, he was intense," Hal said. "He had every RangeMan employee and twenty contract workers out looking for you. We knew you disappeared at Stiva's because I was monitoring your bike. Tank and me started looking for you before Ranger even landed. You told me you were coming back and I got worried."

"You were worried about me?"

"No," Hal said. "I was worried Ranger would kill me if I lost you." He shot me a look in the rearview mirror. "Well yeah. Maybe I was a little worried about you, too."

"I was worried," Tank said. "I like you."

Hot damn! I leaned into him and smiled, and he smiled back at me.

"We went through the funeral home, and we went through the undertaker's home," Hal said. "And then Ranger figured they might own property someplace else, so he got the old lady in the tax records to open the office. She found that little ranch house under Spiro's name. It was all tied up because Spiro was never declared dead."

Forty minutes later, I got dropped off at Morelli's. I had my wrists bandaged, and I had some powdered-sugar siftings on my black T-shirt. Tank walked me to the door and unlocked the cuffs while Morelli waited, a crutch under one arm, his other hand hooked into Bob's collar.

"She's in your care," Tank said to Morelli. "If Ranger asks, you can tell him I unlocked the cuffs in front of you."

"Do you want me to sign for her?" Morelli asked, on a smile.

"Not necessary," Tank said. "But I'm holding you responsible."

I ruffled Bob's head and slipped past Morelli. He shut the door and looked at my T-shirt.

"Powdered sugar?" he asked.

"I *needed* a doughnut. I had Hal stop at Dunkin' Donuts on the way across town."

"Ranger called and told me you were safe and on your way here, but he wouldn't tell me anything else."

Ranger was going to take Stiva down, and he didn't want anything going wrong. He didn't want to lose Stiva. He wanted to do the takedown himself, without a lot of police muddying the water.

"I accidentally got lost trying to find the memorial service and happened to stumble into Con's personal work-room. I tripped an alarm and Con found me snooping."

"I'm guessing he wasn't happy about you snooping?"

"It turns out Spiro is dead. Con said he found Spiro's ring in the fire debris. Con needed a scapegoat and decided Spiro was the ghost for the job. So Con's been going around in mortician's makeup, looking like a scarred Spiro."

"Why did Con need a scapegoat?"

I told Morelli about the hijacking and the money missing from the vault, and I told him about the mass murder.

Morelli was grinning. "Let me get this straight," he said. "In the beginning, you basically made all the wrong assumptions about Anthony's involvement and Spiro's identity. And yet, at the end, you solved the crime."

"Yeah."

"Fucking amazing."

"Anyway, Stiva locked me up in a casket and took me somewhere to kill me. He left so he could do one last Spiro impersonation, and while he was gone Ranger found me."

"And Ranger's waiting for him to return?"

"Yep."

"He should have told me," Morelli said.

"Probably didn't want the police involved. Ranger likes to keep things simple."

"Ranger's a little psycho."

"Marches to his own drummer," I said.

"His drummers are all psycho, too."

I looked at Bob. "Has he been out?"

"Only in the yard."

"I'll take him for a short walk."

I went to the kitchen and got Bob's leash. And while I was at it I pocketed the keys to the Buick. I was feeling left out. And I was feeling pissed off. I wanted to be part of the takedown. And I wanted to release some anger on Stiva. I'd quit my job in an effort to normalize my life, and he'd sabotaged my plan. Of course, he'd done some good things, too, like blowing up Mama Macaroni and sending my cello to cello heaven. Still, it was small compensation for mowing Joe down and stuffing me into a casket. Maybe I should be feeling charitable because it appeared he was insane, but I just didn't feel charitable. I felt angry.

I snapped the leash on Bob, took him out the front door, and loaded him into the Buick. There was a

slight chance we'd both be blown to smithereens, but I
didn't think so. Blowing me up wasn't in Stiva's plan. I
shoved the key in the ignition and listened to the Buick
suck gas. Music to my ears. Morelli wouldn't be happy
when he heard the Buick drive off, but I couldn't risk
telling him I was going back to help Ranger. Morelli
would never let me go.

I'd paid attention when we left the little ranch house
where I'd been held captive, and in fifteen minutes I
was back in the neighborhood. I cruised by the house.
It was dark. Half a block away I spotted the Explorer.
Hal and Tank were in the house with Ranger. I backed
the Buick into a dark driveway directly across from the
little ranch. I sat with the motor running and my lights
off. Bob was panting in the backseat, snuffling his nose
against the window. Bob liked being part of an adventure.

After ten minutes, a green sedan came down the
street. The car passed under a streetlight, and I could
see Stiva behind the wheel. He was wearing the hat,
and a splash of light illuminated his fake scars. He
turned into the ranch house driveway and stopped. The
garage door started to slide up. This was my moment.
I stomped my foot down on the gas and roared across
the street, slamming into the back of the green sedan.
I caught it square, sending it crashing through the bottom half of the garage door, pushing it into the back of
the garage.

Bob was barking and jumping around in the backseat. Bob probably drove NASCAR in another life. Or
maybe demolition derby. Bob loved destruction.

"So what do you think?" I asked Bob. "Should we
hit him again?"

"Rolf, rolf, rolf!"

I backed up and rammed the green sedan a second
time.

Ranger and Tank ran out of the house, guns drawn. Hal came five steps behind them. I backed up about ten feet and got out. I inspected the Buick. Hard to get a good look in the dark, but I couldn't see any damage by the light of the moon.

Tank played a beam of light from his Mag across the green sedan. The hood was completely smashed, the roof had been partially peeled away by the garage door, and the trunk was crumple city. Steam hissed from the radiator and liquid was pooling dark and slick under the car. Stiva was fighting the airbag.

I took Bob out of the backseat and walked him around on Spiro's front lawn so he could tinkle. I was thinking I'd move back into my apartment tomorrow. And maybe I'd get a cello. Not that I needed it. I was pretty darned interesting without it. Still, a cello might be fun.

Ranger was standing, hands on hips, watching me.

"I feel better now," I said to Ranger.

"Babe."